Praise for

THE
HIDDEN
THINGS

"*The Hidden Things* is a treat: a heist story taken to pieces and expertly put back together at off-kilter angles into a startling, smart, vivid book."
—Tana French, *New York Times* bestselling author of
The Witch Elm

"Greed and revenge collide as Jamie Mason deftly explores an art theft gone terribly wrong. *The Hidden Things* is a wholly original and deeply compelling read that will keep readers on the edge of their seats."
—Mary Kubica, *New York Times* bestselling author of
The Good Girl

"A tense and captivating story of things both lost and found, *The Hidden Things* puts an entirely unique twist on the aftermath of an art heist. A sharp, atmospheric thriller that lingered long after I turned the final page—I couldn't put it down."
—Megan Miranda, *New York Times* bestselling author of
All The Missing Girls

"Mason's innovative plotting with touches of devious humor fuels the story, but *The Hidden Things* is driven by its perceptive character studies of criminals, the criminally inclined and two innocents whose worlds are about to implode. . . .Violence simmers throughout *The Hidden Things*, ready to explode at any moment."
—*Associated Press*

"Captivating . . . Mason combines taut action with an intense character study and hauntingly memorable prose."

—*Washington Independent Review of Books*

"*The Hidden Things* confirms Jamie Mason's prodigious and wholly original talent. In a world of copycat writers chasing trends, she does her own thing—and it's magnificent."

—Laura Lippman, *New York Times* bestselling author of *Sunburn*

"*The Hidden Things* is a model for superb thriller writing. It checks all the boxes: Grabbing us on the opening page, sending us on a roller coaster of plotting, taking us deep into a world (fine arts) that most of us only glimpse from the outside, and offering up a cast of brilliantly drawn characters, noble and evil and everything in between. Mason also proves to be an ace wordsmith, whose sharply drawn prose elevates the novel to an even higher peak."

—Jeffery Deaver, *New York Times* bestselling author of *The Bone Collector* and *The Never Game*

"Relentlessly suspenseful and as hauntingly sinister as any book I have ever read. This dark domestic noir, with greed and bravery clashing over a priceless possession, is irresistibly sardonic and beautifully written, with a complex and textured cast, a twisty contemporary plot, and one of the most endearing and unforgettable main characters you will ever meet. A master class in character and a knockout of a story, this book is a rare treasure—terrifying, heartbreaking, and completely original."

—Hank Phillippi Ryan, nationally bestselling and award-winning author of *The Murder List*

"[Mason] is wonderfully adept at creating multifaceted characters in emotionally complex relationships. Little black and white for these characters—just multiple shades of gray, causing readers to temper their allegiances as the plot thunders to its conclusion. Masterfully nuanced crime fiction."

—*Booklist*

"A smart and hugely entertainingly thriller, with so many sharp twists and hairpin turns that you'll need to hold on for dear life. But it's the compelling, nuanced characters—dark, light, and every shade in-between—who will stay with you long after the last page."

—Lou Berney, nationally bestselling author of
November Road

"Suspenseful . . . the whip-smart, courageous Carly [is] hands down, the best part of the book. Those with an interest in the real-life museum theft may want to check this one out."

—*Publishers Weekly*

ALSO BY JAMIE MASON

Three Graves Full

Monday's Lie

THE
HIDDEN
THINGS

Jamie Mason

GALLERY BOOKS

New York   London   Toronto   Sydney   New Delhi

G 10

Gallery Books
An Imprint of Simon & Schuster, Inc.
1230 Avenue of the Americas
New York, NY 10020

First Gallery Books trade paperback edition March 2020

GALLERY BOOKS and colophon are registered trademarks of Simon & Schuster, Inc.

For information about special discounts for bulk purchases, please contact Simon & Schuster Special Sales at 1-866-506-1949 or business@simonandschuster.com.

The Simon & Schuster Speakers Bureau can bring authors to your live event. For more information or to book an event, contact the Simon & Schuster Speakers Bureau at 1-866-248-3049 or visit our website at www.simonspeakers.com.

Interior design by Jaime Putorti

Manufactured in the United States of America

10 9 8 7 6 5 4 3 2 1

Library of Congress Cataloging-in-Publication Data for the hardcover edition is as follows:

Names: Mason, Jamie, author.
Title: The hidden things / by Jamie Mason.
Description: First Gallery Books hardcover edition. | New York : Gallery Books, 2019.
Identifiers: LCCN 2018047379 (print) | LCCN 2018050258 (ebook) | ISBN 9781501177330 (ebook) | ISBN 9781501177316 (hardcover : alk. paper) | ISBN 9781501177323 (trade pbk. : alk. paper)
Subjects: | GSAFD: Suspense fiction.
Classification: LCC PS3613.A81723 (ebook) | LCC PS3613.A81723 H53 2019 (print) | DDC 813/.6—dc23
LC record available at https://lccn.loc.gov/2018047379

ISBN 978-1-5011-7731-6
ISBN 978-1-5011-7732-3 (pbk)
ISBN 978-1-5011-7733-0 (ebook)

For my daughter, Rianne,
the young Queen of Hidden Things,
who is not Carly, but made Carly real for me.

And for all the fine hidden things that make
all of us who we are.

Try to put well in practice what you already know, and in so doing, you will in good time discover the hidden things you now inquire about.

—Rembrandt

CHAPTER ONE

The video had been watched only forty-four times before Carly Liddell's attacker was identified to the police. Viewer number forty-four was the prize tipster, and it was a good thing it was all resolved quickly. The young man in the video had killed a turtle over a span of hours one dull Saturday a decade earlier, at the age of nine, in the early weeks of the same summer he'd set his first fire. Since then, matches, rocks, the heel of his shoe, the long drop over the railing of a bridge, and other weapons of juvenile destruction had been urgently fascinating to him in ways that got him into trouble when he was a boy, in ways he'd learned to hide over the years.

He'd been stealing things, lately. And watching women.

He always would have made the news.

The video, a sloppy edit of footage from a home-security system, went on to become something of a phenomenon. It had been cut together in a hurry by a tech-savvy officer in the cybercrimes unit who was good with that sort of thing. It went up on the police website less than twenty minutes after the flash drive, loaded with the raw recordings from the home's monitoring surveillance, had been plugged into his computer. Backslaps and high fives all around for that one.

The local news stations had rushed to repost it. It was a civic duty, of course. But at least as good as all that, it was irresistible: a heart-stopper in three acts that clocked in at under half a minute.

By the end of the next day, it had been uploaded to more than a dozen YouTube accounts.

In seventy-two hours, nearly a quarter of a million people had seen fourteen-year-old Carly Liddell come into the frame from the top right, her face pixelated to anonymity in every shot.

The view in the opening clip is admirably long-range, the camera pointing down a concrete driveway, clearly covering the near intersection and eventually fuzzing out of focus a block up the far sidewalk. The feed is tagged in the lower left-hand corner as *Exterior_3*, which would indicate at least two other cameras are outside scanning the bland green agreeableness of the minivan-and-hybrid neighborhood.

Carly comes down the stretch of pavement covered by Exterior 3 in the last yards of her return trip from school, backpack on one shoulder, crossing the screen on a slight diagonal, right to left. She moves with a loping, coltish gait that already shows signs of being reined in. She's so close to grown.

Even with her head high, and with only one reflexive glance at the phone in her hand, she doesn't appear to react at all to the young man slouching beside the hedge on the retaining wall as she passes him.

But even in the grainy farthest reach of the lens, his notice of her is unmistakable. He leans forward, watching, hesitates for a beat, then checks the walkway behind them. It's deserted. He slides into her wake.

If there were only one frame of the video to see—Carly in front, the young man a few long steps behind—in just that single still image it would be clear that one of the people in the scene belongs there and one doesn't.

Her posture is soft, easy in a pleasant end-of-the-day fatigue. She's all but home. It's in the flutter of the flannel shirt tied around her waist. It's in the tilt of her head and the bend of her knee.

But he's rigid, chin down, every bit of his stance just a degree off a natural bearing. Some switch in him has been tripped, and he's not entirely what he was a few seconds before when he was only loitering on an empty suburban block. Now he's a mannequin, a robot, an approximation made of impulse wired through him like opposing magnets strung together. The surging current has pushed his arms away from his sides, pulled his legs slightly bent, the omen of a reflex to come, the windup to a sprint or a spring.

Then the edited video cuts to a different camera, labeled *Exterior_2*, this one mounted on the back side of a decorative column, one of two pillars flanking the front door. Carly and the young man are facing each other. There's no audio, but he's closed the gap and seems to have invented something to talk about, something to keep her poised between being rude and being on the safe side of that door.

The young man's back is to us, still taut and awkward, but now Carly is also rigid. Her key is in the lock, but that's as far as she'd gotten. He's walked all the way up onto the stoop and set his body close to the door's handle, though not quite blocking it—a threat with a built-in plausible deniability that buys time with her doubt.

She's backed away a little to preserve a cushion of personal space, though it meant giving up the easy reach to the door. She'd have to nearly touch him now to finish getting inside. She plucks at the hem of her T-shirt, shedding nervous energy in the repetition. His shoulder twitches. He says something. She shakes her head and glances at the empty intersection, so close and useless to her.

The young man looks down and shuffles back a half step, and Carly either misinterprets the maneuver or takes the only chance she can count on. She dives for the key and the threshold. He lets her get past him. He also looks to the intersection. It's still empty. He doesn't even have to hurry to stop the door as she scrabbles to slam it closed behind her.

The last part of the video is shot from the back of the foyer, by a camera marked *Interior_1*. The light off the paint gives a vague green hue to the indoor footage. Carly is slapping at a control panel on the wall. He pushes her away from it. They both trip and scuffle over her fallen backpack. She shoves with all her woefully inadequate might and gains less than an arm's length from him.

Instead of pulling her in, the young man locks his forearm across his body and drives them on, plowing and pinning Carly into the corner next to her own front door. Her back hits the wall hard enough that the edge of the painting in the foreground jumps and quivers on its nail. Her knees let go, and his surprise topples him into the blank space where her body should have been to receive him.

On elbows and heels, Carly scrambles backward toward the camera, toward the quarter of a million viewers (and each new one, as they come) holding their breath, rooting for her, willing her a way out. She makes it into the sharpest focus yet, her long hair swinging around her shoulder in a sheet of blue-sheened chestnut cascading from the strong side part that's almost close enough to stroke.

He runs at the camera, lunges for her, catching her left ankle as it shoots out in her ungainly crab crawl. He drags her, kicking and thrashing, away from the clear focus that felt like safety, back into the open foyer. He pulls her leg up, tilting her onto her back. He leans in, stooping low to make a short fall of the distance left to be on her, to finally catch her under his control. And Carly Liddell, never a dancer, never a gymnast, never any color belt in any martial art—but ever the natural math and science whiz—becomes trigonometry and physics. And she has cool boots.

Her mind and muscles do the calculations of the arcs and angles as she rises up, torso cocked to the left, then swinging to the right to load momentum into her free leg, which she brings back across her body. The knobby tread of her goth-girl combat boot explodes his grip on her ankle.

In a perfect ballet of Newtonian inevitability, unlearned and unpracticed but as natural as a whirlwind, Carly makes a figure-eight flourish of the follow-through, winding up again, this time to bring her boot crashing into the sweet spot where his jaw meets his ear, dropping him like a bag of gravel.

She rolls onto her hands and knees. She pushes up from the floor and looks down at her fallen foe. *Run!* thinks every single person who will ever watch the footage.

And she does.

It's magnificent.

But short-lived. The video freezes and the cybercrime tech destroys the triumph and tension with a quick electronic red circle, drawn to bring the audience out of the drama and into the lineup. The young man's face, sideways in forced repose against the foyer tile, is largely in shadow and not terribly in focus, but it's lit up enough that someone who knows him well might peg him. To the stranger, he still looks rough-hewn and indistinct. But viewer forty-four had already picked up her phone by the shot of him coming off the retaining wall. He was arrested just a few hours after Carly walked past him on the sidewalk.

It was a good day for Good Samaritans. It was a good day for law enforcement. It was a good day for the local news outlets that vied to make the most appealing special report of the pulse-racing video and happy ending.

And it would have been a good day for John Cooper. His elaborate security system, which his new wife teased him for, had caught the reckless and newly bold young man who had attacked his stepdaughter, and it got the boy before he'd done all the terrible things he'd been whittling vivid in his mind for years.

The system had worked just as designed, its clarity and clever placement revealing what had happened and when and how, and most importantly, by whom.

In the longer reach, the video had captured a moment of heroic self-preservation that would go on to inspire many people in both the abstract and even occasionally in practical application.

It could have been a good day for John Cooper, but it wasn't. His wife and stepdaughter knew of the perimeter cameras. They knew about the door chimes and the alarm codes and the motion-detector lighting. But they hadn't known about, nor would have they agreed to, Interior 1, the camera inside the house. And they didn't know why he had needed to put it there in the first place.

CHAPTER TWO

John Cooper's silenced cell phone shivered against his leg again. The barrage of text alerts from the network of cameras always ramped up around the time Carly came home from school, but this was getting ridiculous.

Until he'd become a self-taught expert in home security, John had never much noticed the all-hours parade of mundane creatures flitting, scurrying, snuffling, moseying, and waddling all over the 360 degrees he was worried about. On nice days it might crest over into a circus, and occasionally, in some clairvoyance of weird weather, you'd get a full-out episode of *Suburban Wild Kingdom*—flex-eared cats stalking small things in the grass, hackles-raised dogs making sport of the cats, squirrels losing their minds, and blue jays dive-bombing the whole spectacle. The cameras dutifully reported these scenes to John's phone in text messages. And they reported. And reported.

It didn't relent in the evenings, either, but the cast of the after-hours show became slightly more exotic and leggy, and sometimes even toothy when a curious coyote would venture down out of the hills. The night footage had been fascinating for a while. He'd never realized so much was going on out there. His household winding down into whatever passed for tranquillity at the end of each day didn't mean all that much to the rhythm of the world. Other creatures still had things to do. Some of them in John Cooper's yard even.

When the neighborhood went lights-out in every direction, it was the sort of place made of early-to-bed people. They'd be up productively soon. But if sleep wouldn't come to you, then at least the ritual quiet was expected of everyone in the tidy darkness, even if you were wide-awake and staring at the shadows on the ceiling.

In the first weeks that the security system was live and pinging, John had watched a selection of deer, raccoon, opossum, and fox, all careful and walleyed in the night vision, picking their way in singles or sets over the lawn and around the trash bins. Their flat white stares were disturbing in their unblindness, pairs of blank spotlights snapping up out of the grass, alerting to things in the grayscape that John's cameras didn't show him.

He wondered if it was the same animals he saw night after night. He tried a few times to study the videos to see if he could tell one from the other, to recognize a familiar snout or rack of antlers, but he could never be sure. In reviewing the daylight recordings, he easily kept track of the different people he regularly observed on the sidewalks in front of his house, and of the expected neighborhood cars that drove by without slowing.

His phone buzzed again in his pocket. The cameras' sensitivities had been lowered to a balance that hit somewhere between vigilance and sanity, and John had turned down the vibration of his phone to barely there. But he still got so many notifications each day that, through sheer repetition, he'd been trained out of startling at most of them. But this time he flinched.

"John?" His boss for the past three years at BabySafe, Inc. was staring at him with a strange little charged-up look, shocked, as if he'd felt the tingle of the text in his own pocket. Both of the sales managers who relied on John's projection reports to steer their strategies for rubber spoons and scuff-free safety gates were gaping at him, too. As were the four random worker bees from other departments around the table with them.

John felt the heat in his face of absorbing a sudden salvo of expectant looks.

"Huh? No, I'm good. Sorry. Everything's fine. I just got a text and my phone startled me. That's all."

"No, look," said his boss.

All their gazes slid past John, over his shoulder and through the conference room's glass wall. John turned in his chair to follow their attention.

His office was one door to the right of dead center of the conference room's glass. He'd left it open when he'd walked over for the meeting, and now two uniformed police officers were leaning in, searching the empty room for him.

Every thought evaporated from his head and dragged the roots of his hair to attention as they went. His breath stalled between inhale and exhale, then caught fire in his chest. John watched the police look for him, their starched blue backs filling up his office doorway across the hall. They were only one turn from finding him.

His heart slammed into a full gallop and he forced himself to blink, and to release his grip on the armrests of his chair.

He'd had this idea in the abstract plenty of times: cops looking for him. He'd composed scripts to answer any number of questions they might have. He wanted to be ready if they ever came asking. *If*, though, was the fear, and each day that passed—nearly four years' worth of them now—was the hope. More days, more hope. But his memory had an unkind habit of now and then pushing back on the progress he'd made into that confidence.

It had been better lately, with Donna and Carly and all this pretend normal that he played at every day to pass the time. The setup he'd made with them—the house, the routine, and the job he didn't really need—was more than the sum of its convenient parts. It was nice. They were nice. But still, when his memory kicked up the things that it occasionally did—sounds, images—*her blood dried dull on the cuff of my shirt, like coffee or chocolate—*

"John." A woman's voice called him back into the moment.

He looked at the lady beside him and wasn't certain he'd ever known her name to forget it.

She touched his arm. "I'm sure it's nothing."

"Why would it be nothing?"

Her eyebrows stayed concerned, but her mouth twitched into what was supposed to be a reassuring smile. "I mean, I'm sure it'll be okay."

"Okay," John said. "Thanks," he added, and felt stupid for it.

"Go ahead, John. It's fine. We'll finish up later."

John looked back to see which of the men had said it. Though he'd heard the words, he'd lost the voice in the hum of all the possibilities clamoring in his head. But everyone was nodding at him in a just-said-something kind of way, even whatsername sitting next to him. All in agreement, all of one mind, every one of them eager to let the guy with the cops in his office go on in and collect his disaster while they all sat there and watched it happen through the glass.

There was nothing for him to do but go. Even the doors out of the office suite were on the far side of the conversation. He'd have to walk past the policemen just to leave.

Inevitability is gravity's cousin. It is its own force of nature, one that pulls both the ready and the unwilling along, not toward the earth, but toward consequence. And it can stand in, quite nicely, for a paralyzing lack of resolve. John's starved lungs dragged in a huge openmouthed breath, and he got out of the chair on autopilot, vaulting the fear in his guts.

He was standing behind the two officers in less time than he would have liked. The blur of his dash through the hallway sharpened into focus around him, and he was there before he'd figured out what he meant to say.

"Can I help you?"

The cops made the turn that John had been dreading and looked at him. He felt their eyes land on him like weight.

"John Cooper?"

"Yes?"

The one on the right, trim and baby-faced, smiled encouragingly. "Don't worry. Everything's all right."

True or not, it was nice to hear. Hope fluttered in John's chest.

The other cop, less trim and less dewy, scowl-smiled. John's flutter hunkered down.

"Mr. Cooper, your wife's been trying to reach you."

"Is she okay? I was in a meeting."

"She's fine. Not to worry. We just came to see if we could find you while she was trying to get you on the phone. It looks like we got here first. Now, Mr. Cooper, I do need to tell you that there's been an incident at your home." The cop raised his hands, palms out, staving off the reaction that blazed up on John's face.

"Was my house robbed?" John grabbed his head between his hands, all ten fingers flexed to exclamation points. "Jesus Christ, was it a robbery?"

"No, sir. Everything in your house is fine. And your daughter's fine, too, but I'm just sorry to have to say that she was attacked in your home."

"What?" John dropped his hands onto his thighs, leaning over like a spent runner. "What? Carly? Oh, God. Is she okay? Is she hurt?"

"She's okay. A bad kid forced his way in as she was letting herself into the house after school."

The cop continued his story, but John didn't hear him. Relief and fury flooded his mind, a chemical no-no of two feelings that don't mix well.

The police weren't there for him. He tried not to wilt. The deliverance from that specific terror threatened to buckle his knees. But the lump in his throat, the sudden rush of acid and heat from the thought of anyone hurting Carly, overwhelmed him. And surprised him, too.

"—and she was already over at the neighbor's house, but they both saw the little punkass run across your lawn while they were on the call with 911. He must've woken up and taken off like the devil was on him. But your wife said there are cameras and we—"

"Woken up?" John was disoriented by the Goldilocks detail of a story he'd missed most of. "He was asleep?"

The younger cop glowed with amusement and surrogate pride. "She got him good. She knocked him out, Mr. Cooper."

"Carly knocked somebody out?"

"Your daughter's a little pistol. She's really something."

"Stepdaughter," John said, and winced at the nasty impulse to distance himself.

He'd lost track of his face. John tried never to lose track of his expression. Words were important in convincing people. Keeping your story simple was security. But body language was everything.

A shadow crossed both of the police officers' faces, and he was fairly certain that neither man had consciously realized that John Cooper had just stepped out of the good-guy lane, maybe just one foot, maybe only a toe over the line. But noted, nonetheless.

"Mr. Cooper, your wife says that your security cameras are motion activated. This guy should be all over your recordings. We need to get this footage. This attack was incredibly bold."

The younger cop couldn't contain his affectionate admiration. "And she's really fine, don't worry, she's totally okay, she's awesome."

The older man smiled in agreement. "But this guy is really dangerous. We need to let the public know. If you've got a good picture in there somewhere, somebody will recognize him. Somebody will tell us who he is. We can stop him before he gets to someone who can't handle him."

John Cooper felt the trap of his own devising snap closed. While the police pointed and nodded enthusiastically over his shoulder as he pulled up the video clips, one after the other, his mind was already far ahead into what came next, into what he would say.

He watched as Carly found a way to be okay in all her thin, kind, funny, sweet, brilliant, not-nearly-wary-enough unreadiness. He watched her win the day with no help from anyone after pounding away on an alarm system that had been disabled because John Cooper couldn't let a computer call the police to his home, no matter what. He couldn't let blind chance tug its way off the leash.

With the officers behind him, their distractingly laden belts squeaking against their cuffs and guns, John kept his shoulders down and level. He was thankful for the setup that kept them behind him so he could have the privacy of his own face while he went through the recordings.

They watched for the best shots to use for their website and to send out to the media outlets. They had to find this guy before he could hurt someone else. And John had to help them.

The calculations played out, and he wrestled the twinge in his heart at Carly's desperation and triumph on the screen. *Let it go. She's fine.* He had to think. The calm he mimed was at odds with his body's urge to hand over every file, to let them have everything, anything, if it would only let him get in his car and not stop driving for days.

But he fought it all. He didn't know how he was going to get away with three things, three things that stood in the way of the part of him that wanted to see this through. That part of him was frantically writing new lines into the script to clear his path.

He needed to decide what he would tell his wife and daughter—stepdaughter, damn it—about why they had been filmed coming in and out of the foyer of their own house for better than half a year when they didn't know it. And why the panic button might as well have been the thermostat for all the good it did for poor Carly to bang away at it.

And the painting. Goddammit, why had he never thought about what else it could mean to have even a little bit of it in view of the foyer camera? It had never occurred to him that anyone would see these images. Not from any of the cameras, but especially not from that one. It was the entire point.

Interior 1 was only for him, only there at all because he hated that the painting was hanging out in the open. It didn't look like much, but if anyone, inside the house or a delivery person or salesman peering in through the sidelight window, ever stopped to look at it or gave it any special notice, at least the camera would let him know. He would see them looking. He'd gauge the reaction. Then he could decide what to do about it. But that had been the end of the plan. He'd never imagined that anyone besides him would know a camera was there.

Only a corner of the painting was in the recordings anyway. The unframed panel wasn't all that big to begin with. Just a triangle of the lower left corner, no more than seven inches deep, took up a slice of the camera's capture in the far right of the shot.

The cops, no surprise, hadn't reacted to it at all. That was something. But it wasn't everything. Some people out there would know what it was.

More than one person in the world would recognize even a small section of that painting and know its worth. Beyond that, a few would know what all it had been through.

He'd already dealt with three of them. One, still alive and an eternal pain in the ass; another who made John wonder about how hot a grudge could burn and for how long; and one who'd bled out all over his shirtsleeves and the pavement under his feet four years ago.

CHAPTER THREE

The whole thing was over so fast. Her favorite song was longer than that. Just a few minutes, start to finish. Finished. It was over now. It would always be over.

It didn't quite feel that way, though. Carly couldn't stop fiddling with it in her mind. How could everything fly around in less time than it took your favorite song to play and then land in a different order?

What Carly remembered most, once the guy was inside the house with her, was an overriding, all-caps, red-font chant: *NO! NO! NO! NO! NO!*

No. *No* in some animal way that wasn't a word. It wasn't even a thought, really, just an overwhelming refusal in every scrap of matter and energy that made up Carly Liddell.

No was her skin, and her eyes gone hot in her head. *No* was an itch in her teeth to sink into any warm thing that came close enough to bite. *No* to him. *No* to the terror rising up in her throat to choke her. *No* to the thought slashing through her mind like lightning—*He's too strong. I can't stop him.*

Any recollection of what she'd actually done in those few not-song moments was far away. Like on another planet far away. *(And how long had it really taken, anyway—how many real minutes and seconds? It felt like infinity, as if in some way it was still happening, as if maybe it would always be happening. But no.)*

In a memory that should have been fresh, almost every image and sound of the struggle in the foyer was vague and skippy. She'd kicked him or something and he'd fallen down hard. The wet thud of his head hitting the tile, that was kind of clear. But she wasn't very big and she didn't know how to fight, so it didn't make much sense. She really did not know exactly how she'd gotten away.

The first clear impression, after he was down, was an electric giddiness that blazed up her every nerve. The doorknob in her hand, cool and solid, reeled her in from overload and let her catch the scream that was rushing up into her mouth. She wrapped it up tightly, that scream. She strangled it in her throat like her fist squeezing down on the brass. The only sound was the gasps of air sawing over her dry tongue.

The guy was silent. Carly strained to hear any movement behind her. He was—(*NO!*) The scream in her throat wriggled to be free at her instinct to turn around, to check to see if he was getting up.

She didn't look. She cranked open the door. She still didn't scream.

She ran, her boots sinking into the spongy grass of the lawn— three strides, four, five, six—and she shoved down the crazy laugh that tried to bubble up into the floaty space that not-screaming had stretched into her throat. *No* was fading. Carly was coming back online. For her to laugh about this was just nuts, and that would make her cry. She kind of thought she should be crying.

Where her head had been full of nothing but *No!* now the swerve and dance of random thoughts, the weaving hum of thinking, came back to her. She was aware of being aware.

A stop-and-start afternoon rain raised a warm haze off the street. She breathed up the smell of oil, metallic dirt, and the ghost of spent tires. Her elbows hurt. She wanted things. To be far away. A milkshake. Her mother. To not have left school yet.

Ada flared brightly into Carly's mind. She wanted to talk to her best friend, to tell her what had happened. They were usually together after school, but Ada had to get new glasses today. That's why Carly had come straight home.

Ada played the ukulele. Carly drew. Carly had stacks of sketchbooks filled with cartoon characters and portraits of her friends and family. Ada wanted Carly to teach her to draw, so Carly had bargained for lessons on the ukulele. She'd never gotten past messing with the tuner the day before. *Just yesterday? Really?*

When Carly plucked a string, the tuner caught the vibrations out of the air. It measured what she'd done and delivered a little electronic verdict, a pixel needle wagging through the red toward the green zone, the sweet spot. Turn the peg, get closer to the green. Turn too far, and overshoot it back into red. It was like a game. More fun than the little guitar.

Carly did look back just once as she ran, when she was flying across her side yard into Mrs. Carmichael's. He'd never catch her, even if he was back on his feet now.

But she ran faster anyway. Concrete to grass. Grass back to concrete. The pavement disappeared under her long, sprinting legs and it rose up into two short stairs and a stoop. She pounded on the green door of the neighbor's house. The silk-flowered wreath jumped off its hook and rolled away.

That's when things had gotten frustrating.

Trying to explain what had happened—to Mrs. Carmichael, and later to the police and to her mother—was like trying to tell a dream as a story right after you'd woken up. She kept stammering through backtracks to fill in the details of what came before to make it all make sense.

It was important to them, in a different way than it was important to her, that she set the links in the chain in the right order. The story had to go smoothly from then until now, for everyone's sake. Carly needed to be able to see it correctly in her mind to sort it out. They only needed to know how to catch him.

In Mrs. Carmichael's house, Carly finally fought the tingle of tears, but more from not being able to get the story out than from shock, although the shock was certainly there. Her body was shaking with spent adrenaline. Her teeth chattered as she tried to talk. The aftertaste was metal and ashes.

Something turned and tightened in Carly as she watched Mrs. Carmichael react to her story. Carly didn't know Mrs. Carmichael well. She was the nice neighbor, the woman who carved half a dozen amazing jack-o'-lanterns at Halloween and lit her porch with them for three nights running. She was the lady with the little white dog and always a smile and a wave. Now she was the first person to pull Carly into a fierce hug after what had happened. But there was a message in the embrace.

Mrs. Carmichael's hug felt charged with more understanding than Carly felt for her own idea of the last few minutes. *No!* But yes. Something had happened to Mrs. Carmichael, something that made her know what Carly had just been through. But Mrs. Carmichael knew more, knew worse. In the tremor of her arms, Carly could tell.

Instantly they were part of the same set, even though Carly was only almost fifteen and Mrs. Carmichael was way older than even her mother. Carly wanted to know, but was sure that she would never ask. She could feel the woman's fingers trembling, holding Carly's face in her hands the way Carly imagined a grandmother would. The wary sadness in the woman's eyes. The way she pulled her mouth into a lipless line, hemming in her own story behind a tight sadness, Carly knew that this was as close as they would ever get to talking about it. It felt both right and wrong.

She thought of the ukulele. The peg turned.

Carly told her story, over and over. First, to the EMTs from the fire truck that got there while Carly and Mrs. Carmichael were still calling it in. She'd told Mrs. Carmichael that she wasn't hurt, but the word *attacked* had been part of the 911 report, and that's all it had taken. Carly told the story to the police as they arrived next, two sets of two, minutes apart. Then to another man in regular clothes. They said he was a lieutenant, who seemed like the boss. Everyone said the detectives were on the way. That sounded like a big deal, so she tried to get the story better, get it ready.

She couldn't talk at all, at first, when her mother came rushing through Mrs. Carmichael's front door.

There is no proper term, no single word, for the tidal wave of emotion on the far side of a near miss. It's made of a fear that's completely after-the-fact. There's nothing to fix. Everything is fine except the trembling and the terror spiked with fury at the carelessness of the universe. It's resentment shot through with bright pangs of superstitious gratitude toward whatever Power intervened to make it a horribly lucky day. It's love concentrated to a strength that's nearly poisonous.

The worst of it, though, is the gift of preview—that cold ghost of grief that whispers that it is still out there for you, simply waiting for some other day.

Carly and her mother shared all of it in an unbroken look as they scrambled past the small crowd of policemen and Mrs. Carmichael's barking dog to get to each other. Her mother grabbed her up, trying to hold her, stroke her, and look into her eyes all at once. Carly couldn't breathe, pinned by the desperation on her mother's face to be sure, all the way through, that she was okay. They told each other in sobs and nods. She was fine. They would all be fine.

But the clutching quickly lost its practical power. Muscles relented. Breath slowed. Mrs. Carmichael's grandfather clock clucked its second hand at them, and everyone else ran out of places to look to give them the privacy of their reunion.

Carly turned back to the police.

The story was her job right now. Their expectant looks gently reminded her of it, so she went back to work. They seemed happy enough with what she told them, fired up even. They always smiled at the part where she knocked him down, however it had happened.

But her recollections became more frustrating to her as what happened became a script instead of an actual memory. The whole narrative took on the order of recitation, and she lost the reality of where she'd stood, what he'd said, why she had bolted inside the house instead of out into the street for help, what he'd done, what she'd done, how she'd made it back to the door and beyond. The details of it receded as the tale of it bloomed. She was the foremost authority on the subject, and she wasn't sure she believed any of it.

They took a break to move the whole circus back to the Liddell house. From the porch Mrs. Carmichael watched them leave. Carly looked back and tried to let her know with the right-temperature smile and steady eyes that she understood what had passed between them.

The parade of cops and their pair of guarded civilians crossed the two front yards, properly on the sidewalks this time, not in the grass. (*That's the square where he called to me and I stopped. I should have kept walking. Or started running. Infinity.*) Carly was steered across the stoop with her mother's shoulder set against her own, her mother's arm around Carly's waist. The door was unlocked, so the police went in first. Each of them stepped over the lump of her backpack, but Carly picked it up and put it on the bench as she would have done if it had been a regular day.

And just like that, everything looked normal. As if it—whatever it really was—had never happened.

Carly excused herself to the bathroom and stared into the mirror. The only difference she could make out was in the urge she felt to pull a face. She bared her teeth at her reflection. But that was the wrong kind of different. She flushed the toilet and ran the water in the sink to buy more time.

The beep of the sensor on the opening front door zapped her heart back into her throat. But that was stupid. It wasn't like the guy would come back. And it wasn't like she was all alone this time.

Still, the best she could manage was to lean her ear to the door, listening, her heart kicking in her chest. Someone rushed past the bathroom. Then she heard her mother's muffled cry: "John!"

Carly flung open the door.

They'd been a family of two since Carly was a toddler. Her father had left them, divorced them, and evaporated before she'd ever known him. Her mother, though, was a hard, unstoppable, high-speed engine of shake-it-off. Carly sometimes wondered if part of the reason her father was so thoroughly gone was that her mother was so thoroughly fine with it.

But it only took two to live a good life. Carly didn't remember being anything but happy enough with just the two of them. It was still her default setting: me and Mom.

But Carly was better than halfway to genuinely loving her step-father. He was fun. He hadn't made her mother different as Carly had feared he would. He'd blended into the background of Donna's bustle, as if he were happy enough to be a nice nothing. Everything was almost the same except where they lived—their regular life plus one, with barely a ripple. He made them three, but Carly had not yet thought about him as part of this insane day.

John looked up from the crook of her mother's neck and gently maneuvered out of her arms. He took a deep breath, came to Carly, and wrapped her up.

"Holy shit, Carlzee."

She liked the nickname and liked the softball curses he sent her way sometimes, even if her mother didn't. He was there with them. It was nice. She smiled into his hug.

He pulled her away by the shoulders and fixed her in a hard stare. "You okay?"

She nodded, but had to hold her bottom lip with her teeth to keep her from crumpling into ugly cry face.

John shifted his gaze beyond her, to the cops milling around the living room. He pulled in a deep breath and sucked his teeth, sizing them up like bad weather.

Carly felt forgotten in his grip, and John's scowl made her look back over her shoulder, too, to double-check that the same nice men she'd been talking to were what he was laser beaming.

"What's wrong?" she asked.

But when his eyes met hers again, the question cranked in her head to a loud, looping *Whatswrongwhatswrong-ohno-whatswrong?*

They both tracked for what they could read in each other's thoughts. She saw . . . what exactly? And he saw that she did . . . *something (NO!).* The corners of John's mouth turned down and he shook his head, just a little. Did he want her not to worry? Was he saying sorry? Sorry for what? The questions hummed in the air between them.

"Mr. Cooper?" The taller detective walked up, hand outstretched. "Nice to meet you. Glad my guys found you. Thanks for your help."

"Sure," John said.

"I just got a message that the video clips are up on the website. Do you have somewhere where we can all look at this together? We'll see if maybe you guys recognize him."

The security cameras. Carly had forgotten about them. "Oh, wow! You can see him? You saw him—"

Her mother talked over her, grabbing at John's arm. "Did you get a good look at him? Are the pictures clear enough? Can they use it to . . ."

John chewed at the corner of his lip and nodded. "Yeah. Yeah. Uh-huh."

They filed into the study, Carly, her mother, John, and the five cops left in the house, to see what the local police had posted to their Alerts web page.

Carly discovered, while watching the video, that there were actually two of her in the room, not counting her image on the screen. There was the Carly who could feel her body. She was standing just to the right of her stepfather, who was sitting at his desk manning the mouse and the keyboard.

That particular Carly's hands were cold and her eyes burned from lack of blinking. That Carly trembled. That Carly felt a little sick watching the video and making a new memory of what had happened. And of what had almost happened.

The second Carly, Carly 2.0, was born where she stood, and she was made of both no and yes. She'd been on her way all afternoon. Carly had felt her stirring with the doorknob in her grip, on her feet, breathing, booming, growing brand-new into her skin. This Carly knew that breath and movement and chance were the parts of the physical fight she was watching on the screen. But she saw an entire machine inside her, a system of Other Carlys that would try things and do things and figure things out at a speed and ferocity that regular Carly didn't direct.

She was breathless in the hold of discovery. It burned. Tingled. It sang. She was watching with her own eyes something that would never, could never, have been in her memory. That terrible minute was hers again, but from the one viewpoint that she alone on planet Earth was barred from seeing. Outside herself.

A whole silent, hidden life was inside her body waiting, vigilant, to be called on. There were worlds within worlds. The layers between them broke away like sugar glass when they needed to. When they had to. She couldn't look away from her other self doing the unimaginable.

On the screen, she watched Other Carly give Carly the aim, the strength, and the break from thinking. Other Carly made her try and took away the idea that it wouldn't work.

If all that, then what else? Then there was more everywhere. Something was working away underneath it all. Everyone, without knowing it, was getting ready. Constantly. Making things. Having ideas they wouldn't have time to ask permission for. Everyone was inventing fast plans to plug into problems, ways to cope that stayed hidden until, suddenly, they didn't anymore. Everyone thought they weren't ready. But that wasn't all the way true.

The peg turned.

Then Carly felt what was wrong in the room.

The cheerful line of cops behind them were laughing it up, commenting on the looping video. One man slapped his hands together with glee when on-screen Carly's boot connected with the guy's head again, and he crashed into a nerveless heap on the tiles.

But the heat of trouble came not from the strangers behind them, but from the left. Her stepfather absorbed most of it, stiff and grim at the computer's controls. Carly's mother glowed like the sun, mouth agape.

In a moment of discovery and wonder, Carly had sped right past the obvious thing. *Since when are there cameras in the house?*

Carly, in the last year or so, was only beginning to appreciate that her mother might be beautiful. In that final hour, after the entire group watched and rewatched the video together, the hard set to her mother's jaw, her flush, and the careful mask of composure managed to light her face and posture like a work of art on display. The image of her, incandescent and restrained, convinced Carly to look at her mother in the way the other people, all men at the moment, must see her. Donna Liddell was lovely. And she was furious, but you'd have to be well versed in her usual expression to notice.

As the police finished getting what they needed for all that came next, Carly watched their eyes—helpless, not predatory—drawn over and again to her mother's face, her glittering eyes and tight, full-lipped smile. And Carly saw they didn't get it, but her stepfather did.

She noted the chain of appraisal: John, when he wasn't casting measuring glances at Donna's pointed avoidance of him, was watching the other men watch his wife. He didn't look jealous, though, which surprised Carly. He seemed worried, but more in the way of a juggler. As if one too many bowling pins were flying around, and maybe someone just tossed in a carving knife. He looked as if he were doing hard math.

John saw the last cop to the door. He closed it behind the lieutenant, whom he watched through the side window all the way down the driveway. Carly stood next to her mother at the back of the foyer. The room was oriented around the two of them as they faced John nearly to the angle of how it appeared in the video. Carly looked over her shoulder for the camera.

At the turn of the wall was a motion sensor tucked into the corner, pointing toward the front door and the hall table with the painting over it, where they all stopped on the way in and out of the house for their keys and sunglasses. He'd put in a system that turned on the lights when you walked through the house. That's what he'd explained to them. The camera had to be somewhere near it, or even in it, maybe. Her eyes roamed the smooth span of wall, crown molding, and baseboard. None of it hinted at anywhere else it might be. Carly moved to her mother's right side, more out of its path.

John turned around from the door like someone who didn't want to.

He didn't try to hide that he was drawing in a big preparatory breath. "Okay. There's a lot to talk about, but let's try to keep things in perspective."

"Really?" said Donna. "*That's* where you want to start? You sure about that?"

"Donna, listen—"

"Wow. No. Stop. Do not make the word *listen* or my name sound like you think I'm being unreasonable."

"Come on, I'm sorry. It's not like I put a camera in the bedroom or near the bathroom or anything. Nobody's naked in the foyer."

"Obviously I have no idea where there might be a camera in my house. So where they're *not* is hardly the point."

John's hand came up, defensive, placating. "I know. I know."

"I don't think you do."

John let his hands fall back to his sides, his shoulders loose under the weight of defeat. *Or at least to look defeated,* Carly thought, and cocked her head in concentration.

"What do you want me to say?" he asked. "Where do you want me to start?"

Surprise, like a little pinch, startled Carly. She looked at her mother and saw that Donna hadn't heard him all the way. Her mother didn't realize it wasn't a rhetorical question. It was bait. John wanted her to tell him what would fix this. But *no.* Filling in the blanks would be less like explaining himself and a lot more like scratching where her mother said it itched.

Carly's focus went wide and she looked into the thousand-yard distance, listening to the two of them. The match struck and went into the tinder. The argument burst into flames while Carly sorted out how different her mother's unfiltered, uncalculated upset sounded from her stepfather's precision in answering her.

The call came in the middle of their fight. The police had caught the young man who had pushed his way into the house. Carly wasn't supposed to hear that the boy had a knife in his pocket when they'd found him, but her mother, putting the phone on speaker, the angry conversation with John on pause, had hit the button too late.

Carly couldn't decide how to feel. The fact of his knife bumped up against the fact of her win. More danger made her mother sag with breathy talk of "so incredibly fortunate." Carly didn't want luck to make it seem like she cheated. It didn't change anything. The freak never got to his pocket.

Carly could tell by how fast and scattershot her mother was yelling at John that it was more convenient for her to be furious than to think about what other night they could all be having right now. They'd all be doing something different—in a police station or in a hospital or someplace worse—if it had gone another way. Carly understood because she didn't want to think about any of that stuff either.

But she found it hard to be mad at John, even though he was wrong and being somehow really weird about it. He should have told them. That was true. He should have asked.

If there hadn't been a camera in the foyer, though, or if he'd asked beforehand and her mother had said no, the video wouldn't exist. Carly would never have known what really happened. That guy pushing her, grabbing her, trying to—*Come on, NO, don't think about that.* Her taking him down and getting away. Everything was always going to be different after what had happened. Carly thought of Mrs. Carmichael.

But without seeing it, without really knowing, it might not have been a good change in her.

While John and her mother were arguing, Carly had replayed the video over and over on her phone from the police website. Without John and his bad decision, she wouldn't have had that jolt, the radioactive spider bite that made her feel so electric tonight. Everything was sharp. Everything glowed. Everything sounded so clear.

It wasn't right, what John had done and how he was acting. Was a lie of omission as bad as a regular lie? She didn't know. And she also didn't know for sure that there weren't other kinds of lies in the story as well. Hearing and listening had become slightly different tools in the last few hours.

John said there was a man who'd stalked him when he lived in San Diego. But he said "San Diego" as if the words were unfamiliar in his mouth. He said that the man was a nut, a pitiful loser, but that he didn't want to ruin the poor guy's life if it was something John could handle on his own. So he'd put in the cameras and monitored them closely.

John said the man wasn't a danger to Carly or her mother, but Carly heard a wrong note. The peg turned. He didn't believe it when he said it. Of that, she was sure.

Carly's phone lit up with two notifications, and another as she read the screen. Her friends were starting to check in: *Is that YOU?!?!*

The video had jumped into the social media stream.

CHAPTER FOUR

Once the police explained to John what had happened at his house, he'd kept one track of panic running, and one of face management. Hours of concentrating against looking too worried to the police, or not worried enough to Donna and Carly, was just about to the limit of his talent.

When they'd caught the little shit who had tried to hurt Carly, John let the adrenaline divert fully to the Donna problem. He let hope tamp down the immediate concern about the video, about its being out there on the police website. The cops had kept the media down at the end of the block, and the case was solved fast. It would sink. Everyone would be well on their way to the next thing in hours, if not sooner. It would be great if a celebrity death or a terrorist attack or something else happened in the next ten minutes. But either way, this was over. That part of it, anyway.

But he was exhausted. There wasn't enough juice left in him to be as good in the fight as he needed to be.

As fast as he could make it up and say it out loud, the playback began, with a twinge at every point he could've been smarter. He

saw—just too damned obviously—all the moments as they sped by
when he could have made a better choice of words or gestures.

Donna, in a slow spot in the argument, made him show her all the
cameras. When they came back inside, she'd gone quiet, but opened
a bottle of wine. She poured two glasses. He took that as a good sign.

"I don't get it, though. Why did you only put one camera in the
front hall?"

Most people didn't realize the value of not speaking when they
didn't have to in a tight spot. Vacuum, meet nature. John wasn't most
people. He fought that little fact of the universe and always tried to
keep his mouth shut when it served him well to do so.

He squinted at what she'd asked and shook his head, a perfect picture of innocent confusion. At the very least, the maneuver bought
time. Seconds were money in a tricky conversation. And sometimes a
bewildered look made a generous person discount their own questions
as nonsensical or unfair before they'd let the other person feel too bad.

She looked away from him and into her wine. "I mean, what if
somebody, that guy you're so worried about or someone else, what if
they broke in through the back door? Or had come in through the
garage?"

Shit. He was tired and dull. "I don't know, babe. I didn't think
about it. I put that one camera in to cover the front door, and then I
just realized how much money I'd spent and how maybe it was overkill already. . . ."

Her head snapped up, eyebrow a hard arch over a sparking glare.
"Overkill? You thought it was overkill, but you canceled the monitoring? The one thing that could have actually helped in an emergency?
That doesn't even make any sense. It doesn't even seem like you. It's
not like you to let something go at that. It's so . . ."

Donna stopped, her mouth working around the rest of her sentence. It set off a warning tingle in his jaw. She took a big bolstering
gulp of her wine.

"It's just so half-assed."

John had to clamp down hard not to react. Bitch. The muscles in his legs jumped. His chest craved a huge breath to yell back out. He ached from holding still against every instinct. But too much ground had been lost to even suck air in a way that looked out of place.

He had to move, though. The energy had to go somewhere. He reached out, put his hand over hers, tensing to keep the gesture gentle and steady. He curled his fingertips into her palm. "The important thing is that Carly is okay."

Donna's head dropped in exhausted resignation and she slid her hand out from under his as if it were slimy. "Do you really think I need you to tell me how great it is that nothing worse happened to Carly?"

Donna dragged herself out of the chair shaking her head. She refilled her glass from the bottle on the coffee table, clearly on her way out of the room.

But not without a parting shot. She turned at the doorway, watching him over the rim of her glass, and he dared not look away.

"Why are you so bad at this?" But she didn't wait for an answer. "Carly!" she called. "Get a bag together. We're going to Ada's."

There had been punishment in Donna's threat to go, but even beyond the upset of the fight, they were all restless in the house. It didn't feel right, standing around in the alien echo of trespass.

A parade of strangers had sized up their foyer—the bargain-wood bench stained to make you think walnut, its basket cubbies and jacket hooks above, the granite-and-iron hall table that weighed like a piano, the oil painting right above it that weighed a hundred times more than that in worry. They had peered at the things that were the backdrop to any normal night at home. The creep who had attacked Carly, the police, and the uncounted number of clickers who had already watched the video, all of their scrutiny had left everything feeling pawed.

With all three at the end of their energy, it was like trying to settle into a museum display. It was what normal looked like, but not what it felt like.

But even after everything that had happened, Carly said she didn't want to leave. The guest room had been her idea, a compromise that kept everything simpler.

"There's no way this night isn't going to be weird no matter what," she said. "But why does it have to be that weird? Can't you guys just sleep in different rooms until this gets worked out? Tomorrow will be completely stupid if we leave now. Mom, you can stay in my room with me, if you want. If that's better."

Carly looked to John, wordlessly pleading for him to say something right, to *do* something right. He was surprised that she'd wedged her way into the conversation at all. She usually took in everything from the sidelines, pretending not to be paying attention. But she never manipulated a situation. She was easygoing, always looking for the laugh. She didn't wheedle or angle for advantage. She wasn't the obnoxious kind of kid who hopped up and down for the pat on the head for being precocious. Thank God.

In truth, he was grateful for her interruption and her suggestion. She'd managed to resupply the choice of exits from this mess. He was wrung out. But a jab of recognition startled him. He saw in Carly something privately familiar, a sense of double exposure when he returned her gaze. She was there in the moment, talking and participating, but she was also separated from them. Even from herself, in a way. She was removed, measuring, watching her influence, gauging her reach. She was both an active player and a fly on her own wall. It was a hard trick to manage, as John well knew.

Impressed and unnerved all at the same time, he hooded his notice of it, giving her the privacy of her newfound dexterity. He threw in his lot with Carly and made a case for the spare bed.

All night long, he never sank deeper than a wheel-spinning doze that kicked him awake every time a thought caught traction. The house sounds in the guest room were different from what he was used to. The clatter of the ice maker down in the kitchen came from the wrong direction. It startled him the two times the ice dropped in the night. The bed was aligned fully opposite from his own that he shared with Donna. The streetlight streaming against his closed eyelids came from a strange angle. No tall dresser loomed by the door, so the air moved through the room in a weird way.

John was also terrible at sleeping in hotels or at other people's houses.

He cherished the peace and reassurance of predictability. He'd been killing time with it in the marriage and the new house. It was almost two years since he'd met Donna, both of them captive one afternoon in an airless stint in the holding pen of the DMV. She'd made that ugly time evaporate.

He'd had more ugly time to kill.

John still had a long run of hours, days, months, to go before he would feel free to do what he really wanted to, so he'd been inspired by Donna, her spark striking one of his own, to try his hand at being irresistible. She hadn't resisted, but that wasn't solid proof that he'd actually succeeded. She was beautiful and busy, quick to laugh and slow to cry. He didn't want to be needed, but he admired the little tugs of jealousy and insecurity that pushed him to keep wooing her, and also Carly. The whole diversion was in the game to win them.

But he was addicted to fresh starts. He loved being comfortable, but the urge to break things always held the promise of what to replace it with. His will was a hammer.

John had been enrolled in fourteen schools before he graduated, and he'd been a different sort of kid in each one. He'd made a new Jonathan at every chance, on purpose, for fun and profit. A hammer was a building tool, too.

But it always took him ages to get used to a setup, to dig a self-shaped hole into the pattern of days. He was dug in good this time. Jonathan was John Cooper more than he'd ever been anything else.

The morning after, John knew he had felt worse before, but he'd never been as tired. Donna ticked a glance his way as he walked into the kitchen, but that was all that was on offer—an acknowledgment in place of a greeting. He stopped at the end of the counter, feeling like an intruder with every step into the sunlit room full of everyone else who lived there.

Carly was shoving her quilted lunch bag into her backpack. Her mother fidgeted next to her on the seating side of the kitchen island. Carly, the fact of her and the hope for her safety and happiness, was the only thing that ever rattled Donna. Her only real soft spot.

"Are you sure you want to do this?" asked Donna.

Carly smiled at her mother. "Ye-e-e-e-s. Do you believe me yet?" Carly zipped closed her bag. "Hey," she said to John.

"Hey."

Carly moved to the other side of the island. "Do *you* think it's okay if I go to school?"

The question was on pace. The inflection was right with just enough teenaged exasperation to suit it. But Carly was watching him more steadily than the weight of his answer should warrant. His opinion didn't matter in this. Everyone knew that. She was well aware that in all things parenting, John was neither qualified nor particularly interested. He was a friend to Carly. Someone to joke around with and get rides from. He was her mother's husband, not her father. Everyone was fine with that arrangement, and none more than John.

But Carly had removed herself to the far side of the island, and not by accident. That's what the pointed look was all about. She'd left John and Donna on a level on purpose, with her in opposition.

He held her gaze and slid one symbolic half step toward Donna. "I don't know, Carlzee. You sure it's a good idea? Maybe you should take the day off."

Carly's mouth tightened down against a flash of a knowing smile. "Oh my God! You guys are impossible. I'm fi-i-i-i-ine."

John fought his own smile and reached across to the fruit basket for a banana. Donna didn't move away. It seemed like a good sign. He sent it back over the net one more time for effect. "Are you sure? It was a hell of a night. I don't think anyone expects you to be there. We sure would understand."

Whatever her mission, Carly was satisfied and itching to leave. "No, seriously, I've got to go. Damage control. I've already had ninety-one tags and messages and—" Her phone buzzed and twitched on the counter, and then again before she could pick it up. "Ninety-two, ninety-three . . . See? I gotta go. This is going to get out of control." But she was smiling.

Donna shook her head at John. "It's been nonstop."

Carly swung her backpack onto her shoulder in full stride toward the door. "See ya! It'll be fine."

"What do you mean?" John asked Donna. "What's been nonstop?"

"Mom!" Carly called from the foyer.

John let Donna lead, but they went to the front of the house together.

Carly had gotten all the way to the door. She turned from the narrow sidelight window alongside the stupid dead security panel, with its one glowing, lying green light. John pushed his tongue against his back teeth and looked away.

The high color of cleverness and fizzing excitement drained away from Carly's face. Her mouth had gone loose, unsure.

"Mom, everybody's down there by Ada's block waiting for me. I'm going to make them late. But I don't want to . . . by myself. Can you just . . ." Carly looked back out the window.

Donna was across the floor and wrapped around Carly in an instant, stroking her hair. "I never got the mail yesterday. I'll walk out with you. I'll wait till you get to them," Donna said against Carly's ear. "Let's go."

John caught up to them as Carly reached for the doorknob. The last time she touched it would have been yesterday, when she ran. Maybe for her life. The thought stabbed him and he darted his hand under hers and gripped it first. They looked at each other.

"Have a good day, Carlzee. Go get 'em," he said past a tight throat, and kissed her forehead. He caught Donna watching them through tears. He smiled at her, with her daughter wrapped in his hug. She smiled back, thawing.

In the few minutes that Donna took to make a slow circuit of the path to the mailbox and back, while Carly regained her swagger, her boots striking the street in growing determination, the worry came back to him. A big, heaping scoop of it.

"What was she talking about?" he asked when Donna was back inside, pouring more coffee. She slid a mug to him but didn't put the cream in. Halfway home, maybe. "What you said about it being nonstop? She said it was getting out of control? What is?"

"Oh, the video clip. The police website has a Twitter or Facebook thing. Some of the kids' parents saw it, and, you know, this stuff just flies. I don't know what's going to happen with it or how it's going to go over with everyone. I just hope it's not too much for her. Do you think I should call the school?"

John would have thought he'd burned through all his control the night before. Standing there as the bottom fell out again, it fell hard, but not far. He found that he owned another level of pushback, another subbasement of resolve. He wasn't ready for it, but somehow he was ready for not being ready.

He told Donna to wait and see. No need to make a thing of it if it wasn't going to be a thing. He managed his face. He managed his voice. He showered and didn't cut himself with the razor. He dressed and set out for a few errands.

He stopped by his office to get the things he needed to work from home for the rest of the week. They understood. They'd seen the video. They told him to take all the time he needed.

Donna was shaken to the soul. She didn't need a lot. Almost nothing. That's why he liked her. That's why it was easy. But she needed him now and that was kind of nice. Or it was convenient. Maybe both. Then John wasn't sure what the difference between those two things might be.

When he'd driven up to his office, he hadn't seen the coin on the ground on his way in. But he might have been lost in thought, or a cloud may have passed over the sun, tamping down the glare off its shine. If it was there when he arrived, he must have stepped right over it.

When he came back into the parking lot with the papers and his laptop and the midday sun blazing down, a quarter, heads side up, lay centered on the curb directly in front of his car. Precisely set and never to be confused for dropped change.

He straightened up and swept the full circle around him. How in the hell would Roy Dorring have found out about this so soon? He lived in his truck, for God's sake.

John's first thought was that it was the last thing he needed. It'd taken just about all of what he had left to hold it together with everyone in the office wanting to relive the video with him. They wanted to add their upset to what they assumed was bothering him. His escape from their sympathy had been a fine performance. He was practically vibrating with the need to stop pretending.

John Cooper was the box that held Jonathan Spera, the careful veneer that kept Jonathan distanced from his troubles. John Cooper was nice. Responsible. Easygoing. Patient. Very patient. Jonathan Spera was angry and bored and stuck waiting to resurface.

Jonathan wanted daylight. He wanted his space and his freedom, and nothing so much as to let other people know what he thought of them. And Jonathan Spera didn't have to hide from Roy Dorring. If the sniveling little shit was going to be a problem, it might be nice to let loose on the one person who never fought back and couldn't say a thing about any of it. But it might be disastrous, too.

John was definitely pent up from all of his playing nice, day in and day out, even when it felt actually nice, as it so often and so surprisingly did these days. He wished he knew if Roy had been skulking in the cypress hedges when John had driven up, watching, cowering in the shadows like an oversize rat. Like an ugly-ass opossum. Goddamn Roy. Seriously, goddammit.

John gave the trees the finger anyway and drove off.

CHAPTER FIVE

A lifetime ago, after high school graduation, while all the other kids his age were tending to their mullets and switching out their music collections to cassettes, Roy Dorring had been persuaded that three milk crates full of 8-track tapes were worth almost half the money he'd saved from stocking the shelves and cleaning the Slushee machine at the Q-Mart. The fourth time he broke the Slushee machine was the end of that job. His grandmother, brandishing a broom handle she'd used on him before, threw him out to go learn the world. He never did learn what to do about the world. But he'd kept the 8-tracks for years.

Long after his 8-track player finally died, he discovered that the miles of polyester tape inside them were good for creative repurposing—for braiding up replacement straps for overstuffed duffel bags, for holding together bundles of curtain rods or rags or whatever needed bundling, and for tying down his possessions in the backs of borrowed pickups when he had to move again.

He'd once even used a length of 8-track to splint his broken index finger to its neighbor when he couldn't afford a doctor's bill. It had worked, too, more or less. He never could make a proper fist with his left hand after that, but he'd never really been a fighter anyway.

Roy didn't throw things out. He wanted, with a faintly hollow ache, almost whatever he could gather and keep. He liked having stuff in the way some people liked a big meal. He liked the feeling, the ambient pressure of plenty. It didn't matter if it was frayed or dented or obsolete—he wanted it. You never knew what might grow a purpose when the going got odd.

But everything he owned these days had to fit into an old Ford Explorer with enough room left over to put the seat back so he could sleep. The mess was piled roof high and axle wide, but everything in there was only waiting for the right run of happenstance to be just what somebody needed.

That he was smelling bacon frying this morning was proof that he was right. And if that alone weren't enough to renew his faith in his philosophy of keeping stuff (which it totally was), Roy sat up and stretched and discovered that his back felt like—well, like nothing. It felt like a plain old back, not a web of knots and fishhooks.

After a decent night's sleep, he didn't feel young, exactly, but he couldn't feel every second of the hard fifty-seven years in his body either, and that was near enough to bliss to make him smile.

He'd had something useful in the truck the night before. Of all things, this time it was an old board game. Inspiration wasn't a familiar feeling to Roy, but it had come and goosed him in a moment of need and he'd gone scrabbling around next to the fifty-five-gallon fish tank he kept near the bumper end that held his clothes and important papers.

Because he'd had it, he'd been able to avert a fight between two men he barely knew. In reward and celebration, they'd given him a number of beers that he'd lost count of.

And for a whole night there had been laughter and no fear. Roy had slept a full nine hours on sofa cushions instead of waiting out the darkness in a restless doze on a cold, cracked vinyl bucket seat. He'd had a pillow and everything.

He'd tagged along with Mikey and Byron and the other guys from the worksite, a corporate landscaping project so vast that Roy could reasonably hope for cash under the table for weeks. The guys were headed out for a beer or five to close out the workday. He hadn't exactly been invited, but he wasn't expressly uninvited either. He'd been feeling the blues coming on. He couldn't afford to waste money on bar beer, but he was afraid to be alone.

Roy had been scraping by for the last few years with day work and side jobs and the occasional extra $20 or $50 from John. He'd leave a quarter where John had told him to—in front of John's car by his office, or on the curb where he parked at the YMCA—the old signal between them. It was a pointed joke. Painful, but Roy was a good sport. He wasn't mad. He wasn't.

Shortly after they'd met, he'd won a coin toss for the chance to do some side work for John, to earn some extra money. That moment was so far away it felt like a different life. A different Roy. He'd aged a lot in five years.

And it had all gone completely *old-dynamite wrong*, as Roy's mom used to say.

Roy and John were bound up together in the long fuse of that old dynamite.

John figured that Roy owed him and reminded him of it often. *You lost big when you won that coin toss, Roy. And isn't that just like you? Lose every time, even when you win.*

Roy *did* owe John, from one way of looking at it. The woman who died was Roy's fault. It was an accident, but it didn't change the truth of what Roy had done.

But when Roy downed enough vodka and energy drink, he could admit that John, after a fashion, owed him, too. It wasn't a safe case to make, especially when asking for money. No matter, though. It was true. John owed Roy just as much as the other way around.

Roy was tired all the way through. Things were hard. Life. Work. Hanging on. He hated asking John for anything. But he wasn't getting any better at being hungry, cold, and sliding into the lonely groove that led him to watch the oncoming traffic from the sidewalk and wonder if it would hurt much to step off.

So Roy would have to withstand John's eyes glittering in hateful hope for Roy to get lost or get dead. It didn't matter to John how things went for Roy. Or maybe, more likely, it mattered to him a lot, just not in a way Roy wanted to think about. He'd seen the sparks of temper in John.

Sparks, fuses. Old-dynamite wrong.

But this last night, with a little bit of patience and a fierce grip on his nerves, Roy had found the sweet spot between being needy and being invisible. Roy had taken care of the night, then the night had taken care of itself. Things were looking up.

Mikey and Byron had asked the four guys standing around to come back to Mikey's place to play video games and drink more beer. Three guys declined, and Roy, the only one arguably too old to go with two twentysomethings to play video games, was included only by accident of his standing there within earshot. He'd said yes before they could bend the conversation away from him, and finished the dregs of the warm pint he'd been trying to make last for better than two hours.

But a single flipped light switch and two steps into Mikey's nasty little hole of a house and the plan was undone. The pride of the house (there was no reason to think any of the other rooms held more promise) was a seventy-five-inch TV. It had probably been top-of-the-discount-store-line right up until someone had put a roundish cave-in into the screen with shatter cracks flung to every corner of the glass.

Mikey threw a fit and cussed the walls over who might have done such a thing, while Byron scratched at his scalp and tried not to laugh, which didn't go over well. Roy watched between them both, counting in his head to keep the anxiety pushed down, listening hard to figure out whom to side with to keep the night from going over to fists and ending too soon.

Then he remembered the board game in the truck and convinced the boys to go old-school with the entertainment.

Mikey and Byron had never played Monopoly. They were young. Though even if it all came down to just age, Roy had to admit that it was hard to imagine Mikey or Byron growing up in a household where there'd ever been family game night. Feral, that's what they were. Cats with no collars.

They'd laughed when he'd brought it in. The wear and repair on the box had left the bottom more duct tape than cardboard, the white-and-red top frayed to fuzz along the edges. The play money had been so thoroughly thumbed that it was all more or less the same dingy color. But even after almost three decades, every bit of it was still there—every playing piece, every property marker, all the Community Chest and Chance cards. Even the original dice.

And in the random chemistry of some nights, it was great. There was beer enough on hand and the laughter was contagious, and by the time everyone was bleary-eyed and completely, if temporarily, over the busted TV, Mikey disappeared down the hall and came back with a tattered lace-trimmed pillow and pointed vaguely past the kitchen and reminded Roy that the bathroom was back that way, if he needed it.

So here the next morning, with the sun blazing through the bent blinds, was the smell of bacon, and after some clomping and door slamming, a good bit of noisy chatter coming from the kitchen.

Roy walked in on the end of an argument. A young woman with yesterday's mascara smudged down to her cheekbones had her glittering club shoes swinging by their straps in the fist she was jabbing over the table at Mikey.

She cut her eyes at Roy as he crossed the kitchen's threshold, but homed back in on their host, who went rigid under her wrath.

"And you can ask your asshole brother. I haven't been here for almost a week. I don't know what happened to your stupid TV, and there's no way I'm on the hook for it. I just came to get some of my shit." She shook the drawstring bag that was scrunched in her non-shoe fist. "And to get my pillow, except that you let some random hobo sleep on it with his greasy-ass head." Her shoe-clutching hand flung out toward Roy. The heel swung wide and nearly took the nose off of Byron, who was sitting quiet and goggle-eyed next to Mikey at the table.

Byron sputtered out a laugh at Roy's expense.

"And I don't know who you are," the girl said to Byron, drilling him through with a bloodshot glare. "But you can fuck right off, too."

She abruptly ran out of steam and sighed. The bacon sizzled and smoked. The girl dropped the bag and her shoes on the linoleum and crossed to the stove. She turned the bacon with tongs while the three men stared at the window, the clock, the tabletop.

She turned around, hands on hips, then retrieved her stuff. She walked the long way around the table and kissed Mikey on the top of his head, then clonked him over the skull, right on the kissed spot, with a dull clatter of stilettos on bone.

"Ow! Fuck!"

"Tell your brother to call me." The hinges of the screen door screamed in protest as she banged through. "And you owe me a new pillow!"

The silence settled around everything but the spit of bacon grease.

"That bitch needs to chill." Byron stared after her on her barefoot way down the sidewalk.

"Nah. She's okay." Mikey rubbed his sore head and winced. "My brother's kind of a dick." He brought the bacon to the table on a paper towel.

Breakfast was almost-burnt bacon and beer and a splash of orange juice from the bottom of the carton, split three ways into red plastic cups.

The scant discussion turned to how nice it would be to have some weed to soothe their hangovers. Mikey and Byron both had reasons why none of their money could go toward a trip to the house on the corner.

Roy hated weed. The lightness that other people seemed to feel when they smoked was lost on him. The woozy high rose up in him like helium, stretching him like a balloon, but with no lift, only pull and itch and worry that something would bust.

At the table with his new friends, he struggled for the right tone. He didn't want it. He couldn't afford it. And if he didn't help them, they might make him leave. "I mean, it's totally fine with me if you guys do. I don't have any problem with it. I just don't . . . it doesn't . . . I just can't."

"It's cool. No problem," Byron said. But it wasn't true. His voice was thick with a disappointed problem.

"Hey"—Mikey looked at Roy—"have you got a gun?"

Roy felt all the blood speed away from his head as if he were doing it on purpose. Because he absolutely would do it on purpose. He would happily drain his head like an oil pan, if he could. Anything to unplug the idea of having a gun, touching a gun. He'd do just about anything to hold the door against the memory of the roar that went with a pulled trigger, the gasp and gurgle through a bullet-torn neck.

"Hey, hey! Dude!" Mikey reached over and grabbed Roy's shoulder. "Dude, dude." Mikey was laughing now. "You should see your face. I didn't mean it like you would rob anybody. Not for weed. Don't be crazy."

Roy looked at Mikey, bewildered. His neck was cold with sweat. His hands were icy and damp.

"Damn, man. You need to chill," Byron said.

"No, hang on. I've got an idea." Mikey left the room and came back with a terry-cloth-wrapped something that he thunked down onto the table.

Somehow it was obvious that only one thing in the world would make a noise like that. Mikey unwrapped the gun, a black .38 revolver, bullet tips glowering from their nests in the barrel. Roy might have been less alarmed if the guy had uncovered a coiled snake.

"Here's what I'm thinking," Mikey said. "You live in your truck, right?"

Roy had been in Mikey's house for just over fourteen hours, with Byron, and briefly some girl, and a game and some jokes and more untroubled sleep than he'd had in months.

He'd woken not even noticing his hope, well rested beneath his jacket, but on top of a pillow that smelled like flowery perfume. He'd forgotten about the truck and the several hundred pounds of useless junk in the back. None of his heaps of nothing had crossed his mind in more than half a day, and he'd forgotten that he was worried about feeling low. Some pound-puppy part of his mind had curled up as if he were home, as if he'd been adopted.

Byron chimed in, "Ray, man, it's okay. No shame that you have to stay in your truck sometimes. You're getting by, man. We all get by as best we can."

"*Roy,*" said Roy.

"What?"

"My name is Roy, not Ray."

"Oh. Right. Sorry, man."

"So I was thinking," Mikey continued. "Anybody who lives in his truck should have a gun. You don't know what could happen. You might need it. There are assholes out there who *need* to see a gun to believe you. And I'll sell you this one for a hundred."

"You're going to sell your brother's gun?" Byron asked.

"He's got, like, six of 'em." Mikey nodded to his own decision. "Plus, fuck that guy. He's probably the one who broke my TV. And, yeah, fuck that guy."

Roy jammed his fingernail down over a bottom tooth. "I don't want a gun," he said around his chewing.

"You probably do, seriously, but whatever," Byron said. "If not, just buy it and sell it, if you want." The hope for getting high had returned to his voice. "It's worth way more than a hundred dollars. Bet Mikey here would take a little less, right, Mike?"

And there it was. The bargain. The hook of usefulness. Roy wasn't mad that Byron didn't know his name or that they wanted him to leave. He wasn't. He didn't want the gun, but it could be useful. Spend money to make money. He'd heard that. Right. Do that, sell it, and maybe then you don't have to ask John for anything anymore. Maybe there's a way to get a step up, a little boost to get a payday ahead, just even one. Then you're on the way to a place to stay and a real job and a girlfriend who forgets to wash her face, but turns the bacon and kisses you on the head.

In the end, Roy gave Mikey $80 for the gun, almost everything he had. Mikey and Byron clapped Roy on the back and told him to take care and that they'd see him later at work. They said it had been a good time, but they said it on the front stoop with their eyes already cast to the end of the block, watching the foot traffic in and out of the last house there.

Roy didn't like the weight of the gun in his hand and insisted that it be wrapped up before he took it. He didn't trust it not to slide across the truck's seat or floor when he took a fast turn in a sharp bend. He didn't want it in the glove box, either, with his registration, should he need it—the registration or the gun.

So he put the Monopoly box back where he'd gotten it in glee the night before, in a mood of belonging. He took the gun wrapped in the hand towel and layered it in with care inside the dry aquarium, beneath the board game, cushioned in with the undershirts, stacked newest to rattiest, the seven work shirts and two pairs of blue jeans, and the sad wad of shredded boxers and holey socks.

He put his jacket on the passenger seat. It was folded over the perfumed pillow he'd tucked inside it when Mikey and Byron weren't looking. The girl said she'd wanted a new one because Roy had put his head on it. It was embarrassing, but he understood. He wasn't mad. He wasn't.

But he was down $80, plus the little bit he'd spent at the bar. Now his cash wouldn't last him until next payday. He realized he didn't know how to get rid of the gun. It wasn't like a normal thing to sell, not a normal question to ask. He didn't know anyone who might know what to do with it.

So he stopped by the store for three raspberry vodka minis and two energy drinks. He downed the whole mixed potion fast, like medicine. The polluted buzz would be just near enough to not giving a rat's ass anymore. It would let him get things done.

He took out his stopwatch and got what he'd say down to sixteen seconds, even with a lot of *please*s and *thank-you*s. He nudged his finger through the loose change in the cup holder to see if he had any quarters. He'd leave one for John so he'd know they needed to talk.

CHAPTER SIX

John had firsthand experience with the run-and-hide reflex. He knew what it took. Everyone thought it was the go-to move when things fell apart, but that was only for people who'd never actually had anything truly fall apart. It wasn't just a response. It was a commitment. Evaporating out of the twenty-first century wasn't easy.

Jonathan Spera had found an old painting. That bit of good luck met three things: a gap in his knowledge, a gorgeous art dealer, and an idiot called Roy Dorring. These ingredients, when blended together too fast, made a disaster that, at first, looked like easy money.

Jonathan Spera's mistake had been in thinking he could unmix the batter and rethink the recipe after the oven door was closed.

He'd offered Roy $5,000 to scuttle the sale. Five thousand dollars was ten times more money than that witless weed had ever had to his name at any given time. If Roy had just shown up and disrupted the meeting, just enough for Jonathan to back out so he could rethink and renegotiate without Marcelline, he would've gotten paid.

But that's not what Roy did. Roy had shot two men in a panicked sort of on purpose—and Marcelline entirely by accident.

That night, after the gunfire, Jonathan had escaped with more than he'd intended to. The cash was a lucky stroke, but no one was supposed to get hurt except maybe Roy.

No one giving chase knew who Jonathan was. They didn't know where he lived or worked. They didn't know how to contact him. They didn't know his last name.

So he could use his credit cards. He *did* use his credit cards. He'd used them to get off the street and watch from a hotel room's television all that next day to see if anything would rise to the level of the local news from the mess he'd left.

But there was nothing. It was as if it hadn't happened. And it wasn't even a little bit reassuring. All it made him know for certain was that the people he was dealing with could make a bloody, noisy open-air firefight vanish, and a parking lot littered with dead bodies somehow unnewsworthy.

Back then, he'd been able to unplug from his life legitimately. Sell his condo. Quit his job. Move. Change his name the proper way and do it far away from anyone who might care. And still, it was nerve-racking.

John Cooper had thoroughly unanchored from Jonathan Spera, which should have made John Cooper more likely to get hit by a bus than caught.

The only loose end had been Roy.

Roy Dorring was the only one who knew John Cooper used to be Jonathan Spera. Roy was the only one who'd known Jonathan Spera was connected to the painting.

But he could handle Roy. Roy was an idiot. Roy would always be an idiot. John was pretty sure that it would take him all of six minutes to convince Roy that the earth was actually flat and spinning through the universe like a fucking Frisbee.

Four years ago, John had told him a different, more useful lie about how the world worked. John told Roy that he hadn't been able to retrieve the painting. He told him they were safe because the buyer's guy, the one Roy didn't get a chance to shoot, took it.

If they kept their heads—meaning if Roy did what John told him to do—they could make it. Roy had believed him, and John had spent the last four years trying to scrape him off his shoe.

Roy's blundering had put John's life on hold. But now the video.

It might be better if they just had it out. Waiting and wondering what Roy was thinking, however pale and pointless his thinking ever was, wasn't going to do anything good for John's mood.

Roy needed to get it out of his head, right fucking now, that he was getting anything out of this catastrophe. John felt it might, for once, come down to physically knocking the idea out of Roy. With a wrench on his skull, if need be.

It had been less than twenty-four hours since any possibility of anyone connecting John Cooper to the painting, and already he was exhausted by the whole thing.

You can pay for a hotel room in cash, but they'll notice you. It wouldn't do to be remembered when the type of people looking for you can keep mayhem off the news. He didn't have time to outrun his new name. If he had to run, this time it would be cash running, which was the hardest kind.

The painting had to come down out of sight. If there was going to be any margin to find, any hope to try to sell it or disappear with it, it couldn't stay on the wall. He had to be cool about it. If he could manage to walk away instead of run, he might be able to make this work again.

The plan, when he got home, was to redecorate the foyer. He would replace everything and take down the painting from where Donna had insisted on hanging it.

When they had bought the house and moved in together, she'd found it wrapped in blankets during the bustle of combining his meager belongings with hers and Carly's. She'd nailed it up before he could stop her.

But he'd tried to.

Oh, wait. I didn't have that out. Don't . . . I mean, do you really want that there?

It goes great! Look, it's perfect. I didn't figure you for an antique-y type.

I'm not. It's not really my taste.

Don't get defensive. It's sweet. Do you really not like it? Is it just a sentimental thing? A gift from an old girlfriend or something?

No, no, nothing like that. It's just . . .

A family heirloom? Hang on, is this thing a real antique?

No! It's . . . it's fine. It's just a little embarrassing. Yeah, I bought it. Some people have comfort food. I've got comfort . . . colors.

Well, I like it. And I like that I learned something new about you just now. And that it wasn't some deal breaker that I'd have to do something drastic about. It's adorable.

She'd kissed him, a little turned on by the softer side of him that really wasn't. And that was that.

It didn't really look like anything more than a wall hanging from a fake-cinnamon-smelling décor-and-knickknack shop. He'd had no choice but to laugh along. She'd thought it looked perfect there and John hadn't been able to think of a way to make the case against her happy discovery without turning it into a topic of contention or, God forbid, further conversation.

To keep Roy from pissing his pants every time he came up against the next thing he couldn't manage in his life, John had invented the emergency measure of the call system.

John designated three spots he'd always use at the Y or his office so that Roy could signal him, if he could just hold himself together long enough to find the car. He'd made it plain to Roy that he would actually, physically kill him if he ever attempted to contact him at home or on the telephone.

John had been convincing to an easily convinced moron, but he idly doubted that he'd be able to bring himself to really hurt Roy. It was useful to give him a scare every now and again, a little peek under the lid of John's temper when plain words wouldn't do. But John wasn't a killer. Probably. Sometimes that was a relief and sometimes it was a speed bump.

The passing of time wasn't improving his opinion of the idiot or tamping down how irritating he found Roy's sad-sack face. John tried not to think about it. Thoughts became things and he didn't know how to end anyone's life outside of a daydream. But as the months turned to years, he found that he wasn't any less inclined to kill Roy.

If John found a coin, he was supposed to meet Roy at 6:00 p.m. or 8:00 a.m.—whichever he could manage within the next day—in the back parking lot of the closest McDonald's.

With Roy's latest signal weighing like a lead sinker at the bottom of John's otherwise empty pocket, he wandered around the house-wares section of Target. Necessity would get him over the hurdle of his lack of imagination. With exactly one exception, he didn't give a shit about what hung on the wall.

Once home, he put the painting in the back of the guest-room closet and nailed up a three-panel metal scrollwork in its place.

"Wow." Donna waved her hands at the frenzied wreckage of cardboard boxes burst at the staples. "What are you doing? What's all this?"

John startled and nearly swallowed the last nail he'd stashed between his lips while he worked.

"I thought a change would be good. I got a different mirror, too, see? After I get this up, I'm going to put that new bench together." He pointed to the long box leaning against the wall. "Goodwill is scheduled to swing by tomorrow to pick up all the old stuff. This place feels all bad mojo now. Thought I'd try to make it feel new. None of us needs to be reminded what happened every time we walk through the door."

Donna came to stand beside him. "It's really nice. I like it. I've always said you have good taste."

John dipped his head, surprised that the satiny stroke of the small compliment even registered in the moment.

Donna tapped her lip, thinking and turning a circle in the foyer. "But maybe the other picture would look really good over the fireplace. What do you think?"

John's heart kicked his sternum. "I'm just going to get rid of all of it. The whole point is that Carly has to live here after all of this. I don't want her to see the same things she saw when . . . I want to do this for her, okay? We can paint in here, too, if you want."

Donna touched him for the first time in more than a day and a half. "Okay. That's very sweet."

CHAPTER SEVEN

Emma O'Connor hadn't had braces on her teeth for more than twenty-one years, but she still ran her tongue over her front teeth whenever she was lost in distraction. In some remote part of her mind, she'd never quite gotten over the feeling of the difference once the brackets and wires came off. Even as a grown woman, some small part of her remained right there at that transition of her teenage self—transformed from wrong to right, at least in the teeth.

The habit of feeling for it, for reconfirming herself to herself, became a time slip, a subconscious touching base when she fell absorbed in a task.

The scar running up the right side of her neck into the sunken place that should have been the squared turn of her jaw was a souvenir from a more recent metamorphosis, this time from right to wrong. And also to *wronged*.

The scar had finally faded to a quieter shade of pink on the white field of her skin, but it had always been too high to cover with a scarf, so she'd grown out her hair to hide it, as much as it would ever stay hidden.

The tall, slick, sharp-jawed urban pixie, in good suits and a constant hurry, wouldn't recognize the shaggy-haired woman in T-shirts and worn-through jeans that she'd become.

Dragging her fingers along the knotted track of damage and repair on her neck was now part of the ritual fidgeting, along with the habit of sweeping her straight white teeth with her tongue, unconsciously revisiting the reminders of her milestones. She did these things when she was lost in thought—daydreaming, puttering, reading, and especially when she was at the computer, as she was now, clicking through the social media feeds.

Her mother's page was set to private, so Emma only caught electronic glimpses of her whenever she commented on someone else's post. Her brother's son had become quite a good photographer as his high school years spooled out, so mostly there were just pictures by the dozens, imported from his Instagram feed. But her sister was a Facebook champion.

Regular days and holidays, big events and little nothings, Bethany chronicled it all. She was so thorough in her updates that some days Emma nearly forgot that they hadn't spoken to each other in four years. But time had definitely passed. There was a new baby in the family, and also a niece by marriage she'd never met. A favorite cousin had passed away after an illness he hadn't yet been stricken with when Emma last saw him. There were new jobs and house moves and achievements and sometimes pictures of what someone had for lunch. Everyone got cartoon cakes in their birthday messages.

But each year on Emma's birthday, her sister stayed off-line. No one ever mentioned Emma in the lively discussion threads that Bethany hosted. Emma was the ghost at the never-ending cyber-reunion, watching unnoticed, ungreeted. Always and never there.

Her own social media accounts were not in her real name. They weren't in the name Emma O'Connor either. The profile picture wasn't a photo of her. She'd learned to use proxy servers to keep even more distance. She watched her family from more than a thousand miles away, with layers of electronic anonymity protecting everyone from her, and her from maybe no one. She could never be sure.

When her sister posted something that generated a conversation—with friends and relatives all having their say in back-and-forths that scrolled down the screen—it felt like a gift. Emma checked the feeds throughout the day, pinging home all the time, though they never knew it, but she saved the longer posts and conversations like a sweet treat, a dessert for after the eating-her-veggies part of the day.

She had the internet and her sketch pads to fill her evenings. And wine. She didn't bother with the television. It was a showcase of all she couldn't have in the world, and her jaw hurt if she got clenchy with rage. Beyond that, all the good TV was expensive. The budget bridged the bills, but not with a lot of slack.

Emma had come into town with a little cash for getting settled. She'd had a suitcase full of clothes—more than half with the tags still attached, a laptop, a box of books, and an art case. Her new life fit into the trunk of an uninspiring but reliable used car. The Toyota's lines seemed modeled on a squashed loaf of sandwich bread, and it was bread-crust brown, too. She used to care about the finer things, including good, not-brown, cars. This one's engine gave a pouty yowl when she asked too much of it, but it got her around. And most importantly, if things ever went wrong, it would get her out again with the go-bag she'd been told to keep on board at all times. She never let the gas tank run below half-full.

Her cover was that she was an artist escaping an abusive marriage. She hated that story so much she'd surrendered her outgoing nature to keep from telling it. She would only ever break it out to get by in the unavoidable social crossings that required a little history to get through. And she tried to tell it only to men. Women might want to console her or to share their own angers and terrors, and Emma would be left lying way more than she was good at.

So she talked to men when she talked at all. She'd say the word *abuse* and their eyes would drift to the scars on her face and neck. Discomfort would close their mouths. And they wouldn't open them again until the topic had changed. So she would obligingly let them off the hook and talk about something else to get what she needed in order to return to her sketch pads, internet, and wine.

When she'd needed a job, the Craigslist search led her to Eddie Delahunt, who, like every other man, squirmed under the weight of her tale and lowered his eyes from the implied nightmare of the right side of her face. But she was pleasant and still exuded her old competence, and he hired her on the spot to care for his eighty-six-year-old mother, June.

The pay was a small weekly stipend and a garage apartment with a bed, a desk, four cane-backed chairs around a glass dinette set from the eighties, and an internet connection. Bare bones. Anonymous, but friendly. The stuff that fresh starts and soul starvations were made of.

Caring for June had slowed Emma's days to the speed of a body that had seen nearly ninety years. There was so much to notice at that pace. The bottom line—that there was only this one life and what you chose to drag through it—worked at Emma's conscience. Haunting her family electronically reminded her of what she used to be not all that long ago.

Her sister's latest Facebook conversation beckoned. With June full of her bird's portion of dinner and her last vice, a nightly gin and tonic that was practically homeopathic for its mere whiff of Bombay Sapphire, Emma tucked her into bed and raised the safety rail. The evening's pills went down with a little Ovaltine, and June's dentures went into the soak. Emma brushed the old woman's hair and felt herself relax in tandem with her. She kissed June's cool forehead, furrowed as it tended to get in the later hours, as the confusion rose with the moon. Emma put on Rosemary Clooney's greatest hits and set it to auto-repeat.

She'd come back later to check on June before she went to bed herself. Eddie had already called in for his nightly debrief of his mother's day. His conscience jousted with his work schedule, and it soothed him to know how she was doing without having to do it all himself.

Emma poured a glass of Malbec and clicked into her sister's feed. Bethany had posted a video that had already kicked off a roll of commentary. If Emma was lucky, she might even catch a post snapping into the chain while she was watching. It always startled her. A little thrill to be psychically caught by the only people she'd want to be caught by. Could they feel her there, watching as they typed?

She previewed the stacked responses first. *Hi, Mom,* she thought, as she always did when their mother showed up on the screen.

Emma took a big swallow of wine to put a different kind of lump in her throat.

Several people she knew (because she couldn't bring herself to admit it was *had known,* unfixably past tense) had commented—*Wow! Grrl power! That was awesome! That poor baby.*

She started the video, primed with interest, fully ready to be with them in spirit and as impressed as everyone else, trying to be content to click on what they had clicked and watch what they had seen. With them, but not.

The video had a nature-show feel to it. The built-in dread of the camera's vantage point stopped Emma's wineglass halfway to her mouth—a young girl in the role of the antelope, with a grim young lion-guy prowling after her. Emma watched him close in and corner the girl at her front door. The next camera shift brought up the interior of the house.

Even if the advancing progress bar at the bottom of the frame hadn't shown that the adventure was almost over, the natural rhythm of narrative did. The fight, life-or-death, would happen inside the house. One way or the other, it was nearly The End.

But all Emma knew in the moment of the scene change was the burning spur of a beginning. Not a starting gun, but a cannon, a bomb blast. Heat swept up her body as she stared at the screen in disbelief. She moved her glass toward the desk, but the base hit the edge of the wood instead of landing home. Emma barely flinched as it crashed into shards on the floor.

The foyer of the house on the computer screen was bog-standard suburban. A six-panel door. A plain glass light fixture up above, full of flame-shaped bulbs. Big beige tiles set in a diamond pattern on the floor. A bench along the left wall faced off with a hall table against the right.

The desperate struggle played out between the human animals in the middle of the image, but Emma couldn't pull her eyes away from the right side of the screen. The historian, the expert hiding within the scarred, quiet caregiver, stirred.

Above the table, with just a corner showing at the edge of the field of capture, was a painting.

This was no print. The light didn't slide off it as it would against any slick, glossy paper. This surface drew in light as only oil paints could. Its texture simmered the plain ambient sunlight in the colors: russet ocher for the mill and the waterwheel, strokes of slate and white that called to mind the silver ridges on peaks of river water flowing over stones. Even in this rough resolution, she could make out a fine web of craquelure in the ancient varnish that spoke to its age. Centuries.

Decor stores sold aged-looking replicas of all sorts of great masterworks. But not this one.

Emma could envision the rest of the painting without trying—a smallish, fairly tame terra-cotta and green landscape, the tree trunks, the bridge, the terraced land stepping off into the background. The mountain plateau. The pair of travelers in the foreground seemed brushed in as nearly an afterthought, as if they were put in self-consciously when the painter remembered mankind. The greens of the foliage were interesting, the finest element of this work in her opinion, the painted light on them converged in the center of the picture, well rendered in carefully layered shades of color under a storm-surly sky.

The odd ivory obelisk at center left would be just past what this video's angle showed. She wanted to nudge the screen, to drag the cursor as if she could bring the painting down to show her what she knew was there, to prove that she was right.

The value of story could make a treasure out of anything. In the art world, a good story, a heavy history, could take a mundane landscape and make it priceless, make it something worth killing over.

The painting, *Landscape with Obelisk* by Govaert Flinck, long mistaken for a minor work by the master Rembrandt van Rijn, was a case that proved the point.

Emma doubled over in her chair, her arms gripped around her middle, holding in a sob. The shock of seeing the Flinck without warning had wrung the heat out of her. She was freezing. But her scar burned.

It had been a fantasy to know what had happened to it. And what had happened to Jonathan. She'd dreamed of using that knowledge to get her life back. The dream had been her companion, her coach, the air in her lungs.

After Jonathan, she'd spent nearly a year disappearing and healing, learning to talk and eat naturally around a jaw that didn't work quite right. The task after that was surrendering to the truth—that the danger in getting caught trying to find the painting and force a homecoming was too great. For her and for her family. It was too dangerous for her even to research. So she hadn't.

Anyone looking for the painting (and people had been looking for it for nearly thirty years) would be dragging the electronic net for anyone else who might be searching for it. They would all be her enemies. Jail or worse, depending on who found her first.

She'd tried letting it all go as the months wound out, click by click on the computer, her friends and loved ones and the hope of ever righting this wrong fading from the forefront of her thoughts. After four years, the heat of wanting it was all but lost at the vanishing point. She'd acclimated to a shortened focus, to days made of helping June through fits of oddly happy, if uncooperative, dementia. Emma's nights were spent drawing and drinking and cyberstalking her people.

And now a reset. Revenge was her heartbeat again. The painting was right there on that flat, cold screen, but also very much on a nail on a wall in a house somewhere.

Emma was unsurprised by the jolt coursing through her, and at the wild urge to grab a few things to add to her duffel in the trunk of her car. She wasn't even shocked by the sudden satisfied rage, the mental image flaring back into her mind's eye after all this time, the ugly but good daydream: Jonathan bleeding out and her just letting him.

But what did knock her sideways and press a howl out through her gritted teeth was the fear of that hope, of failing and of having to let it all go again, and the sudden wish that she'd never seen the video at all.

CHAPTER EIGHT

Waiting suited Roy. He kind of liked it. Other people got upset over their minutes ticking off into the air, or draining away into the floor under their feet, or soaked up into the pavement under their slow-rolling wheels. The chance to get ahead of their to-do lists dried up, and it meant a lot more to most people than it did to Roy. He never minded the blameless moments that trickled out in between the things he should be doing. He found them peaceful.

Waiting in traffic wasn't too bad. Or on line for a lottery ticket, or in this case just passing an hour in his truck with his eye on the corner where John would be turning into sight.

He didn't ever count time spent waiting. It was the easiest time of all. In delays that couldn't be blamed on him, he could disappear without trying. And hiding from the world was practically his part-time job. It was better not to be seen at all than to be seen screwing up. It was self-preservation.

He craned to look farther down the road, between the buildings, watching for the flash of John's red car.

The envy of how easy life seemed for other people was an injury that Roy couldn't really feel anymore. It was an old pain, part of the background hum of being him. But just like being able to put your hand on your knee with your eyes closed, no fumbling, he knew where to find that feeling. It was the YOU ARE HERE marker that flagged his place in the food chain.

No matter what *it* was, he was well aware he was about to get it wrong. In some small way, or in a big way, someone would be annoyed with Roy. Someone would be disgusted. Someone would be furious or done with him altogether. Or worse, someone would have something to say: a curse, a recap, a lecture, or a lengthy, earnest sermon of advice.

And he, being on the wrong side of whatever, would have to withstand it and agree and say he would do better next time. He'd have to nod a lot and try to keep from shrugging or looking sad. They hated that. It was blood in the water for some people. And Roy couldn't get angry when it was only true. So he didn't.

Roy couldn't tell if other people worried about the same things he did. He didn't know if anyone else always had an ear cocked for bad luck slinking up behind them, ready to climb their pant leg and ride them like a horse into the next mistake.

Waiting was a chance to rest.

Roy stretched against the seat and stole a glance away from the road to dig out the half-empty bag of barbecue pork rinds crushed against the center console by all of the God-knows-what that was crammed into every inch of space on the passenger side.

He settled back into his seat and checked the road again for John's car, watching the street for every second of forewarning he could get. He only needed a little money to make it through to payday. Just twenty bucks. Thirty at most. It wasn't anything he hadn't asked for dozens of times. But it didn't get easier. John hated it. So did Roy.

He wondered if he should offer the gun to John for a good price. It would be less like begging. But John holding a gun, even just as a picture in Roy's mind, gave him the chills.

He dug around in the bag of pork rinds with the hope of discovering one with all its corners intact. There weren't any good ones left, only airy shrapnel and crumbs. He ate the biggest pieces first, pressing his lips together to keep from crunching too loud.

He looked away from the road again, this time for the last mini-bottle of raspberry vodka he'd hidden in the seat under a wad of napkins in case anyone walked by or rolled up on him. He poured it into the warm half-can of Red Bull waiting in the cup holder, and he shoved the empty bottle back under the tent of paper. He swished the can in a tight circle to mix the brew. It tasted like courage and melted SweeTarts.

Two minis were already burning in him, and a can and a half of the energy drink. He'd save the rest. It would top him off while he was talking to John. If he rationed it out just right, it would keep his bravery afloat. And he could always take a swallow of it when he needed to buy five seconds to think of something not stupid to say.

A wink of red over the rim of the can zapped him like a cattle prod. He took another big sip.

The tires of John's car squealed lightly in his fast turn into the parking lot where, at the back, behind the grassy median, Roy waited for him. Sunlight streaked over the clean finish on the wheel flares in blinding, sinuous arcs. John's car jerked to an angled stop next to Roy's. The door flew open and John dodged around it as it slammed home.

"You piece of shit." John reached through the truck's open window and hooked Roy's neck and dragged his head down. John's hand was fever hot. "You piece of shit. Do you think you can get in on this now? After what you did? Do you think you have any claim, any right to anything?"

"What? John? What? Wait!"

John wrenched open the truck's door and Roy spilled out onto the blacktop. He scrambled to his feet. The Red Bull can rolled away and chugged the rest of its magic onto the blacktop.

There had been a few shoves from John before that could have been written off as just kidding if Roy wanted to, which he did. It could have been worse.

This was worse. John had never come at him for real. Roy put out his arms to stop John's charge. "Wait! Wait!"

John slapped Roy's arms down. "Wait? Are you kidding me? Asshole, you set a quarter out on the curb. Today? In the middle of all this shit? You summon me up here, knowing fuck all about what is going on. But you think you do, don't you? All of a sudden, you think you're smart. Don't you dare put your hands up now and squeal *wait* like a little bitch. Do you think this changes anything for you? Do you think you have something on me? Did you think I'd just roll over?"

"John, wait. Come on." Roy stepped back two stumbling strides and ran his hands through his dirty, graying hair. It had been a good few days since he'd been able to shower. He could smell himself. "I didn't mean to make you so mad. I just wanted to talk."

John scanned him head to toe, and Roy wanted to fold flat under the miserable spotlight of John's anger.

"How did you see it? Huh? Did you get yourself a *smart*phone? Dummy got a smartphone now? Is that it?" John sneered as if he were going to spit. Roy almost couldn't imagine John spitting. People with ironed shirts and shiny red cars didn't spit.

John was still midtirade and Roy came back on task, almost sharp with caffeine, but still drifty with the vodka.

"—do you get Wi-Fi in that heap-of-shit truck? Did one of your homeless buddies get YouTube pulled up on the internet for you? 'Cause I know they didn't let you into the library looking like that."

"I'm sorry." Roy didn't know all of what he might be sorry for at that particular moment, but he felt quite a bit sorrier than usual.

John stared at him, his shoulders rising and falling with the heaving of his breath. Something was off—really off—and the caffeine side of the seesaw lifted Roy into a short swell of clarity. He chanced a solid long look at John's face. He was tight around the eyes, as if he couldn't let all the way go of a squint. The little ridges between his eyebrows looked almost sad. He was pale and fighting to keep his shoulders straight. If Roy could recognize anything in the world, it was a back that wanted to stoop.

"What's wrong? Is everything okay?"

"What's *wrong*? What's—" John leaned back and looked at Roy, regarded him fully up and down with an extraslow, searching pass of Roy's face. For once, it didn't feel like being scraped with a wire brush. John was checking for something.

Then John sent his own word back to Roy. "Wait."

Roy shuffled back another small step, sneaking in another few inches between them, a bit more head start, just in case.

John tilted his head, and the more usual mocking study of Roy warmed back up on his face. His natural smirk bloomed and brought a little of his color back with it. "Is this just a regular day for you, Roy? What do you mean 'Is everything okay?' "

Roy looked down at his wrecked boots. "I don't know. I mean, I know you don't like it when I need to talk to you. And I don't mean to bother you. I never do. But . . . I don't know, you just seem different." Roy checked John's expression. John seemed more like himself, and that was both good and awful. Roy kept on. More apology always seemed to help with John. "I just didn't know if something else had happened to you to make you so upset. I didn't know if you were okay."

"That's it? You just want to know if I'm okay. Well, wow, Roy. What do I do with that? And if I'm not okay, then what? Are you going to help me out? You gonna come to my rescue, Mighty Mouse?"

"No. I don't know. I mean, I don't know what you need."

"From *you*? Let's see, what do I need from you? You're a pain in my ass, Roy. You've *always* been a pain in my ass. The only thing I need from you is never to have met you. That's what I wish for on all my birthday candles and every shooting star. Did you know that? But since I can't have what I wish for on fucking candles and comets, if you *really* want to help me out, Roy, then maybe just drop dead. That would do it. That would work fine."

Roy's throat clenched and his pulse banged into his vision. He hadn't always been a pain in the ass. That wasn't true. John wanted it both ways. He wanted it all the ways. *Hey, Roy, need a pack of smokes? So wash my car. Do it real nice. Meh, that's not good enough, Roy. You missed a spot. So, hey, Roy, how 'bout you cut my grass for pocket change? Hey, Roy, you stupid shit, I know you about broke your back doing my yard work, but get up early and clean out this garage, whydontcha. . . .*

Roy hadn't been a pain in the ass all the times he did everything John asked of him. He hadn't been a pain in the ass when John had given him a gun and told him to come to the parking lot and point it at the people who would be buying the picture of the storm coming up over the waterwheel and the mountain. It was a nice picture. Roy had liked it.

Of course, he'd done it all wrong, which had ruined everything, but he'd never said a word or done a single thing that got them in trouble for it. He'd done everything John told him to do.

But here on the McDonald's blacktop, Roy remembered that he'd never won an argument in his entire life.

John actually did spit. "Goddamn, I'm thirsty."

Roy was usually unshockable. Not so in this moment. He very much wanted back the time earlier that morning when he decided to leave the quarter.

"What do you want, Roy? Why—fucking exactly—did you call me out here today?"

"I'm sorry, John."

"You really, really are." John opened his wallet, pulled out two $20 bills, and shoved them into the pocket of Roy's best work shirt. He hadn't wanted to put it on over his dirty undershirt, but it was as good as he could manage in getting ready for their meetup.

John shook his head at him. "I swear to fucking God, Roy. . . ."

John got back into his car and drove away.

CHAPTER NINE

Owen Haig's seatback was in the fully upright and locked position and he twisted the clip on his tray table to secure it for takeoff. The latch set home with a satisfying little click that was more felt than heard. Owen was a big man, but trim, and he fit into his economy-class space with no room to spare. He could afford business class, if he were buying. Which he never was. Hell, his boss would be happy to pay for first class, if only Owen would ask for it. But it would be ski season in Satan's back acres before Owen would float his ass in a plush leather recliner next to someone who had paid for the distinction.

Coach was fine if it got him where he meant to be more or less when he meant to be there. And with his luggage. He did, however, fantasize that people were much less inclined to chatter at strangers way up there in the front of the plane.

Owen wore dark suits with dark sunglasses, even indoors when it wasn't ridiculous for him to do so. It wasn't that he particularly liked navy, hurricane gray, or dead-star black for a palette. It's just what they wanted him to wear. For him, it was nice that it made the dangling cord of the white earbuds more obvious.

At six foot six with covered eyes, blocked ears, and a disinclination to smile, he would've thought it might have been enough to guarantee that he'd stay alone in a crowd. But it wasn't foolproof. Like a lighthouse rising out of the sea of everything, the fools sometimes found him anyway.

Between his employer's expectations and his own efforts at generating a force field, Owen's look was fairly specific. The Anningers, especially Mrs. Anninger, preferred their staff to present and act as if they should have a staff of their own—a collector's set of nesting dolls of privilege. If the butler had a housekeeper, and the chef had a cook, and the personal shoppers all had harried assistants, the Anningers were just that much more buffered from all the sadness and tedious work in the world. Work that they possibly only grasped at the level of fable.

Of course they scheduled inoculations of misery into their itineraries with tours of Mumbai slums and Cambodian orphanages. But closer to home, none of them ever seemed keen to drive from the pavement to the gravel to the dirt in Appalachia, and they found reasons not to set a charitable course through the less manicured areas of Chicago or Dallas. But Mrs. Anninger always told Owen to send checks with the regrets when she turned down domestic outreach events.

They weren't evil. Not really. Only remote, nearly alien. Owen wasn't convinced they understood the concept of generosity, but they had to do something with all that money. The Anningers were generations removed from the merely wealthy. They were practically a different species.

Mrs. Anninger would have liked it better if Owen had put more effort into letting everyone know how well they paid him. It would have been good for what passed as a conscience' sake, but he suspected they also liked the friction of a stubborn employee they could choose to suffer over.

His employers were easily bored, so he was busy. He did for them in capacities secretarial to diplomatic. He researched things; procured things. Sometimes he stood in as proxy to make matters easy for them or to make a point of their absence when they thought it necessary. He was a high-end errand runner.

By looking at him, some people wrote him off as a bodyguard, an enforcer. That was useful at times and it amused his bosses. But his size and his strength and his specific inclination to violence were his own, and as not for sale as his cock. He had applied all of those things adjacent to his professional duties at times, but on his own terms and without comment or suggestion from anyone who wanted to keep on his good side.

He did their bidding as he pleased and tempered it with the bare minimum of the image they wanted. He wore decent suits and bought the Mercedes, a sleek thing that he might have actually loved a little bit, once upon a time. Beyond that, he withstood being the source of their favorite discontent.

His costume made him look like an asshole. Owen had to admit that he might very well be an asshole. He pinged himself at least three times a day to better understand humanity in that regard and got nothing but his own brand of joy. He was an asshole in a world of different varieties of asshole.

Today he had the window seat.

A woman scanned the numbers along the aisle bulkhead and stopped next to Owen's row. She drew back at the sight of him. He was used to it, if not almost all the way pleased by it.

"Wow! I'm glad I'm little. Bet you're glad, too. They don't leave us a lot of room, do they?" She shoved her bag, bright and unscuffed at the corners, into the overhead bin. "If you split the difference between me and you, you'd get a normal-size person out of it."

She wasn't that little. Average size. Cute. Curvy. Tight enough in the important spots. But still. You could tell a lot about someone by the yardsticks they used to measure themselves. She was utterly delighted to be traveling.

Owen cared not at all.

She kept her lid on until the first pass of the drinks cart. Owen asked for black coffee.

"I'm going to splurge," she said, leaning into him as if it were the key to a conspiracy. She ordered wine and handed over her credit card.

If a screw-top split of economy-class chardonnay is a splurge, lady, that is also a yardstick.

But he nodded when she declared it not too bad.

In ten minutes, he knew her name was Charlotte (which she felt she had to clarify after introducing herself as Charlie, lest he think she was a Charlene or transgender), and he knew that she was headed to her sister's wedding. Charlie herself had a wedding band on, but didn't mention any husband.

Said sister had been married once before. She had three kids from that first marriage and *still* snagged herself a new man who was financially well-off and, get this, almost five years younger. The new husband didn't even have any kids himself and treated Charlie's nieces and nephew just like his own.

"Must be nice," said Charlie, but she sniffed as if it didn't exactly smell so by her estimation. The happy couple was making a huge, elaborate production—white dress, sit-down dinner, a string ensemble and everything—and Charlie thought that was fine, because why shouldn't people celebrate good things?

Owen could only agree out loud and wish an aneurysm on her silently. He started calling her Ann in his mind and wished he believed in wishes. Aneurysm Annie. He fought the corners of his mouth as she blathered on.

Owen pulled a pack of gum from his pocket. He carried some with him when he traveled to make his ears pop on takeoff and landing, but the coffee was lousy and had soured on his tongue. He extended the pack to her.

"Would you like a piece, Ann?"

"Ann? It's Charlie."

"Sorry. Right. Charlie." Owen had been told he had a charming smile, but he wasn't quite sure how he managed it. "You remind me of an Ann."

She smiled back, then shielded her mouth with her fingertips. "Do I need gum?"

"No, no. I was only going to have some and didn't want to be rude. Because I'm going to have to be rude now." Owen uncoiled the white cord of his earphones. "I have a program to listen to."

"Oh." Her face fell into a pout. "Sure."

"It's just a work thing." He twisted the earbuds into his ears. "I need to have this done by the time we land. But it was nice chatting with you."

"Okay. Thanks. You, too."

As always, Owen mimed tapping up something on his screen, but he really just opened and closed a couple of apps and slid the silent phone back into his pocket. He never actually listened to anything. He merely enjoyed the peace in those times when the earphones worked as pest control.

CharlieAnn lasted another ten minutes or so, flipping through the catalog from the seat pocket.

She gave him a nudge. He popped out his right earbud and held it in his closed fist so she couldn't hear all the nothing coming out of it.

"Can you believe they charge sixteen dollars for Wi-Fi? I mean, I didn't even know you could get internet on an airplane. That's great. I love it! But sixteen dollars? After what I paid for this flight?"

Owen pressed his lips together and nodded in what he hoped looked like sympathy. He didn't care if she felt validated, but it seemed a better gamble at getting her to shut up than making a case for $16 Wi-Fi or calling her a cheap, pointless waste of breath and skin.

She drew her shoulders up in a little shiver of naughty glee. "I think I'm going to splurge," she announced again.

"Go for it," he said, and worked his earpiece back into place.

For sleeping, Owen preferred dark rooms, no company, and a locked door. He almost never slept on planes. But he was nearly there. He'd drifted numb and weightless, with a dream just ahead, something bright and good, something he wanted to see—

She tapped him excitedly on the elbow and he crashed back into reality. His body jerked against the seat and he swallowed past a nap-dried throat.

"Oh! I'm sorry! I didn't know you were sleeping. I thought you were just listening."

Owen was all out of chitchat, and he was also all out of pretending as if there was any more stored away somewhere behind his eyes. So he just let her look at his blank expression and take inventory of the rest of his patience.

She was undeterred. "You've got to see this. Or have you already? It's everywhere. So cool. I love it. It'll make your day if you haven't."

Unbelievable.

And because he literally couldn't think past the oblivious patter from this woman, this airy, happy, impossibly annoying creature, he let her direct his gaze to her iPad.

"Look at this kid. Watch what she does."

Charlie was carbonated with excitement—about this video playing on the screen, about the utterly mundane adventure she was on, about life in general when she got two steps out of her routine. It occurred to him that some people would find Charlie irrepressible. It badly made him want to press her until she cried.

Owen had a blister of fury rising in him at all times, chafed raw by each dull stupidity and sparkling inanity in the world that he couldn't avoid. He didn't hurt people when he couldn't get away with it, but he did catalog how it felt in these moments that he really wanted to. He used it for fuel in the times that he could. A few people paid for all the rest of them.

The girl in the video was being dragged by her ankle. In the mood he was in, Owen vaguely approved.

Then the tug on his attention from the edge of the screen.

Oh, you bitch.

Not Ann. No. She'd gone from useless to his new favorite person in two crashing heartbeats.

The painting. Marcelline. You fucking bitch.

"Do you want me to play it again?"

Owen smiled and nodded at—*Oh, what the hell*—at *Charlie*. She blushed and reloaded the video.

People rarely tried to get one over on Owen. He knew the recipe for the cooperation he collected. It didn't take anything away from his success for him to know what it was made of. And it was made largely of money and intimidation. Only the really clever ones realized they probably had nothing to fear from him. Probably.

Marcelline Gossard had been one of the clever ones. From the very first time he'd walked into the art gallery, she always looked him in the face and never once did that measuring-tape thing with her eyes or flinch when he stepped into her sight line. Owen had made a career out of being a walking omen, eclipsing too much light out of everyone's peripheral vision wherever he went. He enjoyed watching people do the math of what it might mean to find him suddenly there.

But nothing changed in Marcelline's poise or tone when her attention shifted from him to the regal old woman on the gallery floor who probably wasn't going to buy anything, to the FedEx driver, to the little boy who couldn't take the DO NOT TOUCH sign to heart. Owen was no different to her, and it was the most different thing that had befallen him.

The Anningers had sent Owen to the gallery, and by the transitive property to Marcelline, for artwork: four times for themselves, once for a wedding present, and once for a secretive deal with him on loan to a group that Owen was pretty sure was Russian Mafia. He fancied that he and Marcelline had bonded over knowing looks during that transaction.

She was capable in a much warmer way than Owen was, but distanced, a little guarded. There was a barricade of professionalism, but when she smiled from behind the bars, she made you wonder if the fence was there for her protection or for yours.

Before he was scary, before he was cold, before he was brutal, Owen Haig was efficient. Everything about Marcelline appealed to him: from the sleek, short-sheared curve of the crown of her head to the way her ankles didn't wobble in the four-inch heels as she strode across the polished floor. And Owen had felt damned near noble that everything in between the top of her head and those ankles, he'd counted as equal. All of it.

She was beautiful, but her posture, her voice, her confidence, her expertise, the fast math she could do with no calculator, the astonishing speed of her typing, it all rolled over him like cool velvet across his skin, across his thoughts. She soothed him, instantly and effortlessly.

They'd worked together the half dozen times, then nothing for months. He'd only been a little disappointed when her number rang in on his phone and she only wanted to talk business. No matter. She was still calling him. Work and solitude were mostly all he had, so business was his road to everything that wasn't.

"Mr. Haig. You told me to let you know if I came across anything interesting that the Anningers might like."

"I did. The gallery has something good?"

"No. They don't have it. Not yet, anyway. I have it. Want to talk?"

Did he ever.

The tribe his employers came from was a rare phenomenon in the world. That was a good thing. Too many of that kind and we'd all be back in caves in short order, eating our enemies and making carved keepsakes of their bones.

Some families could never own enough houses or boats. They bought and sold companies, real estate developments, shopping malls, office buildings, ore mines, small dictatorships.

Fleets of private cars and airplanes moved them around. But when it came to the things they could hold in their hands, the ornaments of their fingers and necks and cabinets and walls, they liked a little history with their sparkle. Sometimes the word *history* was a euphemism for *notoriety*.

The Anninger magpie was half-vulture.

There was silver in a sideboard that had been stolen in a coup, the aristocrats of that country hanged and burned while their homes were looted. Mrs. Anninger had a brooch, two rings, and a necklace that had been Nazi plunder. There were gun collections that should, by all rights, have been haunted by their accomplishments, and the oldest Anninger son had two goddamned shrunken heads in the library of his favorite house. Artwork that could be traced back through theft and raid was practically commonplace.

But Mr. Anninger Sr. and his only daughter shared a taste for the truly infamous, with displays and stashes of contraband and ghoulish souvenirs that made Owen hate them. It also made him work the hardest for those two in particular. It was a pet project of his. He was curious to see how far they would go. How much money would they burn to warm their boredom? How many dim thugs would they stack into the dangerous spaces, ordering their hirelings to climb over one another to reach the forbidden fruit for their dessert—the only thing left for them to want after their endless feast of too much of everything else.

The painting that Marcelline had acquired was one of a haul from the largest heist of personal property in history. It, along with its gallerymates, hadn't been seen in more than twenty-five years. But that much legend would only get it to Mrs. Anninger–level unsavory.

The selling point, the sticky bit of trivia relayed to Owen from Marcelline's perfect mouth—*How did she not get lipstick on her wineglass?*—was that this piece had more story than the others, and a story that not many people knew, possibly because it might have been bullshit. But rumor was good enough to turn up the want in a certain kind of person. In an Anninger kind of person.

This painting was arguably one of the more minor works stolen from the museum. It wasn't the most missed or the most sought. But it had been the only one seen, or at least reported to have been seen, in the trophy room of a famous, and famously murdered, music producer. There had been whispers of bragging. There were always whispers of bragging. That was the game. That was the entire point. The long story of the painting was better than the quality of the artwork itself.

Per Marcelline, it was theirs, off the books, and the price was negotiable.

Yeah. If there was a chance of blood on it, Mr. Anninger would want it. Or his daughter.

When the sale had gone completely wrong, and the scrubbed-up tweaker had walked up and opened fire on them all, Owen, to his shame, had looked first to Marcelline. He didn't care about the money. He didn't care about the painting. He didn't care about the Anningers. Disappointment was such a rare, bitter treat for them, he often wondered if they actually loved it best of all. No, he cared only to see if Marcelline had known, to see if she had set him up.

He still didn't know, even now.

When he'd picked her out of the shadows and the movement in the chaos of that night, she'd been curling toward the pavement, hands clawing at her neck, blood already raining down in a narrow torrent as she folded.

The man who'd come with her was already there at her side. At the start she'd introduced him to everyone as Jonathan, and he'd been the one who brought the painting to the meeting. Now this Jonathan knelt next to her. He leaned in and pulled her hand away from her throat, looking, checking, but no. He took her other hand, too, holding them both away from her thrashing instinct to push against the pour of her blood. He just let it flow. Jonathan rose up, prying her fingers from around his wrist. And he ran. When Owen got to her, Marcelline was fading unconscious, no story to tell.

Owen had let him run, and he also ignored the Anningers' hired help, some guy and some girl who looked like a guy, neither of whom he'd met before—one clearly dead, one rolling around grunting, looking all but done for. He'd lifted Marcelline, his biceps pressed hard into the wound, her blood invisible as it warmed, then quickly cooled, into his black suit jacket.

He had access to essentially every resource of the Anningers. They never asked him to account for anything. He'd made the call with Marcelline dying against his arm to dispatch two warm and upright retainers to retrieve the two cold, dead ones from the lot.

At his place, a quiet doctor and a couple of see-nothing-say-nothing nurses were easy enough to get. They went to work on her. He'd stopped a nurse hurrying past him in the hallway. She'd held a metal bowl grim at the bottom with blood and bits of bone.

Is she alive?

She is for now. She's hanging in there.

She needs to make it. Do you understand me?

I'm sure she wants to come back to you as much as you want it. I know you're worried. But love is medicine, Mr. Haig. I believe it. Hold on to that. Have faith.

You're not getting it—

Ow. You're hurting my arm.

She needs to wake up long enough to talk.

We're doing our best, Mr. Haig.

Then let's hope that's good enough. Now, take that shit back into the room. I'll bring you some bags. I will personally take care of whatever *needs to be disposed of. We're clear?*

Absolutely.

And Marcelline survived long enough to shine him on, get strong, and steal his fucking car.

She'd vanished with a thoroughness that could only have been professionally mediated. Or else she'd died before she could slip up. He would have found her if she'd made a mistake.

He got the car back, eventually, but it never felt the same.

Owen couldn't remember the last time any of the Anningers had specifically brought up the lost money or this particular void in their art collection, but he also couldn't remember the last time a *Do you think you can handle this?* sneer wasn't attached to everything they asked of him.

Now, after years of looking and nothing but dead ends to show for it, the painting was on the wall in that video of a little girl kicking some shithead in the face. Charlie had played it for him three times.

Over the intervening four years, he'd read everything he could find about the painting. He had seen it over and over in articles, and, of course, once briefly in real life. The one in the video could have been a print, but why bother? Who would? It was nothing special to look at, by a guy no one had ever heard of, a half curiosity that it was even taken in the first place.

But it was the first clue he'd had to Marcelline in years—through an accident, by the pestering of a ditzy woman who was all too happy to be out of whatever hidey-hole she called home.

The last place you looked wasn't ever the end of anything. *Found* was always a beginning, whether it was your car keys or a lost art treasure. Find it and you start the thing you'd been kept from.

When they landed, Owen convinced Charlie to have a drink with him. It turned into two and a half glassfuls as she chirped and giggled and flattered him until he had to fuck her against the wall of a private room nestled away in the labyrinth of the VIP lounge. She seemed unhurtable, though he tried a little, driving up and into her with a force that knocked her head against the doorframe.

She was flustered and glowing when he was done, chewing the corner off a nervous smile as he zipped up. She was unfathomable, delighted again, with her unmentioned wedding ring and her pristine luggage and her newly mussed hair. He saw the approving up-and-down glance she gave to her reflection in the long mirror on the wall.

Owen meant to walk away without a word, one last dig to make it sting, but she was between him and the door. Of course she was.

Before he could stop her, she took his face in her hands and kissed him, sweetly, her elemental thrill tingling against his lips. He stood, stunned stupid. She pulled out of the kiss first and smiled into his face.

She sighed, a short, happy sound, and patted his charcoal lapels. Charlie was finally out of noise. She took up the handle on her roller bag and walked away.

The clip of her heels faded into the next surge of airport crowd and Owen was finally alone. Confused, but just slightly infected by her excitement, if not exactly kindly so, he flexed his wrists to settle his shirt cuffs and headed toward the parking deck, to find the car he used to love.

CHAPTER TEN

Nothing could have stretched an already desperate run of hours into an impossible grind like trying to get Miss June through her day. It should have been good—a cheerful, lucid granny and pretty weather. But Emma wanted to be anywhere else.

She tucked June into her recliner with her two blankets, three pillows, and tea, diluted just right. Emma switched on the television to a roundtable gossip show.

She wanted to be alone, to think. To rewatch the video. To decide what to do about it.

"Emma!"

She pulled back from her deep drift. "Yes?"

"You worried me, honey. You're a million miles away. I called you. It's like you didn't hear me. I thought I'd died and was the last to know it." June's blue eyes sparkled in humor that disguised the slight tinge of the actual fear of confusion.

"I'm sorry! You called me?" Emma looked down at the phone in her hands.

"Called your *name*, for goodness' sake."

• • •

Marcelline Gossard had been answering to the name Emma O'Connor for nearly four years. She'd left her real name behind, shedding it unknowingly at first, in Owen Haig's apartment. He'd made a magic trick of Marcelline Gossard. Her coworkers had seen her leave for the day. A few people, all now dead or fled, had seen her at the secret meeting to sell the Flinck.

Then poof. She vanished. First, from her own train of thought.

The first time she woke up in his spare room, not that she recognized it as such, it was like clawing up through miles of crumbling darkness that dragged against every gain she made toward thinking. She'd swim up, pulling and fighting to hold on to an idea or even a question. She'd get as far as the wall of pain, then slip back to sleep before she could make sense of anything. She slid so deep that she hadn't been dreaming. She couldn't swear that she'd even been breathing except that she was still alive to wonder about it. She was just gone, unplugged, then plugged back in for rebooting. Over and over.

She was there for nine days, with the first two only accounted for by working backward on a calendar. Then nearly three days of the molasses swimming.

When she saw Owen for the first time, she thought she might finally be dreaming. Or possibly dead. He was wearing a long-sleeved T-shirt and jeans. Marcelline searched her catalog of impressions of him and realized that she could never have pictured him in anything but a dark suit, buttoning and unbuttoning the jacket when he sat down or stood up—smooth, graceful, as automatic as a machine.

A rippling soft crewneck on Owen Haig was all wrong. He had his costume like a paint job, as if he hung himself up in it every night and shrugged free of the hanger each morning, already set for business when he hit the floor. She could imagine him shooting his cuffs and straightening his tie, but that was about it. She slid her jaw sideways for a bolt of pain to test reality, just to be sure.

It was real.

And he was real.

He was there in the room with her and he didn't always wear suits, and he had, apparently, given her a lot more thought over the time they'd known each other than she'd ever given him. She tried to make his having saved her life stay up top of the growing list of things that were on her mind.

Everything came back into focus. Gains were made by the hour and the day. The pain became understandable, and thereby bearable. She rediscovered her voice and a way to talk through a mouth that didn't move right. She found that she could now remember, from one sleep to the next, where she was and what this was all about. But she wasn't inclined to show her progress. Owen was kind, almost sappy, when she was weak and aching, but he sharpened as she did. He had a lot of questions about what had happened. She had a lot of questions about what was happening.

Her phone was gone. The clothes she'd been wearing, too. She didn't have any shoes. He took the medicines out of the room after dosing her, but left her bottles of water to drink.

She had doctors and nurses to tend the damage to her face and neck, but Owen wouldn't let her have a mirror. She burrowed into the bed, deliciously piled in softness and warmth, when the painkillers kicked in. The curtains kept out the light, so she could rest and heal. But it took hours, not days, to realize that the room was actually a well-appointed cell.

She'd asked for her phone, any phone, every time a nurse or doctor or the timid housekeeper came into the room. And every time, they'd avert their eyes and say that she'd need to talk to Mr. Haig about that.

When she did, Owen, in a tone with no inflection, had asked her if she'd be willing to call her partner. He obviously expected her to say no. He didn't mind showing that the question was a prod. He watched her for a squirm. Her heart revved in her chest.

"He's not my partner, Owen. I swear. I only met him a few days ago. He wouldn't talk on the phone at all. I don't even have a number for him."

"Hmmmm. That's a shame. But okay. There's no reason for you to have the phone, then. But you can have the battery."

He slid the silver-and-black square onto the bedside table.

Even the cell signal of Marcelline Gossard was gone. No one would find her that way.

Over the first days, the situation sketched in. Jonathan had taken the painting and the money in the interrupted sale. That was only known "in-house," as Owen put it. The two people who came with Owen were dead. That was also being kept private. Marcelline Gossard had been officially reported missing by her family. Owen said her picture had made the news, but the nurse had gone pale and shut her down when she'd tried to plead with her to get a message out.

On day five, Marcelline started practicing standing and walking on her own. Her legs trembled and her heart pounded her blood into a froth that carried not near enough oxygen up to her head. But she did laps to test her stamina when she heard Owen in the shower or on the phone. She couldn't help but notice that he never left her alone in the apartment.

She wasn't ready for it on the day she had to leave, but Owen had asked her if she needed anything.

"No."

"Okay." He turned to go.

The stabbing pains in the constant yammering ache were keeping her from deep sleep, especially at night, but she was trying to take less medicine. She was exhausted and stir-crazy, then just regular crazy on top of that from trying to hide that she was feeling well enough to walk around, count hours, and churn.

The urge to tip something over, to give a spur to the dragging clock, won out.

"Actually, I do need something," she called out to him. He came back to her bedside. "I need to know what you're going to do."

The disappointment in Owen's expression was the freezing part. He was furious. He was frustrated. But his reaction to everything had matured into a kind of acceptance. He was wounded, but somehow bored and ready to move on.

He sighed, but never raised his voice out of the soft near-monotone. "I don't know. Losing cash by the quarter millions isn't what I'm hired to do. Having not a fucking thing to show for it doesn't help. No painting. No hint as to where it might be. Two dead people . . .

"If you won't give up your partner, then it's either you or me on the hook for this whole mess. But really, in the end, no matter what, it's only me, isn't it? I let this happen. I trusted you.

"Besides, everyone's looking for you, so that's a consideration. They'll want interviews and press conferences. If they were to find you, in this—" He touched her cheek above the bandage. "I can't be sure of what you'd say. Or what any of your family would say either. There's not a lot holding this together."

She didn't let him trap her in a hard stare. Instinct warned that softer was better, shoulders dropped, eyes gently out of piercing focus on his. "I wouldn't say anything. They wouldn't say anything. I'd make something up about my face. You have to know that. You saved my life. You think I don't know I'd be dead without you? Jonathan is *not* my partner. I'm sorry, Owen. I'm trying to remember something that will help us."

She put a quiver on *us* for sparkle, then again on *we* and *our* and every word that made her part of a pair with him. "We will figure this out. It's not our fault, neither one of us. He did this."

She stopped babbling. He hadn't relaxed into a single pleading word she'd said. The clock wasn't plodding anymore. It was flying.

Owen ticked his head, only half a nod. There wasn't nearly enough agreement in it to make her feel better.

Marcelline had forced her voice down to a pained rasp. "Actually, if it's okay, can I have a couple of those Percocets? My jaw is killing me."

She palmed the pills and fought to keep a grip on her fear, to keep the terror in its lane. She invented and discarded plans, burning through to a useless blank far too soon. She couldn't think. Her ears strained at the quiet.

She watched the clock add minutes to her desperation. Owen didn't come back in. Marcelline turned her head deep into the pillow so when the housekeeper checked, she saw her sprawled in the pose of narcotic oblivion.

Marcelline heard Owen walk past her room into his own.

But then the front door opened and closed.

When she heard the shower come on in the master bathroom, her fear whispered that she shouldn't trust it, she didn't know why the housekeeper had stepped out, or for how long. Marcelline was too weak, and where the hell would she go anyway? But then the plastic clatter of a dropped shampoo bottle bouncing off tile was like a starting gun. No plan necessary. Just go.

She peered from the open bedroom door, listening. All quiet except for Owen in the bathroom. She wobbled from her room out into the unfamiliar apartment. She was across from the laundry room.

Shedding the string-tied hospital gown that the nurses swapped out for a clean one each day, she ransacked the dryer for an enormous T-shirt. She yanked it down over her head and, in her rush, scraped over the bulky bandage at her jaw. It pulled free and the gauze dangled onto her shoulder. The air hit the wound and lit up the damp, tender wreckage, mapping the extent of the ruin that she hadn't yet seen. Her stomach rolled. Suddenly, running seemed like a terrible idea. But she pushed the tapes flat, as best they would go, and swiped at the thread of fresh blood that tickled her neck. It didn't hurt much. Terror was almost as good as morphine.

The shorts she tried wouldn't stay on her hips. She kicked them away in frustration and snatched up the discarded gown and tied it around her waist as a ragged skirt.

Her medicines were lined up on Owen's bookshelf, and she raked the orange bottles into a fold of the giant T-shirt she wore and held it closed against her body. Straining her ears to both the front door and the steady rain of the shower, she pulled open the desk drawers in the office, looking for her phone, for money, for anything that would help her.

Near the top of a loose fan of business cards scattered in the center drawer was a plain white card, a silver stripe in the middle separating a phone number below from the embossed initials above: S.K.

Marcelline had taken the card, an empty manila envelope for the pill bottles, and a nasty-looking letter opener for just in case she ran out of alone time or strength in her legs before she got out.

The sound of water still hissed from the master suite. Marcelline closed the door to her room, tucked the laundry back into the dryer and eased it shut, and considered Owen's gym shoes by the door. That would never work. They were way too big. But she took his socks, still grotesquely damp, from the pile of towels and gym-bag flotsam that he'd left on the floor by the breakfast counter. His keys were there, too.

She'd never given much thought to Owen Haig when they'd worked together. Rich people and their minions were a staple in her life; their polish and bling and attitudes were wallpaper to her. But Owen's beautiful silver Mercedes, with its muted orange calipers, now *that* had caught her eye, she had to admit.

The silence thunked into place as Owen cut the water. Marcelline's Jell-O heart tried to stop in her chest. She folded her fist around the keys to keep them from clanging, double-checked the room for anything obviously out of place, and tiptoed out the door in Owen's sweat-soaked socks.

Adrenaline had gotten her down the elevator and through the garage in Owen's building, first to find the car in a frantic, swivel-headed stagger through the gloom of the concrete cavern, then driving through the exit, trembling behind the tinted glass. The gate lifted with no alarm, and she turned onto the street, gripping the steering wheel until her fingers ached.

She'd burned through the last of her energy in only a few miles. She was exhausted and anemic, sweating and gasping for air—and all of that was before she'd even gotten out of the apartment. Her once-booming heart now limped along in her chest. Her teeth chattered. The car was conspicuous, and too much of her concentration was diverted to wondering if Owen had discovered her gone yet. A few days of confinement with too much of it spent being unconscious had warped her sense of time. She hadn't looked at a clock on the way out. He might have showered more than an hour ago, or she may only have been gone ten minutes.

She'd ground the bumper of the Mercedes over a too-high curb when she'd pulled in between a dog park and a line of shops.

In her own wallet, wherever that was, Marcelline had the same business card that she'd taken from Owen's desk.

S.K. was Samantha. Marcelline couldn't remember her last name, something long, lots of letters. She didn't know what the woman's official job title was either, but the handful of transactions that had involved Samantha had been with the shadiest characters Marcelline had ever seen in the gallery.

Whenever Samantha was part of the exchange, the layers of discretion were the answer to their own questions: Don't ask.

Samantha's personal style was changeable. A tousle of the hairdo and one accessory more or less and she'd blend into a school board meeting or an audience with the queen, a get-together in a pub or a church. It wasn't hard to imagine her charming bikers and politicians alike. Her appeal was sparkle eyed and harmless, and Marcelline enjoyed it, but didn't buy it for a second.

In the work they'd done together, Samantha was somewhere between an ambassador and a greased skid. She got things done. She erased negotiation and replaced it with introductions and efficient payments and everyone feeling like friends in the end. The last time they'd met had been with the Eastern European heavies who dealt with the Anningers through Owen.

Samantha would have been the next person Marcelline would have called if the Anningers hadn't wanted the Flinck. As it was now, she seemed like the only person Marcelline could call at all.

So she did.

She'd refolded her makeshift skirt to look a little less obvious and steadied her hands and breath. She'd checked the mirror and wished she hadn't. At least the bandaged, hollow-eyed wreck that she was in the moment wouldn't likely remind anyone of any photo the media might have used in the search for her.

Marcelline had fished the stream of passersby and went for a kindly, confused-looking older woman with a flip phone that had to be a decade old. She begged to borrow it. The call went through and Samantha remembered her.

Samantha had done three circuits of *Holy shit!* in the first moments of that call and never acted shocked about a single thing beyond that.

Once Marcelline described where she was, Samantha told her to get out of sight, directing her, with her keyboard clicking over the line, checking online photos and maps, to a row of trash and recycling containers at the far end of the run of buildings.

"Wait there. Oh, and delete this call from that woman's phone before you give it back. Don't worry, we'll take care of the rest from this end."

"How—"

"Don't ask. Hang in there. Sit tight."

When she was retrieved to Samantha's office, then fed and medicated, Marcelline's story, all of her regret and terror, flooded out past any good reason not to. She had no energy left to spare on defense.

"Let me just finish one thing, here," Samantha said, looking from her keyboard to the screen. Marcelline's story had wound down to exhausted silence. "Then I'll take you home with me."

"Why would you do that?"

"You need rest. Also, because I have an idea. This is interesting."

Marcelline worked up a weak smile. "I'm not sure I can handle any more things that are interesting."

"Don't worry. I can help you." Samantha looked away from her work. "Do you believe me?"

Relief filled up Marcelline's throat. She could only nod.

"Good. All it will cost you is a little blood. Not that you look like you can afford to lose much more."

Marcelline closed her eyes. It was work to even lift her lips into a better smile. She should laugh. It was the kind of thing people said as a joke. Why didn't it sound like a joke?

Samantha noticed. "I'm not kidding, actually. Sorry. I'll have someone come out to the house to draw a little blood tomorrow. It'll be okay. We won't need much." Samantha emptied a small brown-paper shopping bag of its lunch leftovers and held open the sack toward Marcelline's shoeless feet. "Put his socks in here."

Samantha's grin was adorable, mischievous even. A gray swoon of unreality threatened to tilt Marcelline out of her chair. "Why?"

"Why? Because you're a missing person. And not just plainly missing. You're gorgeous and well missed by good, upstanding photogenic people who pay their taxes. That's why. It's quite an opportunity. A little mingled DNA on some artfully hidden socks can be very compelling to police and juries. Did you never see anything about the OJ trial?"

"You're going to set him up? But Owen didn't do anything to me. I mean, I don't even know that he would have. I might have over-reacted. It might just have been his way of making sure I didn't know where Jonathan is."

"You think Owen Haig is all talk?"

Marcelline couldn't bring herself to say yes, but *no* would have been close to a lie.

Samantha sighed. "I know it's horrible and terrible. It's also not fixable. And, no, I'm not *necessarily* going to set him up. He didn't do anything to you, but he didn't get the chance, did he? Let's just say that your concerns for your well-being—and your family's—weren't ridiculous. He's humiliated. It's not safe to make him angry. You'll have to trust me on that. Seriously."

"But the socks . . ."

"Right. In our weird world I actually like Owen, for the most part. But he gets in my way. And I get in his. Being able to divert him, should I ever need to, is a gold coin. The police crawling up his ass over a missing person like you?" Samantha laughed, delighted. "I could drop that little bomb for years and it would still play."

The guilt made Marcelline's stomach lurch.

"Look. I probably won't ever do it, but leverage is very impor-tant in what Owen and I do. It would probably be just as effective to send him one of the two socks and tell him what it is. It's worth taking you on as a little side project just for this piece of rainy-day insurance.

"I know you think this is a disaster. And from where you're sitting, it is. For me, though? This, dear M, is easy. And maybe even worth-while."

Samantha called everyone she liked by the initial of their first name. She'd started calling Marcelline *M* the second time they met in the gallery, and Samantha picked it up again now, automatically, in the moment of taking her on as a pet project.

After a few weeks of lying low at Samantha's, they'd come to a decision. The two of them together, S&M, was a joke—funny because it was a little bit funny on its own, and funny because their situation demanded honesty that was true to the point of pain.

M couldn't stay. It wasn't safe to be so close. She couldn't hide there forever. Marcelline's family was frantic over her disappearance. Owen Haig was on a rampage. And no one knew where the painting was.

When Samantha was prepping Marcelline for her next life, far away as someone else, picking her new name had been the hardest part. Well, not the first name. That had been easy. M—Em—Emma.

S had been typing, her ever-present purple manicure flashing quickly over the keys, the clicking a soothing white noise over Marcelline's anxiety. It sounded sure. And competent. And not crazy. This was crazy.

"Okay, for the last name, just pick one of someone you love. A name that always means good things to you. You'll answer to it quicker that way. That's the hard part, responding naturally when your new name is called. So, what do you think?"

The prospect of not seeing her sister sprang to Marcelline's mind. "Bethany."

Samantha sighed. "I know. But Bethany is a weird last name. Emma Bethany? That won't work."

"Okay."

"And you have the same last name as your sister. So, that won't work either. What else?"

They settled on O'Connor after Marcelline's third-grade teacher, a woman she'd adored and who had let her take home the class rabbit over the summer as her first pet.

"I assume you were fingerprinted for the gallery?" Samantha asked.

"Yes. They had to do everyone."

"That's what I thought. So a life of crime is out. Got it?"

"Probably should have told me that a couple of months ago."

Samantha smiled and kept typing. "No, really. Don't get arrested. Okay, now all that's left is—" Samantha had stopped short, hands hovering above the keyboard.

All that's left had drawn a hiccuping sob from Marcelline.

"It's going to be okay, M. I know how to do this. I know you're scared, and I am, too, which is weird. I've never had to do this before for someone I care about. And I don't have a lot of friends. But I'm good at my job. I never get to save the day. I'm not going to screw this up. Okay?" They'd stared into each other's tears, a pin in the map of their odd new friendship. "It's going to be good. You're going to be fine. We'll work this out. I promise."

Samantha scratched her nails over Marcelline's shoulder. A friendly, reassuring grand gesture from the least touchy-feely person Marcelline had ever met.

"And now you need to pick a birthday that's a holiday—What? It makes the date easy to remember. And it makes good stories that are easy to come up with. Fourth of July, Christmas, Halloween, something, any of those. And"—Samantha snapped her fingers—"you need a trauma, a reason not to talk about things, a reason not to be on social media."

Marcelline had looked at Samantha as if she'd turned into a beetle on a path straight across her foot, and cupped her hand over the sunset palette of scars at her jawline. "How will we ever think of anything?"

Samantha shook her head. "Right." She looked Marcelline over. "Okay. Simple. You've got a psycho ex-husband. You ran. He's cut you off from your family. It's PTSD and you won't even say his name." Samantha looked unselfconsciously at the scar when Marcelline dropped her hand. "They'll believe you."

So in her new life, whenever she talked about herself at all, Emma O'Connor said she loved having a birthday on Halloween. The story was that all her life there was always a masquerade that no one had to go to any extra trouble for. And she was effectively a refugee from a horror that would be cruel to prod. It was the exit to any conversation she didn't want to have.

Her official paper trail was shallow, but reliable. Marcelline Gossard was gone. Some people, a lot of people, thought she was dead. Knew she was dead. Counted very much on her being dead. Samantha stayed close, always there by phone and text, and kept a watch for who looked for Marcelline online.

Emma watched the video dozens of times after June was once again situated for the night.

She read the comments on the different postings, searching through the *You go, girl,* and cheers and horrid troll commentary for clues as to where this attack had taken place. As to where the painting was hanging right now.

She wrenched her eyes off the taunting wedge of it in the video to study the girl, the street, the direction of the late-afternoon light to orient the house to the compass.

She sifted the internet chatter for leads. She found the police website, and the map of the town.

Her eyes burned. She finished the wine and rolled into a paralyzed sleep. She waited ninety minutes after she woke up, watching the clock in a blank trance, before she set about packing her bag and calling Eddie to plead a case of a family emergency. The fictional family of pain needed her. No one could ask her to deny the drama.

Eddie was sweet and understanding, as Eddie could only be.

She called Samantha as she settled south at highway speed.

"I don't understand, M, tell me what this video is. Send me a link. Let me check into this."

"It's okay. I'll be careful. I have to try."

"You really don't. Just come back. I'll fly in. We'll talk it through."

"Owen thinks I screwed him over. You didn't see how he acted. He was . . . It wasn't just the money and going back to the Anningers empty-handed. He was so upset that it was me. He thinks I set him up. I'm the only one who can fix it. It has to be me. If I can bring back the painting, he'll see—"

"Okay, that's one hell of an *if*, and it doesn't really undo what went wrong that night. Owen has been in the naughty corner with his bosses for four years. Can you imagine how that is for a guy like him? You can't ever make that go away. I don't need to have seen him to know what you're saying. That's exactly why I'm not convinced the painting can be traded for a clean slate."

"I want my life back."

"Um, one small detail—you have to be alive to have a life. You could make a new life if you'd just get out a little bit. I know it's hard. But you don't have to be a hermit. It's making you crazy. This is crazy. Your cover is solid. It's at least solid enough to try to live a little. Give me some credit."

"It's not you. I owe you. I owe you everything. I know that. But it's not just the painting. What if I could give Jonathan to Owen? Let him see for sure that it wasn't me?"

"You don't even know that Jonathan is still in the picture. He might not be anywhere near there. What if he sold it to someone else?"

"Sold the Flinck to some random people who hung it up as a decoration in the suburbs? Come on. It has to be him."

"I don't even want to remind you that if you break in and something goes wrong and your fingerprints are on anything—"

"I know."

"Sure you do. You're the expert. Oh, wait! No, that's me. This thing is only as good as you *not* delivering yourself on a platter to the police."

"I know."

"You say that a lot. But if you don't listen to me now, you'll definitely know soon, one way or the other, about a great many things. And if it goes a particular way, you also have to know that I can't help you."

Emma chewed her bottom lip. "Are you saying that because you think it'll stop me?"

"No. I'm saying it for the other reason."

"That it's true."

"Yeah, if you think you can trust me," Samantha said.

"I'm sorry. Shit."

"No shit, shit."

"I'll be careful. I promise," Emma said.

"Uh-huh. Just call me."

Emma watched the exodus from across the street in front of Gordon Hawley Middle School. It felt impossible to sift for any single kid in the liquid rush of young people pouring from the doors. They wore different colors and carried different things, but in the distance, they all seemed as alike as a romp of otters. And just as energetic. You only noticed any particular one of them when they drew some leaping attention to themselves.

Some of the kids split off for a line of buses. Some milled around in front of a queue of cars, waving their goodbyes as they matched to their rides home. But the girl in the video had been walking when she was attacked. So Marcelline looked to the margins of the crowd as it went ragged in all directions into the surrounding neighborhoods.

There. It had to be her. Same hair. Same stride. A plaid shirt tied around her waist an awful lot like the one in the video. Her features had been blurred out, but Marcelline had seen her on the screen so many times now. She was with another girl. It had been eleven days since the attack. Marcelline watched her for wariness.

Marcelline dropped the transmission back into drive and blew out a deep breath. She didn't know how to follow anyone. She didn't *want* to know how to follow anyone. The girl turned the corner with her friend, heading up the hill and out of sight.

Like the inverse of Emma's family, who had become just images on a screen to her, it was strange to see this girl in three dimensions in plain daylight. Emma had sought her out and studied this girl's life the way she had her sister's. Emma felt both predatory and protective of her. Why and how the Flinck came to be in the girl's foyer, none of this was her fault.

There were roughly a hundred ways this could go once she found the right house. And only if she discovered a streak of stealth within herself that let her get close enough to do anything about it. But sneaking wasn't much like her. Emma was untested, but Marcelline had always been a by-the-horns kind of person.

She ran her thumb over the braille of her ruined jaw, the pits and peaks of the scar retelling the story of what was lost to her. And with whose help.

Jonathan had only thought he'd found an old painting, but once she'd explained what it was and the infamous Boston gallery heist, they'd decided together to skip the media attention and the pat on the head and the splitting of the FBI reward for only one small part of the Gardner Museum's lost haul.

It was unethical and clearly against her contract's details, but in a business that dealt with rarities every day, the truly unique was understood to be tempting, and not terribly difficult to get away with.

Collectors who bought on the sly tended to stay sly about it, and their impulsive purchases could change the lives of garden-variety art dealers. Most of these transgressions were forgiven in principle, with the understanding that if you got caught, the payoff had best be enough for you to fade into an entirely different circle of friends and colleagues.

Still, even as the doldrums set in and her thirties became the fixed grind that they were for most everybody, it wasn't anything Marcelline had ever entertained. She'd gotten out on the wrong side of the bed on the morning she'd met Jonathan, and not figuratively. Normally she slept on the right side of the bed, with the left side too-long vacant until the next time she fell in love, or at least into deep like.

But on that day, the sooty morning light had put an end to a night's restless sleep. She'd woken up before her alarm went off, way over to the left side of the bed, stuck in a sweaty tangle of sheets. She'd kicked them away and crawled out, feeling headachy and off and in the perfect storm of a weirdly expectant mood. Ultimately, it didn't disappoint.

After lunch, a guy walked in off the street with a photo of the Flinck on his phone and the skeleton of a story of wanting to sell it.

After the decision to go rogue with the painting, and after too much wine and kissing beyond that, the next morning the left side of her bed was full of a hungover Jonathan. Always just *Jonathan*. He never told her his last name. He wouldn't. He thought it was funny.

And a few days later, he had left her to die. It could possibly have been forgivable. Anyone would be afraid. Something had gone horribly wrong. Anyone could panic.

But Jonathan hadn't been panicked, and that's what was unforgivable. She never saw a ripple of raw worry on his face. For all the world it looked as if he'd shaken off the shock of it as if a fly had landed on his sleeve. He'd knelt and looked her over, but not into her eyes. He was measuring. Adding. Subtracting. He'd pinned her hands down as she tried to hold in her own blood. He looked across the lot to check how far away Owen was. Calibration. Triangulation.

And he knew the shooter. *For fuck's sake, Roy! Get the hell out of here!*

Jonathan had looked up at the sky, shaken his head regretfully, almost annoyed, mouth drawn tight. Marcelline had seen the decision settle in through his shoulders. Her fear, the warm river of blood pooling under her shoulder, the look in her eyes, none of these things figured into his sum. She grabbed his wrist. She believed the last thing she'd ever feel was fury. He would look at her, goddammit. She wasn't letting this go without that. He would look at her.

But he didn't. She'd had the strength of cobwebs, and he flexed his wrist in her grip and brushed her fingers clear. Then he ran. The scene went dark and silent, and the next sharp moment was realizing that she had become something like Owen's catch-detainee-responsibility-pet.

Now she was close to . . . well, something that was the next part of this painting's story.

The two girls came back into sight as Marcelline's car slowly crested the hill. Jonathan might not be a part of this scenario. If he was here, if he was still part of this story, well, that particular what-if dead-ended at a curtain. But she wouldn't look behind it until she knew for sure.

Marcelline unclenched her teeth. The ruined side of her jaw was aching. It reminded her to be angry. The watch-and-wait phase was a whetstone for sharpening that feeling into something useful.

CHAPTER ELEVEN

In the two weeks since it had happened, Carly always called it the *thing*. She didn't know what else to name it in her mind because it wasn't just what the guy had tried to do. It was what had tightened and sharpened in her while watching the playback of it. In seeing what she'd done, seeing what it looked like to be better than she thought she was, all the good and the terrible of that day had become bound up into one electric, snapping *thing*.

On the second day after the *thing*, Carly's gym teacher started calling her BK Liddell. *BK* stood for *Butt-Kicker*, and she liked it. She laughed along with everyone else. Carly figured that under his mostly gray buzz cut, Coach Marshall was really thinking *Ass-Kicker*, but he made a big deal about being a deacon in his church, so he wouldn't say *ass* to a bunch of eighth graders.

The next day, her math teacher had hugged her on her way into the classroom. The principal knew her name all of a sudden, and the janitor high-fived her and called her Girlie when he'd never called her anything before.

It didn't matter that the police had scrubbed her face out of the video. The neighbors saw the cops and the fire truck and the news vans on their street. Her friends recognized the rest of her—her hair and clothes and her backpack, and her house. Then those kids showed their parents. It didn't matter that it was over so quickly. It wasn't hard to put together. The next day it was all over the place.

The thing spilled over the borders of the school grounds. The desk clerk at the Y asked her if she was the one, and Carly had to try to not giggle because it sounded so high drama, like *THE ONE*, in her head when she heard it. The high schooler at the ice cream kiosk in the grocery store kept checking her recognition against Carly's actual, not-blurred face by staring and trying hard to look as if she weren't.

Every several hours that passed from the thing to whenever she noticed again, it seemed that the catalog of new reactions had grown by half. So many variations on a theme. It got to the point that she could feel the eyes on her, scuttling over her like butterfly feet, but soon she didn't need to turn to find the source. It didn't matter who it was. They needed to look, but she didn't need to look at them looking.

Just looking was good enough for most people, but some kids, and even some of the grown-ups, insisted on more. They were positively itching to see what Carly was about in real life. And it wasn't enough just to stare. It needed to be a circuit with Carly actively looped in while they checked what they could tell about her with their naked eyes. They measured her to see if she matched up to the video.

Some maneuvered into her peripheral vision and got so obvious about it that she had to peek over at them just so that she didn't seem weird. There was on-purpose paper rattling and throat clearing to draw an involuntary glance from her, which some people would then make into an invitation to chat. Much of it was friendly. They wanted to say they'd seen the video, that they were glad she was all right. Sometimes they wanted to tell her about something that had happened to them, or to say they thought it was cool what she'd done. But sometimes they asked her to tell them the step-by-step details, to narrate their memory of what they'd seen on their screens. They wanted her fear and her pain and her almost-maybe-dying without thinking about how she might feel about the *thing* she'd actually lived through.

But whatever looks or words they wanted to trade with her, what Carly understood was that none of this was the real want, the real need. They wanted her to look at them, yes, and they wanted her to know what they were thinking about when their eyes met. But the demand of attention, even from across the room, was a type of touch. As much as if they'd put their hands on her, it was a reach and a catch that she saw with her eyes, but felt in her throat.

Her bad thing was any bad thing—accident, illness, attack, ruin in all its million forms—that everyone, not so deep down when they looked at Carly, knew was possibly close by. Maybe even standing invisible at their own shoulder in that very moment. Any bad thing could be on its way to them. Their lives could be on the to-do list for disruption, or even disaster. And so they forced Carly into contact, and it was a weird little bravery for them. They wanted to touch it before it touched them.

Strangely, she didn't mind. She felt like a freak, but it wasn't unpleasant. It made her feel real. Somehow, and with a pang, she knew this feeling, this certainty, wouldn't last. It would end. She would forget. She was already forgetting.

The Carly of two weeks ago felt far away. The reality of Other Carly was fading. Normal life was blocking the view. Right at first, she'd been like the Venus flytrap on the windowsill in the science lab. Sticky and spiny, grabbing things that landed on her attention and then digesting the idea of them, breaking them down to know what they were made of. But now sometimes she was just what she was. She forgot to pay attention. Dumb as a regular plant.

She was still changed. She thought she was. What if she wasn't? What if she didn't get to keep it?

Whenever this thought nipped at her, she located that feeling she'd had since seeing herself on the security camera, the glue and the grip of it. It lived behind her eyes. She turned it up and pointed it at loved ones and strangers alike. *Use it or lose it, BK Liddell!* He made them scream back *Yes, Coach Marshall!* when he hollered out his encouragements like drill orders and laughed into his whistle as they ran or jumped or did sit-ups or shot baskets.

In line with Ada at the doughnut shop, Carly watched the cashier scramble through order after order, and the girl with the black headset and cool nose ring running the drive-through, and the couple bristling at each other at the only table she could see without being too obvious about it. She chewed over their gestures and postures, trying to glimpse everything more in their movements, everything she knew was there in every moment. The fishing was good today, and every day that she remembered to try. So many little things she could catch that were always happening everywhere.

The lady in front of her turned around and put her hand on Carly's arm. In the past two weeks, there had been other people like that. Carly told her friends they were freaky, but in truth the touchy ones were usually nice.

"You don't know me. My daughter goes to your school. She's over there at the table. She's in the seventh grade, so you probably don't know her. Anyway, you're wonderful." And then to the cashier: "And I'll pay for whatever she's getting."

The lady smiled back to Carly, and Carly looked at Ada, drop-jawed at her side.

"Oh, I'm sorry! I didn't realize the two of you were here together. Of course, you, too," the lady said to Ada. "Both of you get something. My treat."

Carly paid more in thank-yous and blushing than she would have in money for the sweet coffees and sprinkled doughnuts. She and Ada walked back through the crush of people, their eyes on the goal of the last two swivel stools at the window. The line was from the counter to the door, packed with Friday-charged students and a few adults.

A boy from her class stepped clear of a knot of other kids in the middle of the line. His name was Dylan and Carly had hated him since the third grade. Dread pulled down on her stomach, even as her heart sped up to pounding. Dylan had his phone pointed toward her, tracking her, recording.

"Oh, look! It's the famous Carly, gettin' free eats. Maybe we can catch her doing something *awe*-some. C'mon, Carly, do something *awe*-some."

Carly could handle the tickling curious looks from regular people, but the bully's spotlight pressed hard. Dylan wasn't the beat-you-up kind of scary. He was just mean. And he was on all the time. Ready constantly. A real asshole. She wanted to say it, to give him the finger and coolly walk out. She daydreamed the scene right where she stood, with Ada and everyone else looking at her, waiting for their cues. She imagined rolling right out the door and leaving Dylan to deal with the drag of half the crowd's expectant attention and the air-sucking awkwardness of the other half who were averting their eyes.

But the load was all hers. She owned the hope of everyone pretending they weren't leaning in for the payoff—either a sad story for them to tell in school next week about the poor picked-on girl, or a triumphant one about the whip-snap burn served up by the one who didn't care at all about a reject like Dylan Davis.

She hated that she couldn't do anything but crumple up inside and wish she'd never come in here.

"Let's just go," Ada said, close and low.

They hadn't set down their snacks or even stopped long enough for it to be a real spectacle yet. They could just keep going, almost as if it weren't happening. It would be the next best thing to being awe-some. *Awe*-some.

Of course, the next best thing to awesome would feel like a total loss, but Carly let Ada pull her along anyway.

"Hey, Carly! Why'd you kick your boyfriend in the head? Might've been your only chance."

She heard Dylan step out behind her, cutting loose from his circle and sliding into her empty lane. Ada was a length ahead, still carving a path for them to the door. Carly sensed the gap behind her and turned back. It didn't matter. No one's closeness would have made it anything other than just him against her. He'd steered it that way on purpose. It was his talent, making a show out of people who didn't want it. He'd already won the first round.

The ones who laughed made Dylan bold. So did the ones who didn't, holding in their exhales so as not to miss anything. They couldn't help it. They were just like her, everyone breathless to know what came next. They were exactly as uninformed about what he would do as Carly was, and just as riveted, only not in the crosshairs.

Carly could almost feel the rise of his blood in him, so like her own, but in a different chamber of the heart altogether. He wanted to strike as badly as she wanted to turn to smoke and blow away.

He held up the phone, lining up his camera. His friends jostled and snickered in his wake. "You should've given him a chance," Dylan said. "You might have liked it."

More than anything, *it* was a concept. An idea made of giggles and rudeness and wonder and heat and a couple of partial diagrams from a rigorously straight-faced health class lecture on the biology of *it*. It was loaded into a slingshot of shame when the idea was pointed at her or the other girls, but she didn't quite understand why the joke was funny for the boys, but definitely not for her. She was embarrassed by *it*, but even more embarrassed just for being embarrassable in the first place.

Nothing waiting in the queue of her thoughts would make any

sense to say out loud. Fire bloomed into her cheeks and the maddening tingle of tears felt like a hand around her throat.

Dylan smiled, starting to collect his reward as the people in the room helplessly took score.

No one was on his side, but the balance tipped. She could feel their acknowledgment. He certainly could as well. The cruel, smooth, ancient part of the crowd brain tilted irresistibly toward not what was right, but to what was strong.

Carly saw the woman seated to her left watching with her folded hands pressed to her lips. She shifted in her chair and leaned forward, enthralled. But the woman didn't settle back. Instead, she got up and walked toward Dylan and the other boys, smiling.

She was tall. White shirt. Jeans. Really good boots, with cool buckled straps wound around them. As she went by, Carly saw that the woman's jaw was messed up. The right side of her face was tight at the far edge and puckered with scars.

The woman walked all the way up to Dylan, arms crossed, back bowed into a casual slouch. She looked amused.

"You know, you might be the bravest boy I've ever seen."

Dylan tried to smirk, but the color went patchy on his face. A sudden rash of alarm crept up out of the neck of his T-shirt.

"No, really. That was unusual. Not a lot of people would be that . . . that . . . I don't know. What would you call it?"

Dylan shrugged.

"What's your name?"

He stiffened to keep from squirming. It was plain he wanted to shrug again so desperately that Carly felt her own shoulders rising in unwitting sympathy. He dropped his gaze to the level of everyone's knees.

The woman ducked her head into his sight line. "Oh, come on. Don't lose the fire now. What's your name?"

One of the boys behind him cough-shouted into his fist, "Dylan!"

The woman dropped her smile and uncurled from her friendly slump to her full height. She rolled her hand over with a flick of her wrist, palm up. "Give me your phone, Dylan."

Dylan struggled in the trap of his age. He didn't have to give her the phone. But he wasn't all the way out of the reach of authority. Not just yet. Everyone in the room knew it. He glanced out the window as if he were hoping to see a meteor on its way through the glass. No one said a thing, and now even the front of the line and the cashier and the girl with the headset and nose ring were all watching. The couple at the table had forgotten their argument.

Carly trembled with the thrill of it and also with some stupid measure of guilt at his agony.

The woman fluttered her fingers and snapped her palm flat again. Dylan rolled his eyes and scoffed in the back of his throat, but he gave up the phone.

She turned it over, lit it awake, and handed it back. "Unlock it."

"C'mon. I'm sor—"

"No, no, no. Don't do that. It's not time to be sorry yet. Unlock it."

Carly could see only half of Dylan's expression and none of the woman's, but whatever he read there made him clench his jaw and jab at the screen. He slapped the phone back into her hand and wheeled away as if he would walk back to his group, who had already pulled an extra step of distance from him.

"Wait," she commanded.

He did.

She circled around so that they were facing each other again, never taking her eyes from the phone, slow steps, bootheels thocking on the tiles. She ticked a glance at his face to make sure he was watching her. He was. Carly could see her a little better, too. The woman launched the video he'd just taken and turned up the volume. *C'mon, Carly, do something* awe-*some.*

Carly's mouth twitched in the fight against crying. Dylan rolled his eyes again.

The woman tapped the screen. "Okay, well, that's gone."

Dylan put his hand out for his phone.

She shook her head. "Not just yet."

The woman scrolled through his pictures, all her reaction playing out in her rising left eyebrow.

Dylan shrank with every flick of her finger across the screen, going paler until his freckles and two panicked spills of red across his cheeks were all the color left in him.

"Oh. I see. Wow." She looked up. Calm, Carly saw, and a little rage rippling under it. "Really, Dylan? Do you think we should show this to, I don't know, your parents? *Their* parents, maybe?" She studied his photo gallery again. The last passes of her fingers were in a tight-lipped hurry. She looked up and sighed. "You have a real problem, Dylan. Do you know that?"

He quaked and nodded. The drive-through kept running in cars and order-box static, oblivious to the frozen crowd inside. The girl with the headset was going to give herself whiplash trying to both do her job and not miss out on the show.

"I'm going to do you a favor," the woman said, her fingers flying across the screen of Dylan's phone. "And delete all of this."

She handed the phone back to Dylan, tears now running in shining tracks over his furious blushing. He put his fingers around it, but she didn't release her hold on the phone or his gaze. She did, though, take a small-arc step to the left, Dylan in tow, turning the conversation and angling their bodies, Carly realized with a startle, for her benefit. She could see them both in full profile now—Dylan's wrecked humiliation and the woman, at once scarred and beautiful, in complete control.

"Fresh start," she said to him.

He made a little choked sound in his throat and nodded helplessly again.

She pulled the phone like his tether and reeled Dylan in toward her. "You're going to get a lot of shit for this, Dylan. For what's happening here, right now."

Carly felt the antennae of all the young people in the doughnut shop buzz to life, remembering their world.

The woman continued, "But it won't last long. It'll pass. I want you to get over it. I want you to be fine. I really do. But I want you to remember it. Every time you go through your new, nice—regular—pictures, remind yourself."

Dylan bobbed his head, agreeing to anything to make it end, quivering in place, pinned there in all his wrongness.

"Don't be a terrible person, Dylan. In the end, you never really get away with it."

She let go of his phone first, then of his eyes.

Dylan melted into his group and they went straight for the door like a single creature. The room broke out in chatter.

The woman said to Carly, "Take my table. Catch your breath." She gathered up her bag and her book, and moved her coffee to the far side to make space for Carly and Ada's things.

"Thanks," Carly said. "I mean, not for the table. I mean, yes, for the table. But for . . . you know. Thanks for helping."

The girls arranged their treats in front of them, but the doughnut now looked gross to Carly. She was lost-in-the-desert thirsty, but the clear condensation on the outside of the cup was more appealing than the thought of the syrup-sweet drink inside.

"You can repay me." The woman smiled at them for checking each other's worried glances for the right answer to that. "And by that, I mean you can show me your drawings." She nodded toward Carly's spiral-bound sketchbook. "I used to be an art expert. I can smell an artist a mile away. Either that or I saw you showing your friend here while you two were in line. Take your pick."

Carly laughed and passed over the book. Shy and proud all at the same time, her face burned again, for what felt like the hundredth time since she and Ada had come in the door.

"I'm Emma, by the way. You're Carly, or so my new best friend, Dylan, tells me."

The girls giggled.

"And you . . . ?" Emma left it open for the answer.

"I'm Ada."

"Do you also draw, Ada?"

"Nah. That's her thing. I'm a musician. And a nerd. DC, *not* Marvel. Puh-lease."

Emma flipped through Carly's drawings, pausing, turning some of them into the light. She wasn't kidding about the art thing. Carly had seen lots of people look at her drawings.

When she drew, it was a different kind of thinking. A pointed blankness in the front of her mind and whirring concentration in the back of it. But the moment when other people looked at what she'd done, when her ideas went into their heads in the first pass of their eyes, that was amazing. She felt both impossibly close and spacewalk-distanced from anyone who was looking at her work.

Everybody liked them. They liked them because they were good. Carly knew this, though smiles and shrugs were all anyone ever got out of her in reaction. It was the weirdest kind of thanks to give when someone had liked the work that was private and public all at the same time.

But this woman, Emma, could really see what the drawings were made of. Carly watched what she paid attention to on the page. Emma knew exactly how Carly's pencil moved, where she'd started with the shadows and edging. Emma knew everything about what she was looking at.

"These are very good."

Carly smiled and her shoulder moved toward her ear as if it couldn't help it.

"No, really. These are excellent. Truly."

"Thank you."

"You're welcome. So, I see Disney here. Some anime. Some original stuff, too." Emma wound the pages back to the beginning. "But what else? Who do you like? Old Masters? Renaissance? Or more recent stuff?"

Carly didn't know the answers to those questions. She had only the vaguest idea of categories and famous names.

Emma watched her with a steady patience, waiting for an answer.

"I . . . I don't really know what I like."

"Well, what do your parents like?"

"Oh, my mom doesn't know anything about art. She can't even play Pictionary. She's a disaster with a pencil." Carly hoped her smile was nice and that what she'd said hadn't come out snotty. She hated getting stranded on the unknowing side of a knowing smile. When adults talked about *Oh, teenagers* as if they were all the same and all out-of-control obnoxious, it made her wish she'd never said anything at all—ever. "I don't think John knows about art either."

Emma closed her mouth and tilted her head. Carly saw her take a slow inhale that lasted forever. She hadn't moved. That was it. That's what was different. She'd gone statue still.

"John's her stepdad," said Ada, never to stay forgotten in a conversation for long. "I got to be in the wedding. Junior bridesmaid." Ada nodded at her own commentary, wise with pride. "Me and Carly had matching dresses. They itched."

"They were the worst," said Carly. "But, yeah. I just draw on my own. I get comics and cartoon books from the library sometimes. Just to look at. Mom and John are really nice about my drawings. Really supportive. But they don't know anything about art."

"Is that right?" Emma said. "That's interesting."

CHAPTER TWELVE

John didn't know anything about art, but he knew a fair bit about things that were old. He'd grown up with the vague idea that his father had a dedication to three things: root beer, real beer, and flea markets.

As Jonathan got toward adulthood, he understood there was more to it, that his father was ill, wrung in cycles of hopelessness that didn't seem to obey any rules of cause and effect. But the truth was that John never really gave a shit about any of that. He didn't have much of an attention span for wondering about the invisible weight that pressed his father.

His mother had always made up the practical difference anyway, sometimes with three jobs at once and always with a watchful eye on her husband's frailties. He wouldn't protest as she'd donate a truckload of his accumulated junk and move them on to the next town, and into the invigorating distraction of a fresh start.

It was time to go if the man of the house bloomed in enthusiasms that swelled into days-long impassioned rants. He'd quit his job at the grocery or hardware store and spend his time instead bringing in carloads, sometimes even borrowed-truck loads, of plunder as he discovered this, that, and every ridiculous other. At one point, they'd owned four washing machines and two refrigerators, a blocky white Stonehenge of appliances in the living room, all just as useful plugged in as not.

It was equally worrisome when he quit talking altogether and got to slurping sweet suds and hoppy ones as the television channels ran through their schedules in front of him and the clock wound circles on the wall.

His mother's vigilance had a whiff of warden about it. Something truly bad might've happened if she didn't mind the fences of her husband's moods.

She slept no more than three or four hours a night until she didn't wake up at all one morning two days before she would have turned forty-six. Jonathan knew it was a sad thing. Tragic even. But she'd brought it on herself. No one made her everyone's keeper or made her stand sentry until it killed her.

Jonathan had spent hours—months' worth of hours probably—trotting along on the trail of his father's obsession with the minutiae of secondhand sales. His dad was animated by abundance, sometimes the shabbier the better, and by the suspended animation of all that stuff just sitting there in between belonging to someone.

Flea markets, swap meets, and pawnshops were his father's favorites, but the peripheral booths at gun shows and trade fairs would do, too. He wasn't above enjoying a yard sale either, but his wife made him promise that the lawns of their neighbors, in whatever town they were living in, were off-limits.

Jonathan Spera the Elder was warm and happy and competent and just a touch holier-than-thou when he roamed the no-expectation zones of the world with a little cash in his pocket. In tow, Junior watched the traffic on the road, fantasizing where the long-haul truckers would end up when they pulled in and unhitched their trailers.

But the knowledge of the worth of things, and specifically of how a span of years magically transformed the worth of things, soaked into Junior and became reflexive.

After his mother died, Jonathan didn't have the patience that she had for calibrating each day against his father's ability to cope. So he'd introduced his father to marijuana and plain cigarettes just to keep him calm.

He smothered the embers of his father's chemical swings with blankets of nicotine, caffeine, sugar, and THC, until his dad was up to slightly better than three packs of cigarettes a day and just under an ounce of weed every two weeks. A few cases of protein drink, a few economy-size tubs of instant coffee, an assortment of junk food, and all the root beer and Pabst his father could drink was the standing order. That and a paid cable bill kept the old man effectively paralyzed. Happy enough, as far as Jonathan could tell.

The government checks and his mother's annuity covered it until it didn't. There was never any left over, and the last few days of some months were tense with Jonathan's phone lighting up in spasms of his father's anxiety, hunger, and permanent hangover.

But not until his father died after nearly nine years of the routine, alone in his chair with the TV on and a cigarette burned fully through to the skin, did Jonathan truly understand himself.

When he found his father with his tongue dried to a shriveled leaf-looking thing in his slack open mouth, he'd turned off the TV and switched on the overhead. The smoke-stained glass fixture dribbled yellow light over a room chock-full of junk, and entirely empty of life. And it was Jonathan's own personal sunrise. In the sudden echo of release, and thirty-two years young, he knew what he was made of.

The burn on his father's thigh was disgusting—deep and dry by the time Jonathan found him, but a howling blackish red and clean edged. His father clearly hadn't budged while the cherry seared through the flannel and his skin. He'd never made a single move to save himself. Just as always. No struggle at all.

Jonathan had thrown a blanket into the old man's lap, and cleared his throat to make room to wedge a sad sound into his voice and called 911 for a pointless ambulance.

Then life moved on.

When Jonathan sold his father's house, he hired out for all the hot, boring, dirty, splintery work of making the place look as if it had been even a little bit cared for. Out of the crew that came to pressure-wash and repair the deck, Roy was the only one who didn't look like a criminal. Roy looked like a mess, no mistaking, but not as if he was eyeing up everything that wasn't nailed down, or as if he was ready to carve a few extra holes into anyone just for the sport of it.

Roy Dorring was a mule—dull, plodding, and reliable in a narrow beast-of-burden kind of way. But the shiniest facet of Roy, as far as Jonathan could care about, was his stubborn insistence on being pathetic. It was a rustle in the grass, a whiff of prey on the breeze. And Jonathan had a stinger, a restless vestigial tail on his personality.

That's what he'd realized once his parents were gone. He was free, but he couldn't sink his disapproval into a memory. It didn't satisfy. It was distracting. He'd been too long without a target, and the venom was backed up in him. Roy drew the barb as if it were his one true calling.

After the deck, for the rest of the grunt work, Jonathan flipped a coin between the two broke-ass fools who most needed a job, cheating the spin to let Roy win the jumping chance to ask *How high?* Out of the two likely candidates, Roy was the weakest, and therefore the best.

Jonathan set him on various errands and projects and exorcised his irritation on Roy's cringing back at every fumble and misstep.

The leaching worked. Jonathan felt better. He acted more friendly with other people. He slept more deeply. He got things done. When diagrammed out, it was the upstanding thing to do. Everyone whom Jonathan encountered benefited from his heaping a little extra shit on a guy who didn't notice the difference.

Roy, like John's father, also had a weakness for junk. His truck was full to blackout at the windows with it. Jonathan had called him over for the sneezy, gritty chore of clearing out the old man's garage. The endless heaps of everything had Roy as distracted as a toddler in a toy store.

Jonathan was hot and exasperated until the discovery of a box bowing at the sides with old magazines, loose art prints in plastic sleeves, and a painting sticking up from the rest—a mill with a water-wheel next to a river, a bridge, a tall tower off on its own in the middle distance. Boring.

When Jonathan pulled the panel out and saw the faint inscription, *R. 16*, something illegible, then an *8*, brushed in at the right corner, the painting just sitting there in a box in his father's garage, propped up among the ridiculous crap and the marginally useful crap, he doubted it at first. But he'd seen enough old junk to recognize time. And that looked like an awful lot of time.

He'd sharpened his sneer to shoo away Roy, who was peering over Jonathan's shoulder, cooing over the stack of papers and art prints as if it were sweet.

Do you need something to read, Roy? Can you even read? Take this shit if it interests you so much.

Jonathan had topped off the box with a pair of dry-rotted snow-shoes that Roy had been eyeing, and shoved him out the door to be alone with this possible treasure.

It had been overcast and the daylight hadn't gained much of a reach through the rolled-up metal door. Jonathan squinted to make the most of the weak, gray glow as he studied his find. Then he believed what he saw: that the first two digits of that number would be worth a lot. But to whom?

Jonathan had dared hope that the painting could be worth five figures. It turned out to be worth millions. But how to unload it? It was the best worst problem he'd ever had. No regular person knows how to do that. All of a sudden he had this thing he suspected was valuable, but then what?

He had to find someone who did know what to do with it. Nothing in his education in special trash had ever offered a suggestion of how to get the most out of a nearly four-hundred-year-old painting.

Yellowed newspapers, bubbled glass, vintage advertising signs with their logos rusting off, buffalo nickels, toys they had wisely stopped making once better fun had come along, obsolete electronics—if it was quaint and old, or just quaint or just old, Jonathan would have had an idea of where to start. But as it was . . .

Lots of experts were available online, but his instinct had been to go in person, with only a photo of the painting on his phone. He'd strolled through a huge auction house and two high-end galleries, sizing up the people there, comparing their treasures as best he could against what he'd hidden away at home. But he hadn't been inspired to talk to any of them before he met Marcelline.

She was beautiful, both warm and cool at the same time, and that never hurt anything. But watching her work through two phone calls and one in-the-flesh transaction had convinced Jonathan he'd find an angle, a set of dials he could control in the exchange. She was interested in her work, but passionless about it.

That assessment of her burned to the ground when they'd realized, together, what he had wrapped in a blanket in his closet at home. Marcelline had sparked up, so glittering and intense with excitement that Jonathan couldn't even look at her without feeling it in his balls. It wasn't just the money for her. It was the story of the painting, the history, the old Boston museum heist.

They talked each other into selling it themselves without involving the gallery or the FBI. She made calls. Took a promising meeting.

Then they talked each other through two bottles of wine and, ultimately, into bed.

When he woke up in her apartment, he'd still been convinced of the wisdom of the private sale, but perhaps not of the rest of it. He shouldn't have slept with her. Maybe he shouldn't even have shown interest in her idea. He should have left and said that he would think about it and be in touch.

He was angry with himself. It wasn't as if she hadn't telegraphed with her sleek look and liquid grace, climbing atop him, smooth legs parting over his lap on her sofa, mouth tasting of wine, that she was fast, decisive, aerodynamic even.

The sale was set up, bird in the hand as it were, before he knew anything about feathered friends and birds of prey. Too fast. He'd have to split it with her, whatever she could negotiate. Jonathan was an only child to the last cell in his body, unaccustomed to sharing.

So he'd quick-plotted, using the simplest tool he'd had. He could control Roy with a minimum of explanation to rattle the buyer, some rich prick named Anninger. Easy. Hell, if it went wrong the right way, it would have been fine with Jonathan if they'd killed Roy or beaten him into a coma. Either way, it would have been the excuse Jonathan needed to duck out and reschedule—without Marcelline. After her indiscretion, with her career in the balance, she'd hardly be able to complain.

They all had guns, and Roy managed to ruin everything by spazzing at the trigger finger when one of buyer's guys pulled his hands from his pockets. Both the small- and medium-size thugs fell, but the big guy, the absolute hardest-to-miss target outside the buildings themselves, had nothing but the noise to slow him down. Roy also killed Marcelline.

The double cross had closed off the legitimate route forever. Jonathan's new enemies were possibly worse than jail. So four years on, instead of millions, he still had a little cash and the painting. And he still didn't know how to get rid of it.

He could look for another Marcelline. Someone else out there would be as knowledgeable. Other people would be bold and greedy enough to slide this painting off to its next owner without involving the law.

Or . . .

Jonathan had to admit that he did know more now than he had back then. He knew at least one person who was willing and able to pay for the painting. He knew the name Anninger, and their guy, Marcelline's contact . . . Oscar? Oliver? Owen, Oren, definitely an O name.

John pushed back from his desk where he'd been staring out the window until his eyes had gone dry. Donna was out of the house with her to-do list. Carly and Ada had packed up the art supplies right after school and run off again. They'd been living at the library over the last few days.

He'd been going in late to the office and coming home early. Everyone was so understanding of his need to be with his family at a time like this. And that worked great for John, who more needed to be with his painting at a time like this, even hidden away as it was.

The stillness of the house was gnawing at his nerves. He checked the drawer where he kept a little slush fund, but found only four twenties left.

He pulled down the attic ladder and craned to listen for the garage door. The sound of nothing spurred him on to full speed. The quiet wouldn't last.

Up the ladder in three pulls, he moved a box from in front, and one from on top of a locked trunk, and took the key from the gap between a pair of raw two-by-fours.

Hiding the satchel and the painting was tricky, but the money wouldn't be worth less after aging in the heat and the cold of the attic, or after a plumbing mishap in the basement. Money, dry or damp, would still spend.

At first he'd put the painting, wrapped against humidity, down in the skeletal unfinished basement, behind the open, raw-wood stairs with the boxes and cobwebs and mousetraps where no one ever wanted to go. Then he decided he didn't trust it.

If anything good was about the Flinck's being on the wall in the foyer, it was the air-conditioning in the summer and the soft gas heat in the winter. Even the sunlight didn't get to it where it had landed.

He drew a short stack of bills from the dwindling green bricks. It had been four years of pocket money and expensive indulgences, but not the life he wanted, not the life that was so tantalizingly close.

He'd found a way to bide time before selling the Flinck, to buffer his trickery and accessory-after-the-fact vulnerability with a thick sheaf of calendar pages. It meant being a different person again, and that was kind of fun.

Donna was gorgeous, the sex was great, and a courtship and a wedding kept the schedule full of something other than waiting. She and Carly both had been so much better than what he'd needed to pass the days.

In his attic, their attic, above the rooms where he'd been part of a happy, laughing routine he dropped his hands to his sides, struck suddenly heavy and unsure by how fast the time with them had flown. It wouldn't have if they'd been less than they were.

An ache swelled into his throat, but he shook his head against it. It didn't matter. Anyway, he didn't have to decide right now what this meant for them as a situation. He wouldn't call it a family. *Family* felt too inevitable, something you didn't choose. He chose this. He could choose to cut it loose. Or he could choose to find something in between.

John resecured the trunk and its camouflage, stowed the key, and eased the attic access door closed. He listened for the garage door. Still nothing. He swiped the grit and insulation dust from the floor with a static mop and smiled at the small success. Anything that went well in these last few days felt like getting away with skipping school.

He replenished the petty cash in his desk drawer, then went out and bought a prepaid phone with some of the rest of it. He sat in the car, setting it up and trying to remember all he could of the Anningers' man who worked with Marcelline. John replayed the conversations he'd heard, what she'd told the guy in setting up the sale, listening to her play up the notoriety of the painting because she'd said the Anningers liked a side dish of darkness with whatever they were buying.

He tried to imagine what that night had looked like from that other guy's vantage point, across the alley from Roy's poor performance. Was any of this still an option?

A little cybersearching turned up a number for an Anninger-held business back near his old life, not far from the gallery where John had met Marcelline. He set his tone for harried, but friendly, ready to plead his case to the clipped, professional drone at the other end of the call.

"Hi. I'm wondering if you can help me. My phone died and I've lost all my contacts. I'm screwed. Everything's gone. I was working on setting up a sale with one of Mr. Anninger's associates, a big guy named—"

"Let me put you through to sales."

"No, no wait. I just—"

Click. Hold music.

Call after call. Calls transferred. New numbers suggested. Exasperated verbal shrugs.

"I'm trying to locate one of their associates. He's a real big guy. His name is Oscar or Otis or something. . . . I'm almost sure his name started with an O. I'm terrible with names."

The man laughed through his nose, but John heard promise in it. The car had gone stifling with heat and with the boredom of too many dead ends. Goose bumps on John's scalp was almost as good as a cool breeze.

"I think you mean Owen Haig."

"Owen! Yes! That was it."

"Yeah." There was tapping on the line, a keyboard in the background. "Except now all I'm going to be able to think is *Otis* next time I see him, and that'll get me killed for laughing at him. So, thanks for that." The guy chuckled again. "*Otis*. Fan-friggin'-tastic. Here's a number for their call service. Just tell them to put you through to Owen Haig's voice mail. Got a pen?"

John Cooper looked at the number now typed onto the screen of the throwaway phone in his hand. His pulse throbbed in his head. He watched it banging into his eyes, hypnotizing him. His mind wanted to run away to anything, even into the strobe of his own heartbeat.

He was worried about pinging the Anningers. He was worried about getting this wrong. And he almost couldn't take any more worry on top of everything else. But just doing nothing was a constant needling itch in his skin.

No one might ever notice the painting. The video could have its flare of fame with the internet generation absolutely oblivious to the sliver of waterwheel and bridge. The best thing might be exactly that—stalling and waiting and letting this whole fiasco glide right over him so that he could move the painting when he felt good and ready to do it. That's what all of this had been for.

But if he was wrong and the fuse was hissing up behind him, it had all been for nothing anyway.

He dragged his hands over his face, his wedding ring pressing a track against his left brow and cheek.

The phone could go under the tire of his car in the next ten minutes if he needed it to, if this didn't go well. Owen Haig didn't know anything about him. Which meant the guy didn't know anything good, but he couldn't know anything all that bad either.

Their one meeting had been a disaster. John had seen the way Owen looked at Marcelline; saw a big man with his heart in his throat who didn't know how to chew and swallow a simple crush. John had felt the unlikely urge to put his hand on her ass and wink at Owen just to see what color he'd turn.

But the guy was huge and serious in a way that discouraged any jokes. No hint of a gentle giant there, just one so stone-faced that it wasn't worth finding out if he could take a little ribbing or not.

Jonathan had taken the money. And the painting. That's all Owen Haig knew about him. But Haig didn't know why any of it had happened. There could be a scenario sketched out that would explain it all in a better light. In a show of good faith, the whole debacle could be worked in as a discount, a concession in the new asking price if that helped make it feel more right to Owen and the Anningers.

Jonathan cocked his head, deciding what he should sound like in this call, figuring out which John he needed to be to get things moving again.

If Roy had gotten it right that night, John would always have had to make a call like this to renegotiate with the Anningers. He was always going to have to make Marcelline look bad to justify it. In a way, this was easier. She was hardly in a position to argue her side of it. The original plan, more or less, was possibly salvageable.

That was the answer: act as if nothing had gone irreversibly wrong four years ago. Handle it ice-cold. Nothing more than the unfortunate hazards of doing business in the big leagues. That was the extralarge goon's shtick. That's what he would understand.

John cleared his throat to make room for calm confidence in his voice and dialed Owen Haig.

CHAPTER THIRTEEN

Owen leaned back against the headrest of his seat and closed his eyes. He pressed the phone against his ear and replayed the message for the third time. He'd listened to it in the first go-around on the car's hands-free connection. He'd been making use of the driving time to clear out his voice mail. All boring stuff. But he'd pulled over into a neighborhood swimming pool's parking lot and sent this particular message back into the handset once he'd realized, in the first ten seconds, who had called.

"Mr. Haig, my name is Jonathan. You may remember me. We only met once, a few years ago, but it was kind of a standout experience. I have to think it was for you, too. A sale . . . hit a snag at the last possible minute. It was unfortunate. I'll be honest, I still don't know what to think.

"You and your employer probably hold me responsible. But considering all that happened, you might understand why I've been reluctant to reach out. Our mutual friend, what happened to her, well, I've had a hard time moving past it, myself. It was easy to think it was you, but, to be fair, I didn't know her all that well. I wouldn't have thought she would do anything like that. But I just don't know. Either way, I trusted too much—you or her. That's my own fault. It kills me that I'll never know. I'll never hear her side of it. So . . ."

The pause cut down to a silence that was clean enough to have Owen thinking it was the end of the message.

But then the guy started up again after a sharp, resigned breath, in and out. "Yeah. So. Things being what they are, I'm in a strange position. The item is still available. Of course, there would be a lot to talk about. And I would need much better assurances than I had last time. I realize that this ship may have sailed. Your employer may not want to acquire this piece anymore. And really, it might be better, safer, for me to simply start all over.

"But after everything, this thing seems . . . cursed. Not that I believe in that sort of stuff. But if that doesn't bother them, or you, I'd prefer to be rid of it. I don't know, maybe the history of it is a deal breaker. That's fine, too. In light of everything, I just thought I'd extend the first gesture. Maybe to try to set things right. If you want to talk about it, call me back at this number. I look forward to hearing from you."

Owen closed the voice mail app, his fingers firm on the edge of the case so as not to accidentally hit a delete command out of habit. He'd be listening to that message again. He was sure of it.

What the fuck was this guy playing at?

Jonathan, *the* Jonathan, put his head up like a prairie dog in the middle of all of this shit and acted as if Marcelline had died at the scene. He seemed completely unaware that Owen knew, firsthand, that she hadn't. Which, if he wasn't lying, would only mean that he hadn't spoken to her since that night. And that meant she'd been telling Owen the truth. She and Jonathan weren't partners.

The air felt thick in Owen's throat.

The other possibility was that perhaps she'd not made it far after her little joyride in the Mercedes. Maybe she'd tried, but never made it back to Jonathan and their plan. Maybe she died of a blood clot or sepsis as a fevered Jane Doe in some undiscovered place, and Owen had for years been looking for someone who didn't exist anymore. It would explain some things.

He caught himself gripping the seat's edge in his fist. He flexed the painful lock out of his knuckles and blew out a big deep breath. Now what?

There was no coincidence that Jonathan had surfaced after all this time, ho-humming aloud—today—if Owen knew that the painting was still available. *You're a ham-handed little asshole sometimes, aren't you, Jonathan?*

The delivery of the message had been smooth enough, but the real question still blared out around the polished edges. This wasn't simply about what Jonathan wanted Owen to think of him. This was about what Jonathan wanted to know. Had Owen seen the video? Jonathan wanted to know what kind of trouble he was in, and then how to get out of it.

And what kind of trouble *was* he in from Owen?

The Anningers had cooled toward Owen considerably after what had gone wrong that night. Blue blood had stripped cunning from them as surely as it had dialed up the sensitivity in their asses for a pea under a stack of mattresses. Their punishments were blunt and unsophisticated. Petty. They rolled their eyes at him and had relegated him to a series of dull special projects that made him want to break jaws just to keep himself awake.

He had an ear and an eye for the structure of it all, why they were the way they were. But he never had a reason to talk about it outside the few conversations he'd had with Marcelline. He'd lost himself in that connection, in those exchanges that brushed the line of what was not okay to say about the people they both worked for.

The image of her, of Marcelline looking up from her paperwork, eyes smiling at him from under her long lashes, it pulled him awake on the pillow so many mornings, still after all this time.

A tingle climbed the rungs of his ribs. Everything else could burn. He cared a lot about this one.

This Jonathan character had said way more than he meant to in his message, perhaps mistaking Owen for a simple gamecock that could be useful to him, if only Owen could be convinced to believe the right things.

The leather on the steering wheel of Owen's C63 had an irregular dark patch at about two o'clock, right where the smooth-grain leather wrap gave over to the grippy padding. A similar smudge was at the edge of the center console, rubbed nearly invisible by the people who had detailed the car after he got it back. A few of the white stitches in the cover on the gear selector weren't cream colored anymore. The dealership had wanted to reupholster the stained trim, but Owen had declined.

Marcelline had bled a little in her flight. He never knew how to feel about that.

So Jonathan wanted something from Owen that was probably as simple as a lot of money and to be rid of an item that could land him in quite a bit of trouble. It would be nothing for Owen to make that happen. It was his job to do just that.

If Marcelline was in fact dead, all that was in it for Owen was the chance to know what had really happened, to maybe finally be sure whether she'd set him up. And if she wasn't dead, it was the same thing, but with even more potential.

He scanned the dashboard, a beautiful thing, really. He admired the mellow sheen of his trouser leg. The fine, carefully crafted things in life. He thought of Marcelline, who never got closer than his guest bed.

He keyed back into his voice mail and listened to the message again.

She was there in Jonathan's script. The bit about the curse of the painting and all the Br'er Rabbit dissembling over how the bad history of the piece might be a problem for the Anningers. *Please don't throw me in that briar patch.* Owen could practically feel her smirking.

Jonathan had known her better than he let on. Or he'd been paying better attention than he wanted to admit, as any straight man would in her presence. Either way, she'd left enough of an impression to write lines for him to speak when he wanted to wield her influence, even all this time later.

But the *I've had a hard time moving past it, myself* was pure, pointed fabrication. Owen knew what it meant to have a hard time moving past Marcelline. He knew exactly how it felt to not make much progress toward not thinking about her, in wondering if she was a conniving bitch who had found him disposable. And for nothing more than money. He knew what that feeling would sound like in someone's voice. But it wasn't there in Jonathan's message. They were not brothers in disillusion, no matter that the man thought it was a coin for him to spend.

Owen had only a few images of Jonathan in his mind: the blandly handsome, stoic mask at the handshake; the hooded interest in the formalities of the exchange, trying not to look on high alert, as if he weren't counting the number of steps to the exits.

But the image of him prying Marcelline's hand off her neck, her mouth in a shocked little O and the quick lurch of blood as he pinned her arms down, that was vivid. Had Jonathan been helping her or hurting her? He'd looked over at Owen, unreadable.

There were things yet to know.

Goddamn, the Anningers' silly wants were so boring.

Owen watched across a lane of parking spaces. Beyond the chain-link was a line of boys daring one another into the deep end, nudging, close to shoving, heads swiveling to take the measure of the others. Everything they knew about the world was obvious in the curve of their spines and the tension in their shoulders. But in that half-naked lineup you couldn't tell what they would become. The short, skinny little twerp might be due for a growth spurt. The fat one might discover offensive tackle or physics. The one who stood a half step away, straight as a soldier, might find luck and opportunity that took him to places he'd never imagined but cost him his soul.

Owen took up his phone and tapped into the service's message details for Jonathan's number. He wouldn't pick up. Of course he wouldn't. He'd want to hear Owen's tone on his own turf. He'd want to analyze Owen's words and inflections to know whether to destroy his disposable phone or to roll the dice and take his next turn elsewhere.

Owen put his hand over the stain on the steering wheel's leather and squeezed. Marcelline.

"Jonathan. Good to hear from you. Of course, I remember you. Who forgets something like that? You're right in that there's still interest and much to talk about. But I think it's better, for everyone, if we talk in person. If you give me twenty-four hours, I can be wherever you'd like. You say where, you say when, I'll make it happen. Text me the particulars, if that's easier."

Owen paused, then gave Jonathan the least of his own sentences back.

"I look forward to hearing from you."

Owen closed the call and cranked the Mercedes's engine back to life. He didn't want to love the car. It had an axle in both worlds—too showy in one and too humble in the other. He felt weak in that, at his heart, the car was in the same category as his rain-shower fixture in his bathroom and his underwear and his bedsheets and the occasional woman who touched his naked skin. The car was something intimate, a beautiful chain to the world that other, lesser people seemed to enjoy.

He thought of wacky, economy-class Charlie and the day he'd first seen the painting in the video. Something somersaulted inside him—then and again now.

He dropped the Mercedes into gear and pulled out into the mild suburban traffic.

He'd told Jonathan to give him twenty-four hours notice to meet up. But Owen didn't need twenty-four hours. He probably didn't need twenty-four minutes. He'd been in town for a day and a half, not knowing whether the girl, whom he'd watched walking home from school with her friends, deep in conversation punctuated in the occasional wild, uncontrolled gestures of youth, was heading to the plain little house that linked back to Marcelline, Jonathan, or some unknown and unlucky soul who would eventually tell Owen, with a last breath if need be, what he wanted to know.

CHAPTER FOURTEEN

Marcelline was growing convinced that the sense of knowing yourself was a delusion. The smackdowns you delivered in the bathroom mirror rarely happened to a foe who wasn't your own reflection. The scripts you wrote in your head were almost never performed. You knew what was important to you, but you didn't insist. You knew what was right and still steered around it. You took self-defense classes and could, in theory, stay frosty and flip an attacker over your hip. But in the end you still stood there and got shot in the neck.

The thing that bothered her, though, was wondering which was the real Marcelline. Was it the one who planned, or the one who abandoned plans and principles in the face of life rushing over her?

She wanted to see Jonathan, wanted to lay eyes on him. A plan about what to do would start with getting a second first impression of him. She'd only known him for a few days a long time ago.

There weren't any photographs, not even of the painting. He wouldn't send it to her. He wouldn't give her his number. He never even told her his last name and made a big joke of it, promising it for later when all was said and done. And deposited.

She couldn't even be sure if what he looked like in her mind would match up to reality. Every time they'd been together, she'd been buzzing with distraction. They'd had sex in the dark after a lot of wine. And in the last moments there was the moon, for all the help it was to see clearly by, and patches of streetlight along the weedy lot. But the darkness had swallowed most of the detail of that night. The last she'd seen of him, she was sure she was dying.

She knew sharply what she'd felt toward him in that moment, but the specific features of his face wavered uncertainly in the memory. Marcelline had this recurring horrible fantasy that she might have walked right past him on the street between then and now and not even noticed. In her ugly daydream, he turned as she went by and smiled at her blindness.

She needed to see him because she needed to know how she'd handle it. She was afraid of what it would do to her to know, to recognize—not just remember and guess—what he looked like. She was desperate to put a face, the right one, on this thing.

Or so she said. So she thought. But instead, here she was in the library with Carly and Ada for the fourth day in a row.

"It seems like cheating," Carly said. "I'm just copying what these great famous artists did. That's not very right, is it?"

The table was covered with art books opened to iconic paintings: *Starry Night, Girl with a Pearl Earring, Guernica, A Sunday Afternoon on the Island of La Grande Jatte, Water Lilies.* In front of her was Michelangelo's *The Creation of Adam.* Carly peered up from her paper every few strokes, checking it against the zoomed-in detail of the famous fresco.

Her sketch pads and pens, two full rainbows of colored pencils, and a set each of oil pastels and charcoals took up the rest of the table-top. Ada had brought along a mandala coloring book and a big box of crayons that Carly had frequently borrowed from during the lesson. But Ada had left off the coloring and was flipping though an art book that covered most of her lap.

Marcelline looked up from her own book that she'd been hiding behind to think. "I'm not suggesting you sign your name to it and try to pass it off as your own idea. It's just an exercise. Brain training. You look at it and try to decide what medium and technique you'd use to get something like that effect. You guess at how to duplicate the strokes you see, or think you see. You make the leap and find out how close you were to right. All it costs is paper and time.

"However it goes, it doesn't matter. You'll know more about what your hand can do, and your eye, and your materials. And I think, really, trying to understand how they did it makes you feel a little closer to these guys. It's a time machine." Marcelline swept her hand over the open books. "Besides, what do you think you're doing when you're drawing Peter Pan and Pokémon?"

"Those are just cartoons."

Marcelline went wide-eyed at Carly. "I am going to pretend you didn't even say that. Cartoonists aren't artists?"

Carly blushed. "No. They are. I know that. I mean, it's just not serious. . . ."

Marcelline smiled to reassure her. "Yeah, it is. And so are you. So don't forget it. And be careful with your thoughts. They matter."

Ada held up her open book and showed them Munch's *The Scream*. She wrinkled her nose. "I've seen this before. I don't like it."

"No?" Marcelline said.

"It's kinda cool, though." Carly nodded at it.

"It's creepy," Ada said.

Marcelline could only agree. "It is. But why do you think it's famous?"

Ada scoffed. "Because people like creepy stuff. *Some* people do. Creepy people do."

They all laughed, but Carly stopped first. Marcelline watched her study the picture. "What are you thinking?"

"About maybe why it's famous," Carly said without looking away from it.

Marcelline dropped her gaze to the tabletop to keep the weight of her own stare off Carly. She kept still so as not to cause a ripple of distraction. These things were fragile, and self-consciousness could crush it in a second. She gave it its elbow room, letting the possibilities click together in Carly's head.

Carly leaned back in her chair. "It's famous because it's really good."

Ada was indignant. "What? No, it's not. It's weird. And it's ugly. Sorry. Just being honest. I don't know why it's even a thing. I mean, who even let him? It's creepy."

Carly kept staring at the picture on the page. "Yeah, but it's good because that's not what creepy looks like." She wiggled her fingers at the image. "Nothing really looks like that." She leaned back again and pointed to punctuate her conclusion. "But that's *exactly* what creepy feels like."

Ada was shaking her head.

"No, no," Carly said. "No. See? If it actually looked real, like something real-life creepy, it would be less creepy, because creepy is a feeling, not a look." She turned to Marcelline. "Right?"

Marcelline sucked in her cheeks to keep from beaming. "I'm not sure it's ever been explained better."

Carly beamed for the both of them.

Ada shrugged and went back to her book. Carly took up her pencil.

Marcelline tapped the photo of the Michelangelo. "Try just the hands. Clean sheet. Use . . ." She hummed over the tray of charcoals and drew out a slim vine stick. "Try this one."

Carly went straight back to being lost in her work, and Marcelline into her thoughts. The room faded to vague around her, Carly's scratching charcoal and the library murmur receding to nothing. Marcelline ran her tongue over her teeth and drew her fingers along the track of her scar.

She knew so little about Jonathan. She was acting as if everything hinged on the moment she saw him, as if as soon as that was confirmed, she'd know what to do. But that was a bit of wishful thinking. Sure, she'd probably rattle the bejesus out of him. As fun as that sounded, she hadn't survived and come all this way to raise his blood pressure for a few minutes.

She took inventory of what she actually knew. With as much power as she'd given him to launch her into an entirely different life, it was embarrassing how little she could say for sure about Jonathan. She didn't even know how he'd come by the Flinck. He'd been as cagey about that as he'd been about everything else.

The painting they'd been dealing with was only one small part of the haul from the Gardner Museum theft.

He couldn't have all of it. What-if tugged for attention.

Marcelline's heartbeat skipped wild in her chest. She pulled over one of the largest collection volumes and checked the index and found her page. She stuck in a pencil as a bookmark and went back to the index. She held the second place with her finger.

"Hey, Carly."

Carly looked up. She'd managed to rub charcoal under one eye. She looked like a boxer two days after a bad round.

Marcelline wet a napkin from her water bottle. "Here, you've got . . ." She motioned for Carly to wipe her face.

"Oh, thanks."

"Hey, so I liked what you saw in the Munch, in *The Scream*, and the way you figured out your reaction to it. I want to see what you think of this one."

Carly lit up with an eagerness to collect more pride, to win the gold star of Marcelline's approval. That it was just a ploy for information made the smiling back at her hurt a little. Marcelline winced, but stretched it into, hopefully, a more convincing expression.

She opened the book to Rembrandt's *The Storm on the Sea of Galilee*, one of the missing treasures from the Gardner Museum. She watched Carly's face for a jolt of recognition.

There wasn't one. "It's nice. Good. It looks big. Like it should be big." Carly's expression was tight in concentration. "Is it big?"

"It is, yeah."

"It's pretty. But is it weird that I like the other one better, even though it's not as pretty?"

"No." Marcelline covered her disappointment with more conversation. "But it's interesting to know why. Can you tell me why?"

Carly shrugged. "I just don't feel like I need to look at it for more than five seconds. Like after just a quick peek, I'm all done with it."

Marcelline nodded. "What about this one?" She flipped to the other saved page and held her breath.

The biggest prize from the robbery of the Gardner Museum was a rare Vermeer, *The Concert*. When it was stolen, its value was marked at around $200 million. As a black-market trophy, it was almost hard to imagine what it could go for.

Carly bobbed her head, eyebrows up, alert. Marcelline's heart slammed against her breastbone.

"Same. Yeah. It's nice, but not as interesting as that other one."

Marcelline pulled a breath down over the pressure in her throat.

Carly's back went rigid. She pinched the fingertips of her right hand, massaging them unconsciously. "I'm sorry. Was that lame? Are these special and I missed something? Can I look again?"

Marcelline sagged. "No, honey. Not at all. I mean, yes, they're special in that they're works by famous artists, but you never need to apologize for your opinions. There's no question that if you studied them, you could give a clever analysis. You're a natural. I only wanted your basic reaction." She swallowed a hard lump of guilt. It felt shitty to make Carly doubt herself, yanking on her budding confidence.

"Please don't worry. It wasn't a trick que—" Marcelline shook her head and forced a smile. "There was no right answer. You're fine. You did exactly what I asked of you."

The three of them worked and read in companionable silence for nearly another hour. Marcelline stewed in feeling lousy and in doubt of everything she'd done since she'd left. She was sitting here manipulating a sweet kid because she was too chickenshit to figure out how to do what she'd claimed to want more than anything else in the world.

Carly clearly had never seen the other paintings. That didn't mean anything. The Flinck was definitely in the footage of Carly's house. A phantom itch skittered over Marcelline's neck. She drew out her phone and angled it away from the girls and watched the video again. Just to touch base, to make sure she wasn't crazy. Or not crazy like that, at least.

Later, in the stacks, Marcelline put back the art books they had taken out, but she withdrew, again, a single volume.

"Hey, Carly. One more. What do you think of this one?"

Carly came to stand with her. Her eyes swept over the page Marcelline held open. She had only known Carly a handful of days, but would swear the kid was taller than when she'd first found her. Growth spurt, in both height and art appreciation. Expanding in every dimension. Concentration was cute on her face, but also formidable. Carly could turn off the kid in her like a tap. Then she ran just pure can-do.

"Oh, wow! Yeah. We have that one at home—wait. Ha! No. It's not the same. Wow, that's weird. It looks so much like it. What is it?"

"*Landscape with the Good Samaritan*, by Rembrandt."

"Huh. I wonder if he did the one we have at home? I mean, not *the* one, of course. It's not fancy. It's just something my mom likes. It was John's, I think. But that's funny. It looks a lot like that one."

"Do you like it?"

Carly grinned and shrugged. "I still like the screaming one better."

"Fair enough." Marcelline smiled back, false and genuine both. Carly was adorable, and the Flinck had been mistaken for a Rembrandt landscape for centuries. It was the reason Isabella Stewart Gardner bought it in the first place, and possibly the reason the thieves had bothered with it at all.

The painting was at Carly's house.

But Carly could not, would not, get hurt in this.

In the parking lot, as Marcelline unlocked her car, the girls moved past her, cheerfully lugging all the art supplies the few blocks back home. Each day after their time in the library, Marcelline had wanted to offer them a ride, wondered if they thought it was strange that she didn't. They'd never mentioned it or looked put out. They didn't again today.

But the risk. Marcelline couldn't run into Jonathan by accident. She was too close already. The town wasn't a tight knot, but it was still only a few miles in all directions. The chance of just bumping into him wasn't zero. She'd played the scenario through, rehearsed what she might do if he'd shown up for some reason at the library. A big public place had its advantages. But getting caught on his street or idling in his driveway while his stepdaughter collected her things—no.

Ada was pulled off course by a woman walking a dog in front of the book drop.

Carly lingered and asked, "Is everything okay?"

This throwaway line was something people said more as filler than real inquiry. Like *How are you?*, your response was supposed to be *Everything's great*. But not this time. Carly was asking the actual question.

"Absolutely," Marcelline said.

"I just wanted to say thanks, in case we didn't get to do this again."

"We'll get to do this again."

"Okay. It's just most grown-ups can't do this kind of thing all the time. And your out-of-state plates . . ." Carly shifted the art case in her arms and put a toe up toward the bumper of Marcelline's car. "I just don't know what you do. You know, for a job or anything. I didn't know if you can keep doing this with us, if this is something that can just keep going."

The back of Marcelline's neck went cold in the breeze. "I'll be around. I'm enjoying the nonstop art party."

"Me, too. Us, too. It's been weird lately, you know, with the . . . Did you watch the video?"

A spike of alarm straightened Marcelline's spine. She didn't think Carly could have seen her at the table.

"I mean, it's okay. Everybody has. And the first time you saw me, Dylan was making such a big deal about it, so I figured you had seen it at some point."

"Yes, I saw it."

Carly looked over at Ada, who had the dog on its back, leg pedaling from a belly scratch. "You know what the weird thing about movies and books is? You get all into it and it seems real, even though everything that happens is crazy different than regular life—but then it just ends. They never explain how anybody just does their usual stuff again after the aliens leave or the monster gets killed, or . . ." Carly stared past Marcelline's shoulder. "Or the bad guy gets stopped. They never show how it goes back to normal."

"I guess that's not the part everyone finds interesting."

"Unless you're one of those people in real life. *I'd* think it was interesting." Carly looked at Marcelline's scar with open curiosity.

"You'll get back to normal," Marcelline said.

"Did you?"

The question crackled in the air. Carly couldn't possibly know what she was asking, but Marcelline had the uncanny feeling that, on some level, somehow she did.

Carly didn't yet understand how far from normal that video had taken her, or that it had brought the two of them together on this sidewalk outside the library. Her stepfather's shadow covered both the video that had turned Carly's life upside down and the scar that had spurred her to ask that incredibly intimate question.

Carly didn't know that the turn back to everyone's normal was still well ahead of them.

But what Marcelline knew about Carly's circumstances and near future made sense. What Carly understood about Marcelline's was pure dialed-in attention.

"Normal? I don't know," she said, and thought of years' worth of nights spent sketching and drinking and clicking through the internet. Carly had been just as unreal to her, just as out of reach on the screen as her own family was. But Carly was here now, right in front of her. Carly was real. So was she. The sun warmed the space between her shoulder blades. "It's there if I want it enough."

Carly opened her mouth to ask more. She was about to go full geyser with questions, but Marcelline shook her head. "Not now." They left it at a shared smile.

"Carly! Let's go!" Ada called.

In the car, Marcelline typed fast into her phone, hitting send before she could talk herself out of it. *S, I'm going to get it. This is going to work.*

The car was too hot. Marcelline started the engine. Her phone finally lit up.

I don't know what to wish for you. Maybe just that there was another way. But no matter what, just get back to one of your lives alive, please. And call me when you can.

A tear splashed the glass of Marcelline's phone. She wiped it against the leg of her jeans. She put the car into drive and pulled out of the library parking lot.

She'd wanted a swim, to cool down to the temperature of the water and let it block her ears and turn everything a shimmering blue for a while. She wanted to exhaust herself with laps so there would be no fighting sleep afterward.

She checked the clock.

It wasn't too late in the day to do something. Confront him. Or don't. Blow up Carly's life. Or don't. She'd already made the vow to get on with it to Samantha. But S would only cheer if she broke it.

Tomorrow. She would swim, sleep, then do something tomorrow.

Her YMCA membership was good for a dozen guest passes to the facilities here. She'd walked over from her hotel on her first night in town and had been back every night since. The gym was nothing special, but the pool was brand-new and glorious.

Memory is a weird thing. Marcelline had been preoccupied with the nagging uncertainty that the picture of Jonathan in her mind wasn't accurate. The placeholder for his face in her plans was fuzzy and generic.

The mechanisms of recall are mysterious, even to science.

In the parking lot of the Y, a skinny man with his hair rucked up at the back of his head, as if he'd slept on it wet, was crouching in front of a red sedan. It was a strange thing to do. He reached out, set something on the curb, then straightened up quickly. He swept the parking lot with an exaggerated swivel of his head and shoulders. Everything about him was begging not to be seen.

Marcelline froze behind the wheel to keep from drawing his notice. Then froze again from the inside out.

Some things were completely clear in her memory from that night. If she cast back for it, she could still feel the sickening hot tickle of blood sliding backward over her scalp, not like liquid but like a feverish finger tracing the base of her skull, a thin snake parting her hair like grass. She'd felt herself weakening. As if she'd been pinned to the earth. Heavy. Then heavier. Then pulled motionless against the ground, metal to magnet.

The one thing she remembered without a doubt was amazement—Jonathan, kneeling beside her, then looking over his shoulder, calling back to the shooter in an angry whisper:

For fuck's sake, Roy! Get the hell out of here!

For all the worry that she would not recognize the man she'd seen in broad daylight, the man whom she'd vaulted her good reputation for, whom she'd slept with and stood next to at the most ill-advised betrayal of her common sense in her entire life, it was with all the wrenching brilliance of being struck by lightning that she instantly recognized the man who shot her.

CHAPTER FIFTEEN

Roy wanted a bottle of iced tea. But if he bought a scratch-off lottery ticket instead, and if it paid out even $5, he could get the tea and put a gallon of gas in the Explorer. He stood at the door to the refrigerator case, not letting his focus fall on any particular flavor in case it would tip the craving over into a decision before he was ready.

His pay had been docked for leaving equipment out. The stuff hadn't been stolen, but it was a lesson. That's what they'd said, a lesson because they'd told him before to make sure everything got put away. So the $40 John had given him instead of a beating hadn't lasted. He hated to bother him again, and especially so soon. But John had missed the six o'clock check-in.

If Roy got the lottery ticket and it didn't pay, he still had an empty tea bottle in the truck that he could fill with water from the tap in the bathroom. It wouldn't be as good as tea, but it would be okay. And he probably had enough gas for tomorrow. Maybe.

He left the wall of cold drinks and walked over to the colorful spools of scratch games to see if it felt lucky. The woolly-bearded cashier scowled and tracked him across the room.

The bell on the push bar of the door clanged as someone came in, and in a storewide reaction to the jangle, the new customer took all the eyes off Roy. The cashier looked over to the door. The sneering pockmarked guy with the knit cap who was keeping the cashier company looked over, too. The only other shopper, a guy in workman's coveralls, with a can of WD-40 in his hand, glanced up from the row of air fresheners shaped like Christmas trees. The waitress who was always there, running the half dozen diner tables, turned to see who had come in and what it might mean for her.

Roy didn't look. He just enjoyed a moment of everyone's attention being elsewhere.

He was in here all the time and had never shoplifted so much as a candy bar, but they always watched him as if they were sure that their staring at him was the only reason he hadn't. When he had money, he filled his gas tank here, and he sank quarters into the laundromat attached to the store, and he ate in the diner whenever he could. They made really good tuna salad. He always told the waitress so. Sometimes he bought scratch tickets, and whenever he won anything, he went straight to their aisles and spent that money here, too. But it didn't get him anywhere with the staff.

He turned his back to the room and studied the tickets. He was going to get one, he'd decided.

Someone came up and stood beside him. Roy stepped to the left to let them see the rack of lottery choices. In his peripheral vision, he could see it was a woman, almost as tall as him. He edged a little farther away to give her more space.

But she turned to face him and leaned in. "If I screamed that you tried to kill me, do you think you could make it to the door before they tackled you?"

That she'd spoken to him at all startled him out of truly taking in what she'd said. For the most part. Some of the words had gotten straight through. *Scream. Kill. Tackle.* And *you.* A yammering terror collapsed his throat, and his heart was floundering in arcs as if it had gotten loose in his chest.

"What?" He looked at her and felt the breath and bones go out of him before he'd consciously connected this woman with a solid memory. It was bad. There was only one thing that bad. *Oh, God.*

Her voice was low and shaking. Her whole body was shaking.

"I said, do you think you can get past them? How many hero types are between you and the door if I scream?"

He'd seen her only one time, or really two times in one night. He'd watched her from where Jonathan had told him to wait, hidden from view of the open lot where he was supposed to go once everyone got there. She had strode up the sidewalk right past him, hands shoved into the pockets of her long, flowing coat, her boot heels striking the concrete like a metronome, even and solid. She was glowing. Drawn straight and tight as a bowstring.

She was the kind of person you couldn't help but look at. Everything going crazy didn't change that. She'd whirled to the clamor that Roy started, those first shots a mistake, a complete surprise to everyone, including Roy. Her coat flared out around her in the turn; the streetlight ran a halo over her shiny cap of hair; her surprised expression lit up and fell into shadow as she moved.

The aim follows the eyes. He hadn't meant to do it.

Her hair was long now. She was wearing regular clothes. Her face was rounder, but her jaw tapered away at the right side, uneven. The edge of a thick, pitted scar twisted up her neck and disappeared into the curtain of her hair.

Roy's eyes burned. She'd spoken quietly, but he had only enough air in him for a whisper. "I'm so sorry. So sorry."

Her face trembled with rage. "Don't you fucking dare. If you say *sorry* again to me, I *will* scream and say anything it takes to make them beat you to death right here."

The cashier called out to them. "Everything okay, ma'am?"

She stared into Roy, fighting to keep her shoulders from heaving with her shuddering breaths, quaking. John had told Roy that he'd killed her. This should be better. It was better. And it was breaking him. He thought his throat would tear from the cry trying to come up over top of the breath that was trying to go down.

"I'll do whatever," he whispered.

The woman glanced back at the cashier. "Yes. It's fine." She turned back to Roy. He couldn't stand her looking at him. He wanted to die. "We know each other," she called over her shoulder.

The woman scanned the layout of the little store. "We'll go sit down."

Roy waited to follow her over, but she didn't move from facing him. With a furious double tick of her head toward the diner, he felt stupid. Of course she'd never turn her back on him.

That was new and awful. No one trusted him to get things right. In this place they didn't even trust him not to steal. But no one had ever been afraid of him before. He had to go first so she could keep watch on him. It felt strange to lead the way.

"Wait. Give me your keys."

Dozens of times a day, Roy patted his pocket for his keys with an irrational lurch of terror that somehow they wouldn't be where they were since the last time he'd panic-checked. The loaded truck was literally all he had. But he handed this woman his keys without hesitation.

The waitress came over, one eyebrow already high with skepticism. She looked between Roy and the woman, back and forth more times than could be mistaken for anything other than making a point. She wasn't buying it, whatever it was that was happening here, and she wanted them to know it from the outset.

"What can I get you . . . two?"

"I'll have an iced tea," said the woman.

"And for you?" The *you* was the anchor of the waitress's doubt, and she let the eyebrow inflect it for her.

Roy shook his head.

"Just get something," the woman said through gritted teeth.

"But . . . I was going to get a scratch ticket. I don't have enough."

The woman he'd shot closed her eyes and exhaled slowly through her nose. "Just bring two teas, please. Thank you."

The waitress stalked away with a semi-scowl and turned back to show it one more time in case Roy had missed it somehow every time he was in here. She disappeared into the back.

The woman across from him rolled her eyes to the ceiling and did the slow breath again.

The worst feeling in the world wasn't being hated. It was being tolerated. It burned in Roy's face.

"So are you related to him?" she asked.

"To who?"

She blinked at him.

Roy felt as if he were swimming in quicksand just to think. "Oh! John? Right. Of course, John. I'm sorry. No! I mean, I'm sorry that I said . . . don't scream. I didn't mean to say it."

She was just looking at him. Blank as a wiped chalkboard.

A hot tiredness slid over him. He let his head dip down and watched the dots in the pattern on the Formica tabletop blur together. "You said you would scream if I said I was sorry. And, no, I'm not related to him."

"Then why are you here? What all do you do for him?"

"I don't know your name." He didn't have a good answer for her question, and that he didn't know her name was bugging him. So many terrible things tied to this, and she was right here, not at all as John had said. A stranger, but more important than any random person should ever be to another. Back from the dead. After everything, it seemed wrong not to know her name.

"You wouldn't know my name, would you? It's not really necessary in your line of work, I guess."

"What do you mean?"

The waitress brought the drinks and banged them down onto the table with no comment. She pulled two straws from her apron pocket and slid them into the middle of the table slowly, deliberately, still signaling some sort of disapproval that Roy couldn't fathom.

The woman tore the paper from her straw. "Why would you need to know the name of the people you shoot?"

"No! I don't shoot people!" Roy felt like he was drowning. A thick, crawling desperation of not wanting to be inside himself rose up, filling in every bit of breathing space like a flood of syrup. All his life, sometimes this happened, for a reason or for no reason, this blinding fear. Like he had to hold in a wet scream that was turning him inside out. But he always fled when he felt it coming on, so no one could see. But she had his keys.

She tilted her head and he didn't know if it was on purpose that she moved so that her hair slipped back over her shoulder, dragging the cover from her scar.

"I wouldn't. Never." His throat clicked closed and he coughed.

She leaned in. "You did. You do."

"No, it was Jonathan."

"Oh, he made you do it?"

"I mean, he told me to. He told me to be there. But not that. I screwed up. I can't . . . I shouldn't have a gun. I didn't mean to."

The woman hands gripped hard around her glass. Roy didn't trust himself to touch his, but he was so thirsty.

"But he paid you. He paid you to do it."

"No." Roy shook his head. "Not to do that. Just to be there. I was supposed to make a fuss so that everyone would leave. That's all." Roy risked a sip, no straw. His hands weren't going to be able to deal with unwrapping it. The sweet, cold drink was so good in the middle of something so bad. He blinked fast to clear the tears that were starting. So stupid. He cleared his throat. "He never did."

She'd gone silent. Each time Roy darted a look up from the table-top, she was just staring at him with her mouth closed, drawn down a little at the corners.

"He never did pay me, I mean. I didn't get anything for hurting you. Or those other people. I messed up. If I had done it right, maybe he would have paid me. But . . ."

Silence flowed over from across the table. He didn't look up again to see it. "It was never going to happen the way he said, though. I know that now. I knew it as soon as I got there and saw everyone. They had guns, too. I think he wanted . . ."

Roy was getting dizzy. The shallow breathing, and the booming pulse, and the dozens of thoughts slashing through his brain at the same time. He planted his hands on the bench seat to steady himself.

"What do you think he wanted?" she finally said.

"I think he meant for me to get hurt. I think that's what he wanted."

Roy had never before said it out loud. Who would have ever been there to say it to? Getting it out was a subtraction from his overstuffed skull, a small space cleared in his chest, a vent, a release. It was as if he could breathe. Just a little bit.

The woman shifted in her seat. "For Christ's sake. Don't cry. You're not the one who got shot."

His head snapped up. She flinched. Roy heard a glassy crack that wasn't real outside his own mind, he knew. With just a cold little pop, some small piece of handhold broke off, fell away. He wasn't good at locking a gaze, but so much was there. He couldn't not look. She was seeing him, hearing him. There was some overlap between them that he couldn't deserve to crave. She understood.

"My name is Marcelline."

He swallowed and tried to keep his mouth from twisting into something that could howl. "That's a very pretty name. I'm Roy."

"I know." She swiped at her eyes, then wiped the side of her hands on her lap and blew out another breath. Roy's heart twisted a spike of pain through his chest and up his neck. His jaw hurt. He looked at her jaw.

"I didn't mean to hurt you. I never would."

"I believe you."

"He told me you died."

"He probably thinks I did."

Roy snatched up his glass and lost himself in getting through a deep drink of it without dropping it, spilling it, or choking on it.

He dragged the back of his hand across his mouth. "Are you here to . . . Were you looking for him?"

"I don't know. Yes. Sort of. For four years I didn't know anything about what happened after Owen got me out of there that night. I don't even know Jonathan's full name. Then I saw the painting in the video. I had to come and—"

"John doesn't have it. Those people do."

"What people?"

"That big guy. The people that night. They stole it from him."

"Roy, what are you talking about? It's in his house. It's right there in the foyer."

"No, he doesn't have it."

"He does."

Roy didn't want to be contrary. His grandmother had called him so one time when he was a kid, on the afternoon his mother finally died. It seemed like the worst thing you could be in a bad situation, next to stupid.

But John had told him what happened that night after it was all over. John didn't have the painting, and it was all Roy's fault that he didn't. With his screwup, Roy had killed Marcelline and cost John not only the picture, but all the money he was going to get for it. And, of course, the money he'd planned on giving Roy, the payment for going along with the plan.

Not having the painting was the reason John hated him so much.

"No," Roy said, keeping it simple. He didn't mean to argue. He should stop shaking his head, he knew. But he couldn't help it.

"Roy, he took a quarter of a million dollars *and* the painting that night."

He wanted to say no again, but his tongue felt glued to the bottom of his mouth. The back and forth of his head slowed like the last notes of a windup music box.

Marcelline couldn't seem to close her mouth. Amazement. Pity. "You've never been there? To his house? You haven't seen the video. You don't know. All this time. Oh my God."

They talked for almost two hours. They ate tuna salad sandwiches. The waitress glowered for a bit, but seemed to lose interest with Roy blending into the scene like everyone who had ever sat in this diner and ate a sandwich with someone. The two of them sat across from each other, having a conversation like normal people. It wasn't a normal conversation, he knew that. But still.

They sat and ate and she talked, then he talked. Like normal people. She nodded. He did, too. She showed him the video, but he had to take her word for it that it was the same painting. You could barely see it. But he believed her. She wouldn't lie. It was okay.

She laughed when he warned her off the coffee because he figured they swapped out for fresh grounds maybe once every two weeks, and he thought his heart would break from how happy he was that she wasn't dead. And that she wouldn't drink bad coffee because he'd warned her.

She went quiet after she'd paid the check, staring into the hot tea that she'd gotten instead.

"What are you going to do?" Roy said.

"I don't know exactly." She moved the little folder with the receipt and the tip in it so that it lined up just even with the edge of

the table. "If he knows I'm alive, it changes everything. You understand that, right?"

Roy said yes automatically, even though he wasn't sure he did.

Marcelline clasped her hands and slid her arms onto the table to
the elbows, leaning in so that he would tilt toward her, too.

"Roy, if he knows I'm alive, the person it changes everything for
is you."

"Oh."

"You're the only person who can say what happened that night,
the only one who can back up my story. And you were always the only
one who knows who he was before. You're the only one who can put
it all together. Before, it was just his word against yours. And . . ."

"I know. Who would believe me?"

She chewed her bottom lip. "It's not your fault. He made it this
way. He moved everything around the way he wanted it."

Roy nodded.

Marcelline patted the table with her fingertips and looked up at
him from under her study of the tabletop. "I have an idea."

Roy held his breath.

"You can get in and take the painting—"

"He'll kill me!"

"He won't. He won't know until it's all over. And then he won't
be able to do anything about it. Meet him tomorrow like you were
going to. Stay cool. Act normal. Ask him for twenty bucks and get out
of there. Then later, or the next day even, break a window, take the
painting. In and out. I'll pay you."

"It'll be on camera! Just like the video you showed me! He'll
know it was me."

"You'll be gone before he can do anything about it. Do you think
he'll say anything? He can't."

The panic was back in Roy, climbing his throat. But so was the
shining want of something that someone was offering. She was selling

him a way to not feel so awful. A way to not have to ever see John again. Roy wanted to do what she said. He wanted to make this end with her not hating him, with him not hating himself.

She kept going. "If I do it, if it's me on the video, he'll know I'm alive. Then you're a danger to him, for real. You have nothing. Do you think he'll ever let you have anything? You have no way of getting out of here, Roy. Where I am, I can't even help you. But if you get the painting, he'll never be able to say anything about it. What could he do? You'll be gone.

"I can get rid of the painting. I know how. I don't know if I can get my life back. I don't know if you can get your life back either. But maybe we can have something else. Something good. And we can take it away from him."

There it was. He could make the worst thing he ever did right. Or righter. Something good.

He said yes. He'd never owned much of a no.

She told him where John's house was. She showed him the video again so that he'd know just where to find the painting. It was right inside the door. Five steps, max.

Marcelline bought him a tank of gas and gave him $20 that made him sick to take. She said she'd be at the same pump at six o'clock at night and eight o'clock in the morning for the next three days, just like John's times so it would be easy to remember.

"You can do this," she said.

Roy nodded. "I'm sorry."

"I know." She smiled, a small sad twitch at the corners of her mouth that had nothing to do with her being happy, but everything to do with trying to help him not be too sad. Or too scared. He wanted to die.

John didn't show up the next morning at the eight o'clock time either. Roy waited until ten. It felt weird. He counted to sixty to cancel out the sick flutter in his middle and to see if he could make his counting match up to a real minute. One twenty. Two minutes. Six hundred. Ten. John had never missed both times of a meetup before. Marcelline was relying on Roy, but he didn't know what it meant that John hadn't come after Roy left the quarter on the curb.

Roy avoided the service station and Marcelline, burning up gas just to drive miles out of the way around it. He went back to the McDonald's at six. Just in case. No John. He didn't know what to think. Maybe John hadn't seen the coin. Maybe someone had picked it up. Maybe something had happened to him?

Would that change anything? He owed Marcelline this.

Roy had plenty of gas in the Explorer for a change, but he'd only had a bag of pork rinds and a bottle of tea since the sandwich with her at the diner. His stomach squeezed down into a grumbling knot and stayed that way, twisting and stabbing every now and again to remind him that it was still empty.

The twilight thickened into nightfall, and Roy drove old back roads to a spot he'd found where the crumbling asphalt bled into a sloping grassy verge so close to the riverbank that it flooded when it rained. But it hadn't rained in a while, so the run down to the water was nothing but bare, bent grass. Roy pulled the truck off the lane and rolled down the windows. The frogs were louder than the old engine's idling.

John didn't hate him because of the painting. John hated him to keep him easy, to make him do what John wanted him to do. Marcelline had understood this. So she forgave Roy for shooting her. Did she know that her forgiveness also kept him easy? That it made him do what she wanted him to do?

He was so tired, but he hated sleeping. He couldn't remember a time when thinking everything would be okay hadn't turned out to be a trick of the light. Peace was a feeling that seeped away as soon as it ever settled in him, something that blended into the air with every breath he let go of. And just as meaningless.

The thought of breaking a window in John's house held surprisingly little glee for Roy. Just another ugly thing in an ugly life. He tried to picture delivering the painting to Marcelline, her triumph, her hugging him in happiness and even gratitude. It would pay. He could maybe . . .

Hope hurt in his already-groaning stomach. He wasn't the only way for her to get the painting. She could do it herself. He was so tired.

He put the truck into neutral and let off the parking brake. His right foot held the whole thing in place. He pumped the brake, rocking the big truck on its exhausted springs. The tree frogs chirruped, call and response. The truck was so full that it would sink like a boulder.

Roy knew that he would be able to stay still as the water rushed into his lap, into the crook of his arms as he held the steering wheel, all the way up to his unscarred jaw.

But he didn't know what he'd do when it closed over his head. Would he sit still and just let it happen?

He slid his foot off the brake. The truck lurched down the bank a full roll of the tires, slipping backward toward the water, then a little faster into the next rotation.

Roy jammed his foot back down and stomped the parking brake into place. The truck snapped to an obedient stop, just waiting for its command. Give it gas and go forward, back onto the road and into tomorrow, to do what she'd asked of him. Or give up the brakes, pull up your fool foot and let it go, relent into the slide, and surrender backward. Either way was fine with the truck. It didn't mind.

He grabbed up the lace pillow that still smelled of flowery perfume only at the edges. He covered his face with it and screamed.

CHAPTER SIXTEEN

"**M**om, where's the picture that was hanging in the front hallway?" Carly asked.

Her mother looked up from her computer, distracted, mentally replaying the question that she hadn't clearly heard when Carly asked it. "Um, John took it down when he nailed up that new thing, but I don't know where he put it. I think he got rid of it with the rest of the stuff. Why? Did you want to hang it up somewhere? Is there a blank space we need to fix?"

"No. I was just going to take a picture of it to send to Emma. We were talking about it. She showed me a painting in one of the art books, and it looked so much like the one we have. Had. I thought she would think it was neat."

Her mother smiled and went back to typing. "I should come over one of these days with you and Ada. It's been so crazy around here, but I do want to meet her in person. I look like Mother of the Year leaving it at just the one hello text. Plus, it would be fun to see how you guys work, to see how she teaches you."

"You'd like her. She's awesome. Ada still won't draw anything, but you can't tell her she's not an art expert now."

"That's fun. Ada can be an art expert if she likes. Just look at me. I'm great at eating, a total foodie, but barely any kind of cook at all. Are you guys meeting up with her this afternoon?"

Carly stifled a sigh. She knew they couldn't meet up *every* day. "She said she can't today. She's busy. Maybe tomorrow, though."

Her mother looked up again. It took nothing these days to see her expression fall into a version of that same look she'd had on her face when she came running into Mrs. Carmichael's house. After the *thing*. Her mother was still worried, and every time she got that look, it rattled Carly into a reminder of all there was to worry about in the world.

"Ah. Okay. I'm sorry about today. I know it's disappointing. This kind of sad feeling is the downside of great stuff. And I'm so glad you've found something new and positive. It's good timing for that, yeah?"

"Yeah."

"It helps me—a lot—to see you happy, to see you getting out there, doing what you do. That's the way it should be. I like you bouncing around."

Carly stuck her tongue out and bounced on her toes, rolling her eyes.

Her mother smirked and shook her head. Carly hoped she had a smirk like that.

"And Emma sounds very nice. It's great that you have an outlet for your drawing, and some artistic advice, too. I'm not a lot of help to you in that. You're so talented, honey."

"Mo-oom."

"What I'm saying is that I'm trusting this. It seems like a very good thing. You know I'm okay with you going to the library—with Ada, always with Ada—but you don't go anywhere else until you've told me. We *all* need to get over this, but I need to know where you are. Right? If Emma, or anyone, wants you to do something else or meet up somewhere else—any changes like that go through me first. I need that. Okay? Or call John if you can't get me on the phone."

Carly felt a spark of indignation at the suggestion that she wouldn't know when to call in, but she reined it back. No one was over the *thing* yet. Her mom still got that look on her face all the time. John was jumpy, either too quiet or too chatty, making sure everyone was okay all the time. Ada mostly wouldn't let Carly walk half a block by herself, then watched her on a tracking app they shared with Carly's mom when it couldn't be helped. It wasn't a bad thing. If they weren't over it, it meant she didn't have to be either. She didn't have to be alone with it yet.

"I know," Carly said. "I promise." For extra points, and because it felt good to be good, she walked over to the table and hugged her mother.

Her mother tried to be cool and poke at the corners of her eyes as if they itched. "All right. Good. Glad we're in agreement, because it's nonnegotiable, anyway." That smirk. Her phone rang. "And double-check with John about the picture," she said quickly before answering the call.

"Okay."

John was in his office, leaning against the window frame, typing into his phone.

"Hi," she said.

John slid the phone into his pocket. "Hi!"

"Did you get a new phone?"

"What? Uh, yeah."

"Oh! Cool! Can I see it?"

"Not right now, Carlzee. I'm kinda slammed. What do you need?"

Over the last few days, every foot closer she got to John was like walking under power lines. It seemed as if she could feel him through the walls, a teeth-buzzing hum overhead when he was upstairs.

This was the worst yet, though. He was trying so hard to look normal—a mighty thick layer of trying, too. A John mask, or a full face of TV makeup that wasn't quite the right color and too smooth by a lot.

Carly shoved her hands into her back pockets to keep them from being awkward. It always took at least two to play the normal game. She'd gotten good at the face part lately, since all the people with their questions and comments and open stares. But her hands definitely didn't know the rules. "Everything okay?"

"Yep." John took his keys from the corner of the desk. "Just have to run out for a bit."

"Where are you going?" she blurted out, then wondered about the question as it flew. Why would she care where John was going? She didn't. She just wanted to tug on the mask. It was bugging her. There was a whole other *why* for that one, but she would watch first and pick it apart later.

John ticked his head to the side, a little flinch of the eyes and mouth in puzzlement that he erased as soon as it had arranged itself on his face. "I just have a few things to do. What do you need?"

"Nothing."

"Well, you came in for some reason." His voice had an exasperated edge that she hadn't earned.

He was right, of course. She had come in for a reason, but a better one flared up behind her eyes. *Not. Normal. Your. Move.* She pulled her hands from her pockets and jammed them down onto her hips. She conjured up a look made of a slack sneer and half-mast eyes, and gaped at him like he was the stupidest person ever to take a breath. "Um, because it's a *room*. In my *house*. And I *live* here, if that's okay with you? God! What is your problem?"

Her heart pounded. Her cheeks burned. Normal John would call out not-normal Carly. She would never speak to him like that. She would never speak to anyone like that. Normal John would ask her what was wrong. Or maybe get mad. It would be worth it.

"Okay! Jeez!" He put up his hands, keys still clutched in the right one, in mild surrender. But he looked relieved, as if he'd gotten an easy out. "Excuse me for living. See you later, Grouchy." He walked past her and called his goodbye down the hall to her mother.

She was still on her call and waved to him around the corner of the wall.

Carly hovered in the doorway to the dining room, which they never dined in. It should be the homework room. Or the wrapping-presents room. Or one-of-the-places-Mom-takes-her-laptop-and-talks-on-the-phone room. Just not the dining room. The call went on and on and Carly paced the foyer in meandering loops down to John's office.

She listened for sounds that the conversation was winding down, but it was rolling like waves—a listening silence, her mother's turn to talk, listening silence again. Carly lapped John's office, looking at the books on the shelves and the labels on the row of craft-beer bottles he kept for . . . She didn't know why he kept them. She circled as if she didn't have a plan to open the desk drawers, which she totally did.

Notepads, a couple of flash drives and chargers. Pens, paper clips. *Her* stapler that she'd been looking for. There was money in one little drawer in the hutch, and Carly tamped down that unnameable little zing of what-if that leaped up at the sight of a stack of unsupervised cash. *Did everyone feel that automatically?* She would never steal. That was way low.

She heard her mother laugh from the dining room, and the longer Carly went unable to ask her mother what was wrong with John, the less she wanted to. If there was something wrong and her mother knew it, what were the chances her mother would say anything but *Nothing, everything's fine*? And if her mother *didn't* know that something was wrong with John, the answer would still be the same and it would just give her mother a new, different kind of worried look on her face that would also be Carly's fault.

The doorbell rang her right out of wondering if this was the wrong way to think of these things.

The pattern in the glass made a mosaic mountain of the man on the other side of the front door. Like one of the shattered-looking Picassos in the art books. All Carly could see was that he was tall, wearing a suit, and not standing like a cop.

When the police had come back to the house for follow-ups, they would always position themselves turned slightly out, maybe to keep a wider view of what was around them, or maybe just not to look so *there* and so like a solid wall of bad news. They put you at ease with at least a partial view of the way out. This man took up the whole door.

"Carly, who's that?" her mother called, leaning out from the dining room with her phone still to her ear.

Her mother was right there, watching. So Carly opened the door to find out.

The man was totally comfortable standing full on at her, shoulders straight parallel with the threshold and his empty hands loose at his sides. They weren't folded in front of him or tucked in his pockets or linked somewhere behind his back. That was just weird. Carly realized that nobody stood at a stranger's door like that.

He stepped back, a maneuver to tune down whatever he was reading off her. But she'd seen that trick before. It didn't mean anything. It certainly didn't mean she was safe. She kept her hand flat against the back of the door to shove if she needed to. She'd be much faster this time.

But the man smiled. "Hi. I'm looking for Jonathan."

"John's not here right now. My mother's here, though. Do you want to talk to her?"

"You must be Carly."

There was no answer for it that wasn't smart-alecky, and she wasn't feeling it at the moment. She nodded.

"He's talked about you. Nice things."

That feeling of *NO!* launched from where it lived now, somewhere right under the hollow of her throat. John hadn't said any such thing. This guy didn't even try to make it ring true. He wasn't very good at making people comfortable, but he didn't care. That was obvious. One step back, one little lie, and she'd bet everything she had that he had already run out of concern with how comfortable she was.

Carly's mom came into the hallway behind her. The man lit up just a little, but well in control of his response to her mother's face and everything else she had. Most men didn't catch their reaction so fast. Carly felt her eyebrows go up in spite of herself, impressed. But the man noticed Carly's assessment of him and she looked quickly to the floor.

"Can I help you?" her mother said, sliding a warm hand onto Carly's shoulder.

"I was just looking for Jonathan. We were supposed to meet up, and Carly here says I've missed him."

Carly's mother pulled the door a little wider to stand fully next to her and take up most of the rest of the doorway. "I'm sorry, have we met?"

Carly fought her eyebrows this time. No one didn't remember meeting this guy. The man flicked his eyes to Carly's face again, ready to catch her taking the measure of that one, a small spark of humor in his eyes like a dare to be in on it with him. He knew what she was thinking, teased her about it in a glance as if it were okay for him to do that, but it went cold in her.

He put out his hand. "I'm Owen. Jonathan and I worked together a while back."

Why does he keep calling him Jonathan? It's just John.

Her mother and Owen shook hands, and a rush of warning swept over Carly. Her mother handled this fine. She was cool and calm in her personal space, in her words and gestures, but that's not all there was. That's never all there was. Carly felt small and not strong and too aware of where they were standing, knowing that luck was a thing that sometimes happened and sometimes didn't. A crawly wave slipped through her middle and up under her shoulder blades. It didn't match at all the polite smiles and the blue sky and the little bit of familiar street that she could see around Mount Owen.

"I'm Donna. And, yeah, I hate to say it, but you did just miss him. He left maybe ten minutes ago."

"Hmmmm, weird." He nodded, smiling, and it didn't go with the puzzled noise he'd made. Owen shifted a half step to his left, just a widening of his stance more than anything, but it put him more directly in line with the gap of what she and her mother couldn't fill of the doorway. Carly tracked his eyes across the foyer wall and up to the motion sensor that was also the camera. He swept a fast look across the hall and back, catching again on the camera and then again on the metal curlicues that John had bought for the redecorating project.

He'd seen the video, and without a good reason, it pissed Carly off. "He's really not here."

Owen swiveled his big head on his bull neck down to meet Carly's looking up at him. She let her eyebrows off the chain just a little, a small, real flash of what she'd played insincerely on John. It was right there for her to use, warm in her cheeks, primed and ready. "I mean, if *that's* what you're actually looking for."

Her mother laughed a little, unsure. "Carly! But, nope, he's not here. Sorry. Do you want me to get him on the phone or . . . ?"

"It's fine. I'll just call him later. No problem. I'll catch up with him, I'm sure." He turned for his car. "Sorry to bother everyone, but nice to meet you."

"No problem," her mother called back. "And nice car."

"Thanks. It is," he said from the driver's door. "And the mechanic's bills never let me forget how nice."

They laughed to each other, everyone ending on even ground. Because that's what you do when you're grown up and in charge of the everyday world and everyone pretends that everyone else is the same amount of strong, but only when no one wants or needs anything at the moment. Carly, in her own contribution to the dance, slammed the door over the end of it.

"You okay?" Her mother reached for her.

"Uh-huh." Carly slipped past her, getting out of reach with just a glancing arm rub.

Owen and his fancy car hadn't been gone five minutes before John came screeching into the driveway.

Carly and her mother converged in the foyer at the sound of too-fast tires on smooth concrete. The door swung wide. John was sweating. It was warm outside, but not that hot.

"Hi!" said her mother with the questions already right there in the greeting, stacking up at the slightly electrocuted look of him. "You okay?"

Carly was beginning to think that was the question of the day. Maybe of the week.

John glanced around and pulled himself together like a costume change in front of their eyes. "Yeah. You okay?"

"Yeah," her mother said. "But you just missed your friend Owen. He was here looking for you."

"I know. I saw him on the system." John wheeled his finger around in a vague circle of everything. "You know, from the text alert. So I came back. Uh, you know, try to get here before he left."

Her mother nodded. The security system was still a sore subject, but after the *thing*, she'd wanted it left on. For now. "Why didn't you just call him?"

"I did." John dropped his shoulders and the tension slid from the rest of his posture in a ripple that went all the way down his arms, his legs, out his shoes, into the floor. Carly felt herself relax with it, like yawning because someone else had done it. She stopped when she realized it and wound the springs back tight in her. Still not normal.

"I just got ahold of him. We're going to maybe get in a game of racquetball. So I need my stuff."

Carly's mother stifled a giggle. "You're going to play racquetball with that guy?"

John smiled back. His smirk was more artful than her mother's, less nice, but it was the cutest face he had. "Why is that funny? Because he's bigger than me? Nah. Big doesn't help you in racquetball. It can be a disadvantage, really. Big and slow. I'm fast." He swung at an invisible serve, all smiles now, loose in the joints, putting on a show. "And you should know—I've never been beaten at racquetball on my home court."

Say racquetball *again and I am totally going to lose it,* thought Carly. *Nope. Not. Normal.* "Hey, can I get a ride to the library?"

Her mother turned to Carly. "I thought you said Emma couldn't today."

"No, it's just me and Ada this time."

"I really gotta fly, Carly. I'm late already," said John. "Sorry."

"But it's on the way," said Carly.

"Can you just please walk?"

"Yeah, no problem," Carly said with sunshine in her voice and no trace of her earlier sass, wanting him to comment on her reversal of attitude. He could applaud it or give her some crap about it, just something. Just notice it. Because he did. She knew he did.

"Thanks, kiddo." John went to get his gym bag.

"I just need to get something out of the car," Carly told her mother.

She texted Ada on her way to the door: *I'm coming to your house in ten minutes.*

In the driveway, Carly opened the door to John's car, silenced her phone, and slipped it into the seatback pocket.

Back in the house, John wasn't in his office as Carly walked by. She crept inside one step, trying to hear where everyone was over the sound of her own breathing, loud in her head. She listened through two more careful steps. She would never take money, but she would also never mouth off to John or to a stranger bigger than their refrigerator. Except that she had. *Just if I need it. Why would you need it? I don't know!* And that train of thought got her all the way across the room and to the desk.

She opened the little drawer, peeled four bills off the top of the stack, and was back in the foyer, shaking all over, before she talked herself out of it.

She heard John rounding into the hall from the far end, but he was all in silhouette as he turned into view—the light from the front door and window panels couldn't get to him. The glow was bright at the glass, green in the open foyer, fading to gray down the funnel to the focal point. John, looking back to her, would be just as blind to her details as she was to his. Very artsy. Emma would approve of Carly's eye. *Not-Normal Man with Gym Bag.*

She grabbed a sketch pad and one of the art boxes at random off the bench.

"Bye, Mom!" And she was out the door before she would have to look John in the face where they both could see.

"But you texted me from your phone," said Ada.

"I know. John was going to give me a ride, but then he was a jerk and he didn't, and I didn't get all my stuff out of the car. I forgot it in the seat pocket. Let's just double-check that he's at the Y and we can go get it."

"I don't want to walk to the Y."

"It's five minutes from the library."

"I don't want to go to the library either. Besides, it's more like ten."

"Fine! I'll go get it and meet you there, then."

"You're obsessed. And a freak. We don't have to do art every day. Can't we just stay here and play my ukulele and make cookies and chill?"

The disappointment that Carly was not in the mood for any of it showed on Ada's face. Carly sighed. Ada sighed back and pulled her phone from her pocket. "Fine!" She tapped the tracking app to life. "He's not even at the Y."

The *I knew it* dropped straight through Carly like a hot stone. She came around to look at the screen with Ada, who zoomed in on the map, to the little blue flag with Carly's face on top.

"It looks like he went to Town Center Plaza."

It wasn't the library as Carly had told her mother, but she would still be with Ada. It was good enough. There wouldn't be any harm in going. He probably wouldn't even see them. Definitely if they were careful. It wasn't wrong to go. *What do you need? You came in for some reason?*

"Want to go to Town Center?" Carly asked.

Ada started an eyeroll for an answer. It was a long walk.

Carly slid her hand into her pockets to keep them from being awkward. It turned out that sometimes it only took one to play the normal game. She felt the folded money rake the side of her finger. "I'll buy us Starbucks and new comics."

CHAPTER SEVENTEEN

Owen slid into the padded booth he'd been escorted to by the black-clad hostess. The table was a glossy expanse of dark wood that would have adequately seated six. The glass-globed candle burning at the far end was still a stretch away, even for a man with a seven-foot wingspan. The setup would be elbow-room overload for a party of four, an embarrassment of riches in dining real estate for two. But it was the only kind of table they had here, a subliminal suggestion at the outset that you'd already been pampered before they'd served you a single thing.

The whole place was a bit dim and romantic for an appointment like this. A Waffle House would have served Jonathan better. Safer. Owen would have stood out more. But he figured that Jonathan hadn't thought it all the way through. Jonathan wanted to impress him. With what? His good taste in slick suburban quick-eats?

Another restaurant ninja materialized at his side. "Hello. I'm Courtney and I'll be taking care of you this afternoon. Can I start you off with one of our craft cocktails or a glass of wine from our Reserve Select collection?"

"Black coffee is fine, thank you. I'm meeting someone."

"Of course."

She disappeared without so much as a rustle. The place had the acoustics of a sponge.

Owen took out his phone and sent a text to Jonathan: *I'm here. You're late.* He set the phone faceup on the table and waited. He wouldn't have made it to ten if he'd bothered to count. The silenced phone lit up and shimmied in a fit of vibration. He ignored it.

Courtney reappeared with a glass of ice water. She stopped midway to setting it down as the phone burred like a drill on the table. "Do you need to get that?"

"No." The call went dead, then almost immediately rang its angry droning again against the wooden continent between them. He looked at the hovering glass of water and back into Courtney's questioning eyes.

Across her face he read the confusion of a young person who couldn't comprehend *not* responding to an electronic summons.

"Is that for me?" he asked about the glass in her hand.

"Oh! Yes. Of course. Sorry." She put down a napkin and the water he didn't want.

Courtney was a psychic. She shrugged and nodded, apology already glowing in her cheeks. "I brought that just in case you were thirsty while you waited. They're brewing fresh coffee."

"That's fine. Thank you."

"Would you like to hear about today's special features and our boat-to-table catch of the day?"

Owen liked eye contact, and never more than when his focus met up with that of someone who didn't know what to do with it. It was one-stop shopping for a quick dose of entertainment. Drama, tragedy, horror, comedy. Poor Courtney.

"No. The coffee is all."

"Oh. Sure. Okay. No problem. That's fine." Courtney stammered through every expression of cooperation she could think of while Owen blinked over her efforts.

"Don't worry. I tip well."

"No! You don't have to. I mean, I wasn't expecting . . . It's no trouble. Coffee's easy. No big deal. Really. I'll just go check and see if it's ready."

"Thank you, Courtney."

She evaporated into the gloom.

The napkin went soggy as the water glass sweated down its sides. The door opened and Jonathan came in, red faced, searching the room for Owen with little birdlike jerks of his head. Owen raised his hand to flag his attention. Jonathan nodded, just an angry up-snap of his chin, and puffed himself smooth with a big, bracing breath. Owen watched him trace the maze through the giant booths. It was hard to do, navigating the murky feng shui and trying to look tough doing it. Owen almost felt sorry for him.

He didn't get up as Jonathan dropped into the seat across from him. "You son of a bitch—"

"Take it easy."

Jonathan leaned in to make more out of his furious whisper than it was ever going to be worth. "Don't you tell me to take it easy."

"No, seriously, take it easy," Owen said at normal volume, and looked up over Jonathan's shoulder. "Hi, Courtney. Thank you."

The waitress, with Owen's coffee saucer pinched in both nervous hands, swallowed hard and came on the last few steps to the table.

"Jonathan, this is Courtney."

The two looked at each other, helpless to go against the rules of introduction. Courtney, so far off script, seemed at a loss for words.

Owen helpfully broke her silence for her. "Can she bring you a craft cocktail? Perhaps the boat-to-table catch of the day?" Owen winked at the girl, whose bewilderment was taking on an edge of real worry.

"Nothing for me, thanks." Jonathan stabbed at Owen with a glare.

"No? Okay." Owen leaned back, pressing into the deep padding of the backrest to get his wallet from his pocket. He took out a $100 bill. "Tell you what, Courtney. You've been an angel. Go ahead and close out the check. No need to bring it to the table. Or any refills. And keep the change, of course. We'll just need a little time to talk."

Courtney took the money, mumbled a thank-you, and fled.

"Think she'll remember us?" asked Owen.

"What the fuck was that?"

"You seriously need to calm down."

"And you seriously need to stop saying things like that," Jonathan said, baring more capped and polished teeth than Owen was sure he was even aware of. Feisty.

People who defied Owen fascinated him. Everyone else made sense. This guy was all loose cork and short fuse. And better teeth than he'd had four years ago.

"Jonathan, let me give you a tip—when I stop saying things like that, you've run out of time to try to get it right." Owen took a sip of his coffee before it went too cool to enjoy. It was delicious. Just about perfect. Transporting, even.

Owen, for everything else he was, had decided a long time ago to be a man of simple pleasures. It soothed him, which made everyone safer. He thought a little kindlier of the silly place. "The waitress won't forget us anytime soon, and that's good news for you. I'm just trying to set you at ease."

"By doing that? And after pulling that bullshit—showing up at my house?"

Owen drank more coffee. A glance over the rim of the cup seemed to dry up Jonathan's next comment. Owen set the cup down, watching it the whole way, slow and precise, into the ring of the saucer. No clatter.

Owen let a nod stand in for any more warnings. "I know you want to grab this conversation by the scruff of the neck. You're just squirming to be in charge. And I might let you—if you can give me a good answer to just exactly what the fuck you're going to do if I get up and walk out right now? As far as I can tell, you'll be left holding a *very* expensive, yet functionally worthless bit of paint on wood and looking over your shoulder for as long as you have a shoulder attached to your . . . looker."

"There are other people who would buy it."

"And that would solve half your problem."

Jonathan readjusted his face and his ease in the seat. He wasn't bad at it. Erratic, but convincing a good bit of the time. He was obviously a practiced chameleon, taking on the look not of his surroundings but of his own desperate will.

"Fine," Jonathan said. "So you came here to threaten to leave? That's a lot of work for a hundred-dollar cup of coffee."

"Not much work at all, really."

Instead of surrendering and going more unsettled as he should have done, Jonathan kept moving the mood around like stage scenery. He breathed in a satisfied sigh, as if they were finally maneuvered to where he'd been steering all along. "Just to be clear, you didn't need to pull that stunt. It didn't do you any good. The painting isn't in my house anymore. It's not in my office either. It's safe. And it's hard to find. Carly and Donna don't know where it is either. So all that was for nothing. Sorry about that. You could have just asked me."

Owen let the little speech hang in the air with only his own wry smile for company. If a guy puts his dick on the table for measuring, there was always the option to go for his own zipper to do dueling inches, but he was more inclined to let a little time pass. It doesn't take long for most people to realize that pulling their dick out without a good reason is actually pretty embarrassing.

Owen matched Jonathan's posture. The seat really was nice. The restaurant was growing on him. He wondered if Courtney would cry if he beckoned her back for a reconsidered refill of just-about-perfect coffee. He turned his saucer clockwise in the crook of his thumb and forefinger and listened to the hollow rub of porcelain on varnish.

Jonathan looked comfortable with the standoff for longer than most people would have, but the cracks came. A twitch in the cheek. It looked as if his nose itched. Owen could tell Jonathan was feeling every second of it now, fighting the fidgets, timing his blinks. Not too rapid, but not spread out enough to let his eyes water.

"I think you misunderstand me," Owen said finally. "I didn't go there looking for the painting. If it were leaning against your knee right now, I wouldn't take it from you. I can promise you this: if I ever so much as set a finger on it, it'll be because the Anningers paid for it, and in an amount you agreed to. I don't care about the painting."

Now that made Jonathan uncomfortable. Owen only tried a little not to smile.

"Okay. Great," Jonathan said. "So can we get on with that, then? *Do* they still want to buy it?"

"Hang on. I didn't say there was nothing I wanted in this."

Jonathan sighed as if his patience were any sort of lever in this exchange. "Then maybe we can get to that. Something. Anything."

"How much was it they were going to pay before? Six?"

"Seven and a half."

"Seven and a half. Hmmm. And you and Marcelline were going to split it straight even?"

Jonathan held Owen's stare. He didn't like it, Owen could tell, but he was trying to read and stay unread at the same time. He'd lose at both by looking away now. "Yes," Jonathan said.

Owen stoked the staring contest. "The balance wasn't tilting a little toward her for the expertise and being able to find a buyer? Or heavier in your favor for having it in the first place?"

"What difference does it make? We talked it out—between us— and agreed on splitting it down the middle."

"And yet that didn't happen. Who are you going to split it with now? Donna and Carly? Or do you have a bag and your passport in the car?"

From the collar up, Jonathan's color deepened. It was too dark in the booth to tell if he was the bright-red or the brick-red type.

"What is that to you?"

"It's nothing to me. But it's nothing at all to either of us unless I decide I want to take your offer to the Anningers."

Jonathan leaned in. "What now? What are you . . .? They don't even know yet? Are you fucking with me?"

"Come on now, are we already back to *take it easy*? Why did you wait more than four years to get in touch?"

"What?"

"I'm just curious. I wasn't hard to find, was I? It would have been just as easy to make the call the day after we last met. Or three years ago. Or two. Or even last month. Why now? Did you just wake up the other day with a seven-and-a-half-million-dollar hard-on? Was that it? Or did something happen to make it seem a little urgent?" Owen smiled at Jonathan, all spoiler, and watched it sink in.

"Okay, so you've seen the video."

"Yeah. Hot potato. Not really all that fun outside of kindergarten."

"And that's how you figured out where I live."

Owen just nodded and drank most of the rest of his coffee. He never drained a cup or glass all the way or cleaned a plate to crumbs. He never left anything looking as if he might have wanted more.

"Mmmm-hmmm." Owen decided to sip the water, too. Might as well. "So, that night. What do you think happened? You think Marcelline's man turned on her? For what?"

"Huh? I don't know. And I don't know that he turned on her as much as he just lost his cool and shot wild. I mean, he was a basket case. An idiot all the way to the bone. That was obvious. Besides, I thought maybe it was you, that he was your guy, not hers. Although now that we're sitting here talking, I think probably not."

"No?"

"You don't seem the sort." Jonathan risked a smile as if they might be approaching common ground.

"You make quick decisions, don't you? That ever come back to bite you in the ass?"

"I do okay, thanks," Jonathan said. "You, on the other hand, seem to belabor the shit out of everything. Is there a point somewhere on its way anytime soon?"

Owen could practically see the chill of rising hackles trace up Jonathan's spine, pulling him straighter, more ready. "Are you in a hurry?"

"Oh, enough about me," Jonathan said, actually out of real patience now, not just the theatrical kind. "Let's talk about you. Look, I get it. What happened that night is stuck in your throat. Nobody likes getting caught out, to have things go that far off plan. Especially not a guy like you. You were in charge and it fell apart and you had to eat shit for it and you want to try to piece together what happened. You want to know whose neck to break because you lost your bosses' money and maybe some of their respect for not getting the job done. I get it, but I can't help you. You lost face. That sucks. I'm sorry for your trouble."

Owen surprised himself with the delighted sound of his own laughter. It was musical. Loud music at that. Courtney looked around, startled and still tense, from where she'd been inclined in conversation with the bartender.

"Do you have any idea how many double crosses I've yawned through? How many times I've had to go back and forth because another greedy little fuck gets cute or bold or somehow mistakes a rising burp for a bright idea?

"The Anningers have already bought my time. I get paid either way. I have to do something all day.

"What happened that night was a pain in my ass. But you're not special. And for them? Right now they're getting more mileage from the story of losing the painting and the money. It's almost as good to them as having it. Maybe better. Who can tell?

"Don't embarrass yourself. You scrabbling around like a squirrel with a golden nut doesn't make you a high roller. You've seen too many movies, Jonathan. You have no idea how these things work."

The shade of Jonathan now made Owen decide he was probably the brick-red type. Bright red would look shinier by candlelight. But either way, Jonathan surely didn't like being laughed at.

He was quaking.

Owen pressed on. "So you say you didn't know her well?"

Jonathan didn't lose momentum as much as he gave it up freely. He did it so abruptly that Owen felt himself wanting to tip forward into the void of pressure loss. The fury melted out of Jonathan and he relaxed back into the seat, making Owen's seat just a little less cozy than he'd been enjoying in these last minutes.

"No. I didn't know her very well." Jonathan fought, but not really, a knowing little smirk. "Did you?"

"Not really."

"She was fine as hell, though, wasn't she? It was a shame to see her cut down like that."

"Yes." Owen resisted the tingling in his face that begged for release in a lip curl or a squint.

Jonathan let a quiet beat go on longer than a natural pause. "A *real* shame, unless it was just that she got caught up in her own plan. That sort of thing is a big risk. And I don't think she seemed like someone who would have done a lot of that. Do you? She seemed too sweet, I think. And if that sweetness was all just an act, it was probably too easy for her to get her own way with everything else she had going for her. Ooof." Jonathan let out a slow breath that would have been an appreciative whistle if he'd pursed his lips more. "Maybe that's why it went wrong, I'm thinking. Some rookie mistake. When I remember Marcelline, I can't help but think of the whole *play with fire and you might get burned* thing. I think she made a dangerous choice screwing you over."

Jonathan had started running his finger back and forth along the edge of the table, but it wasn't nervous energy, Owen saw. Jonathan was stroking. It was metaphorical, whether Jonathan realized it or not. Something had changed and this guy had gone from deploying scattershot swagger for any kind of advantage in this negotiation, all the way to his being turned on in some fashion.

Owen eased his spine and shoulders to their full spread. "Why did you take the money that night?"

"Why wouldn't I take it? Somebody was trying to kill me and rob me. It was hazardous-duty pay."

"I don't recall that you were anywhere in the line of fire."

"You know what? I already addressed this. That money will be rolled into the sale price."

"If the Anningers still want to buy it."

Jonathan let the smirk go wide. He twisted away and stepped out of the booth. "You know what? This is bullshit. I guess we're done. Or I'm done at least. You're fucking with me. This is business. You don't care about getting the painting, great. And you didn't care about getting left holding the, well, whole lot of nothing at the original sale. Fine.

"And money, and stuff that people actually find worthwhile, and, I dunno, success in your work, and self-respect—it doesn't mean anything. You're just above it all."

Jonathan put one hand back onto the table and leaned in, not a full-badass lean-in. Tentative. Out of his league, but fired up. Almost that good. This guy was pinging like crazy, lit, all over the place and clearly not yet done, even though he was perilously close to having gone too far already.

"But you're not *really* above it all, are you? Not *all* of it. That's your car outside, right? The silver one? If you really didn't give a shit about anything, you wouldn't put sweet rims and orange calipers on your bank statement and drive it around for everyone to see and yank me every which way for the sad chance to talk about a woman who died before she could disappoint you."

Owen's spit turned acid in his throat. "Obviously, you've lost your mind."

"This is pointless." Jonathan stepped fully clear of the table.

"Sit. Down." Owen bit the words like meat.

He was relieved to find that he hadn't lost complete control of the conversation. Jonathan's knees buckled him back into the bench as if they were on a string that Owen had pulled.

He had to give Jonathan his moment of insight, even as Owen fought to keep from launching across the table and slamming the fancy teeth out of his mouth. Owen shifted his attention from the knots of his fists, clenched under the table, to the air flowing in and out of his nose. Controlled. Cooling.

Jonathan was an amateur, but not without talent. But instead of enjoying and using it to his advantage, the asshole let it get away from him. Instinct had struck a match and made him desperate to blow something up. Reckless. He would almost certainly burn himself down in the end.

Just look at him. Jonathan was still sputtering sparks when he'd gone and poured gasoline all over himself.

Jonathan dripped sarcasm, also flammable, into his words. "Oh, I thought there was a point to you waving around hundred-dollar bills and working up poor Candi over there just about to the point of tears. I thought I was safe. Or was that just conversation, Owen, something to keep me here to give you someone to talk to?"

"Courtney."

"What?"

"Her name is Courtney."

"Okay. Candi, Courtney. Whatever. So fucking what?"

Just as surely as Owen had given himself away moments before, the hole in Jonathan's soul was right there. They were both unused to being seen for their baselines. They'd traded turns getting knocked onto their back foot.

Both Owen and Jonathan had little use for people. But unlike Owen, Jonathan had to work at it. He fought influence—not by his nature, but by his insistence. He was a self-made man on his own island, but not abandoned there. Not stranded. No. He'd hacked it free of the mainland himself. But sometimes he felt bad about it. Clearly, it made Jonathan resentful to feel anything.

Owen's voice went mild. "So fucking what? The little people, Jonathan, they count. Take yours, for instance. Donna. Carly. I know their names. I wouldn't call them Dana and Carrie. I've met them. Talked with them. I've seen them in their own environment. It would be unwise of me not to have paid attention. It would also be dismissive. They don't deserve that. According to YouTube, they've been through a lot lately. And they don't even know what's at stake, do they?"

"Are you threatening my family?"

"Would that make it easier for you?"

"Would that make what easier for me?" The warning bell clanging in Jonathan's head showed, rising into the expression on his face.

"Hmmm." A sincere *hmmm* was always a tricky pitch for the batter. "I *wasn't* threatening them. I don't pick on little girls or their"— Owen raised his water glass in a mock toast—"or their superhot mothers. Are you worried that I was threatening them? Or were you hoping for it? You know, looking at you, I'm not sure you weren't doing just exactly that."

"Fuck you."

"That's fair."

Jonathan scratched his hands through his hair. "This is getting out of hand. I have the painting that your employers might want, even though you think it's stupid. I know the price needs to be renegotiated because of what happened. I get that. But the—I'll admit—impulsive down payment I took was with my head ringing from goddamned gunfire, I'd like to remind everyone. But all this"—Jonathan raked the air back and forth over the table between them—"this isn't necessary. There's no reason for it."

"You forgot to mention that Marcelline is dead in your little recap of history." Owen watched him closely. Jonathan had spoken of her only in the past tense. But would he flinch, a truth reflex, when Owen did?

Jonathan sniffed, a flicker of a sneer as he looked down at the tabletop. "You're right. I didn't mention it. I forgot. But bringing that up seems to be your part-time job, not mine. It's been four years. Maybe get another hobby."

There it was, that hostile pout. Jonathan didn't care that she was dead. But he hated that he was supposed to. According to his story, Marcelline got only what she'd deserved. And why would he think he was supposed to feel anything about that? Because he knew better. The double cross was his.

Marcelline had been telling the truth.

Owen was going to kill him.

The whole revelation, silent and white hot inside Owen, seemed lost on Jonathan. "I wonder why you don't bring up the other people who got hurt that night? You know, those people you actually came with? Your coworkers. Remember them? The little people, who mean so much to you? But the names stick better if they're pretty, yeah?"

"Touché. There's a lot about that night—"

For the second time, a person over Jonathan's shoulder stopped the conversation. Owen had just said her name no more than a minute before, but it didn't feel as if it were anywhere within reach for him to remember it now. His mind was emptied of everything by the look on her face. The rest of her was trembling in the struggle to keep the tears to a thin glistening line on her lower lids. Jonathan's stepdaughter. The girl in the video.

Jonathan followed Owen's gaze and looked behind him.

"Carly? What the . . . ? Are you . . . ? Why are you . . . ? What are you doing?"

The girl was defiant, her mouth tightened down over a barely quivering chin. "I left my phone in your car."

She said it plainly, a dare blazing up in her wet eyes for either of them to make it seem like not a good enough reason for her to be standing there in the self-consciously grown-up restaurant in her yellow high-tops and braids.

She was too old to be cute. But Owen was more or less immune to cute anyway. She was too young and furled for him to even wonder what she'd be later. She was in one of life's middle grounds, adrift on frustration in the sea of not-quite-old-enough-to-know. She had nothing to gain or lose, except to insist that she wasn't stupid.

"Is everything okay?" She spoke to Jonathan, but she looked sidelong at Owen, and he realized with a little sting what she had delivered expertly in that look was that she would cast her allegiance in the direction of whoever told her the truth. He'd bet his whole wallet on that.

"Honey, here." John scooped his keys out of his pocket. "Go on out to the car. I'll be right there."

"Go home, Jonathan," Owen said. "I'll get back in touch with you."

Jonathan searched Owen's expression for clues as to what all that could mean.

Owen rolled his eyes. "What?"

Owen looked at Carly. Carly looked at Jonathan. Carly looked back to Owen.

He wondered what she wondered about, how much she'd heard or intuited, then he wondered that he gave any thought at all to what a kid might be thinking. Sometimes people surprised him, and sometimes cheesy restaurants had the best coffee. Strange.

"Keep an eye on him for me, Carly, will you?"

Owen got up and saw in the margins of his vision everyone track his rise toward the ceiling—Carly, Jonathan, the people at the massive table across the aisle, Courtney, still by the bar, and the bartender, too.

Owen snapped his arms straight to settle his cuffs, buttoned his jacket, and walked out.

Once he was in behind the steering wheel, having pointedly avoided admiring the sleek flares that ran the length of the car's flank, or the sun splashing in the silver flecks in the paint, or the orange enamel winking at him from behind the spokes of the wheel rims, Owen sent Jonathan a text:

Didn't get around to it four years ago. Didn't get around to it today. There's possibly more money in any offer that might come down if there's useful information about how you came by the Flinck.

CHAPTER EIGHTEEN

John gathered a storm cloud of silence over his head the whole way to Ada's house. If Carly materializing over his shoulder in the restaurant had been a shock, finding out that Ada was in the comic book shop on the corner waiting for them was right up to the edge of what he could believe for this day.

He set a grim face and hoped it held a perimeter against any conversation. His time for questions, for looking before leaping, was all but gone. He needed to think and go—forward or underground.

John had never once been eager to talk to Roy. Well, not exactly. Sometimes hearing Roy's truck pull up, whining on its burned-out springs, or watching him walk over on his bowlegs with his shoulders all hunched and stiff, John would grow a not entirely unpleasant pressure in his jaw. Like the tight, rising tension in knuckles that need to pop. The anticipation wasn't awful. It was a sure thing. An itch that would get scratched.

But those little exorcisms of irritation aside, Jonathan had never, in any way, been bursting to talk to Roy. He often daydreamed about getting news that would signal the end of having to deal with him at all. Of Roy breaking his neck while crashing down the stairs. That'd be great. Totally something to look forward to. Or him getting struck by lightning. Or finding out that he'd finally caved in and let that mopey-ass face have what it—deep down—really wanted: a hose run from the tailpipe of his rolling junkyard right in through the window. Carbon monoxide, an hour, and a classic-rock mixtape to sing him over to the other side.

So, of course, for the first time ever that he actually wanted to talk to Roy, he couldn't. He'd blown off the meeting. Another quarter left on the curb at the Y had just come in at the wrong time, in the middle of everything. Something had to give and Jonathan had let it be Roy.

He wondered if the jackass was still showing up at the McDonald's every evening and every morning for the last couple of days like a pathetic tide.

John looked at the clock, then over at Carly in the passenger seat and back to Ada in the rearview mirror. He'd never make the six o'clock meetup. He'd have to try to find Roy in the morning.

It had been easy not to talk about the painting with Roy. They'd never really discussed it except for Jonathan telling him it was gone. And Roy certainly didn't want to talk about it after that night. Not ever. It was a boxed topic just trembling at the hinges to fly open and spill all over everything.

The memory of Roy's face from that night would come to Jonathan out of nowhere, sometimes when he was trying to sleep or eat or watch a show, or like now when he needed to think. The horror. Shame. Regret. Panic. The wheels coming off everyone's wagon.

It had been contagious, that awestruck, begging look. It infected Jonathan and made him briefly sure they'd never get away with it.

Now he had no choice but to risk the third rail of Roy's raw conscience. John needed to know if anything worth the Anningers' time and checkbook was in the box of stuff Roy had taken from his father's mess. Anything at all worth their forgiveness.

He could almost imagine forgiving Roy, too, as the door hit him on the way out, if he had anything in that truck or in his lukewarm brain that John could offer the Anningers. Selling the painting to them was only as useful as it balanced the account to their satisfaction. And to Owen's.

He hated dealing with Roy.

But Jonathan knew what to do with other people's upset, to this or that end. Out of everything he could use, nothing was finer for getting to what you needed to know—and for getting people to do what you needed them to do—than winding them up.

Carly was next. Then Roy.

She'd been quiet on the ride sitting next to the inevitable argument. But she was soft in her posture, with her arm unselfconsciously near Jonathan's elbow on the padded console. As unconcerned as Carly looked, there might as well have been the Macy's parade beside them for how hard poor Ada had been staring out the window. She was practically pressed against the glass, as close to being outside as she could get at fifty miles per hour, straining to the limit of her seat belt in an obvious wish to be riding in a sidecar, in the trunk, anywhere that was not with her friend who was in big trouble.

He pulled into her driveway.

"Thanks, Mr. Cooper!" Ada leapt out with the door already slamming home before the car had rocked back from stopping. "Bye, Carly! Message me!"

She bounded over the tidy bed of pansies to shortcut the walkway to her front door.

Jonathan dropped the car into reverse and drifted backward toward the street.

"Wait," Carly commanded.

He hit the brake hard, expecting Carly to point out a cat or a toddler in the way.

She didn't look at him. "You're supposed to wait until she gets inside."

Of course. That should have been automatic. It was fundamental to his role of fatherly not-father to act as if he cared about things he didn't. But he was curious that Carly somehow felt bold enough to deliver the stern poke of *you know better*. She needed to be in a more useful mood. All his obvious brooding hadn't been enough to get her there.

He needed more time. "We need a few things from the store. And you and I need to have a talk before we get home."

She nodded and took up a more Ada-like interest in the street rushing past them.

"Carly, what the hell were you doing showing up there?"

She whipped around in her seat. She'd been spring-loaded for him to say anything. "Me? What were *you* the hell doing there? It sure the hell wasn't racquetball!"

Carly should have been easier to play. She was a kid. "Don't say *hell*."

Her pink cheeks went neon.

He and Carly had a side-door communication. He wasn't her parent. He wasn't her peer. Neither of those approaches would have been the way in. So from the beginning, he'd teased her. He delivered most everything he needed to say on a joke with only the faintest edge of authority, and they'd always understood each other. As much as he ever wanted to be understood by anyone, she'd been the best. "You're not good at it. The *hell* thing just isn't working for you. Your mother will—"

"John! Stop it!"

"Okay! Fine. But seriously, what were you doing following me? What were you thinking? It's crazy. I mean, I'm not mad. We'll get past it. But this is not okay."

Carly turned toward him in her seat, burning her opinion into the side of his head.

He glanced back from the road to see where they were in this. He didn't recognize her. Jaw set, eyes sparking. And the strangest thing yet—that she didn't mind being seen like that. She didn't wilt into the grumbling fourteen-year-old expected thing. Under challenge, she didn't look down or flinch to a lower wattage.

An icy flutter, a little flurry of premonition, dove through him. For the first time, nice wasn't going to work on Carly. It surprised him how much he didn't want to go the other way. But it didn't stop him.

John dug his tongue against a molar to flex his jaw. "You need to get control of your face, young lady. You have been gunning for me all day. And I don't appreciate it. I've been easy on you. Maybe too easy. I don't know what you think you're doing. If you've got something to say, say it. But you'd better say it respectfully. Don't you glare at me. And don't you ever follow me around again and barge in on private conversations. Is that clear?"

When she didn't respond, John didn't look away from the road. "You've got nothing to say? Really? I said I wasn't mad because I was trying to be nice. But, yeah, I'm getting pretty angry right now."

"But you're not, though." Her voice was the flat confrontational match of the expression he'd seen on her face.

"What? You're saying I'm not angry?"

"Yeah. Actually, I don't think you are. You've got five thousand things on your mind right now, and you want me to think you're angry so that I'll feel bad and be quiet. Like maybe I'll try to get on your good side by not asking questions. But I don't actually think you're mad at me. Not yet."

"Wow. You are really something these days. It's like I don't even know the person sitting here."

She said nothing. The icy flutter grew tendrils and he fished his mind for a new tactic.

She got there first, but with a new waver in her voice. "You told Mom that the cameras were for some guy who was stalking you. But you said he was weak. Like some homeless guy or something. That he wouldn't hurt us."

"That wasn't him." He snatched a quick look away from the road. "That's not who I was talking about. That's not who the cameras were for."

So that was it. The worry of Owen had put Carly on her mission. She was just barely on the dry side of crying. This he could work with. "It's not him, Carlzee. I promise."

"Then who is he?"

"Just someone I did business with a while back."

"Did business?" Tears forgotten in an instant, she was straight back on offense. "What does that even mean? Did you work with him?"

He didn't have time for her hyperprimed attention to detail, but he couldn't help being impressed. "Yes. As in *did business*. That's what that means."

"No-ooo. If you work with someone, you just say *work with*. Why is this *do business* instead? That's like trying to say something without saying it. Why is it different?"

"You're making a big deal out of nothing, Carly."

"Why did you say you were going to play racquetball?"

"I didn't know how long I'd be gone."

She was quiet long enough that he thought she might be done. He'd run her fresh out of moves with a nonsensical answer. It was a good strategy.

But a slight psychic whir of gears still moved the air between them.

"Is a game of racquetball longer or shorter than forever?"

Jonathan let a sigh stand in for trying to outdo her, dodge for thrust. But her comment tingled at the base of his skull.

He resisted drumming his fingers on the steering wheel as the plan of what to do took on its edges. She was right. It was time to go. He slowed the car and dragged the wheel over into a hard U-turn.

"I've changed my mind. Text your mom. Tell her we're coming to pick her up. It's been a long day. I don't feel like going to the store. I'm thinking Don Julio's for dinner."

"Shouldn't she just meet us? We're almost there anyway." Carly stretched into the back seat behind him for her phone.

"No. Let's just all go together. It won't take long."

She flopped back into her seat, scooching deep into a slouch, thumbs tapping out the message.

She couldn't keep it up forever. She was a kid, not a practice partner for his mental chess. He slid a sideways look at her and nodded at the phone in her hand. "And I'm going to want to see exactly what you said to Ada to drag her into this. Your friend is not going to thank you for getting her into trouble, too."

But when their eyes met, a little jolt rocked Jonathan's heart in its nook. She wasn't gassed out for the sparring. Not by a long shot. She was glowing and more than happy to blow up his bluff.

"You want to talk more about why I wondered where you were? Really?"

She wasn't off guard. He was. A riptide of embarrassment pulled at him. Jonathan fixed his stare on the road ahead and locked his posture against reconciliation. "No. I want you to text your mother like I asked you to."

Carly went back to her typing.

His face went warm and the heat sank all the way through him, prickling under his shirt collar. "This smart-ass phase isn't going to go well for you."

Carly shifted at the edge of his vision, looking at him for a few weighted seconds, then turned her face to the window.

His thoughts shifted to the trunk.

Owen had nudged Jonathan with the little wisecrack about having a packed bag and passport in the car. As it so happened, he did. The meeting with Owen, Jonathan knew, was either a beginning or an end. Depending on how things went, he knew it might've even meant leaving straightaway from the restaurant.

Going for the Anningers had been both risky and also the only thing he could think of. Selling the painting for pocket change to someone who didn't know what it was, and what it was worth, was pointless after all he'd done, after all he'd been through.

If he'd known about the Flinck at the outset, he would probably have settled for a slice of the FBI reward and a pat on the back. And he'd have an entirely different life now.

But here he was. Here they all were.

So Donna and Carly didn't know it, but he'd said his goodbyes back at the house, paying attention to everything that had been part of this brief new life. He'd looked carefully, loading the house, the light, their faces, into his mind for use in memory. Just in case.

He was glad he had.

Right before Carly had intervened in the conversation with Owen, Jonathan had caught a whiff. When he'd gone too far, he could actually smell it. Several times in his life everything had depended on it—with a psychotic bully he'd once taunted in school, with his dad's drug dealer on a bad day, at Roy's first pistol shot in the alley that night.

There at the end of the confrontation in the restaurant, there'd been a change in Owen's demeanor. Jonathan hadn't noticed it outright, but something signaled to him in a faint smell coming off his own skin like fresh raw meat and warm metal. Somehow his body knew the danger, warned his survival instinct when his mind had run ahead of it, reckless and unheeding.

Real or imagined, he took the omen to heart. Sitting there in the booth across from a man he was now convinced would kill him when the timing was good, Jonathan was glad of the suitcase in the car.

Except for he had lied about the painting. He'd claimed it wasn't in his house. But it was.

He'd tried to move it for safekeeping, but every place he'd tried to leave it had made it impossible for him to function. Having it in the trunk of his car made him sweat every lane change and intersection. Millions of dollars could be reduced to splinters—and ones that could still land him in prison—in a single fender bender.

He'd rented a small storage unit and tried putting it there. That lasted nine hours.

The house was the only safe place he could watch at all times. With Interior 1 trained on the foyer, John was a bird on a full nest. He could tap it up on his phone whenever he needed to double-check it, to calm himself when the worry rose like mercury in a thermometer.

So he'd zipped the painting into the garment bag that held his worn-twice tuxedo and hung it in the foyer closet, in view of the camera, and he found a way to be okay with it. But he hadn't considered that Owen would show up there.

But he had.

Until Jonathan could talk to Roy and deal—or not—with Owen and the Anningers, he wanted the painting, and himself, gone. It didn't matter where, just anyplace Owen couldn't find him.

Dinner at Don Julio's would end in a fight with Donna. John would see to that. Carly had hand-delivered the kindling for the argument. It would be easy. He'd leave them, pick up the painting, and get triple-digit miles away before the moon came up.

Carly switched from the front to the back seat for the ride to dinner. John kept the conversation light and conspicuously not about the last hour. He felt Carly watching him and caught her studying eyes in the rearview mirror.

They settled into a table by a stuccoed wall hung with sombreros and a driftwood-framed Aztec print.

Donna ordered margaritas. Jonathan prepped the stage for the blowup. He hadn't looked at or spoken to Carly since they were all together. By now Donna would have noted it, even if not consciously. He felt Carly scorching him with scrutiny from across the table.

The drinks came. He cleared his throat. "So. Carly. Do you want to tell your mother what happened today or should I?"

He felt like a slow learner. He expected her to go red to the ears. He thought she'd give way in front of her mother and he'd deliver a quick, righteously offended attack. Donna would take her side. He would leave. Then whatever happened would be the next thing in his life. He might come back. He might not.

But what he got instead, when he finally acknowledged her, was a Carly who leaned in, nearly sprawling on the tabletop, lowering her chin to rest on her loosely crossed arms. She was interested to the point of amazement. "Nah. I'm good. It's all you, John-zee."

Donna looked between them, caught between alarm and amusement. "What's going on? What happened?"

Rage made syrup of his blood, slow and achingly heavy, and for an ugly instant that hot lethargy dragged against the idea of slapping Carly. He didn't need this shit.

He took a quarter of his margarita in a single, cold pull.

"You know what? I'm going to hit the restroom first." Jonathan took another sip, set his glass on the table with a restrained bang, and pushed back his chair. It scraped across the tile with a stuttery yowl.

Donna called after him, "John!"

His phone buzzed a double notification into his pocket just as he hit the door marked GUAPOS. He thought Donna might be checking in with him, short quick notes of allegiance or *what the hell*. She wasn't used to seeing him angry. It had never been useful to have her worried about that. So he had always made angry look like anything but. He let it smolder under the banner of being tired or busy or *everything's fine.* He never raked his chair across the floor and stomped off with a mouthful of margarita.

But the text read: *Alert: Exterior_1 Driveway*

Alert: Exterior_2 Front Door

Another came in as he tapped the app open to see the images.

Alert: Exterior_3 East/Front

The phone buzzed in his hand, alive with message after message.

Oh, fucking hell. Jonathan felt slack, like a spool of twine that had lost its spindle, his train of thought falling off him in unraveling threads.

He should never have ignored Roy. The driveway camera had snapped a photo of his truck as he'd rolled in. Exterior 2 showed Roy moving toward the front door. He'd left his truck door open.

Roy had crossed over to his right. Exterior 3 showed him slip past the office window to the side of the house.

Alert: Exterior_4 East/Side

Jonathan sucked in a cold breath that needled in his teeth. In a short pause in the stream of alerts, he looked around the corner of the restroom alcove, back toward the table. Donna and Carly were deep in brow-furrowed conversation. Carly raised her hands in a big, angry non-Carly-like shrug. Jonathan's chest ached at the sight of it.

Alert: Exterior_3 East/Front

Alert: Exterior_2 Front Door

A foggy blankness covered the place in his mind where he kept his plan. He couldn't fit this into what he could no longer see clearly. Roy was probably banging on his front door right now, croaking out his brokenness on John's front stoop for everyone to hear with that stupid dilapidated truck idling in the driveway. Shit.

Alert: Interior_1 Foyer

Roy was inside. Jonathan sprinted for the parking lot.

CHAPTER NINETEEN

Before he set out for John's house, Roy wanted to time himself with the stopwatch. It would help him to know how long it would take, how long he'd have to hold on to get through the list: break the window, open the door, walk in—six steps at the most—lift it from the wall, six steps back, The End. His guts cramped grossly if he tried to imagine doing it, seeing the street sign, what the door would look like, a broken window, John's house. OhJohn'sHouse. The place where he lived. His nice things. How much John would hate Roy for being there.

But if it was just a number of seconds, if he could just think of it like that . . .

He couldn't find it. The stopwatch had been in the passenger seat. He was sure of it. He checked under the lace pillow, under the plastic bags from the convenience store. He shook crumbs all over the seats from a chip bag and one from pork rinds in case the stopwatch had slid into one of those by accident. This was taking too long. Sweat slipped down his back and glued his hair to his neck. The air felt like he was sucking it through a wet rag. Way too long. Roy started counting as he piled his things on the asphalt, checking everything on the way out, just to double-check the same stuff as he threw it all back in.

Beating the clock was an old trick to keep himself focused, to push worry aside so it wouldn't distract him so much. It kept fear a little bit further away. Like garlic for a vampire. That's what his mother had said. She'd taught him the little habit after she'd gotten sick, to help him get through his chores so he didn't get in trouble with his grandmother. It only took ninety-six seconds to load the sheets into the machine and start the laundry. She bled a lot in those last days. He was eleven.

The next best thing to timing with the watch was counting. It put his mind a little steadier. So he kept counting, then and now. He'd once made it to four hundred and nine when his grandmother beat him with a broom handle.

The sun was searing as he rummaged in the back seat. *Four hundred ten, four hundred eleven . . .*

He knew the stopwatch was in here somewhere. But when the count got to six hundred, he wasn't sure anymore if he was right. He thought he remembered having the watch out one day on the work site. Did he leave it? No, he put it back. He was almost positive. The muscles in his arm trembled. His legs were going rubber. And was he at six hundred going over to seven hundred or should he only be heading into the six hundreds now? He should have parked in the shade.

The timer was under the seat, pinned by a shoe box—filled with coins, an American-flag bandanna stiff with dirt, an empty key ring with a crumbling stress squeezer on it, and a pack of mints melted solid.

He should throw that stuff away. There was a trash can across the parking lot. It was just junk. His eyes roamed the piles of stuff in the truck, the silhouette like a mountain range. He put the box back under the seat.

It took twenty-four seconds to tie his boots.

He could hold his breath for forty-one seconds. Fifty-six if he counted the exhale and dragged it out until his lungs burned.

Marcelline had shown him that the picture on the wall in John's house was close to the door. It might take only as long to tie his boots as to break the window and get inside John's house. Then six steps. That's all. Six steps, twelve round-trip, not hurrying. It only took him twelve seconds.

And he would be hurrying.

Less time than it took to tie his boots plus way less time than he could hold one breath altogether. He could be brave for that long. *Please.*

It would be done. Done. Done right. *Please.*

Walking in and out of the alley, holding a gun, not shooting it, should have taken thirty-nine seconds. At the most. He'd spent all that day timing himself, and it was what he'd thought the worst case would be—thirty-nine horribly scary seconds. It would be less time if he could be better, if he could not be pulled under a tidal wave of freezing fear. But thirty-nine seconds was the worst that could happen. It wasn't that bad.

He'd been to the liquor store, but couldn't feel the raspberry minis. And he'd already been shaking when he drank the first can of energy drink, so he couldn't tell if that was working either. He'd had three total since putting all his stuff back in the truck, with one vodka each in the first two cans, and two poured into the last one. He couldn't feel any of it. *Please.*

His fingers were numb and he caught himself holding his breath even without the stopwatch.

Please.

Please.

Let it be over.

Please.

CHAPTER TWENTY

The second time Jonathan looked at the dashboard and saw that he was driving better than fifteen miles an hour over the speed limit, he set the cruise control. It killed him to do it. He wanted to fly, teleport, reverse fucking time to be there before Roy had ever gotten to the house. But he needed to be careful. He might actually burst into flames if he got pulled over.

The traffic light on the road ahead jumped up to yellow. *Goddammit.*

He glanced into the rearview mirror, but it was more automatic than informative. Everything was panic blurred. He pressed his foot down hard on the accelerator and took the intersection arguably in time, an argument he begged the universe not to make him have right now. He checked the mirror more earnestly for a cop. Nothing.

Rush hour was at full clog. In clear lanes, he would have made it home in less than twenty-five minutes, but at the twenty-five-minute mark, he was only marginally past halfway there. He was hot and nauseated, his mouth dry, his skin thrumming, and he hated every single person on the road in front of him. He needed to scream and pound the steering wheel, but he didn't know what that could unleash. Once he started, he might not be able to stop.

A clear spot opened up and he changed lanes without signaling and cursed again under his breath. He checked one more time for flashing lights behind him and tried not to count time.

Interior 1 had alerted twice in the first mile that he was out of the restaurant. Speeding was bad. Speeding and weaving through traffic was worse. Speeding and swerving and checking the texts from his home security app was madness. But he did it anyway. He had to know.

He was almost home. Roy hadn't touched the coat closet yet.

That Interior 1 had been silent for almost forty-five minutes was scarcely good news. If Roy had left the house, the exterior cameras would have reported it back. His phone was convulsing with texts and calls from Donna, but nothing from the cameras. Roy was still inside. But he hadn't been back into the foyer in a while. *What the fuck is he doing in there?*

The tires whined in his too-fast turn into the neighborhood. Jonathan eased his foot off the gas. The muscles in his right leg trembled in protest. His throat clicked and spasmed when he tried to swallow nothing down a dry throat.

A neighbor he'd seen before but never spoken to stiff-legged it down the sidewalk in shiny green shorts and a thick white headband that could only have been brand-new. It glowed in the lowering light like a halo that had lost its float. The man pumped his arms unselfconsciously high, smiling as he did it, or maybe wincing.

As Jonathan drew even with him, the guy worked a friendly wave into the rhythm of his postdinner power walk. Jonathan waved back as the man flailed past him. Then he checked the mirror—both to see if the man kept going and also just to see it one more time, to know that he wasn't hallucinating. The exchange belonged in a dream given the murder on his mind.

He forced down a big breath to stretch the tightness in his chest and slid his hands back and forth over the wheel to still the tremors that were threatening to wrench them out of his control. He filed away another huge breath, but the calm it brought faded with the exhale.

He had to preserve his options. That meant absolutely no speeding through the neighborhood. No screeching into the driveway. No running. No yelling. No launching anything—word or deed—that might need to be taken back.

He coasted down his street looking for anyone who was looking at him. No concerned faces appeared at any doors suddenly thrown open. No curtains twitched as he went by. A listless kid at the first house on Jonathan's block was staring off into a daydream while his arthritic old dog raised its leg at the post of the streetlight.

Roy's truck came into view at the bend, slanted across Jonathan's driveway. He'd left his door hanging open, inches from having knocked a ding into the rear quarter panel of Donna's car.

Jonathan startled at the sight of it. The realization settled down over the pounding in his chest a second later. Of course she hadn't beaten him home. Not only had he left Donna and Carly sitting at a table at Don Julio's to wonder where he'd gone, he'd left them there with no way to leave.

That was going to require some creative explaining to smooth over, unless the scene at the table under the sombreros really was the last time he would ever see them. He hoped not. Then he hoped the other way. Then he opted for the middle sort of hope—that he would just get through this. The rest would work itself out. It always did.

The driveway had no space for him to leave his car neatly parked. He didn't like the optics of two crooked cars in front of his house. It could draw attention. The fewer eyes on this mess, the better. He might be able to keep it to just his own two eyes, if he was careful. And if he was lucky.

Jonathan wasn't sure how he would answer if anyone asked him if he considered himself lucky.

So he pulled alongside his mailbox on the street and cut the engine. His phone buzzed in the passenger seat. Exterior 1 had alerted his own arrival. He opened the app and shut down the whole system. The cameras wouldn't take any more pictures or send any more messages.

With the exception of the angle of Roy's truck and its dangling door, nothing looked amiss unless anyone peered into the shade of the portico.

The stoop, under its peaked roof, was flanked by a twin set of bushy evergreen shrubs. Their height and their glossy dark leaves kept it dim enough to grow moss where the concrete met the damp earth. It was getting on toward dark. The deepening twilight siphoned off more detail from the front of the house by the minute. But because he knew more or less what to look for, Jonathan spied the flaw straightaway. The pane of the left sidelight panel was raggedly darker than the one to the right of the door.

The east-side camera had shown Roy bending down right where the runoff slope next to the house was lined with river rocks. In his second appearance at the front-door camera, Roy had been back from the side of the house with a gray-brown something in his hand about the smashing size of a softball.

Jonathan got out of his car and walked to the mailbox. He opened it, then closed it back again, ignoring the sizable stack of envelopes and advertising flyers inside. What he'd really wanted was an excuse to look up and down the street. He'd gotten that, which was good. Better yet, there'd been no one to see.

No lights seemed to be on in the house, but it would have been much brighter almost an hour earlier when Roy had broken the window and let himself in. The motion lights, both outside and inside, didn't activate until dark. But John had shut down all the automation with the cameras. Dark was better right now.

He walked down the driveway, threading between Roy's truck and Donna's car. The dome light was still on inside the truck, giving him hope for the battery and for Roy's ability to get right back on the road as soon as possible, with his tail between his legs or ripped right off if it came to that.

Jonathan sized up the piles of junk in the truck's front seats. The jumble was incomprehensible, but the cup holders and center console were tightly packed to overflowing with three open energy drink cans and a handful of mini liquor bottles, their caps scattered over the seat and in the footwell. He pushed the door closed and bumped it latched with his hip to keep it quiet. The light went out.

Jonathan took his keys from his pocket as he strode up the front walk in a pantomime of a normal evening.

The fury in him simmered. He felt feverish. He hated to fight his own body for control. As if he really needed another enemy right now. But it would be odd if the jangling tension in his belly weren't there. It made perfect, seething sense.

But the dread that he felt, the deep unease at taking the two concrete steps to his own front door, held some unwelcome measure of surprise. He didn't want to see Roy. He didn't want to know what it looked like, whatever had transformed in him to bring him around to such a reckless thing.

Jonathan wasn't afraid of Roy. Not exactly. But a stretch of dark possibility lay ahead—what would he have to do if Roy tried to be scary? He was a little bit afraid of that.

Jonathan wasn't all bark and no bite. He'd bite if he had to, but he didn't even like the metaphor. He wasn't an animal. This wasn't a matter of teeth and claws. He was a man. Nothing as simple as survival was on the line. If he were merely worried about staying alive, he'd get back in the car and drive away.

This was about the kind of life he wanted and the irretrievable time he'd invested in getting near to having it.

The front door was closed, but unlocked.

Jonathan turned the doorknob. The hard stop at the end of its rotation marked the line to cross. Push, and he'd be inside with Roy. Whatever had changed between the two of them, it was likely to change a hell of a lot more before Jonathan crossed this threshold again going the other way.

Or he could open his hand. Let the knob roll back. Let the door stay closed. He could still just leave.

No, he couldn't.

Jonathan pushed open the door. The coat closet was shut. He didn't turn on the foyer lights. The brightness would leap out of the broken window into the neighborhood. It would be a beacon to helpful assholes everywhere as they walked their dogs or strutted back the way they'd come in their crazy green shorts and glowing headbands.

Broken glass from the busted side window crunched under his shoes in the dim entryway.

"Roy, it's me. You want to come out and talk about this?"

The question rang into silence. No answer came back.

Jonathan stepped farther into the foyer. The gloom was heavier every few feet into the house. His ears strained to reel back some clue as to where Roy was in the darkness. All they caught was the ghostly ring of silence.

He leaned into the hall bathroom and flicked the switch inside the door. The foyer dawned into slightly better focus in the soft new light.

Some of the broken glass had dark edges. There wasn't enough light to call it red for sure. But it was red. He knew it. Drops—round, raised buttons of black that hinted at maroon—dotted the beige tiles.

Roy had set the rock he'd used to break the window on the very end of the armrest on the hall bench. Like the quarters on the curb. Centered. A precise call for help. It swept goose bumps over Jonathan's arms.

The scrollwork decoration he'd hung to replace the Flinck had been hurled to the floor and lay in the rubble of its broken frame.

Roy had seen the video. Somehow he knew about the painting.

Jonathan called out again into the quiet house. "Let me rephrase that. You *definitely* want to come out and talk about this."

He chewed the inside of his cheek.

"Goddammit, Roy! This will not go well for you if I have to come looking. Don't make this worse."

All the nothing that echoed into the dark was just what Jonathan needed. The dread evaporated. He'd tear the house apart looking for Roy, and it would be great practice for tearing Roy himself apart once he found him.

Neither turned out to be necessary. The hunt lasted two seconds. As Jonathan rounded the hall that led to the kitchen and the garage beyond, he stumbled over Roy's outstretched legs. He lay sprawled across the floor where he'd slid down from his slump against the wall.

Roy had been in the family room. Jonathan knew this because the bottle of vodka leaning against Roy's thigh had been in the bar cabinet next to the television.

He'd also been in Jonathan and Donna's bedroom. Nobody in the family took any regular medicines, and the uncapped prescription bottle beside Roy on the floor was most likely Donna's Xanax, which had been in the nightstand drawer for when she couldn't sleep before flying or presentations.

The details of what he was looking at lined up on their own to make an awful kind of sense.

"Oh, God. What have you done?"

Roy raised his head as if he would respond, but it wobbled and flopped to the other side.

"Goddamn you, Roy." Jonathan nudged him hard with his toe, but even that little release threatened an avalanche. He pulled back his leg and landed a hard kick into Roy's bony hip.

Roy groaned and struggled up, but only made it as far as propping up on his elbows. He fell back, head thudding into the wall.

Jonathan itched to kick him again, but stepped over his legs and hit the light switch for the overheads in the hallway. He looked to see how much it lit the foyer. Not too bad.

He squatted next to Roy. The pill bottle was empty and definitely used to hold Donna's Xanax. He didn't know how many there would have been. The prescription had been for thirty and was months old, but she didn't take them often. The vodka bottle still had a solid third left in it, but he felt that it had been more than half full. John had opened it weeks ago. He set it aside.

He shoved Roy's head upright and held it there, gripping his hair, the strands swollen with grease, shudderingly slick between his fingers.

"What the fuck is this? What are you trying to do?" Jonathan shook Roy's head in his fist with the rhythm of his words.

Roy opened his eyes and worked his mouth to unstick his lips from his teeth. He heaved in a breath as if his lungs were nearly rusted shut. "You . . . You lie . . . d."

Jonathan let him go and his hands twitched into fists against his thighs. He leaned into Roy's face and said through gritted teeth, "So. What."

That woke Roy up. He coughed and battled for a breath. He raised his head, his filmy red eyes glaring back into Jonathan's—not bold, exactly, but no longer afraid. Accusing. Caught and caged, but safe. As if he knew he was out of reach. Untouchable.

Roy thought he was dying. And he didn't mind.

A little sick feeling rose at the back of Jonathan's throat. His heart pounded out of step with anything he felt about Roy. Roy dead was nothing. Roy dead was absolutely fine.

But dead isn't dying. Dying was a thing, a length of time, a noun, not just a verb, a presence, a third entity in the hallway with them. It had to be dealt with, and it was warm, not cold as they make it out to be. It was a humid, dank thing. He could smell it, feel it stealing all the air around them with its own slow, patient breathing.

Dying can be complicated. Messy. Dying can be tricked into stopping.

Roy's lids slipped closed, but he hauled them back to halfway. Then, of all things out of place in the moment, a smile pulled at the right side of Roy's mouth. He was fucking smiling. But his chin trembled, shaking in a horrible effort to hold the smile in place. Whatever that smile meant to Roy, it also hurt him. His eyes shimmered wet, the red of them glowing at Jonathan through the tears.

Watching him struggle with that pitiful grimace, a shiver slid over Jonathan's back.

Roy grunted to clear his throat. "I didn't do what you said."

Jonathan laughed through his nose. A wave of exhaustion made his crouch too painful to hold any longer. He turned and flopped down next to Roy on the floor, their backs against the wall together.

"You sure didn't," Jonathan said. "And aren't you awfully proud of yourself? I told you I'd kill you if you came here, but you did it anyway. And then went and saved me the trouble." Jonathan swatted the empty pill bottle. It smacked the opposite wall with a plastic clatter. It bounced back and wound down in slowing circles between Roy's pitiful, frayed boots.

This fucking day. Jonathan righted the vodka bottle from the floor where it had spilled some of what it had left to offer. The craving for a burning throatful of the stuff couldn't vault the gross certainty that Roy had put his mouth on it.

Jonathan closed his eyes and tilted his head up against the wall. The hall lights were orange against his lids, almost like daylight. He sighed.

Roy might be dying. Probably was. In the hallway. What the hell was he supposed to do with that?

"Roy, in my father's stuff, in all that junk I let you take, was there anything about where it all came from? Anything else about the painting?"

Roy's head had fallen forward, boneless, chin to chest in a way that looked wrong.

"Hey!" Jonathan nudged him, and Roy flinched to a slightly firmer slump.

"Roy." Jonathan shook him. "Roy! Wake up!"

Roy mumbled and groaned. Disjointed words tumbled out— haunting, high-pitched murmurs in a steady moan of broken-down old-man noises, like a radio grabbing things out of static. "Good . . . okay . . . she's okay . . . fine . . . I will . . . I'll get it . . . but . . . I . . . why is it like this?"

Shit.

Jonathan was back on his haunches again, then down to his knees, getting into Roy's face, ignoring the rotting-fruit-and-rubbing-alcohol smell that trickled out on his shallow breaths.

"Roy, wait. Wake up. Hey!" Jonathan shook him, more gently this time, but faster. "Hey. Hey. Do you still have any of that stuff? From the garage? Is any of it out there in your truck?"

Roy rolled his head in a swinging negation, but didn't open his eyes. "Doan know."

"Not good enough." Jonathan shook him and slapped Roy's cheek, hard enough to sting, but not too bad. Not even close to what Jonathan wanted to do, but he reined in the rest. "Roy! There was a whole box of stuff. You took it all. Do you still have any of it?"

"Din' take it. I worked for . . ."

"I don't give a shit. Is there still stuff in your truck from back then?"

Roy finally looked at him again. His back was sagging more with each gravelly breath. "Did you know? Why . . . ?"

"Goddammit, Roy. Just tell me what you did with it."

Roy arched up, pulling straighter. Eyes closed. They slid open again with a quivering effort. His lips barely moved. "No."

"What?"

"No."

Jonathan's rage burned in his face, but his voice was quiet. "Don't you say no to me, you useless piece of shit."

The ghost of Roy's earlier smile surfaced and receded on his lips. But he kept staring. His shoulder twitched hard. Involuntary or a shrug, Jonathan couldn't tell. "No."

Jonathan shouted into Roy's face, "Do you want to die?"

And that it was possibly the stupidest thing Jonathan had ever said out loud was more than he could take. He went cold all over.

Roy wheezed out a shallow laugh into Jonathan's trembling face. His eyes glittered, remote but piercing.

Jonathan slammed the palm of his hand into the wall next to Roy's head and pushed up from the floor. He stomped through the house to his bedroom. At the back of his drawer full of T-shirts, he pulled out what was, as far as he knew, the only other prescription in the house. Painkillers. Percocet and Vicodin from his own shoulder surgery and dental work, tucked away for safekeeping.

He hadn't taken them for long when they'd been prescribed. He couldn't enjoy being woozy and warm, adrift on imaginary goodwill, quick to smile, and maybe a little too prone to honesty in the hazier moments. He didn't trust the waking dream of nothing to lose. Some of the pills were years old.

He'd only ever taken a dose or two to get him through the worst of whatever pain he had, and the rest went into the drawer for emergencies. That Roy was still breathing right now was an emergency. He didn't know how much time he had before Donna and Carly found a way home.

Jonathan's pulse strobed in his eyesight, throbbing in a sharp head-ache that had sprung up in his temple. What choice did he have? Roy did this. Roy wanted this and was always going to have gotten all the way to doing it at some point.

All the things he'd watched Roy fuck up scrolled fast through his memory, an exercise that seemed in the service of something not quite under Jonathan's control as he came back through the house with the pills. It teased him with images of the unsanded splinters bristling on the deck railing. The brush marks in the paint on his father's kitchen wall. The soap dried in streaks on the hood of his car. The bad green haircut of a poorly mowed lawn. The mountains of useless junk Roy burrowed under like a rat, just like Jonathan's father. Every flinching, whining, mealymouthing, sloppy, inconvenient encounter. Marcelline dying on the ground.

Roy's usual half-assed results weren't going to cut it this time. This wasn't personal. Halfway would be a disaster.

Roy had slid down low on the wall in Jonathan's absence, chin to rattling chest now, sipping tiny breaths between long pauses.

Jonathan kicked him again, just to wake him up. "Hey!" He got down on the floor, straddling Roy's right leg to be in front of him. He shook out a pill and shoved it into Roy's mouth, shuddering at the wetness on the tips of his fingers as he drew them back from Roy's lips. He poured vodka into Roy's mouth over the pill.

"Swallow that."

Roy sputtered and choked. Most of the vodka went down his shirtfront. So did the pill.

Jonathan rammed it back in. "Goddammit. Swallow this."

He didn't, except for some of the vodka again.

Fear bloomed a vine into Jonathan's guts. Cold slithering, twisting, pushing up, crowding his lungs.

He was doing this, so it needed to get done. There wasn't time for this bullshit.

"You sonofabitch." Jonathan lost his aversion to Roy's mouth in the desperation of the situation. He poked two pills deep onto Roy's tongue, poured the vodka, then held Roy's jaw shut and pinched his nose closed. Nothing happened. Was he dead?

Roy gurgled after a moment, gulped weakly, and dribbled copiously. Jonathan pried his mouth open. The pills were still there, stuck, but trailing a chalky white streak of dissolved Vicodin down the back of Roy's tongue.

"Fuck!"

But there was something there, something Jonathan could use. He fished out three fresh pills from the bottle. He put them in his own mouth and chewed fast. The strong bitter tang made his mouth water. He spit into the vodka and threw four more pills onto his own tongue, careful not to swallow any of it. Another huge mouthful of crushed painkiller went into the bottle.

Jonathan swirled the bottle around and held the thin milk up to the light.

He chewed a few more tablets and added them, hacking and spitting into the dregs. He dug narcotic paste out of his molars and scraped the tip of his tongue over the bottle's rim.

Jonathan slapped his palm over the top and shook the whole works, blending it nearly opaque.

He straddled Roy again, scooped him up against his chest, and forced his head back. The mix went down his throat to some success and some weak minor geysers of failure.

Jonathan upended the bottle, and a thread, thick with spit and medicine, drizzled over Roy's teeth.

Most of it trickled down with little resistance. The ceiling lights reflected in what didn't, pooling in the back of Roy's throat.

Sweating and dizzy, his heart rocking and thumping out of rhythm, Jonathan stared down over Roy's slack face, holding his jaw with one hand, his other arm around his shoulders, pulling him close and upright. He slid his hand down from Roy's jaw to his neck, poking and pressing for a pulse. Jonathan couldn't tell if it was his own hammering heart throbbing in his fingertips.

He put his ear to Roy's gaping mouth. Nothing, he thought, but listened longer. Did he hear something?

A shadow fell into the hall from the foyer.

"Oh my God!"

Donna and Carly rounded the corner into view.

"Oh my God," Donna said again.

Jonathan shook his swimming head to clear a path for something to say. "He took some pills. A lot of pills. Get Carly out of here. Take her to Ada's."

Donna's hands were shaking as she keyed into her phone. "Oh, God. I'll call 911."

"No!"

Donna's eyes snapped up from her screen. Carly was looking from Roy's lolling head to Jonathan's face. He was mesmerized trying to know how she was reading this.

A small wounded sound parted Carly's lips. "Oh" was all she said.

"Don't," said John. "I already called. They're on their way. Just get Carly out of here. She doesn't need to see this." He pulled his gaze away from his stepdaughter's, breaking the spell for himself.

"And Donna," he called to her as they turned for the door, Donna steering Carly by the shoulders and Carly looking back at the tangle of Roy in Jonathan's arms. He found a sliver of himself still within reach, still right there in his voice when he needed it. "Come right back. Please come back. I need you."

He listened for the thunk of Donna's car doors. He didn't trust that dying had truly done its job, that it wasn't still there, lingering, waiting to see if it would be more fun to leave without what it came for and watch chaos take over. He waited to hear them back out of the driveway and checked that they'd rounded the corner before he took a pillow from the sofa and held it over Roy's face for a long, slow count. It felt like two hundred plus forever. Counting kept the fear at bay, kept him from rushing it. He had to be sure. Now that Donna and Carly had been there, it could only be this way.

Roy never moved. He never made a sound. Jonathan found no pulse.

Jonathan felt lighter. Some of the painkillers had definitely gotten into him. There was a little of the gilded happiness that lived somewhere in the chemistry of the medicine, a surge of well-being that didn't make any sense in illness, or after being cut open and sewn back together. Or in the postglow of holding a pillow over a guy's face either.

But it wasn't half-bad. And it was twice as useful as even that. He couldn't feel a thing. No nerves at all.

Donna came home, her hair on fire over the lack of an ambulance in the driveway, then all over again at the suggestion that she should please help him put Roy in his truck. They had to leave him for someone else to find.

She told him he was insane. That she didn't even know who she was talking to anymore. How could he possibly think this was okay?

But he kept going. Twisting it to sound reasonable. To sound like the lesser of the wrong turns they might make in this.

He would wash and throw away the bottle Roy had taken from their bar. He would clean up everything. No one knew who Roy was. No one was looking for him. No one would know.

She wouldn't have to do anything but help him—just a little— only to get Roy into the truck and then follow them in her car to bring Jonathan back home.

She cried. A sudden, strong rain of it.

But she couldn't argue that she didn't want the police, and inevitably the newspeople, back in their home and all over their street.

Not after what Carly had already been through. *We have to think of her.* John pounded that point, Donna's weak spot. Carly had to live in this town. It would be a terrible and utterly useless thing to make her life about this. To make their life about it. *It's not worth it, babe.* It can't be undone.

He told her Roy was a rotten person. That he'd even been responsible for a nice woman's death back in the day. *That's what I didn't tell you. The only thing.* He was what the cameras were all about in the first place. *I'm sorry. Please don't tell Carly. Please, it will scare her. I'm sorry. It's over now.* If she would only help him, they could make this truly over.

And, most importantly, none of this was their fault. They hadn't done anything wrong. Roy had done this to himself to punish John for not fixing his broken life years ago. Between this and the kid who'd attacked Carly, it wasn't fair that she kept having to take on the mistakes of other people. And it would be another mistake not to let someone else find Roy.

It was pointless pain.

And if somehow I'm wrong, it's on me. I swear it. I will protect you. I will protect Carly. I love you. I'm sorry. Help us, Donna. Help us get through this together.

She did. "But I don't know what we have after this, John. After all of this. I don't know what to think. I feel like I don't even know you. I don't know what we are anymore."

He didn't tell her that she was right and that it didn't matter. She'd never had what she thought anyway. He didn't tell her she didn't need to worry, that he'd be gone soon. As soon as strategically possible.

Roy's stunt and what they were doing might even be a useful thing. It would keep Donna's relentless strength in check. She wouldn't bend the world to find him. She'd bend it the other way—to forget him. She wouldn't say anything for fear of tonight coming back on her. She'd make it disappear. She'd done it before. She wouldn't leave Carly vulnerable, losing her to whatever penalty this could carry.

It would work itself out. It always did.

John pulled on Donna's kitchen gloves to dump half a fresh, unfingerprinted bottle of vodka down the drain. He packed the rest of his pills into a plastic bag, all props to press into Roy's hands and decorate his dead lap. And he also brought a hose for the tailpipe, and the duct tape to hold it in place. Just in case.

CHAPTER TWENTY-ONE

No ambulance was coming. Somehow Carly had known there wouldn't be, but she was leaning against Ada's bedroom window anyway, ear almost touching the screen, sifting the neighborhood sounds for the rising wail of sirens over her friend's excited babble.

"Holy *sh*—" Ada's eyebrows swooped up and she inhaled the *it*. "Was he dead?" Ada always swallowed the last sound in a cuss word like it didn't count as much if she said it weird.

"I don't know," Carly said. But she kind of did.

Her babysitter's dog had died when Carly was seven. She had been the one to find her. The dog was in her oval bed, lying on her side with her ever-present rope toy next to her muzzle. There was no blood. Nothing looked wrong. But Carly never for a second had thought the dog was merely sleeping. It was just different somehow.

The man in the hallway looked that kind of different. Untied. Empty.

Carly's mother had told Ada's mother that a friend of John's had suffered a breakdown and had gotten into the house and tried to kill himself while they were all out to dinner.

Both women said the word *suicide* the way Ada said the word *shit*.

That recap was plausible, right up to the part where Donna said the guy was John's friend. Uh-unh. John wasn't holding a friend up off the floor. That was for sure. He'd been far more interested in what Donna and Carly thought of the whole scene than whether the guy piled against him was going to be okay.

For the first time in all of this weirdness, Carly had felt afraid of John.

She pleaded with her mother not to go back.

"Please. Please? Just stay here." Carly held her mother's arm, but her mother turned to her and pulled her into a hug.

"Sweetheart, I need to go back. It'll be okay. John's all alone over there. It's horrible." But Donna clung to Carly as if she didn't want to let go.

Carly had an in, maybe. A quick opportunity. The right arguments, in the right order, could be tumblers in a lock. "The ambulance will be there any minute. In just a few more minutes, he won't be alone. Maybe even before you can get there. Then we can go back together. We could both be there. For him. But I want to go back with you."

Her mother petted Carly's hair, hesitation in her stroke.

So Carly kept at it. "There's no reason for you to be there right now. You'll just be in the way. I don't mean that in a bad way! I mean, your *car* will literally be in the way. Please?"

"Honey, I have to go. I can't just leave him there with this. I can't do that to him." Donna peeled herself out of the hug. "It's not right. I'll be back to get you as soon as they've taken that guy to the hospital, okay?"

Carly shouldn't have said there was no reason. That was a dumb mistake. The chance was passed. It was pointless to fight it.

And there still weren't any sirens.

"Okay," said Carly. "I just need to get something out of the car."

So, for the second time that day, Carly silenced her notifications and slid her phone into the pocket behind the driver's seat. Just to see.

Ada was skeptical when Carly suggested they check where exactly her phone was.

"Now you forgot it in your *mom's* car?"

"It's been a superweird day. Gimme a break. I just want to see if John makes them go to the hospital with that guy. I wanted to be there, not here. No offense. This is freaking me out."

Her mother's car didn't go to the hospital. But it didn't stay at home either.

Carly didn't want Ada to know that. She put her back against the wall and held the phone up at an inconvenient angle.

It didn't take long for Ada to lose interest in watching Carly watch the phone. She flopped back on the bed with a peevish "Whatever." The ceiling didn't hold her attention for long either. Ada picked up her ukulele and made the background music to the long movie of Carly tracking the little bubble with her own face on it, scrolling along, dragging the blue line over the map for twenty-two minutes.

The more she had to look at her own face, staring and staring at it to keep track of where her mother was going—trying to picture where it was and if she'd ever been there before—the more her face on the screen stopped feeling recognizable to her. *That's really me?*

She thought of the video of the *thing*. How it had felt watching herself. Here she was again, sitting in as a spectator, in two places at once, cataloging her response to a situation she hadn't created and didn't want.

Avatar Carly stopped and smiled up from the phone, pinned in place for almost ten minutes. Carly kept an eye on the clock and screenshotted the map after the car hadn't moved for a while. She texted the image to her own phone, which was, at that very moment, in the seat pocket behind her mother, tagging along on this ride to wherever. Then she deleted the picture and the text from Ada's phone.

The app turned Carly's face toward home. But App Carly bypassed the real Carly, still stranded at Ada's. The car stopped at their house for another half hour. Then her mother and John came to pick her up, together.

Her mother's forehead looked cramped, stuck in ridges that were propped up by stress-slanted eyebrows. She'd been crying. But she worked hard to sound cheerful and hopeful. Everything was fine. They got him to the hospital in time. The guy was going to be okay. He was getting help.

John was loose in the joints, a freshly oiled machine. He was relieved that the guy was finally where he needed to be. This whole thing, as messy and unpleasant as it was, had been a long time coming. He'd tried hard to keep Donna and Carly out of it. It was ugly. It was his past. He was so sorry that they'd had to see it. But in the end, he was glad it was out of his hands finally. It was over. Things would be better now.

Her mother was lying.

Her stepfather was telling the truth.

He kept checking Carly during the tag-team explanation of things, just as he had when she'd seen him on the floor in a tangle with the dead guy. John studied her, and Carly let her gratitude be the only thing he saw. It was easy to calibrate, to make it look like relief and happiness that things were going back to normal. He smiled at her. She felt Other Carly take control of her face. She smiled back. He thought they were on the road to fine.

But her gratitude was not made of what he thought it was. She was grateful for knowing what she was looking at. And for her new way of listening to people. Carly knew this was all bullshit. They could say what they wanted, but they couldn't make her believe it.

The house felt strange. Again. John had taped a patchwork of cardboard over the broken window before they brought Carly home. They'd cleaned up every spot and shard of what had happened. The house smelled of ammonia and lemon polish, and the flat electrical whiff of the vacuum cleaner. But the air still held a fading haze of wrongness.

Carly wanted them to open all the windows and doors and let the wind sweep through the house. She wanted them to blast music, run the ceiling fans, the oven fan, the bathroom fans, the plug-in fan her mother used for white noise to sleep by. Carly wanted them to crank up the air conditioner and the heater all at the same time.

Change the air. Change the temperature. Pour sound into the corners like witching salt in scary movies. Let it all fly away through the window screens instead of settling over the floor like a ground fog she had to walk through.

But she didn't say any of that. It would be too much for her mother, who only wanted Carly to be all right.

So she was all right.

She barely slept, though. All night she rode waves of thin dozing, sinking down into meandering thoughts that didn't make any sense, then rising back up, overheated, to try to figure out what to do.

She knew what she wanted to do. She wanted to do it right now, but it was ages until daytime and any good excuse to leave the house.

She wanted to go to the place on the map where her mother had gone. She wanted to know what was out there.

But she had no way to make that happen. She'd never skipped school before. She imagined walking in the front door of the school and heading straight out the back again before the first bell rang. People did it. She knew they did. But it was all in the pronoun. *They* did. She didn't.

In the morning, her head hurt and the light reflecting off the countertops was too bright, but she didn't want to make a face that anyone would ask her about. How Carly was feeling was apparently the topic of the day. Her mother found a dozen different ways to ask her if she was okay. John found a dozen more.

So she ate all her breakfast and asked for more eggs and a refill of juice. Who did something like that who wasn't feeling 100 percent? She was extra-portions-fine, as far as they knew.

Her mother practically cried with happiness, and Carly wouldn't let on that she was this close to barfing it all over the kitchen floor.

John hovered over breakfast with them, which wasn't what he normally did on school mornings. He chattered about taking the day off. He'd cut the grass and call the gutter man and order the mulch they'd been meaning to get. And he'd get the sidelight glass replaced.

Yeah. Fixing what the *not-dead* dead guy broke was just one chore among many. No big deal.

Carly didn't trust her poker face enough to look at him even though she could feel him trying to draw her into a good long head invasion, pulling at her with his own stare while he talked.

He asked if she wanted him to pick her up from school later.

No. No, she did not.

But it came out on a smooth fib. "No, that's okay. I'm going to the library to meet up with Emma. We're going to get in some more drawing practice." She glanced up at the grown-ups. "Ada's coming, too." She held out her glass for more juice. "It'll be fun."

Which brought them to what they really wanted to know—what was she going to say today, out there to everybody, about last night?

That was easy. No fib required.

"I'm not saying anything. As if. It's over. It's been weird enough around here lately. And Ada will be on my side. She won't say anything either. Or I'll feed her ukulele to the fire pit."

Carly texted Emma: *Can you come to the library today?*

The read receipt ticked over immediately.

She waited for a reply, bouncing her pencil off its eraser against the lunch table.

"Can you not?" Ada scowled at the jittery drumming.

Carly stopped and Ada went back to her math homework.

Emma hadn't sent back a message.

Carly typed again. *Please?*

Read.

Sure. Right after school?

Yes OMG thanks.

Carly hadn't been able to think of a way to leave school, the daydream plot getting crazier and more unlikely by the hour. She couldn't do it. It was funny what she had in her and what she didn't. But now she had the rest of the day to think of a way to get Emma to take her out there without having to tell her why.

"Did you and Ada have a falling out?" asked Emma.

Carly looked up from the shading that was going into the portrait all wrong. Too dark. Bad angle. She wanted to throw her pencil across the room.

"No."

"Oh. You've just never been here without her is all."

Carly looked back down at the drawing and the tears came. She ripped the page from the sketchbook, crumpled the paper, and shoved the wad of it down the long table. "Stupid thing."

She sighed and yanked the book back, pushed her hair out of her face, and crooked her arm over the next clean white sheet to start again.

Emma pulled the sketch pad away. "What's wrong?"

"Nothing."

"Okay, that's clearly not true. Unless you meant to finish that out as a complete thought, as in *Nothing that I want to talk about.*"

Carly wanted to close her eyes and put her head on the table. But she was also buzzing at the same time as if she'd had a giant-size cof-fee. Her insides felt like pudding.

She hadn't been able to think of any way to ask Emma for the ride. It would sound crazy or rude or both, and Emma might say no and not want to meet up anymore because Carly was weird. Or she might say yes. Carly's stomach hurt to think of that. What huge problem was waiting at the end of a yes? At the end of that drive? How could she keep it a secret if it was bad?

Carly shook her head. Then made the mistake of looking Emma in the eye and blurted, "I can't."

Emma's pulled back, and concern transformed her face. The mood contracted around them, suddenly dense and serious. "Hey, I want you to listen to me. You simply not wanting to talk about something is a perfectly acceptable reason not to. You don't have to talk to me—or anyone—about whatever it is you choose not to discuss. Okay? I will never press you for more than you care to share. But *can't* is simply not the case here. Do you understand? You don't have to talk to me, but you absolutely *can*."

Carly nodded, miserable. A sob pressed against the roof of her mouth. The nodding went crooked and turned back into shaking her head no.

"Hey. Hey." Emma rooted through her purse for a pack of tissues and plucked one out for Carly. The small kindness was almost too much. Carly's throat hurt from all the not-saying and not-crying that was stacking up and crowding out her breath.

Emma rubbed Carly's shoulder. She'd never touched her except for incidental bumps and brushes in the close quarters of the drawing lessons. "Listen. I'm your friend, okay? I didn't expect to be. It was a treat to find someone who I could work out my art geek on. It's been a while. You're a kid. But, you're also a terrific person. Something special."

Carly lost the fight and the tears ran down in sheets.

Emma swept a wider path over Carly's back. "Wow. Honey. Hey. Whatever it is, you can tell me. If you want to. I promise, I'll help. Okay? You don't have to worry."

"I don't . . ." Carly stopped, frustrated. The tears were bad enough. Everything wanted to spill. "I don't think I should. But something happened last night. John . . ."

"John what?" Emma's voice had gone hard.

Carly's heart jumped up in her throat. This was getting away from her. "I can't. It might be nothing. If it's nothing and I start drama . . . And if it's *not* nothing, then maybe I shouldn't say anything at all, because I don't know what will happen if I do."

"Nothing happens just because you tell me something. It can be a secret, if you need it to be. What did John do?"

"If it's bad, you might think you have to do something." Carly let her eyes fall out of focus on the white field of her sketchbook. She was so tired.

"It's all choices. You telling me or not. Or what I do about it— later today, next week, when I'm eighty. No matter what you tell me, if in fact you decide to tell me anything, I will not choose to do anything about it without discussing it with you first. Deal?"

Carly ached to talk, to let it come rushing out, to not be alone with what she wondered and worried about.

Emma took her hand away. "Carly, I want you to look at me."

Emma raked her fingers through her hair at the temples, pulling the length of it back behind her shoulders. She sat straight on across from Carly, head level, completely face-to-face. She let it stay that way—a pose, a portrait—before she spoke again.

"You have a good eye for meaning. For intent. You keep surprising me with it when we talk about this stuff." She pointed at the ever-present art books on the table. "So tell me, just from looking at me, do you believe me when I say that I know what it takes to keep a secret? Tell me if you can see that I know what it means."

Carly couldn't keep her eyes from drifting to the scars, as Emma fully intended. She'd stripped away the shyness of the moment with just the power of her voice, and Carly stared openly at the sunken trench where the point of Emma's jaw should have been. The skin stretched over the cruel worst of it in a thick, shiny twist, and the damage transitioned past a pocked, warped margin into smooth skin, into what she was everywhere else. It hadn't always been like that.

Carly nodded.

Emma nodded back. "Yeah?"

"Yeah."

"Well then, Emma is not really my name."

Carly felt a little drop, like a sudden swoop over a hill in a car.

"What is your name, then?"

"I'll tell you, if it looks like we have to do anything about John."

Emma took her hand away from her mouth.

When they'd spotted the crappy SUV under the thin canopy of trees, her hand had come up to cover her face as if she'd gasped it straight off the steering wheel. The truck was nearly hidden in the shade next to the falling-apart barn at the end of the blue line on the map in the picture.

Carly's face had marked the spot. The idea slithered like snakes. She wanted to delete the screenshot from her phone.

Emma's car limped and rolled across the rutted lot, then rocked to a stop in the lush, knee-high weeds.

The man from the foyer was in the driver's seat. A curve of green garden hose looped from around the back of the truck into the front window.

Carly had slept a good bit of the drive over, wrung out and helpless to resist the whooshing lullaby of the road under the tires. The brief nap had left her numb. She was horrified, but it felt far away, as if the caring part of her brain was still asleep. She did care, but her mind would deliver that package later.

Emma unbuckled her seat belt. "Stay here, okay?"

"Okay." It wasn't difficult. She knew what she needed to know. She'd already seen him dead once.

There wasn't much to read in Emma's (*not-Emma*) body language as she walked to the truck. She'd gone pale and quiet at the story of what had happened at the house the night before—the broken glass and wrecked stuff off the walls, the ragged-looking man who flopped as if he were boneless, John not calling the ambulance, and all of that. She'd said little since she agreed to come out and see what was at the end of the track on the app.

She stopped halfway across the field, then turned and shaded her eyes from the sun. She looked back to Carly and to the road beyond. Then Emma walked on, slowly, to the stand of trees. Carly saw her arms come up to steeple her hands over her nose and mouth when she got up beside the truck, her back settled down into a contemplative curve. She lowered her head, totally still for long enough that Carly wondered if Emma was praying. Or crying.

Emma used the hem of her shirt to pull up the garden hose and to cover the door handle when she opened the driver's-side door. She leaned in, looked, closed the door again. She tucked the hose back into the window. She walked around to the passenger side for a similar routine. She spent some time looking in the back, crawling in partway and coming out with something in her hand.

She came back, grim faced, to Carly's side of the car first and opened the glove box to put in a black gun.

"It's dangerous to leave that out here. A kid could find it," Emma said, answering the question Carly hadn't asked.

Emma started the car and turned it around in the open field.

"What happened to him?"

She steered onto the road. The engine whined high as they sped up. "He killed himself."

"Are you sure?"

Emma ran her tongue over her teeth under her pursed lips, pulling her scar tight and pale. "I'm pretty sure."

"Do we need to call the police? I mean, because they brought him out here? I mean, my mom . . ." Carly's throat collapsed on her voice.

"I don't think so. Not now. Maybe not at all. Don't worry." She looked over at Carly. "I wouldn't do that to you. Okay?"

"But what do you think we need to do?" Carly couldn't keep the hope out of her question. There was the simple kind of hope that Emma would say the whole thing should be left alone. That done is done.

But there was also the hot, silvery thread of a different type of hope that wanted this whole thing blown up for parts. Carly wanted to know what the hell was going on, to see the machine broken down, harmless and safe to examine piece by piece. She wanted to understand what it was—but without it being what it was anymore.

Emma watched the road, lost in thought and driving. "So you felt sure they thought you were okay this morning?"

"I think so."

"Can you keep it up? Acting like you're all right?"

"I think so."

Emma looked away from the road again, back to Carly.

Carly didn't feel sleepy anymore. "Yeah, I can."

Emma looked down at her gauges and back to the road. "Okay, good. I can, too. We'll both be fine as far as they know. I'll drive you home. I think I'd like to meet your stepfather."

As they rode on, Carly watched out the window as the wild green nowhere morphed into a woolly green zone dotted with islands of old, crumbling concrete. Then the balance shifted to fresher sidewalks and pavement with only strategic squares of manicured green as they rolled into the places she started to recognize.

A dark sheet of cloud that had been lurking in the distance overtook them. The rain came suddenly, in loud, uneven plonking that smoothed quickly into a solid roar against the roof and hood.

They'd been silent for some time, each deep in her own thoughts. Emma adjusted in her seat and rolled her shoulders. She turned up the speed of the windshield wipers. Then she spoke for the first time in miles. "Well, the rain will be useful. A good excuse for driving you home."

She twisted again, stretching the muscles in her back. She flexed her fingers off the wheel, one hand at a time. Getting ready.

"My name is Marcelline."

"Mom, this is Emma."

Yeah, that felt weird. Almost to the point that Carly wished Marcelline had held off telling her. Carly had asked her why she'd changed it, but she said it was a long story for another time.

"It is so nice to meet you, finally," Donna said.

Carly was worried. Her mother looked exhausted. Tired was okay as long as it didn't look guilty. Carly wanted Marcelline to believe that her mother hadn't done anything wrong. She wanted Marcelline to love her mother, which was stupid. But people were careful with what they loved.

Before shaking Donna's hand, Marcelline pointed vaguely over her shoulder in the direction of the front door and the squall beyond it. "We can thank the weather for running us out of excuses not to finally meet."

Marcelline took in the foyer in a sweeping glance, pausing on the scrape marks gouged into the drywall, where the curly metal thing had been pulled away and broken.

John rounded the corner into the foyer. In the turn, his expression erased—from a man who was mildly interested in what he'd overheard from the kitchen to a blank that Carly found difficult to believe, much less make sense of. She'd never seen him like that. She'd never seen anybody like that.

It didn't have the slackness of sleep, but every muscle under his skin was without inflection. Perfectly balanced in absence. As if he'd been unplugged.

It didn't seem to affect Marcelline. She smiled at him, but her eyes sparkled with purpose when John came into the room. Carly wished that Marcelline was better at playing as if everything were fine. It was a little too close to the line. Marcelline lit up and was not trying hard enough, by Carly's measure, to keep from letting on that she knew anything was wrong. She was being a little weird.

How could Carly be the best one at this kind of thing? She'd thought Em—*Marcelline* would have been a little bit smoother than that. The air was buzzing around her.

Marcelline started across the foyer, hand extended, jacket dripping. "You must be, *John*, is it?"

He nodded and a prefab polite expression twitched into his face. "Yep. Hi."

"It's nice to meet you. After all this time."

Donna went into hostess mode. "Emma, we were just about to open a bottle of wine. Won't you join us and wait out the rain a little?"

Marcelline looked back to Carly and her mother and answered quickly, but straight to John, "I'd love to."

Donna smiled, welcoming the distraction of something nice and normal, Carly knew. And it would seem nice and normal if Emma could just keep it together. "Great! Let me just hang up your coat."

Marcelline walked back to Donna at the coat closet and surrendered her jacket. As her mom loaded it onto a hanger, Carly looked back at her stepfather. The change in him was horrible. He was looking at Donna and Marcelline putting the jacket away as if he were watching an autopsy. He'd gone a weird color, sickly, and instantly shiny.

He was really not happy about having company.

Last night had gotten to him more than Carly had given him credit for. A hint of hope lived in that. Maybe there was an explanation for everything. Maybe it wasn't completely terrible. Look at him. He was a wreck and trying not to be. Maybe it would be okay.

They turned back to John.

Donna startled a little at the way he was watching them. Marcelline wore that same funny look, a tight little smile that she had pointed out to Carly when they'd analyzed the *Mona Lisa* together.

Marcelline looked as if she knew something everyone else didn't. Which wasn't wrong. Carly just wished again that she'd be a little bit craftier about it.

"Hey," Donna said to John. "Can you get the wine?"

"Yeah," he said, but crossed over to push the closet door all the way closed first.

The adults finished the bottle together. Carly took her homework into the dining room but got none of it done, ear tuned to the conversation playing out in the living room. Marcelline, as it went on, was fine at being fine. Pretty good at it, really. In the end, Carly was impressed, even a little proud of having a friend like her, even in the awful kind of private joke this was. But most of all, she was so relieved. Marcelline was being nice to her mom.

This was going to work. Marcelline talked and laughed. She would see what they were about so she could help Carly figure out what to do. Marcelline steered clear, so carefully casual, of anything that would give them away. She wouldn't leave her all on her own to swim or drown in it.

"Carly," her mom called after a while. "Emma's got to get going. Want to come in here and say goodnight?"

They all converged in the foyer. Smiles all around. John seemed okay again, hands in his pockets, standing in front of the coat closet, face perfectly John-like.

"Thank you so much," Marcelline said. "For the wine and for the shelter. It looks better out there."

"Of course," said Donna. "This was a nice surprise. We all needed this. Thank you for working with Carly. It's been so good for her."

Marcelline pulled her phone from her purse. "So, John, I already have Donna's number, but go ahead and give me yours just in case anything comes up. You know how it is. . . ."

Carly's body reacted to the pointed pause Marcelline left there, but it was over before she could name it.

Marcelline had a steady bead on John, who didn't look away. She said, "You never know what's next in this art business. Right, Carly?"

Their attention snapped onto her so suddenly that Carly jumped. "Right!"

John called out his number in a monotone.

"Great," Marcelline said. "I'll just send a text and then you'll have mine, too. You can put my name into your contacts." She gave her phone a solid little tap and looked back up into John's face. "It's just spelled the regular way."

John's phone chirred in his pocket. "There it is," he said, but didn't check it.

Marcelline smiled at him.

Donna reached around John to get to the closet.

"I've got it," he said.

The women were in front of the door, still in chat mode. But Carly was off to the side, in view of John rooting around in the closet. He'd gone stiff again as soon as he'd taken his hands out of his pockets, and the sick look crossed his face once his head was buried in the shadow of the closet. He was listening, a lightning rod. Donna took a step back toward him and he flinched.

He moved fast, pushing a big garment bag down the rack, and inexplicably sliding the winter coats more to the center after pulling Marcelline's jacket off the hanger. He went better than 50 percent less green as he pushed the door closed.

And as he wheeled back to them, Carly, jangling with a new and indistinct worry, feigned absorption in her fingernails. Her unease didn't answer to any specific thing, but more than she could explain, she didn't want John to catch her watching him just now.

CHAPTER TWENTY-TWO

Marcelline made it to the car before doubling over. She pretended she'd dropped her keys in case Jonathan or Donna or Carly was watching through a window. She couldn't breathe. The wine burned her stomach, which had already been scoured raw by everything else in this day.

Poor Roy. Poor Roy. The idea, the words, the lament of it, had been in a loop since back in the library when Carly described what she had seen the night before.

But worrying whether Roy was all right had been on her mind since the second time he hadn't met up with her at the gas station. She'd been concerned. A little more ill at ease as the hours went by. She knew something was wrong. She'd pushed too hard. She'd convinced him that he had to do it, that it was the right thing, the smart thing, and that he was the one to get it done.

When she'd pressured him into taking the painting from Jonathan, she never stepped past the idea that Roy owed her. He did, it was true. But it wasn't all that was true about this.

She'd known him for about two hours in the diner, and also for less than one minute, years ago, in an alley while he shot her. He'd been easy to read both times. And he'd been easy to read again, beyond all hope, this afternoon in his truck.

The pain of his life was just a fact of his face. He'd never had anywhere to hide it. Not even in death. Roy had only ever had one expression—the fear of high tide, always in up to his neck, stretching for air.

When all of his troubles were over, even that didn't give him the dignity of his face back. In the two hours and one minute she'd known him, she never saw what he should've looked like.

His mouth had been frozen open in the truck. As if he were wailing. And he was still out there now, a ruin-faced stone until someone found him or until nature forced him loose, then took him apart.

She settled in behind the wheel, hoping the darkness gave cover to her crumbling composure if anyone was watching.

Jonathan wouldn't be watching, though, the bastard. He wouldn't risk it, no matter how much he might want to or even need to. He wouldn't get caught looking out the window to see that she was gone.

Whatever passed for peace of mind to him was impossible to imagine. Her sitting in his living room must have pressed on every fear he'd earned. But he'd kept his balance with barely a flicker of concern. He was a high-wire artist. She would give him that.

She backed out from the driveway, nearly all of her concentration bent on getting to the road. In a normal evening, it would be automatic. Avoiding mailboxes and trash cans was easy when she wasn't losing her mind. But it took all she had just to focus on lining up the car between the curb and the middle of the road, keeping the margins steady on both sides while she drove away.

She made it a few blocks up the hill before she had to pull over. Her head was pounding, her mouth watering. She veered to the right and stopped in front of someone's house, jarring the tire against the curb and grinding it along the concrete as she straightened the wheel. She rammed the gear selector into park and let her head fall back against the rest, eyes closed, one loose fist resting against her lips, willing herself not to be sick.

It didn't hold.

Marcelline flung the door open and lost her wine all over the pavement. The retching made her eyes water, and once they started tears, they didn't stop. She leaned over the steering wheel and sobbed.

Roy had been teetering on the ledge for a long while. None of that was her fault. He may never have pulled himself away from the drop. But it wouldn't have been yesterday, and it wouldn't have been like that.

If she hadn't sent him to Jonathan's house alone . . . If she hadn't told him about the painting . . . Hell, if she'd never let him see her at all . . .

Any of it might have been too much for him. All of it was nearly a guarantee. She should have seen that. She did see it. But he owed her.

Poor Roy.

The regret of it surged in quick cycles of calming down followed by a fresh fall of tears.

In one of the deep, shuddery breaths, the absurdity of it lit up in her like a candle—she was crying over the man who shot her. The ridiculous light of it grew. Priceless. Pathetic. With survival instincts like that, maybe it was always going to end in tears and spewed wine for her.

He shot her. He ruined her face. He nearly killed her.

But that Roy had done it, and that she had been there to have it done to her in the first place, shared a common denominator. Something had brought Roy Dorring and Marcelline Gossard together, in a failure of free will to be sure, but both by the same guide.

Although both she and Roy had been weak in the important moments, distracted by the hope and sparkle of their different wants, Jonathan had set it up, then held her arms away from her throat as she almost bled to death.

If Carly was right, and Roy had already been dead before they dumped him in the ass end of nowhere, that piece of shit had watched over Roy dying, too.

She had to move Roy's gun to get a handful of napkins from the glove box. The cool weight of the metal left her fingers tingling. It had been years since she'd been to a firing range, and she never much liked the feel of a pistol anyway. She wiped her eyes and mouth.

She put the car in gear and drove back and parked along the curb next to a shrub-topped retaining wall that faced off with Jonathan's house. A silhouette moved back and forth behind the sheer curtains of the office at the front of the house.

Marcelline took out her phone.

We need to talk. You need to come up with a reason to leave. I'm across the street.

The silhouette behind the curtain stopped walking.

Can't do it. Not tonight.

Find a way. Or I will be a problem. Do you think Donna can take another night of nasty surprises?

There was a long pause.

Give me a minute.

I'll give you five.

I'm going to have to take the car. I can't just go out walking. She won't believe that.

Whatever. I'm up the block across the street. By the wall. Light brown Toyota. Park behind me.

He was almost ten minutes in getting there.

She sent a message she'd put together while she was waiting.

Turn off the car. Throw the keys out of your window. Leave your seat belt on. I'm coming to you. I have a gun because I don't trust you. That's all. Not looking to use it.

He didn't reply right away, and Marcelline was typing a new message when the response finally came.

I'm out.

That's a mistake. You might just have to be okay with not controlling everything for once. I'm not stupid. I don't want attention any more than you do. But if you leave now, anything goes. What have I got to lose?

He waited.

He would be thinking of a way to make this his own. She didn't have any choice but to let him try.

The headlights went out behind her. The engine died. She heard the musical clatter of keys on the sidewalk.

The rest of it she'd have to take as it came.

The fear blended into the purposeful revving of the blood in her veins. She needed the painting, but this is what she'd wanted. The manic edge was effervescent, a dangerous flavor of wonderful. And all of it couldn't entirely erase the ridiculous part. The gun felt outlandish.

Where ludicrous meets necessity, in all likelihood, what's happening shouldn't be. She thought of Samantha in a pang of apology. She would seriously hate this. *I'm sorry.*

And still Marcelline was out of her car and rounding to the passenger side of Jonathan's. She held Roy's pistol against her thigh to camouflage it as best she could in the suburban semidarkness.

Jonathan noted the gun as she got in, but didn't say anything.

A moment of nearly blissful neutrality shimmered between them. Not "John" and "Emma" because those people didn't exist. They were liars. Jonathan and Marcelline, here together now, were rather past the need for all that. She would have back the day she met him for anything. But that was impossible. Here they were. Her shoulders relaxed in the only seconds of freedom she'd had in four years. No need to pretend anything. No need to guard against discovery.

He was the fulcrum of her entire life. She would hate him again in a second or two. That inevitability was bearing down on her like a train. But the span of a few drumming heartbeats protected a moment of pure recognition. Like a disaster or a disease, he had changed everything.

She would change it back.

"Holy hell," Jonathan said. But not about the gun. The comment seemed general—an inadequate caption for all she'd just been thinking.

She didn't have a reply for it. But the hate came back in a rush that wasn't hot or cold or blinding or pounding. It was just the next irresistible thing. The next breath, the next blink, the itch on her cheek. She flicked her fingernails over the spot to scratch it.

"Why didn't you tell me?" he said. "Why didn't you come to me when you found out where I was? Why didn't you let me know you're alive?"

She cocked her head as she would if she were confused, which she wasn't. "I did."

"Not like that. I don't mean tonight. I don't mean showing up at my house with no warning and giving me a heart attack."

"How would you like me to have done it? Please, tell me. I'll take notes for the next time."

He drew a breath that suggested patience with her pain and pique. The gun warmed in her hand, reminding itself to her, as if it hated him, too.

He sighed. "When you showed up in front of my family like that, I didn't get any chance to tell you how glad I am that you're okay. I would have. You didn't give me that chance."

"Well, I didn't get the chance to say, 'Fuck you, Jonathan.' We were both having to be so careful earlier, both of us just busting with so many things we wanted to say. But nothing's stopping us now. So, fuck you, Jonathan."

"I don't know what to say. I don't know what you *want* me to say. You're alive. You made it through. This is incredible."

"That's certainly a word for it."

"There's no way I could have known," he said, oozing warm reason. "You know that. You don't know how glad I am that you're okay. You don't know how it's been for me all this time."

She breathed down into her middle and swallowed a scream. She imagined it was the feeling of a cat retracting its claws. "I'm almost afraid to ask how stupid you think I am."

"Marcelline, look. I was devastated over what—"

She moved her gun hand into her lap. "We're not going to get a lot of mileage out of this treadmill. I mean, you can say it again if you want, but it's starting to piss me off."

"Well, what do you want me to say?" He went quiet, surrendered in both voice and posture for her to lead the way.

She didn't buy it for a second. It was a game for him. He'd use whatever she indicated she wanted for his own ends. He was well practiced in it. She was not.

So she kept it simple. "First, I want you to tell me what you think you ought to do to make this better? I just want to know."

"Does Carly know who you are?"

"You mean, does Carly know who *you* are?" Marcelline had forgotten the ring of a purely mocking laugh. "No. She has no idea." She left it at that, though the desperate desire to say more vibrated in her teeth.

Jonathan stared out his window, all but turning his back on Marcelline for long enough that it was getting awkward.

"We can still sell the painting," he finally said.

The sentence and the sentiment were easy enough to understand, but somehow it jammed her signals. She couldn't move. It was something in the way he'd pronounced *we*. The inflection he gave it. He was about to say something terrible.

Marcelline relaxed her grip on the pistol, opened her fingers a little without being obvious about it, she hoped. She was buying an instant for her rational mind—giving it a head start on the reaction she could feel was on its way.

He looked back at her lack of response. "What? We can. Why wouldn't we? There's no reason we can't pick up right where we left off. In some ways, nothing's changed. We're in the same position we were four years ago."

He didn't say it. He couldn't have. He had. Every loss she'd broken over and every hour of pain she'd endured rushed into her wrist. The hatred crowded down into her knuckles, forcing them to bend around the pistol's grip.

His gaze drifted to the right side of her face, lit by the streetlight across the road. She'd never not known, in four years, where the light was in a room and how it was hitting or hiding her scars. That ache flared into her trigger finger.

A horrible sympathy mask took over Jonathan's face. "I know that must be hard to hear in some ways, but if you just—"

"Stop. Talking."

The gun was up and pointed at his middle, and although Marcelline hadn't felt her hand move, the sense of being ridiculous was gone.

"Okay," he said mildly.

"This is simple, actually. We don't need to have a conversation. In fact, it's better for everyone if you don't say anything else. Give me the painting."

He just looked at her.

"No, really. It's that easy. Give it to me and I'll go away and you can keep on making whatever it is that you're making here, which I have to imagine is some shitty new scheme that will leave any number of people dying in your arms."

He put his hands up in something between a surrender and a shrug. "Can I talk?"

"If you think you understand where we are in this, go ahead."

"I understand why you're so angry. I get it. You hate me. You hate what all of this has done to your life. And you can believe me or not, but I never intended for you to get hurt."

"Oh? What *did* you intend for me, then?"

A weariness dragged down over him. A deflation. But he refilled just as fast with resentment. A circuit of sinking down and rising up against his seat belt. He was tired and angry. Very. And Marcelline was suddenly keen to get out of the car.

But it was too late to be anything but bold. She leaned in. "So that takes care of all the old business. I'll go get in my car. I'll follow you down the hill. You go in, bring me the painting, drink half a bottle of whatever it is you drink, nurse your hangover tomorrow, and get on with your life. Easy."

"No."

She replied only with an expectant look.

Jonathan pitched toward her, snarling. "I fucking said no! Are you stupid or something?"

Marcelline almost pulled the trigger in reflex. But his yelling broke it loose in her, too. "You son of a bitch, I will call the police and tell them where they can find you. And where they can find Roy's body."

He hadn't been expecting that, but Jonathan recovered his expression so quickly that she almost doubted herself that she'd rattled him at all.

"Roy killed himself."

"That may well be. And when they get that all sorted out, I'm sure they will let you go. In the meantime, though, the FBI will find out where they can get their hands on *Landscape with Obelisk*."

Smarmy and angry were no surprise to her, but Jonathan's going amused made the breath catch in her throat.

"And that buys you what, exactly? Honestly, what does any of this? Sure, if you pull some stunt like that, I don't have the painting, but neither do you. But you know what I do have? Even if they cart me off? You—all over my security system.

"And right before I came out here to answer your hissy fit, I cut some nice clear clips together and set them in a timed email to a couple of people who will get it to the FBI if I don't cancel it.

"So you can shoot me, maybe kill me, or get the painting back to the museum. Or shoot me *and* get the painting back to the museum, if you like, but you'll get pulled right into it either way.

"You can run." He looked her over. "You've obviously done a good bit of that. But after a break in the Gardner heist? After all this time? After what we did to the Anningers? And you a missing person, a seriously scarred hottie on the loose? Nah. I don't think you know the meaning of the term *lying low* yet."

Marcelline's tongue felt paralyzed.

He sucked in a big loud breath. "Well, this has been something, but I have to get back. The email, you know, and all the ticktock ticktock."

He moved his hand across his lap, and the zip and clatter of his seat belt sliding up into its slot startled her. He opened his door. She might as well have been pointing her finger at him. The gun meant nothing.

Jonathan turned and straightened out of the car, then ducked his head back under the roofline to look at her as if she were an idiot. "Get the fuck out."

She switched the gun to her left hand to fumble for the door latch, minding that her fingers stayed outside the trigger guard of the stupid thing. Useless. Mortifying.

They faced off across the roof of his car.

He shook his head in disappointment. "I just want to point out that I offered to bring you back into this. I didn't have to do that. I tried to do right by you. Because of what happened. I want you to remember that. This isn't on me."

She couldn't think of a single thing to say.

"Go away, Marcelline. And leave Carly alone."

Jonathan got back in his car and keyed the engine to life. He rolled down the passenger window.

"Or don't. You know as well as I do that, in the end, I really don't care."

• • •

Marcelline drove in circles all night. She nearly drove her tank dry and filled it up again as the dark sky drifted into Saturday's dawn. She caught her reflection in the window as she fought the gas cap with fatigue-numb fingers. The yellow light of the station's canopy lit up the window and turned it into a mirror, and she wished it hadn't. Jonathan was right. She looked haggard. Desperate. A little insane.

I shouldn't be here.

It kept coming to her. Bitterly too late now. It felt true. It felt like the reason for every bad fact of her life, all the way back to the memory of the dirty-metal smell of the blood-soaked asphalt under her head.

I shouldn't be here.

She was down almost a quarter of a tank already by the full swell of daybreak. It seemed wrong that everything was this bright and dewy. As if everything were better than fine.

She'd crossed the town line at every compass point in the night, and the longing to just keep going crested to nearly unbearable every time she did.

She was so tired that her thoughts slipped into almost dreamlike snippets of her old life—her forehead against her cat's gray fur; the clink of champagne flutes after a big sale; shampoo in her short hair; her sister's hands shuffling a deck of cards on poker night; a New Year's party at the gallery; her corner of the electronic world pinging with messages from people she knew, from people who knew her . . .

A shriek of car horns snapped her focus onto the road. She'd drifted far out of her lane into the next turn. She was jangling awake now, trembling. She took the exit and pulled into the parking lot of a church. She called Samantha.

The phone rang and rang. Emma kneaded her bottom lip between her teeth, her throat working to hold down the cry that wanted out.

The line clicked. "M?"

She lost the fight with her voice and all she could do was cry.

"M? Are you okay? Are you hurt?"

Her hitching would barely let the words past. "No. Not hurt. I'm okay."

Samantha blew out a relieved breath into the phone. "Okay. Okay. What's going on?"

Marcelline sobbed into her hand to keep from howling over the connection.

Samantha's voice was gentle. "What happened?"

"It's not going to work." She saw Roy's face in her mind and stifled another wail. *I shouldn't be here.* "I can't do anything. And Roy's dead because of me. It's over."

"Nothing's over. This didn't work out. Come on back. We'll find another way."

Marcelline's phone doubled-beeped. An incoming text. She pulled the phone away to look. It was from Carly.

Are you there?

Marcelline typed as Samantha kept talking, her voice distant, calling to her. "Emma?"

Marcelline texted back to Carly, *Yes. Everything okay?*

I don't know. Another message came up immediately. *No I think maybe not.*

"Samantha, I have to go."

"No!"

"I'll call you back. I promise."

"Em, please, don't hang—"

"I'll call you back!"

She pressed the call dead and texted Carly, *Call me?*

Nothing. Marcelline wanted to move, to pace, to crawl out of her skin. As she started to text again, the phone rang.

"What's wrong?"

"John's acting really weird," Carly spoke fast, breathless. "Did you think he was kinda bizarre last night?" She didn't wait for an answer. "And it sounds stupid, but I thought he was kind of hiding his face in the coat closet. I thought he didn't want you and Mom to see how worried he was. It was sort of like that. But not *really* like that. He was moving stuff around, and it was weird."

"What are you talking about, honey?"

"But then I heard him in the closet again this morning, and he was moving stuff again, and I wondered if maybe he'd put something in there. Like hidden something. Like maybe he had something from that guy who died. Like maybe he's actually bad. Do you think John might be bad? I wanted to ask my mom, but she was with him that night. But she didn't do anything. Marcelline, I swear she wouldn't. I don't want her to be in trouble. . . . I just didn't know who to call. But you'll help my mom? Right?"

Marcelline held her breath, the air washed in ozone like the smell that was almost a flavor before a sudden, violent storm. "Yes. You did right. I'm glad you called. It's okay. What's going on?"

"So John had to go out this morning, right? And I waited and then I went through the closet. There was nothing there. I mean just usual stuff. Except he'd hidden that painting that used to be hanging in the front hallway. It's so weird. My mom thought he got rid of it. He got rid of everything. But not the picture. It's zipped up in a bag with his dress suit. That's not normally in the closet either. I saw it last night hanging up when he was in there. But today he moved it to the floor and covered it up with a blanket and stuff."

The runaway monster of Carly's teenaged imagination was pieced together from what she'd seen and heard. It had been jolted alive by the electricity crackling between all the adults in her life. And it was so close to the truth.

All the lies and omissions, a death, the manipulations—Jonathan's and Marcelline's, too—everything they had pretended to be to Carly, and in the end it didn't look that much different from the real story. After all their best efforts, Carly could still plausibly worry that John had killed Roy for something he'd had to hide in the family coat closet.

Marcelline managed to speak past an entirely dry tongue. "It's in the closet? Where my jacket was?"

"No," Carly said. "I took it."

CHAPTER TWENTY-THREE

Nobody said anything about his impromptu late grocery run after "Emma" had left. Donna and Carly ate the ice cream he bought after dismissing Marcelline, though he'd blindly grabbed a brand they never ate. The conversation fell thin and strained as the strangeness of the past days seeped back into the foreground of everyone's thoughts. Carly disappeared into her room. Donna wouldn't look at him and went up to take a bath. She was asleep, curled tight against the farthest edge of the mattress by the time he came to bed. It was a long night.

Jonathan gave up trying to sleep once the sky lightened from black to gray. He waited until seven to text Owen. *Do you want it or not?*

After half an hour, he had to send another message or throw the phone against the wall. *Going once . . . Going twice . . .*

Owen let that hang in the air for another ten minutes before he called. "Are we in a hurry?"

Jonathan had expected him to be like this, straightaway pissing a perimeter around the exchange. But the urge to throw the phone didn't lessen. "I'm not having any more conversations about this. It's a simple yes or no question."

"You think this is simple?"

Jonathan thought he heard something like the clink of silverware, a muted whir, maybe cars going past where Owen was. Outdoor café? He wished he knew more about exactly where that might be.

Jonathan wanted this too much. He wanted to be out of limbo, wanted it right up to treading on the line of wishing he'd never seen the painting at all. But nearly just as much as everything else, he wanted to be done dealing with Owen. Jonathan wasn't good around him. It was embarrassing. Owen made his hands go clammy.

He wiped them, each in quick turn, on his jeans. The aggressive silence routine was getting old. "Okay. Tell the Anningers I'm sorry it didn't work—"

"Yes."

"Yes what?"

"Yes, they want it."

"Were you going to let me know that at some point?"

"Of course."

"When?"

"When I got around to it." Owen was maddeningly mild. "You realize I exist between our conversations and do other things some-times, right?"

Jonathan pinched the bridge of his nose and willed himself to get through this phone call without losing it.

Owen continued. "So, yes. They want it and they've made the arrangements. Same type of setup as before—some cash up front, then a wire transfer after authentication. Although I still have a problem with calling it simple."

Jonathan hoped Owen took everything in this world that he had a problem with and shoved it up his ass, but didn't say so. His pulse sped up. "Great. How much?"

"Five million. So, minus the two hundred and fifty thousand you took four years ago, four point seven five."

"That's bullshit. It was seven and a half before."

"Well, Jonathan, what can I say? Your urgency is their coupon."

"What's your cut?"

"I don't get *cuts*. Stop trying to get in my shorts."

"I just . . . Nah, that's not enough. Go tell them it's too low."

Owen sighed. "I'm going to give you a second to play that back in your head."

"Goddammit, you know I meant pretty please with sugar on top. You have to know this isn't fair."

"I do? I don't think so. I don't care about this silly little decoration, remember? Are you really going to piss your diaper over having to settle for five million dollars for something that isn't yours?"

Everything that Jonathan had ever gotten wrong tallied to that sum. The shame of it was in all the moments lost to laziness and distraction. In his lack of stamina. In getting too comfortable. He hadn't applied himself as well as he could have. And he could only hate Owen for paying attention enough to make the point.

It could be worse. He could be in prison. At least there was that. So he let the jab go unanswered.

"What's next, then? When can we do this?"

There was a smile in Owen's voice. "Ah, great. Back to the beginning of the carousel ride. So, once again, are we in a hurry?"

"I'd just as soon get it over with." *Especially if I'm being screwed to the tune of two and a half million dollars.* But he didn't say that part. He swallowed the pout. It was a small triumph, a warm touchstone of who he was, a reminder that he'd gotten far on being careful with words and tone.

"We can do it today, if you like," Owen said.

"Well, I'd need to have enough time to go get it."

"Lucky us. My schedule is wide-open. So whenever suits you, suits me fine."

"Where do you want to meet? The same place as before?"

"I don't care where we do it. You can handle that, if it worries you. Tell me when and where. I'll be there."

Jonathan didn't like that. He set the meeting for twelve thirty in the same restaurant they'd met before. It would be busy and anonymously so. It felt solid.

Owen hadn't suggested any adjustments to what Jonathan proposed. That was either because the transaction was going to be all the way straightforward, or that Jonathan had missed something. He knew, on a cellular level, that despite all of Owen's protestations of not caring about the painting and the double cross, he cared about something in this, and in some way that was bad news for Jonathan.

So he made coffee and got comfortable in his desk chair. Jonathan threw a saddle on that paranoid feeling and let it take him where it might.

The restaurant wouldn't be a place for trouble. Too many people with cell phones. Too many security cameras. And all of it too buried in a shopping plaza on a Saturday to get out quickly.

Although Owen was certainly built for it, Jonathan didn't figure him for a blaze-of-glory kind of guy. The Mercedes gave him away. Something in him liked living. No full-on nihilist kept his car that clean.

So it—if there was any *it* coming—would be before or after. It was the same problem, both ways. He was in real trouble if Owen followed him. The only thing Jonathan had after he turned over the painting was Owen's ill will.

Buying him off seemed unlikely. Owen was very proud that he had all he needed. Even if Jonathan offered him every bit of what the Anningers were going to pay, it wouldn't interest Owen Haig. And if Jonathan was going to do that, he might as well have given it to Marcell—

Jonathan grabbed up his phone. *Did you really know she wasn't dead?*

His phone lit up immediately. He let it go four rings in before answering.

"Oh, Jonathan, what are you playing at? Things were going so well."

"You know, I'm not sure they were. I didn't have what you might call a strong sense of security in our arrangement. Not like I would've hoped."

"That hurts my feelings."

"I'm sure. But seriously, did you know she was alive? Because I didn't."

"I can only advise you to get to the point."

"Something weird happened last night."

"As I was saying . . ." Owen's words were still clipped and cool, but the strain was coming through in a slightly strangled grip in his voice.

"She showed up at my house last night. None too pleased, but playing it ice-cold. I had to keep a straight face in front of my wife and stepdaughter, because as far as I knew, she was long since in the ground. I almost had a heart attack."

Owen said nothing.

"Hello? Really? She was bleeding like crazy. Pouring. From her neck. How could I know she made it?"

Owen's breathing was now coming through the handset with little huffing breaks forced in at the pace of hard footfalls. Owen was walking somewhere, and fast. He still managed an exasperated sigh.

Jonathan reworked the basic math of what had happened that night. "So you did know. You've known the whole time that Marcelline is alive."

Owen regained his breath and his regular voice. "Where is she?"

Jonathan heard Owen's car start in a walled roar, the engine noise ringing off cement. The car door slammed. A parking garage.

"So here's the thing," said Jonathan. "You and I have a meeting at twelve thirty. I don't want it to take beyond twelve forty. By twelve forty-five I will be hard at work on getting far away from here. As soon as everything is authenticated and I get the rest of my money, I will put you and Marcelline in touch."

"You'll put us in touch?"

"Sure. It seemed important to you. And what are friends for?"

"And why do I believe this? Why do I not just show up at your house and convince you—however that needs to happen—to tell me everything now?"

"You believe it. I can hear that you do. And you can hear me. You believe me because it's true. This is the only thing I have to get on your good side. And I'm not going to lie, I'm glad there's something I can use. You have to know I wouldn't risk it by getting tricky with you now. But all of it hangs on the fact that I haven't told her you're here. Which I could still do. And if I do tell her, I'm thinking she'll bolt. Seems like you might not want that. It's simple, but fragile."

"You and your simple."

"See you at twelve thirty." Jonathan hung up and grabbed his keys.

Jonathan didn't entirely trust Owen not to show up anyway. In his worry version of the day, where Owen wanted the painting without paying, Jonathan had said he needed time to go get it. If he was being watched, he could go somewhere anyway, miming the misdirection. It would be the best time to discover whether he was being followed.

Freedom was just on the other side of lunchtime. But the painting was still his problem for a few more hours.

He listened for Donna and Carly, but the house was sleeping-in quiet.

He took the bag with the tuxedo-padded painting out of the closet and put it into the trunk of his car. It felt wrong. The back seat seemed safer, but either way, it felt as if he was inviting the most ironic car crash ever. And it would leave him more vulnerable than even that.

If his fantasy of Owen bearing down on him before the meetup was more than just paranoia, Jonathan's not having the painting with him in a bad spot might be the only thing that let him live long enough to make one more plan.

So he put it back in the closet. But this time he folded the bag over in a loose roll and tucked it off to the side on the floor. He admired his handiwork and slid it under the two folded picnic blankets. That looked better. But he leaned the rolls of birthday wrap up against it as more camouflage, anyway.

Carly startled him in the kitchen when he went in to put his coffee mug in the sink, one of his rituals of leaving—everything set in its place. In the back of his mind, it was for the last time. He wouldn't pass through this room again.

He hadn't known Carly was already downstairs, but the surprise was in how glad he was that she was there. He flattened his hand against the cool stone of the countertop and ran it back and forth, feeling it to remember it and let it go.

"Hey, Carlzee."

"Hey."

She was looking at him funny. Again. This is how he would remember her. And, of course, this is how she'd remember him. Everything that had made her look at him like this in the last few weeks would become part of the mythology of *when John disappeared*.

If all went well, they would never know why he'd gone. Donna wouldn't be able to say much after what they'd done with Roy's body. Jonathan would never know how often they wondered about him, or how quickly they might move on.

When Donna had said she was in love, he liked her enough to play along. But it had been more than that. There was no reason not to admit that. The longer he was here, the more he'd wanted to be here. The illusion held together with attention, so he gave it attention. It felt secure and a little bit real. Eventually, the second possible avenue had come into view—sell the painting and stay. Why not? The choice was his. Except that it wasn't.

The choice, it turned out, didn't have anything to do with anyone in either version of his plan. And it was made in the open, caught on video for all the world—and Owen and Marcelline—to see. It was the decision of a rotten, twisted kid whose compulsions drove him right over the wants and needs of anyone who fell into his sights.

Jonathan shoved back on the urge to think of the people who might say the same of him. Truth was a composite.

He wanted to leave it with Carly on a better note, in case he didn't see her when he came back for the painting. He wanted to be friendly, as they'd always been with each other. "Kinda thought you might sleep in. You must be so tired. It's been a hell of a few days, huh?"

"Yeah."

"You've got to take care of yourself, you know."

"I know." She didn't look up from her cereal bowl.

"Hey. Don't let all this stuff get to you. Don't let it do anything to you. The world doesn't make you. You make yourself."

She nodded. "Out of what?"

"Out of what you want."

"That's what you do?"

"Yeah."

She seemed to agree with the counter, since that's where the nods were going.

"You okay?" he asked.

"I'm okay." She looked up at him tentatively, worried and so un-Carly-like that it felt like a punch. "Are *you* okay?"

The words felt bigger than the passage up his throat. "Yeah, sure."

They both had the same lie, that they were okay. So to keep their own, they had to let the other's lie go unchallenged.

"Are you going out?" Carly ticked her chin in the direction of the keys still in his hand.

"Yeah. Just for a little bit. Need a ride somewhere?" The hope for a yes from her was a sparkly, pricking thing. Something was getting lost in this goodbye. It felt important.

"No. But thanks, though. I'm not going anywhere."

On Jonathan's drive, his copilot was a relentless wariness. Watching the cars behind him and assigning intent to their distances from him, their turns and lane changes, all while not ramming into the cars ahead of him, it was a water-torture drip of adrenaline. He was glad he'd left the painting in the closet.

But the security system was killing him. The outside cameras alerted to two separate dogs, each with a person in tow, then two dogs trotting along together with no person at all for some reason, and some asshole on what appeared to be her first outing on in-line skates, wearing a groove into the sidewalk, up and down the street on her wobbly training mission.

He had to check all of this while driving with way too much purpose and hard braking. The whole thing on far too little sleep was a trick almost beyond his reach.

His skin stung every time the phone buzzed an alert. He thought of the painting. Owen. Marcelline. Sweat had his shirt sticking to his back. Maybe he should have brought the fucking thing with him.

When the foyer camera alerted, his relief had a certain logic. For all of Owen's aura of getting shit done, Jonathan was fairly sure he couldn't teleport.

Owen hadn't driven up or walked over to the house or Jonathan would have known. It was just Carly.

Just Carly was very nearly the last thing he ever thought.

The camera showed Carly in the coat closet. And then again, still in the coat closet. And in the coat closet with some of the stuff pushed out behind her. Rolls of wrapping paper were among the flotsam in the images sent to Jonathan's phone.

Interior 1's last alert in the spasm of notifications showed Carly at the front door with the garment bag.

The outside cameras showed her getting smaller, with her arms full, heading up the street.

Oh, God. Something broke in him.

"Carly, you need to pick up the phone. What are you doing?"

Jonathan had called twice and let the second one go all the way to voice mail. Her greeting had never been personalized from the phone company's default message. Voice mail wasn't a thing for her crowd.

He had to get off the road. He flinched for the brake at the first turn-in but couldn't bring himself to drive into the McDonald's parking lot where he'd met Roy so many times before.

Three blocks down had an office park with no such connotations for him. He parked and texted her. *You need to pick up the phone.*

He dialed. She didn't. *What are you doing? I am not kidding. Pick up. Now.*

He felt his lips grinding into a snarl as the ringtone pulsed in his ear. The call rang back through to the generic voice mail. *You will be very sorry if I have to call back after this. Pick up. Right now.*

Carly answered then, but didn't say anything.

"Carly, what are you doing? What is going on?"

The breeze, wherever she was with the painting, was all the answer he got.

"Goddammit, answer me. Where are you? What are you doing?"

The wind sound was eclipsed by Carly's shuddery breathing. Her voice, when it finally came, was just above a whisper. "Why is this a big deal?"

There is a line of what is just too much. Jonathan had felt it waiting out there all his life. There was a seam in the universe that held what you could handle right up next to the vast expanse of all that you could not. It was the line that separated getting by from the thing that would change you into something that no one else would recognize.

He imagined that every person could sense when that line was close—for themselves and also for the people they were about to shove over the boundary.

"Carly, you're on your way back home. You need to just say that you are and then turn around and make it true. I'm also on my way back. And you'd better beat me there. Do not stop anywhere. Do you understand me?"

He heard a fumbling rustle and then nothing. "Carly?"

She was gone.

"Hi!" Jonathan was bright and pleasant, but careful not to be too much of either when Ada's mother answered the door.

"Hi!" She tried to match his tone over the obvious question in her eyes of what he was doing there.

His racing heart sank. "I was just swinging by to get Carly."

"Oh? I'm confused. She's not here. Did she say that she was coming over? Ada's out with her dad this morning."

He felt the line again, sliding just barely under his toes. His expression blanked. He couldn't stop it although he knew the effect was startling to people. Jonathan turned and walked away before he made it any worse. "My mistake," he called over his shoulder.

· · ·

Walking into the house again, the feeling of last chance clung to him as if it had been a web spun across the doorframe. He didn't know what it would take to get this back under his control, but it felt very much as if it had to happen here.

Donna's face would tell him a lot.

She was at the dining room table on her computer. She looked up as he walked in. "Hi." She looked tired, stressed, lovely, and not at all on high alert.

"Hi." His chest ached. "Carly here?"

"No. I mean, I don't think so. Honestly, I thought she was with you. Everyone disappears and no one leaves me a note. Real nice family I've got here."

His thoughts were that dream-running-in-deep-sand kind of slow. She pulled back in her seat to see him better. "What's wrong?"

"I need you to call Carly for me. I need you to find out where she is."

"Why? What's going on? Is everything okay?"

"Yes and no. No. I mean, Carly is physically okay. She's been under a lot of stress lately. Obviously, we all have. But she's in a little bit of trouble. She took something that doesn't belong to her."

"Carly *stole* something? What? Like shoplifting? What the hell are you talking about?"

"Can you just call her please?" He nodded at her phone beside her computer. "Let's just give her a chance to make this right. I don't want to say too much."

Donna's own line of too far was coming for her. John knew she'd outpaced disaster by five steps, always. Her whole life, she'd been faster and stronger than anything that had pursued her. Her competence had been both a shield and a weapon. But since meeting him, more—way more—had been rolling toward her that she hadn't known to outrun.

Jonathan rubbed her arm as she called Carly. "Let's just find her and hear what she has to say."

"She's not answering," Donna said, worried and shaking her head. Jonathan thought his teeth might break from grinding.

"Let me just see where she is." Donna took her reading glasses from the table and swiped and tapped at the screen of her phone.

"You can see where she is?"

Donna waved him off, ignoring his question. She tilted her head at what she was looking at. He swiveled around to see it with her. A map. Carly's face in a circle above a blue arrow on the loose grid of streets.

"She's over by the library," Donna said.

She looked at him. He saw her, but all of his vision had become peripheral as his sight turned inward, watching, seeing how this had arranged itself. He grabbed the back of the closest chair at the table and squeezed until the edge of the wood bit painfully into the pads of his fingers.

They got to the same answer at the same time.

"Was she meeting up with Emma?" Donna asked. "Did she mention that to you?"

"Fuck!" he screamed, and pulled the chair to slam down into the floor. "No!"

Donna had gone white and rigid. He breathed deep and smiled, but it landed like a slap and she recoiled from him.

"It's okay. It'll be okay." He took her phone. "Let me take this. I'll go get her."

CHAPTER TWENTY-FOUR

Carly knew the word *impulse* mostly as a concept, but also as a vocab word in English. It had only been a short time that she'd thought of it as anything self-descriptive. She was the good one, the one who used her head. She was careful. She was courteous, which was only another kind of careful. She was the kid who still asked permission for sweet snacks at home, the one who always said please.

No one ever used the word *impulse* and meant it as a good thing. What was accomplished impulsively was a cautionary tale. Bad. Sometimes ruinous.

But to Carly, the idea of it had gotten hooked to the *pulse* syllable of the word. Im*pulse*. A lurch of the heart that set something off like a starting gun. The thing was, starting guns were never aimed and they weren't guides. Just bang and you're off, and therein seemed to lie the problem.

When she'd seen the video of the *thing*, the one element she could solidly match up to the unclear memory was the pounding of her heart and the way it had somersaulted in her chest just before she'd flipped the whole scene to her advantage. She did remember the leap of *NO!* under her sternum, and the yank of the impulse that had spurred her to do what she did. And it had worked.

After that one moment, all-head Carly, Miss Please and Thank You of the Twenty-First Century, wondered if impulses were always bad, if they always led to trouble. Now she had precedent.

She was shocked by all she hadn't talked herself out of lately.

She'd been basically spying on everyone she knew since the day after the *thing*—rummaging around in their voices, rifling through the words they chose, pickpocketing all they hadn't said out loud. Both thrilled and a little ashamed by it, it was automatic now to ransack people's postures and expressions to steal what they didn't want you to know. She'd taken it all the way to really spying: tracking, lying, scheming, stealing. And today. This morning. It was hard to think past the panicked *wow*.

Standing in the library, she'd been trembling so hard she'd had to clamp down on the shakes to scroll through her contacts to find Marcelline's number after having impulsively hung up on her stepfather.

At least Marcelline wasn't laughing at her. She wasn't acting as if Carly were stupid. She was taking it seriously. She would help.

"I took it."

Carly heard Marcelline make a little sound. An "Oh"-like gasp knocked out of her, instead of sucked in.

Carly didn't want to be in trouble with Marcelline. Defense came tumbling out. "I know! It's crazy. I'm sorry. But I wanted to show it to you anyway. I mean, before. I was just going to take a picture of it, but Mom said he got rid of it. And it's weird that he made such a big deal out of hiding it. Isn't it? I thought it was really weird. So I took it. Do you want to see it? But it can't be about that dead guy? There's no way, right? Can it?"

"Carly, where are you?"

"At the library. The bad thing, though, is John's superpissed that I took it. I don't think it's about the suit."

"He knows you have it?"

"Yeah, he saw me on the camera. He's really mad. I'm kind of scared."

"How long have you been in the library?"

"I just got here."

"Honey, you can't stay there."

A spike of ready-to-run bolted through Carly, but also a blaring *Why?* zipped up her spine. She'd come by herself, but now she felt truly alone. "Can you come get me?"

"I'm on my way. But I don't want you to stay there."

"Should I go wait at the school?"

"No. It's Saturday. You won't be able to get inside. You'll be out in the open. He'll probably look for you at Ada's house and the library, but then maybe the school."

"I could walk to the Y?"

"It's too far. Okay, I know. Go to the back of the library, by the other parking lot. Cross over to the gas station. Go into the ladies' room and lock yourself in. Don't answer your phone, even if it's your mother or Ada. Not just now. Okay? Promise me. And don't open the door for anyone but me. If someone calls to you while you're in there, make like you're puking. Just say you're sick. I'll be there as soon as I can."

"Is this bad? Did I do the wrong thing?"

"No. It'll be okay. Go now, sweetheart. Go fast."

At the back of the gas station, the ladies' room seemed like a terrible place to hide. The heavy, rust-flecked door was kicked in at the bottom corner, bent like someone else had gotten the same idea once and it hadn't gone well. The metal collar on the doorknob spun and clattered when she turned it.

Things weren't much better on the inside. A brass latch and a ragged do-it-yourself hole drilled into the jamb took the place of the bolt that no longer lined up to its slot. It looked like it had been salvaged from a boat wreck.

Carly slid the latch home and twisted the little tab lock in the handle, but wasn't sure it caught on anything. She retreated to the middle of the tiled floor. And waited.

The air was humid and vivid with the smell of wintergreen over plumbing problems. The ceiling pressed down like a low lid and held everything tight under its seal. No sound got back into this corner of the thick-walled building. She could hear herself swallow and breathe, and nothing else.

The painting made the bag heavy and lopsided. The floor was gross enough that she thought all the way to how she would feel about picking the bag up again if she set it down. Instead, Carly hugged it to her chest, redistributing its awkwardness. Her bare arms sweated against the slick fabric.

Her phone rang. The bag slid down from her new one-armed grip as she scrabbled for her pocket. The corner of the painting inside the bag scudded along her shin and jabbed the base of her big toe as it settled.

Her mother was calling. The longing to talk to her seared through Carly like pain. She didn't know what John had told her. Carly didn't know if her mother was mad at her. Or worried. Maybe she should answer, just to at least tell her side of the story. But she couldn't. She'd said she wouldn't. She wanted to. No.

There was a muted jingle and someone turned the doorknob and the door thudded against the clattery latch. The phone stopped ringing.

Whoever it was pushed on the door again.

Carly's eyes went hot with tears and her lungs burned on the expired timer of her overdue next breath.

A voice called out, faint to louder as it came closer. Marcelline.

"Sorry! Sorry. I think that's my girl in there."

There was a shuffling of position in the narrow hallway outside, then a soft tap on the door. "Carly, honey, it's me."

Carly unlocked the door and Marcelline smiled at the unsmiling woman in the hallway, who looked back and forth between them, taking score on how long it would be before she got her turn in the restroom.

Marcelline held up a finger as she squeezed through the door that she didn't open all the way. "We'll be out in just a second."

She slipped in and latched the door behind her.

Carly's face felt splotchy hot under the wet streaks.

"Oh, honey." Marcelline pulled her into a hug. "It's going to be okay."

"My . . . my . . ." A sputtering sob overran her words. Just too much. Everything all at once. "My mom just called. I . . . didn't . . . didn't answer it." She coughed and hitched into Marcelline's shoulder.

"It's okay. It's okay. I know that was hard. You did fine. We're going to get this all straightened out, okay?"

Marcelline unwound her arms from Carly to take her face in her warm hands. She did the serious eye-to-eye thing that usually felt so high drama, but it actually helped this time. The volcano swell of crying surged down in Carly.

"I know everything's been crazy. Too crazy. But it's going to be all right."

Marcelline pulled some toilet paper off the roll and Carly dried her face with the shreds of it as it dissolved in her tears.

They both looked at the bag crumpled in a heap and leaning against Carly's legs.

"May I?"

Carly nodded.

Marcelline didn't hesitate to kneel on the grimy floor. She unzipped the bag all the way to the bottom. She pushed the suit off the painting and worked its corners free.

She made the little reverse-gasp sound again.

She smiled and shook her head and looked up at the ceiling. Her eyes were shiny. "In a gas station bathroom," she whispered.

She looked up from the floor, glowing.

"What?" said Carly.

The door clanged in its frame. The voice from the other side was muffled. The mood, though, came through just fine. "Hello? There are people waiting out here."

"Let's go," Marcelline said.

Marcelline carried the bag out, and Carly couldn't help but notice that she held it as if it were glass. She put it in the footwell first, checked it over, shook her head, went into the trunk for a blanket, and moved the whole bag onto the seat. She bunched the suit under the painting and wrapped the whole thing in the blanket, tucked up tight like a baby in bed. She buckled the belt over the bundle of it.

"Wow," Carly said. "What's with all that?"

"Hop in."

Once they were in their own seats and as secure as John's suit, Marcelline turned to her.

"Okay, this is where I'm going to ask you to trust me."

"Okay." It was a strongly not-okay okay, but Carly couldn't think of anything else to do but agree. Why was everyone so freaking weird?

"I don't want to take you straight home."

It felt like a bubble rising in Carly, the worry that she'd gotten something very wrong. "What, like later? Like tonight?"

"Maybe."

"But maybe not?" Carly's voice slipped up on the bubble.

"Hang on. Listen. Everything's going to be okay. Remember the other day, when you looked at my scars, when I said I could keep a secret? When we found that guy?"

Carly nodded.

"This is going to sound weird, but these scars, the guy, and even why I'm here at all is because of—"

"John!"

Marcelline looked confused. "Yeah, but—"

Carly pointed out the window, bouncing in her seat. "He's here! John's here!"

"Shit!"

Marcelline started the car, hands and feet frantically working the wheel and the pedals. She jerked the car out of the parking space, backward and around, flinging them over the blacktop. Carly shut her eyes over a blur of people, posts, and gas pumps speeding toward them.

Marcelline drove them to the opposite exit, with John coming up through the parking lot. They raced past the pump islands, banged over the tank covers, and screeched out into the street.

Marcelline's car made it through the intersection, while John's got held up by cars turning into the road between them. The street stretched straight ahead with a bend looping off in the distance.

Carly looked back at the traffic light. "He's coming."

"Okay."

Marcelline went a little faster. When the road curved to the right, she hit the gas and the car dove in.

"He must have seen my car. Can he still see us now?" asked Marcelline.

Carly craned farther around to check the back window. "I don't think so." Carly felt the swooping pull of the long turn and tightened in her seat to keep from leaning.

"Okay. Hang on."

The gentle swell of gravity lunged for full tilt as Marcelline cranked the wheel over hard to take a violent right turn onto a narrow road they'd all but passed. The tires whined through the floorboards and Carly grabbed for the door to keep from pitching into the center console.

"Sorry!" Marcelline called to Carly and to the car. She patted the dashboard like a good horse.

"What are you doing? What is going on? Why are we running away from John? Why is he chasing us? I don't *get* any of this."

Marcelline didn't answer her and kept checking the rearview mirror until Carly couldn't suppress the eyeroll and the sound that always came with it in the back of her throat.

Marcelline looked over at her. "I know. Hang on."

Carly's imagination was faster than the minute Marcelline needed to get to a point where she could talk. By the time Marcelline finally started, Carly was prepared for news of the zombie apocalypse.

"This is all going to sound really strange. And I hate doing it while we're driving. But I want you to understand. And I don't want you to be afraid. Not of me, anyway."

"But you think I should be afraid of John?"

Carly looked for the answer on Marcelline's face to measure it against whatever words came out of her mouth.

The scar pulled tight as Marcelline nibbled at the corner of her lip. "I don't think Jonathan would hurt you." She stole a quick glance at Carly. "I really don't. You're not going to hear me say anything good about him. And it might ultimately be way more about you than it is about him, but I don't think he would do anything to you."

"You know him."

"Huh?" Marcelline was genuinely puzzled.

Carly felt sick. "You came to my house last night. You said you wanted to meet him, but you already knew him. I missed it."

Marcelline nodded. "He hadn't seen me in a long time. In fact, he thought I was dead."

"This whole time, you knew him? Is that why you talk to me? Is that the reason we did the art stuff?"

"Yes and no. I wanted to know something about his life before I saw him again. Yes. That's why I found you, and why I struck up a conversation with you. And, yes, that's why I suggested a reason for us to talk more. But the work we did together, all the time we spent, that was because I wanted to. It was great. It is great. Because you're pretty great. Carly, I hope you believe me."

She didn't answer. How could she have missed it?

Marcelline had tricked her with bait—with the art talk, with kneecapping Dylan in the doughnut shop, with showing her what being in control of hard-to-control things looked like.

Flinging the car all over the road, and them all over the car, while they were being chased was hardly what being in control should feel like, though.

Marcelline had baited her with the idea that all of it could fill in the gaps that had been blown into Carly's life after the *thing*. And Carly had taken in every bit of it. Every weird thing to see about Marcelline would have been buried under the obviously weird thing that Carly had done by voluntarily laying out her whole life for Marcelline's approval.

Carly's own shadow had gotten in the way. A surge of embarrassed tears burned her eyes, but faded. She wouldn't get caught out again.

"Why did he think you were dead?" Carly looked at the scar as if it would suddenly be an obvious story that Marcelline didn't have to say out loud.

Marcelline cleared her throat. "Not all of this is worth going into right now."

"Right. Not that I deserve an explanation or anything. You just don't want to tell me."

"I don't want to tell you everything, no." Marcelline cast a hopeful, sad smile at Carly.

But she didn't lie. Not even about the hard stuff. And she didn't hold back that she was holding back. It didn't fix everything, but it was something. Carly didn't feel like crying anymore right now, but that made her feel as weird as everyone else.

Marcelline steered around another bend with a little extra pepper on it. Carly didn't feel much of anything more than wide-awake. "How do you know him? Was it from a long time ago? From before he and my mom got together?"

"Yes."

"How?"

"Ooooh, boy. Whew. Okay. Where to start?" Marcelline was watching the road and her own past, too. "It will make more sense to start in the middle, but you have to understand, none of this is your fault."

"My fault?"

"What happened to you when you were attacked, I don't want you to think that anything attached to it after the fact—anything—makes what happened to you less of a big deal. Everything in life ends up being part of a bigger story, but it's not more important than you. Or what you did. You were amazing. I don't want this to upset you."

"What do you mean?" None of the puzzle-piece edges matched. The zombie apocalypse might actually end up making sense.

"The video. It kicked off something more than just what happened to you that day."

"*Pffft.* Tell me about it."

"Now, what do *you* mean?"

"It changed everything. Just seeing it. I got to see what I did. I got to see how I beat him. It was just weird. Nobody gets to do that."

"That must have been very strange."

"It was kinda great."

Marcelline looked over at Carly, checking for a joke.

"No, seriously. It's like all this stuff happens in the world and we just have to guess how. You're doing it, but then it's over. And then it's just gone. But not me. I don't have to guess. I can see it anytime I want. I know, like in slow motion, how I did it. People can do all these things, but they don't know it, because it goes by so fast that they can't understand. I just can. Now. A little bit."

"Wow."

"Yeah, cool story, right? But why do *you* care about the video?"

"Oh, shit. How?" Marcelline yelled. She was looking in the mirror.

John's red car was streaking up behind them.

Marcelline sped up. A lot. Carly pulled her seat belt at the hip the way her mother did when John drove too fast. Carly turned in her seat to watch him coming.

"Do you know where we are?" Marcelline was looking from the road ahead to the road behind in the mirror so fast, Carly didn't know how she was seeing anything at all.

"No!"

"Can you look? Pull up a map or something? We need to go where there are lots of people."

Carly did. They took a left. Not far down, Marcelline took a right and another right and, like stepping through a door into a party, there was traffic. People everywhere. And no John.

Carly felt the absurdity of her question before she said it, like they were in a movie. "Did we lose him?"

"I think so."

But a few blocks up, his car nosed up to an intersection ahead.

"Oh, come on!" Marcelline smacked the steering wheel. "Son of a bitch!"

A sheriff's cruiser turned in from the left a few cars ahead of them.

"Hey, hey! Look!" Carly flapped and pointed.

Marcelline laid a calming hand on her arm, gently pushed it down, and also eased her foot off the gas. "I see him."

The cop passed John. They passed John. Carly looked over at his straight silhouette behind the windshield, but Marcelline didn't.

"No, speed up!" Carly said. "Catch up to him! Flash your lights or something!"

Carly looked behind them. John let two big gaps pass him by before he turned.

"I can't," said Marcelline.

The cold bubble of fear slipped up through Carly again. "Why not?"

"Ask me later. I cannot do all of this at the same time." Marcelline checked the mirrors a lot and slowly maneuvered them behind the police officer.

Carly watched John fall farther behind until the red flash of his car streaked off onto a highway ramp.

"He's gone."

A green arrow lit up above the left lane. "I've got to get off the road," Marcelline said.

She swerved into the left lane, without a lot of room to spare. Marcelline hissed at the tight fit. Carly winced and saw that they looked together, automatically, to the cop ahead to see if he'd noticed. He hadn't. They sighed in unison and Marcelline looked over. Her in-it-together smile pushed down the fear in Carly.

The story was bigger, whatever it was, but her part in it and Marcelline's were crossed now. And Carly could deal with it. Was dealing with it. *Look at me go.* She could do things.

They took the left and ducked straight into the parking lot of a bustling supermarket. Marcelline turned into a spot shielded from the street by a pennant-festooned van, covered with blue and gold wildcat decals and thoroughly soaped windows urging the Cougars to game-day victory. Number Eight was apparently the star player these days. Three number-eight-wearing, blue-wigged people in gold face paint unloaded bags of groceries from a piled cart into the back of the van, filling all the spaces between the tripod legs of a grill and a massive cooler.

Marcelline ignored the sideshow and rested her lips against prayer-folded hands that were shaking. "Oh, this is crazy," she whispered.

"Where should we go?"

"I don't know."

Carly tried to look at the map, but the focus was hard to catch. Her hands were shaking, too. "What do you think he would do? I mean, if he finds us."

Marcelline swiped her hand over Carly's forearm. "I don't want you to worry. I just need a minute. I'm wrecked. He keeps popping up like the damned Terminator."

A wash of chills rushed over Carly's back and scalp in a gust of discovery. "Oh, no! I know how he's doing it. The app!" Carly held up her phone, gripped in her fist as if it would jump away if she'd let it. "John must have Mom's phone. The app. It's a tracker on this one."

"Oh, hell."

Marcelline looked for Jonathan out of her side of the car. Carly scanned the parking lot from hers.

"Silence your phone and give it to me."

"Turn it off?"

"No. Leave it on."

Carly did and handed it over.

Marcelline got out. "I don't know if you'll get this back."

Carly shrugged. "I don't have bad stuff on there, so it's all in the cloud. Duh." She smiled bravely into her trembling cheeks.

"Right." Marcelline smiled back.

She walked around her car, head down like she was looking at the tires. In one smooth sweep of her arm, Marcelline slid Carly's phone into one of the tailgaters' remaining shopping bags.

She hurried back to her seat, dropped the car into gear, and pulled away from the van. "Go, Cougars."

• • •

"So what *will* you tell me about this?" Carly asked.

They'd caught their breath in exhausted silence.

"The short version is that it's about the painting. In some circles, it's famous. It's worth millions."

Millions. Carly looked at the blanket-wrapped lump buckled in behind Marcelline and realized that millions was a concept in the same category as light-years. She didn't really know what that was equal to in real life.

"And it's stolen."

"He stole it?" Carly went goggle-eyed at the image in her mind of her stepfather as a cat burglar.

"No. Jonathan didn't steal it. I mean, not the original theft. But he ended up with it. People got hurt."

A list of reasons waded into the tears that finally sprang up in Carly's eyes—all of it changing John in her memory into something else, something that pulled so many things in her life out of their happy shape. "Did he do that to you?"

Marcelline clenched her teeth, and the ruined side of her face jumped grotesquely. "Not exactly. But he let it happen. He caused it. And he . . ." She sighed. "Let's let that be enough for right now."

The awkward pause cooled off.

Marcelline took a deep breath. "Anyway, I can't understand how Jonathan would risk hanging it in your house. What a crazy thing to do. But there it was in the video. Just the corner of it. I saw it online. It's what brought me here."

"He didn't do it. Hang it up, I mean. My mom found it and really liked it. She hung it up when we were unpacking."

Marcelline laughed. "Poor Jonathan. He must have just about crapped his pants. I almost feel sorry for him. Almost. 'Poor Jonathan' is not a thought that sits very well in my head." She laughed again.

"You always call him Jonathan, but it's just John. It's not shortened or anything. I mean, not on his driver's license and the bills and stuff.

Just John. But you know what's weird? This big huge guy who came to the house the other day called him that, too. When they were talking, he always called him Jonathan."

Carly replayed the guy filling up their doorway, flirting with her mother, menacing Carly by not trying too hard not to. "Wait. He kept looking at the wall. Marcelline! He kept looking at the place it was hanging before. He knew about it, too! I knew he must have seen it in the video. But he was looking for the painting."

Marcelline hadn't said anything during Carly's moment of revelation. In fact, she'd gone like a hole in the air, dead silent. Staring at Carly, openmouthed.

The driver behind them tapped his horn as a friendly reminder that the light had turned green.

Marcelline ignored him. "A huge guy came looking for Jonathan?"

They parked by a playground buried in a neighborhood miles from Carly's house. At the end of the story, Marcelline leaned back in her seat, hands folded over her lips, deep in thought. "He'll come looking for the painting. The first place is your house. Shit."

"But my mom . . ."

"I know."

When Marcelline reached for her phone, Carly felt a pang for her own. Not having it was like not having her hair. She knew she could live without it, but it felt really weird.

So she stared out the window, listening to Marcelline's side of the call.

"S? Hey, it's me. Sorry I hung up on you. . . . Yeah, I'm fine. Fine-*ish* anyway. . . . I don't know." She smiled at something the other person said. "Yeah. I know. Um, I need you to do something. You're not going to like it. I think I might need you to get in touch with Owen Haig for me."

CHAPTER TWENTY-FIVE

Boxes. That was what allowed Samantha to have both her career and a life.

She disconnected from the call with Marcelline and looked at the collection of boxes that lined her shelves and decorated her tables and spare desk space. There were even more of them at home—little jeweled ones, some with sweetly plinking music, big decoupaged hatboxes, glass, inlaid wood, onyx, resin, leather-covered pressboard. They were all empty.

People thought they were knickknacks. Her odd little collector's fetish. Just what you ought to get Samantha for her birthday or Hanukkah. But that wasn't it at all. They served as pretty prompts to remind her of their metaphorical counterparts, lovely little warnings for her to never forget how all of this worked.

The magic of compartmentalization wasn't in that it kept things separate. That was merely the practical function of containment. The separation let a whole lot of people stay in her life because they thought she worked in hospital public relations. But it also let the president of France's personal secretary have her number in his phone under the guise of a plumbing company. It kept scores of wealthy and influential people from ever knowing they were often talking about the same person when they gossiped, in lowered voices, about knowing someone who could do this or get that. It let her help the FBI some days and thwart them on others. It let her talk to her mother three times a week.

No, the true blessing of the psychological box was in the lid. The idea, the image of it, was a simple mnemonic device that forced a pause into her decision making. When Samantha was about to change something, to open a lid as it were, there was the question *What does it mean to pry this open, to risk getting this mixed in with something else?*

Owen Haig was from the same mold. She appreciated that about him. He knew the utilitarian value of isolation in this type of job, the checking of one's conscience at the door. But he was better suited to it in some ways than she was. Owen did it with fewer boxes. And without the conscience.

He performed some of the same tricks of acquisition and facilitation as Samantha did, but for only one small, albeit substantially wealthy, client, where Samantha's employers were myriad and often at cross-purposes. So Owen got to say yes more often than she did, or he had to say yes, depending on how you viewed it.

"No" could be such a luxury. Such a solid lock for the boxes.

Samantha had expended no small amount of unpaid effort to keep the Owen Haig box and the Marcelline Gossard box unmingled for these last four years. Now here she sat, fingers under the figurative lid of each, at Marcelline's own request.

Samantha didn't have a lot of friends. Most of them were in the group of regular people who thought she got paid to make a chain of medical centers look good. But Marcelline's friendship was entirely unique in her life. Samantha didn't have a husband or kids. She didn't have pets. Her houseplants had to be the hearty kind. So it was the one outstandingly single time she'd ever gotten to play the rescuer, the caregiver.

From their work together in the gallery and the oddness of some of the transactions and transactors, M had known enough to think of Samantha in a crisis that couldn't be handled by calling 911. At the outset, this budding alliance was different from all the other people she might think of as friends. She didn't have to keep M at arm's length.

It was a special case, an exception, something she could keep, if she chose to. Which she had. And Samantha wanted it still. Funny that she and Owen had this attachment to Marcelline in common, if in very different ways.

The Flinck was always going to have gone through Owen. He would have found it eventually. The Anningers would have insisted. They had insisted, in fact. It wasn't even unlikely that Samantha might have been a part of it, however it inevitably happened.

The trouble for her involvement was that, whatever Owen's personal woundedness in all of this, his fury at Marcelline was unfounded. She hadn't betrayed him. Everyone but Owen knew that. And the Anningers didn't care. They only demanded that he fix it.

Marcelline would look even worse to him once he knew what role Samantha had maintained in her disappearance all these years.

Odd Man Out Syndrome was Owen's favorite malady. Sickness as a superpower, really. Except when it came to Marcelline. If there was even more whispering behind his back than he'd imagined, that insult was something he might sink his teeth into. And Samantha had never once convinced him to unlock his jaw off anything.

She picked up a little plush box, colorful beads over turquoise silk. A gift from M. She wasn't thrilled about putting Marcelline in jeopardy. But considering the Flinck was in the wind again after all this time, and that Owen was tangled in it once more, it was better for them to meet on purpose than by accident.

· · ·

Owen picked up right away. "Samantha. Always a pleasure to see your name pop up on the screen."

"You just want me to ask you what name you've saved this number under and I don't want to know."

"You might. It's hilarious."

"I don't believe you. You're not really a funny guy, Owen. Sorry."

He chuckled down the line. Warm-ups. Both of them oiling up their most pleasant voices with all the smiles in them. This is what they did because when Samantha called Owen, or Owen called Samantha, one or the other or both would be reasonably likely to have something negotiable to say over the next minutes.

"To what do I owe the pleasure of your call?"

"Well, it's about the Flinck." In the expected pause, Samantha petted the smooth lavender finish on her squared manicure.

"Hmmm. It's fairly coincidental that you would bring that up right now."

"I'm almost positive you don't believe in coincidences."

"Don't I?" A resigned anger crept into his voice. "I have to, because this is one hell of a coincidence. As it happens, I'm picking up that very thing here in just a couple of hours."

Samantha wasn't afraid of Owen's anger. Not for herself, anyway. "Except maybe not."

Owen sighed. "So, what am I doing then? Go ahead. Say it. What has that pointless little ratfuck done now? I know he wants more money, but, really, Samantha? How did you link up with that piece of shit? It's beneath you."

"It's not him. It's Marcelline."

She knew he'd need another second with that one. She waited, turning the box on her desk and watching the light play through the glass beads, throwing a patchy rainbow onto the wall beside her.

"Oh, I see. Ah. Right." Owen went a stormy kind of quiet again. "It was you. You made her a ghost. That's why I could never find her.

Wow. Of course. You've known where she was this whole time. And now you bitches are playing me, all the way down to this."

"Take it easy."

"Don't tell me to take it easy. You sold me out. I'm this close and you just told her right where she could find it. Why would you do that, any of this, and think you could tell me to take it easy?"

"You know, Owen, we don't usually interrogate each other. It seemed like a respect thing, but at the very least it let me tell you to go to hell less often. No, I didn't tell her where it was. I couldn't have if I'd wanted to. You don't have to believe me, but as a matter of fact, she found it first."

"So, that's not much better. You knew and you didn't tell me."

Samantha scowled. "Funny, I didn't think you cared about the Anningers' collection that much."

"I didn't."

"I can't help but notice the past tense."

"I don't care about their hobbies. I have my own. They send me on their errands, but this was mine. Work backward from the Flinck and I find Marcelline. Because I have questions."

"I know you do. That's why I didn't tell you. Obviously."

"What, are you two in love? Decided you don't like dick anymore?"

"You know, Owen, the whole heart-on-your-sleeve thing over Marcelline was always kind of creepy."

"Fuck you."

"Are you done with your tantrum?"

Samantha heard a muted bang and a clattering crash. Owen really was having a fit.

"Hey! Will you listen? Owen! She's not screwing you over. She never did. She was going to give it to you. She wanted to buy her life back with it. To prove to you that it wasn't her."

"Oh, convenient. That you're in a position to tell me all this now doesn't really give it that ring of truth, Samantha. In fact, it sounds a whole lot like bullshit. This was almost finished. I was just about done with it. You took it out from under me."

"Not as such. It sort of fell into her hands. And up until a few minutes ago, she didn't even know you were in the picture. I didn't tell her anything other than to be careful. I'm not screwing you over either."

Owen didn't say anything for almost a full minute, but she could hear that he was still there huffing and fuming. "What happened to Jonathan?"

"I think Marcelline can explain this much better than I can. Can you keep it together and hear her out? She's worried about the girl and her mother. If you look at this a certain way, with the exception of you getting to lose your shit on your own terms, this isn't that far off from what you wanted in the first place. And not to mention, what you are employed to do. Two birds, one stone."

She instantly regretted her choice of illustrative image.

"I want to meet in person."

"Naturally. But I would consider it a personal favor if you would give me your word that you won't hurt her."

"We're not in the personal favors business, Samantha."

She wished they had more time for Owen to cool off. He was still angry. But her reach was longer than his, and he knew it. She'd had enough of his attitude.

It wasn't a habit of hers to draw a red line. Only two times in all her career. One confrontation had ended agreeably and they were still colleagues. The other ended with a burial at sea.

"Then let me put it this way, you gorilla. I have a pair of your gym socks. Think back. Where did I get them? Where did the blood come from that is all over them now? No matter what, she's still a missing person, OJ. Don't cross me. I don't ask much, but this time, I'm not really asking."

CHAPTER TWENTY-SIX

Owen had kicked the leg of the desk in his hotel room, upending the full water glass over the remnants of his breakfast tray and reducing the juice glass to shards against the plate.

The mess taunted him. Owen wasn't the glass-breaking sort. *Tsk, tsk for boiling over.* He gritted his teeth. The dripping water splatted into the puddle on the carpet at irritatingly uneven intervals. He called the front desk to report the mess. The desk clerk said she'd send someone. The patient weariness in her voice briefly inspired him to break more shit just to make this worth it for everyone.

Instead, he took out a $20 bill for the tip and waited. Waiting while angry was his least favorite thing to do.

In the last few days, he'd come to believe that Marcelline hadn't set him up for a stooge four years ago. The relief was both wonderful and terrible. Mostly terrible. Poorly spent time was the one thing you could never fix. He'd scared her, practically held her hostage. But it was probably worse than that. If she hadn't run away, he might have done something bad. Something irrevocable.

Talking with Jonathan had convinced him enough of her innocence to feel glad that she'd gotten away. He'd even set a longer game to see the end of Jonathan because of it. To avenge her. And that idea hadn't been unpleasant either.

If it had worked the way Jonathan had wanted it to, with him delaying the sale by screwing over Marcelline, it would have been a problem of more like the leg-breaking variety. Maybe some lost teeth. Some teachable moment for Jonathan that would have healed eventually.

But after everything, it was too much to have him sit across a table and shrug off the admission that he had, as far as he knew, let Marcelline die like a dog in the road for his own convenience.

Owen wasn't forgiving enough to let that sort of thing go— losing years to an error of thinking, and falling out of standing with the worthless people who paid him. The Anningers had made Owen's days about regaining what they'd lost and then some.

He had ended up dangling at the whim and greed of an over-reaching, underwitted asshole who didn't know what to do with a stroke of good luck. And that just wouldn't cut it.

So Owen's schedule for the day had been to first get the painting off the Anningers' shopping list, then to get right on with removing Jonathan's heartbeat from his chest. That was the plan.

But his certainty had started shedding.

Jonathan had Owen convinced that he really did think she was dead. But then all of a sudden, Jonathan revealed that he knew she wasn't. He claimed that the two of them had even spoken in the last day or so. Then Jonathan changed the deal. He dangled the chance to talk to Marcelline as some sort of condition of doing what he'd already agreed to do.

And now Samantha, the closest thing Owen had to a colleague, to someone who could imagine what it was like to be him and to have his life, had the bad manners to reveal that she'd known the whole time; that she had played monkey-in-the-middle with his peace of mind for years. She'd threatened him over Marcelline's disappearance.

He paced the shallow carpet between the bed and the dresser. The spilled water squished under his shoe.

He didn't know what to think.

In an essentially desire-free existence, a single want had so much room to grow. And had it ever. It crowded out everything to the point he was kicking desks. Had Marcelline thrown in her lot with that smarmy little fuck? Or had she struck out on her own, saying and doing anything to make Owen useful to her goals? He'd never been good at reading her. Obviously.

Jonathan, though, was pretty easy.

Owen wasn't sure that Jonathan wouldn't let the call just ring through to his voice mail. But he answered it, somewhere near the last possible moment.

"Yeah?" Jonathan was trying hard for a neutral tone, but there was a hint of lava in his voice.

"I understand you're having a rough morning," Owen said.

To his credit, Jonathan didn't make a big deal out of how Owen might know this. They were a bit beyond the smaller details.

"I'm straightening it out."

"The thing is, Jonathan, I don't think you are. I don't see how that's possible. I have a meeting here with Marcelline in a little while that seems to have eclipsed the meeting you and I were supposed to have. Then I'll be on my way home soon and the painting will be on its way to its new owners. It just seems the payee will be different."

"Don't count me out of this yet."

"Oh, how could I? I wouldn't like you if you were just a tenacious little wannabe. But I like you less even than that. You're tenacious not because you want it, but because you think you deserve it. I'm sure you'll still be in it until the end, if you can only find a way. So what are you going to do tomorrow, Jonathan?"

"What do you mean?"

"I mean, I'll be sleeping in my own bed. Marcelline will be, I don't know, wiggling around in a bathtub full of money or something. And you will be? What? Back at home on dandelion row?"

Jonathan didn't say anything.

"Or do you have enough squirreled away to also be somewhere else tomorrow? To get lost like you need to? You don't have to answer right away. Give me a second of dead air for each thousand dollars you still have from what you stole four years ago."

"Fuck you."

"That's what I thought."

There was a knock on Owen's door. "Housekeeping!"

He let her in and swept his hand at the desk.

Owen had wound Jonathan up enough that discerning the truth from a lie should be easier. It should be something he'd be able to compare to what Marcelline would tell him when they met. His pulse sped up at the thought of sitting across from her. Want. Anger. Forgiveness.

"How did you lose the painting?" Owen put the $20 bill on the newly dried desktop next to the maid as she swept glass into a doubled plastic bag. They exchanged knowing nods and she whispered so as not to interrupt his call, "Thank you."

"You were just hours away," Owen said. "It was right there."

"Wait. You don't know what happened?" Jonathan sounded a little hopeful. The kind of hope that makes a man with his foot in a door think more about the other side of the threshold than the relative weight of doors on ankles.

Owen sat on the unmade bed and leaned back on the headboard. "No, I don't know what happened. Let's just say that, tomorrow, when this is all over—for the second time—I'd like to be able to reflect on your candor in this particular moment. I'd like to see how it matches up to what bullshit story she's going to tell me when I see her. Then

I'll know how to feel about this. I'll know if I'm done with this whole thing. Or not."

Jonathan took a moment to decide what to say. The maid blotted water from the carpet with a folded towel.

Jonathan sighed. "My stepdaughter took it."

The housekeeper jumped at the laugh that broke from Owen. "You can't be serious."

Jonathan's confirming silence only made Owen laugh harder.

"Carly again? Well, isn't she just karma's own little spatula."

CHAPTER TWENTY-SEVEN

Five minutes after Marcelline was sure she couldn't take on another worry, positive that her head hadn't a square inch of real estate for another problem, Carly spoke up from the passenger seat.

They'd been quiet, driving in the opposite direction from where they'd end up meeting Owen in a little while. Marcelline wanted to stop looking over her shoulder in the time she had between now and then. If she couldn't sleep, she could at least breathe easy for a bit. And find a place to wash her face.

"What happens after you're done talking to whatshisname?" Carly asked.

"I don't really know. It's not afterward that bothers me so much. It's what happens during."

"I know, but what do you think you're going to do?"

"Well, if he believes me or gets past being pissed in some other way, and he takes the painting to set things right, I guess that's that. It's over. You and your mom are safe. I'm safe. If he doesn't want it, or if he doesn't believe me, there's not much I can do, or if he . . . I don't know."

"But no matter what, you'll go back to where you live today?"

Carly's *no matter what* included things about Owen that Marcelline didn't particularly want to tell her. Or think about at all.

"I guess. I hadn't really thought about it." Marcelline hadn't gotten around to envisioning the actual journey back, how it would start, and under what conditions. She still had the fantasy she always had: Bethany meeting her at the airport. With her cat.

"What happens to me?"

Carly's question, small and worried and gently delivered, landed like a slap.

"What do you mean?" But Marcelline knew very well what she meant, although it hadn't occurred to her to picture that part either until it had been laid out in a single quiet, scared question.

Carly didn't lift her head. "Whatever happens, whichever way it goes, you leave and John's still married to my mom. He lives with us at our house. And now he doesn't have the painting. I don't know what he was going to do before, but no matter what happens now, his plan is ruined." She looked out her window, her mouth working to keep steady under the threat of tears. "Because of me."

"I really don't think he'll hurt you. Or your mother. I still believe that."

"But what does that *mean*? What if you're wrong? You won't be there. I don't even know if *he'll* be there, or if he'll come back at some point. What am I supposed to do? What am I supposed to say? What about my mom? She must be freaking out right now."

Marcelline cast around in her suddenly empty head for something that sounded reassuring. That's what she was supposed to do as the grown-up, as a woman speaking to a child. But fatigue was sand in the gears. She couldn't think. "I don't want you to worry. Whatever happens, nobody's going to leave you to figure this out by yourself. Okay? I promise. You're not going to get dropped off without a plan. It won't happen."

"I don't know what I'm going to do."

"We'll think of something." Marcelline turned into a strip mall with a big drugstore for an anchor. "I promise. Okay?"

"Okay."

Marcelline felt like a traitor to women everywhere. It didn't matter what she looked like. This was bigger than that. Owen's want shouldn't be a tool for her to use.

But she remembered the fear pounding through her when she ran away from him four years ago. All she'd had was flight that day. Every other option had been trimmed away.

His suspicion was dangerous. His weak point was terrifying. Owen had never left her with the impression that disillusionment was anything he'd be willing to float for very long.

Whatever came after disappointment, and how soon, or for how long, or to what end, she didn't want to find out. Not then. Not now.

This time she had the truth and the Flinck to try to soothe him. But she didn't exactly look as she did before. She watched her scar flex in the mirror under the flickering fluorescent lights of the drugstore's restroom. She'd bought a few things to cover up the days of adrenaline and far too little sleep. She washed her face and set to work.

Keeping a steady hand for a smooth eyeliner sweep was difficult on a regular day. Tired and wound tight made it almost impossible. She smudged the bold stripe at the corners of her eyes with her ring fingers. She pulled back from the mirror, blinked, and decided it looked okay. Okay had to be good enough. She needed to get back to Carly.

Carly had stayed in the car with the painting because they both didn't want it to be left alone out in the open. Which was absurd. The more she thought of it, the worse she felt. What was Carly going to do if there was a problem? And why would there be a problem?

Paranoia had seeped into their waiting, and they were both try-ing to plan for every bad thing that could possibly happen—Carly by babysitting an inanimate object and Marcelline by painting her face as if it would level a playing field that clearly wasn't. There was no controlling this, only rolling with it.

Marcelline crooked an arm around the bottles and tubes and their wrappers and plowed the whole lot into the plastic shopping bag. She had a last look at herself and didn't feel as familiar with the reflec-tion as she should. She scratched a tousle into her hair to stand in for something that looked like being at ease. It would have to do.

A mist of sweat surged over Marcelline's body and she broke into a run when she saw no silhouette in the passenger side of the car. Carly was gone. Marcelline flinched automatically to check the back seat for the painting.

It was there, disguised in its bland bundle, and with a sting of guilt for what should have been her first concern, she turned a sweep for Carly. But like the painting, Carly was there, too, absolutely fine. She came across the blacktop with a small white bag from the party-supply place that bookended the run of stores at this end.

Marcelline's heart surged, then paced down from booming panic to a merely headache-making bang.

"What are you doing?" She met Carly halfway so that she was close enough to hear a lowered voice.

"I'm sorry! I had to go to the bathroom. I picked the closest place. I could still see the car from the counter. I was only away from it for a minute. Everything was okay, so I bought some gum. My stomach hurts. I thought it would help. Do you want some?"

Marcelline had a hint of old pennies on her dry tongue. "Yeah, thanks." She took the gum. "Come on. We should get going."

• • •

"You should let me go in with you," said Carly.

They'd taken the long way around the town and now sat in the car, with the air-conditioning running, backed into the last row of yet another shopping center. Marcelline wanted the open view in these last few minutes before going into the little sub shop to talk with Owen. She didn't want him sneaking up on them. He was presumably already inside. His silver car sat out front in a casual display of not-at-all-bothered. Her stomach rolled at the sight of it.

But she cut her eyes at Carly and smiled in spite of the nausea. "You're going to be my bodyguard?"

Carly was all out of humor. "No. But I'm part of this. I want him to remember that." She swallowed and looked down at her hands in her lap. "I want you to remember it, too."

"Hey, I'm not forgetting that. How could I? I was out of options before you did what you did this morning. You've been great. You're very brave."

"I don't know if it was good. Maybe we should just give it back?"

"Jonathan doesn't get to win. He let people die over this."

"I didn't mean to give it back to him. To the museum."

"Oh." Marcelline took a turn at averting her eyes. "Yes. That's an important point. And my answer to it isn't very good. It's not the noblest way to go. But this one painting, it's the least of the collection. It's not really one of the ones they care about getting back. I mean, I'm sure it would be welcomed, but . . . it might give me my life back. I'm not getting anything for it. Not money. Not anymore."

She reached out to clasp Carly's forearm and was relieved that she didn't pull away. "Carly, I hope you understand. I lost everything. If Owen will take it, I'll have a chance. Do you think that's terrible?"

"No. Not terrible. I get it."

"I hope so. I made a mistake when I met Jonathan. I was wrong. We should have just turned it in. But doing it now doesn't undo almost any of it."

"It's okay."

"It's lame. I know it is. And I'm sorry."

"Sometimes lame is okay. Sometimes it has to be." Carly twitched a crooked, sympathetic smile into her cheek. Then she tried to get paid for it. "But you should let me come in with you. It's only right."

Marcelline was impressed with Carly's bargaining instincts. "I have to talk to Owen alone. There are things he's going to want to talk about, and it'll look like I'm not willing to do that if I bring you in."

Marcelline checked the clock. She should go. Her heart wound up again for another hurtling gallop.

Carly knocked it back to her. "Okay, but I could come in and just stay for a few minutes, then come back out to the car."

Marcelline hesitated, and Carly brought the rest of her argument in a high-colored rush of persuasion. "It will be good. I can help. If I'm there, he'll have to calm down. What's he going to do? Kill you when he knows I'm here? You'll be safer. I'll be safer."

Marcelline had to go. They had to go if it was going to be a *they*.

"I don't think he's going to kill anybody in a sandwich shop, but okay. You can come in. Say your piece. Or just be there. I'm not going to tell you how to handle this." She smiled at Carly. "You've shown you know what to do."

Carly smiled back. A real one, a worried one, but brave. It bruised Marcelline's clanging heart.

Marcelline cleared tears from her throat. "All right. Let's at least put the painting in the trunk."

Carly snapped straight in her seat, ready to bolt. "Okay. I'll do it."

Their eyes met. The air felt charged with two sets of nerves pumping electricity into the closed space.

"Go ahead," Carly said. "Pop the trunk. And check in the mirror. Your mascara, it's kinda . . ." Carly waved her finger vaguely eyeward on Marcelline.

She pushed the button to open the trunk for Carly, already out and unbuckling the garment bag, and then dug into her purse for her compact. She'd been sweating though she'd pointed the air conditioner straight at her face. A sooty snowfall of mascara flakes sprinkled her cheek ridge. Swiping helped some and smudged some. She wet the tip of her middle finger on her tongue to fix it.

The trunk lid slammed closed. The dark shape of Carly coming back around to the passenger side sent her shadow through the window.

A red car streaked in from the left across the windshield.

Carly screamed, "No!"

Jonathan's car bucked on its front tires and squealed to a stop to keep from running her over. Carly had dashed out into the lane, just beyond the nose of Marcelline's car.

"Carly, no!"

Marcelline was blocked in. Her thoughts slowed down. Parked cars on either side. Jonathan dead ahead. He opened his door and stepped out onto the asphalt.

The only open vista was behind Marcelline—beyond the sidewalk, the strip of grass that separated the people from the parking lot, and then the road beyond.

It was conditioned into every driver that it was off-limits. A bright green suggestion. But it wasn't impossible. And the curb, too, again more of a guideline, a cement caution, not insurmountable. Literally. The only way out was behind her, past the back windshield, out past the back seat now empty of the Flinck. It was in the trunk. Loose. Unprotected.

It wasn't very art-reverent of her that she'd see it smashed to splinters by backing into suburban traffic outside a shitty little strip mall before she'd let Jonathan have it again.

She dropped the car into drive, revved the engine, and lurched up a few feet toward Jonathan's car. She saw him jump back, unsure if she would plow it through or not.

Marcelline stopped hard and waved her arm at Carly, who stood frozen in the scene, shocked white and tear streaked in front of her stepfather. "Carly, go! Go!"

Marcelline wasn't entirely convinced he wouldn't run her over, if only in his race to catch up with the painting.

She shoved the gear selector to *R* and jammed her foot down over the accelerator. Her car shot backward, popped the curb with a horrible thud and clang. She fought the wheel over to point the nose off the sidewalk and ground the car back into drive.

Her last look into the parking lot showed Jonathan scrambling back into his seat and Carly, gape-mouthed, at Marcelline, seeing her suddenly out on the road and leaving her.

"Carly, run!"

She checked the mirror again as she roared away.

Carly did.

CHAPTER TWENTY-EIGHT

She ran with not a question in her head as to where she would go.

Marcelline was out of sight, with John screeching off behind her before Carly was halfway across the parking lot. Owen's car was a silver smudge as she passed it, and she hit the restaurant's door, pulling up barely enough to keep from crashing right through the glass.

She flung it open, and every head snapped up to the urgent rush of her into the room.

"You've got to be kidding me," Owen said.

She stopped herself, hands slapped onto the table as brakes.

"You have to help her." Carly was gulping air.

"Would you like to have a seat?"

"No! We have to go! He's chasing her!"

Owen turned toward the growing attention of the amazed staff behind the counter. "Would someone please bring her a Coke." He swung back to Carly. "Clearly, we're not going anywhere until you tell me what you think is going on."

"He's chasing her!"

"Stop yelling. And sit down."

It felt weird to Carly that she had no inclination to do it. Her body didn't betray her own judgment. Her legs weren't trembling to fold into the seat just because he said so. Her hands didn't want to fidget. She was freaking out and she was also fine.

Carly didn't defy grown-ups and she didn't hassle people, especially when she wanted them to do something. She wasn't stupid. But she had exactly zero impulse to sit down at the moment. So she didn't.

"Or you can just stand there, I guess," Owen said, unruffled. "So you're saying Jonathan just showed up and they drove off and left you here. With me."

"She didn't leave me here."

"And yet here you are. Instead of her."

"It's not like that."

"Tell me, how do you think Jonathan knew to be here? Are you suggesting I told him?"

She was surprised that she could be surprised today. She'd just taken it as a given that Owen would jump up and follow her out on the rescue mission. How *did* John know? "Maybe he followed you," she said.

"Maybe he didn't need to."

"Marcelline didn't tell him."

"And you know that how?"

"She wouldn't."

"You're a mind reader, too?"

"No, she just wouldn't and she couldn't have."

"She didn't make any calls? Send any texts? You were with her every second?"

Of course Marcelline *could* have. Carly knew very well that they hadn't been together every second. She searched for the words to explain why she knew it hadn't happened that way. Owen, helpfully, gave them to her:

"They're playing you."

Her spine pulled her straight to her full height. She looked down on this man. Huge. Dismissive. And completely wrong. She leaned in, her indignation burning up through her without catching on any checkpoints of embarrassment. "I don't get played."

He pulled back just a little. She marked it with a soaring recognition that it had been automatic for him. He couldn't help it. He saw her.

The victory gave her the okay to sit down. Her legs were tired. This day was hard. She pulled out the chair and dropped into it. A girl with a ponytail under a logoed ball cap put a drink in front of her, and Carly took a long pull of the bright, cold fizz.

"You're a regal little thing, aren't you?" Owen said.

"She didn't set this up."

"You do realize I've been in this position before with the two of them?"

"I don't know what happened before."

"Right. You didn't even know your times tables back then."

"She didn't do this. You have to help her."

"But I don't."

"She's a good person. It's your fault if something happens."

"I can promise that you're testing the wrong string if you think I'm worried about it being my fault."

"You don't care if something bad happens to her?"

Owen blinked at her.

Carly raised her eyebrows to answer him.

He cleared his throat. "Everything about this looks like an ambush. They wind you up and send you in here. I bet you a million dollars we get a message soon telling us where to meet them."

It was the only time anyone had said "bet you a million" that Carly believed there could be that actual bet, on his side at least.

"She's only afraid of you. She thought you might take the painting or even hurt her."

"Do you imagine that's reassuring? Is there anything more dangerous than an animal that's afraid?"

"Do you think I didn't notice that you didn't say you weren't going to do any of those things?" Carly took a sip of her soda. The bubbles went all the way into her blood.

Owen played it like tennis. "And you think I should just take your assessment of the situation? You think it's reasonable for me to forget what I know about Marcelline and her very bad judgment when it comes to this particular thing?"

"But you don't know it. You just wonder about it. Besides, don't you have to buy it no matter what? Isn't that your job?"

"All I have to do is say that it didn't work out. Do you imagine anyone's going to call me a liar?"

Carly looked at him over the lid of her tilted cup. The sweetness was outpacing the wet in the third sip. She wasn't thirsty anymore.

She sighed. "I can tell that you like being different from everyone else. It's your thing. That's always your advantage. Well, almost always. Sometimes it sucks being a unicorn, doesn't it?"

The idea she was having came with a pause here that she only sort of understood, so she took another unwanted sip for something to do while it worked in her.

He shifted just a little in his chair and tilted his head like he was bored-listening. But he was listening just the same.

"But it's not working out the way you planned. And because it's me sitting here and not her, you're mad. You're saying she's being tricky. And that she might be planning to hurt you. You're saying that she's doing what you would do in this situation.

"So you're different when you want to be, but when you don't want to do something, all of a sudden, everyone's the same."

"Did you just call me a chicken?"

"No. Nobody wants to get attacked. I don't blame you. But I don't count. I'm just a kid, not a fancy loner guy." She waved her hand at his slick blue suit to punctuate the point. "It's easy for me to see how you're different from Marcelline. She's not going to attack you. She just wants to go home."

"And what does Jonathan want?"

Carly thought toward John. There wasn't much there. "I don't know."

"So you've known Jonathan for years and Marcelline for a few days, but you understand her more than you understand him?"

Carly found herself a sudden fountain of hot tears, not because it was true, but because she was tired and because it was frustrating not to find the words to explain why it made sense. What she knew about John was muddled with memories from both before and after she knew how to really look and listen. Everything she knew about Marcelline, even about how tricky she could be, Carly had learned the right way.

Owen snatched napkins out of the chrome holder on the table and extended them to Carly. "Oh, for God's sake."

Owen stopped on the sidewalk in front of his car and snap-flexed his suit sleeves into place. Carly stood next to him, done with crying and wishing she hadn't started. Embarrassing. She felt dumb and blotchy.

He pointed down the road, down the way Marcelline and John had raced away. "So you want me to just drive that way until something else comes up to give us a clue?"

"Yes."

Owen sighed hugely. "If you're right, you understand that it really makes more sense for me to just let one of them kill the other and buy the painting from the one who's left. Then *I* can go home."

"That won't work."

He looked down at her. She looked up at him, but the sun behind him made her squint. She looked back down the road.

"They don't have it," she said to the street. "I do."

CHAPTER TWENTY-NINE

Owen didn't want to let on that the jolt had been oddly pleasant. The shock of her was a sparkling bit of fun on a grim day. The distraction of a shooting star.

"I don't suppose you're going to tell me where you've put it?"

"Nope." She didn't look at him and walked to the passenger door of his car.

He unlocked their doors from his side. "And even though Marcelline is worried I might hurt her, you're not, because you think I won't do anything since you're a kid."

"Yep."

"Fair enough." Owen got into the car.

He watched Carly take in the interior of the Mercedes, both of them lost for a moment in her barefaced appreciation of the look and feel of it. She ran her finger over the hashy stripe on the carbon-fiber faceplate, double-checking the illusion of texture there.

Owen felt a gurgle of envy percolating in his chest for the unself-consciousness of the gesture.

He started the car and pulled out to the light on the main road. "So just go that way?"

"I guess." She smiled, a little gift in it for him that she acknowledged the lunacy of their predicament.

His phone rang through the audio system. He checked the screen, then answered, "Samantha, I'm a little busy right now."

"Don't fuck with me."

"Just so you know, we're not alone and you're on speaker."

"Marcelline is with you?"

"No. But a friend of hers is."

"A friend? What are you talking about?"

"It's Marcelline's friend Carly. Say hello, Carly."

Carly looked to Owen for confirmation that he really wanted her to say it out loud, and he nodded toward the dash.

"Um, hi."

"That sounds like a kid. What is going on, Owen? Where is Marcelline? Is she okay?"

"Is who okay? Carly or Marcelline?" Owen cut his eyes at Carly and grinned.

"I'm serious. Do not fuck with me."

"Language."

Samantha's voice faltered. "Owen, have you done something?"

"I have not. It was Jonathan. That's why I'm sitting here with Carly, not Marcelline. He found her and they zoomed off on a high-speed chase. That's the story I was told."

"Did he take the painting?"

"I'm not sure, but that's a reasonable guess." He put his finger across his pursed lips for Carly's benefit. She nodded and the little conspiracy crackled between them.

"So what are we doing?" Samantha asked.

"We?"

"My nerves are shot, Owen. Pick a side."

"No. But I will say that, as it stands, I'm in it for the painting and to go home for now. Any number of things could change how I feel about that, but that's where we are at the moment. If that helps you, great. And all that, of course, is if I can find it." He cast a look at Carly, who returned it solidly, unblinking, unintimidated. Weird kid.

Samantha let some dead air hiss through the speakers. When she spoke, she sounded sad and worried. "That's not good enough."

"No?"

"I want you to help Marcelline."

From the passenger seat, Carly darted in between Owen's shoulder and the dashboard and leaned in. "I do, too," she said, and glanced up at him.

"Carly," Samantha said through the speaker. "Do you have something to write with?"

Carly looked expectantly at Owen, who gave up and pointed at the center console. She took Owen's pen and twisted in her seat to pull a folded paper from her back pocket. "Got it."

"Take down this number. Owen, if Carly here gives me a call later and tells me what happened, I will do a load of laundry for you. Whites. With bleach. Lots of bleach." Samantha read out a telephone number and Carly called it back to her as she wrote.

"Is this a result-based promise or do intentions count?" Owen asked.

Samantha sighed. "I'm sorry for the crack about having your heart on your sleeve. That was unkind of me."

"I don't really know what you expect me to do. We don't know what we're dealing with until one of them reaches out. And then, of course, there's always the possibility that they're perfectly happy, just the two of them doing whatever they're doing and letting me stand around with my dick in my hand." Owen looked over at Carly. "Sorry."

Carly shrugged.

"It's not like that," Samantha said. "It never was."

"If you say so, then it must be true."

Samantha ignored it. "Could you send a text to Jonathan, maybe?"

"I could. But since we don't know which one of them currently has the upper hand in this, or neither one if they're partners and don't need it. . . ." He slid a sideways look at Carly. "It seems like a risk that Marcelline might not appreciate if we make things more difficult for her."

"What are you going to do, then?"

"I'm going to wait, Samantha. They'll be in touch. This would be a pretty pointless exercise if they don't. Hopefully Carly will give you a call before the streetlights come on. Because I won't."

"I'm sorry, Owen."

"That'll be the day."

Owen killed the call from the steering wheel. They drove on for a while in silence.

"You're going to have to tell me where the painting is, you know," he said.

"I know. But I don't want to go home yet."

"Convenient. Because you can't go home yet."

Her head jerked up, testing the air for a threat in that comment. "Why?"

"Look, it's not personal. There's just no way to turn you loose in the world until this is done. God knows what you'd say."

"I wouldn't say anything. But I don't want to go anyway. I want to make sure that Emma is okay. Marcelline."

"I won't let anything happen to you."

"That's not the same thing."

"I understand. But it's the best I can do. So where are we going?"

Carly unfolded the paper, a receipt, that she'd written Samantha's number on. "When Marcelline was washing up, I took it into the party store and asked them to gift wrap and hold it for me. I said it was a present for my mom."

Owen couldn't decide if the tremor in him was nausea or a laugh trying to elbow through his amazement.

"What?" she said.

"That painting is worth a fortune. And you left it at a party store."

"They didn't know what it was. Sometimes there's nothing safer than cluelessness. Ask any kid."

Owen waited at the curb. He didn't like the worry of all she might get up to in there if she changed her mind, but he weighed it against the inescapable fact that he didn't look like anyone's idea of a teenage girl's father, and he was too old to be her brother. People would stare.

Carly reappeared after a tense few minutes. She slid the festively wrapped rectangle into the back and plopped into the passenger seat as if it weren't only the second time she'd gotten in beside him. She adjusted the air flow onto her face and petted the leather of the seat.

"All set?"

"Easy-peasy," she said, but looked as if she might cry.

"What is it?"

"My mother must be freaking out."

"So send her a text. Make something up. Tell her you're at the movies."

"Yeah, I might have thought of that if I had my phone anymore. This is bad. What if she calls the cops?"

Owen pulled into a parking space. "Do you know your mother's phone number?"

"Yes, but she doesn't have her phone. John does."

"Is there someone else who can take her a message?"

"I guess Ada. She only lives two streets over."

"Do you know this Ada's number?"

"Yes."

"Do you know your own phone number?"

"Ye-eess."

"I know how to mask a text, spoof a number."

Owen watched Carly fall lost into the sea of possibilities. She gasped. "Oh, wow. Will you show me how?"

"No."

"Why not?"

"Because you would be an unstoppable menace. But I will send your mother a note so that she doesn't think you're dead."

"I wouldn't be an unstoppable menace."

Owen squinted through the windshield. "If you could only see you like I see you. No. I'm not showing you how to do it."

"You know I still have to make that call later. To tell whatsername what happened so that you can get whatever 'laundry' means in secret code." Carly pierced him through, the cheeky point of it glittering in her eyes, trying to bring him around to meet up with her honesty.

He held his smirk down between his teeth. *God, this fucking day.* "I don't like you."

She buckled her seat belt. "I don't think that's true."

They watched the clear streamers of heat waving on the rim of the rise in the road. Owen sent a text from Carly to Donna via Ada, saying Carly was sorry. That she was upset and keeping her phone off. That she was fine and safe and that she'd be home in a little while.

"I don't want to sit here anymore," she said. "Can we drive?"

"Okay."

"Your car is pretty."

"Yes, it is."

They resumed the ride back in the direction that had swallowed up Marcelline, and Jonathan after her. They hadn't made it four miles past where they'd first set out before they found her car on the side of the road.

"Stop!" Carly cried. "Wait, stop!"

"We can't."

"Why not?" Carly twisted in her seat, ducking out of the seat belt to better see into Marcelline's car as they drove past.

"Well, I don't know. What do you think you'll say to the cop who stops while we're poking around an abandoned car?"

"What if she was in it?"

"She wasn't. She's with Jonathan."

"You don't know that. Please." Carly was winding up to crying again. "Stop! Go back!"

"Listen to me. Calm down. She's not in the car. She's not in the hospital. I promise you, she's with Jonathan."

"She might not be. She might be hurt."

"I didn't say she wasn't hurt. Look, that wasn't a crash. That was a swerve to a stop. The back right wheel was broken, she may have tagged something, maybe a curb, but the car wasn't smashed in. There's no reason to think she was banged up at all. But she was being followed. We know that. So, Jonathan picked her up. The question is whether she was happy or not to go with him."

"You can't know that's what happened. You weren't there. Maybe someone else stopped to help her. Maybe she got away."

"And you don't think we would have heard from her by now if any one of those other things had happened?"

That corked her right up. She wound herself back under the seat belt and chewed her fingernails. Owen watched Marcelline's car disappear around a bend in the rearview mirror.

"Does your stepfather carry a gun?"

"What? No! I mean, I don't think so." Her shrinking confidence on this point dwindled, sputtered, then went out. "I don't know."

"Okay."

"Marcelline had one."

"Well, maybe she got to it first. I still think she would have called by now."

"What are we going to do now?"

"We still wait."

But it was only for a few more minutes. The texts started rolling in.

CHAPTER THIRTY

Jonathan had rehearsed having the upper hand even before he'd ever once in his life had the upper hand. He'd done it since he was a little boy. Instead of getting songs stuck in his head, he looped elaborate scenes about his life, and the life he would have—detailed plays of his saying whatever he wanted to say, doing whatever he wanted to do, having whatever he wanted to have. Having everything, as a matter of fact.

All the practice had made him good within a range.

He'd been born with some talent for manipulation and had dedicated years of thought and testing to grooming his edge. But the second most important thing was knowing when it was all getting away from you. He had a sense for that, too. A knack for self-preservation beyond the basic animal toolset.

In his earlier calls with Owen, there had been hotel and garage sounds. Only two hotels with parking decks were close by, and Owen had been in the first one. His car wasn't hard to spot. Jonathan had tailed Owen to his meetup with Marcelline.

There, he'd tried the simplest thing he could think of—to set things back the way they'd been, to have the painting and reclaim the meeting with Owen. From there, it should have fallen the expected way. He would get paid and get gone, just as he'd practiced in his mind's eye.

Going all the way to hands-on with Marcelline tipped this into a brand-new landscape. He'd felt the difference, the new requirements, in his bones. Then he smashed her facedown onto the steering wheel.

The car had cracked something on her wild, sparking stunt ride out of the shopping center. It held out longer than he would have guessed. He watched it fight its injuries, hobbling down the road at an impressive clip for all the struggle. He imagined Marcelline wrestling physics behind the wheel. But after a few miles, the wobble disappeared in a snap and a hard pull to the right. The chase was over.

He was behind her on the shoulder and out at a fast walk in seconds. She was frantic, grabbing at the clasp on her purse. He tried to look as helpful as possible from the outside. He opened the door and put her under control before she could get clear of her seat.

He'd guided her, dragged her, dazed and wavering, into the back footwells of his own car. Both feet into this strange new territory, he was committed. There weren't going to be any do-overs.

He grabbed up her handbag, which had fallen onto the pavement, so no one would stop for it. He held tight against the instinct to rush. It would draw attention. A mild hurry would have to do, and it would probably keep him from falling over his own feet besides.

But the plan, such as it ever was, ended at the bumper of Marcelline's car. Jonathan checked the back seat. Empty. He glanced back. Marcelline still hadn't risen over the window line of his car. He popped the trunk latch. Thank God it was there. He scooped up the blanket and garment bag, but it sagged—all fabric, no brace of wood—in his grasp. The tuxedo was the only thing under the zipper.

From there, everything else had been a developing exit strategy.

Marcelline fought like hell when he stopped to tie her the first time. Shirtsleeves, jacket sleeves, cummerbund, and trouser legs were the only useful things in the garment bag. Her own purse strap eventually got her feet under control. He pushed her down, struggling, over the hump of the floorwell and threw the garment bag and blanket over her for camouflage. Round two, when he'd gotten to where he was going and had more time and privacy, was even more vicious. He moved her into the front seat. By the end, they were both bruised and bleeding.

Jonathan looked over at Marcelline. Her eyes were closed. The tears had dried in black-streaked, vividly pale tracks over her face that disappeared into the gag pulled hard through her lips. Her hands were tied, clasped in her lap, the broken nail beds still glistening with drying blood. Her left cheek was swollen and red, but going dark in the center where the first strike of the steering wheel had landed. The second blow had almost knocked her out, but the knot was hidden in her hair.

Seeing her like that, tied at the neck to the headrest and at the wrists and ankles, he felt a mixture of guilt and amazement. He hadn't known what all he was made of. Now the creature of his own mind was splayed out for vivisection.

He'd never hurt anyone. Not really. Not directly. True, he'd never stopped any hurt either. He'd even nudged it along before.

But instinct had been honed to habit, and today, habit had succumbed to evolution.

He enabled his father to ruin. Marcelline was the first person he'd hurt with his own hands. Roy, well, Jonathan had escorted him right over the line.

And Roy smelled terrible.

Jonathan had come out here because getting rid of Roy was essentially the only thing that had worked out okay in the last few weeks. Revisiting his last success seemed to be the most hopeful thing to do. But the reek from the truck was already a bigger deterrent than he would have guessed.

He wouldn't take the Anningers' money now for anything. It wasn't worth it. Owen would never forgive this chaos twice. He'd find him. The only way to be clear of it was to be all the way clear of it. The little survival compass in his guts fluttered. He had to leave. He'd find another way.

He texted Owen: *The painting for Marcelline. Then we're done. We're where the truck is. Carly took Marcelline yesterday. She knows where it is.*

The message came back: *She knows where you're talking about. She doesn't know how to get there. She's fourteen, dumbass.*

Jonathan sent a screenshot of his location and a message: *I can see the approach road. If anyone other than you comes down it, they'll have to stop to move Marcelline's dead body out of the road first.*

Owen texted back: *Have you been working up that line for the last hour? You missed your calling. You should have been a janitor.*

Jonathan: *How long till you get here?*

Owen: *About half an hour. So go ahead and put on something pretty.*

It was oddly reassuring that Owen was being a dick.

Jonathan waited. Sometimes he caught Marcelline looking at him, sometimes she was so still he wondered if she'd somehow died.

He got the gas from the back. It was his leash on this meeting. The cheap hunting knife would be the collar. He'd picked up both at a gas station that sold everything. It even had a diner and Laundromat. You could practically live there. The styrofoam cups in the flotsam of Roy's truck had the same logo as the sticker on Jonathan's new gas can. The symmetry sent a nasty little tingle through his chest.

The sting of his blood pressure surged pins and needles into his hands as he worked. He held his breath as much as he could. He opened the truck's doors and poured and splashed the gasoline. He was thankful for every oily, antiseptic waft of the fumes. It burned his throat, but it gave him a break from the constant exhalation of rot coming off Roy and his mess.

It was a strange, miserable thing to do, dousing Roy and all his stuff. It had to be like this because Jonathan had to go as far as he could. And that might have to be all the way.

Of anyone he'd ever met, Owen was the only one who might happily go to that line, take them there possibly only because it amused him. And Owen had a pastime of feeding humiliation to Jonathan. The dose makes the poison. This time, Jonathan wouldn't swallow it.

He rehearsed it in his mind to the worst case, imagining sinking the knife into Marcelline's neck. He had to know if it could happen. The shiny, pleated cummerbund was an accident of necessity that made it more likely. It held her still against the headrest, but better than that, he wouldn't be able to see what he was doing. If it came to that, it would be almost like not doing it at all, just the blade disappearing into black fabric.

Owen had stopped to save her before. That was his line. He would stop to save her again.

Jonathan could do it. He would do it. Owen would believe it if Jonathan did.

He heard the Mercedes coming before he saw it. It had to be Owen. Even cops didn't swagger that much in the tailpipes.

He walked away and lit a pack of matches and lobbed it into the truck as Owen pulled into view. He tossed a second one to land underneath the running board. The initial blast of the cooking gasoline licked at his skin and drove him away at a trot.

Owen got out of the car, setting his cuffs and buttoning his jacket as he came. Carly stepped out into his wake, openmouthed at the fire already busy in the truck.

Jonathan positioned himself at the open passenger window of his car and put the knife against the satin that covered Marcelline's throat.

"Stop," Jonathan said. "You have to be carrying a gun. I would be so disappointed to find out you weren't. So take it out now and put it on the ground. Either that or Marcelline will have to insist you strip naked for everyone's peace of mind."

Jonathan brandished the knife, hoping his hand covered the embarrassing camouflage plastic that decorated the handle. The blade was bright and impressive, though, and he put it back against the fabric.

Carly gasped.

Owen reached behind him. "That would be quite an education for young Carly here."

"Stop," Jonathan said again. "Put your hands up where I can see them."

Owen sagged in exasperation.

"If it's at your waistband, let Carly get it."

Owen unbuttoned again and raised his jacket clear of his body. "It's okay," he said to her. "The safety's on. You'll be fine."

She struggled at the small of his back, then stepped out from behind him holding the gun as if it might blow up in her hand.

The worried, wary look she'd had in the kitchen this morning was gone, replaced with disbelief. Anger. Carly looked disgusted. There would be no *when John disappeared* legend. She would hate him or excuse him or possibly forgive him. But her new expression was a banishment. He'd never know how Carly would tell it.

"Carly, bring that here." He held out his hand for the gun and stepped to the blade-tip limit so that she wouldn't have to get too close. She wouldn't want that. He certainly didn't. He didn't want to see her face change even more when she got a closer look at Marcelline.

"Carly, do not do that," Owen said.

"Carly!" Jonathan called.

Owen smiled at her. "Take it across the road. Throw it down the hill. You know that's what you want to do."

Carly straightened up and scowled at Jonathan. She stomped off across the grass and overhanded the gun down the embankment.

The flicker of the fire in the truck was starting to grow wild sprouts and plumes of dark smoke.

"Carly," Owen said as she came back into their standoff. "Can you please go get your present from the back of the car?"

Panic filled Jonathan's throat. He forced his voice up through it. "Carly, no! Stay right where you are." He risked a threat. "Carly, look at me. Look at what's happening. Do not go get anything for him. Don't risk your friend."

"Relax," Owen said. "It's just the painting."

"I said no."

"Well then, go ahead and stab her and let me get on the road. This is getting fucking old."

Jonathan felt Marcelline recoil the scant inch she could from the knife.

"Honestly," Owen said. "It's the painting. How else are you going to get it? How would that feel in your bladder to see me digging around in my car for something? Do you trust it? I wouldn't. But you do you. As if you could even help it."

Carly's glare heated up. "Just stop. Both of you." She stalked off toward the car without anyone's permission.

"Unwrap it as you come, so he doesn't mistake it for a machine gun," Owen called back to Carly.

She did.

"I'm not booby-trapping her, Jonathan. None of this was my idea, remember? Never has been. I was going to blow you off. Carly made me come here. I already had what I came for. See?"

The comment made Jonathan look at Carly, who was studying the ground and cradling the painting. Marcelline couldn't turn in the seat, but inclined her head. Fresh tears streamed down her face.

Carly's shoulders were shaking with sobs.

Owen brought the group around from the moment of cascading emotions. "What's with the bonfire? I'm not going to say it doesn't make a hell of a backdrop. I could do without the smell, though."

"It's a timer, if you like. To keep this short. Someone is going to see that smoke. They're going to call 911. It might have happened already. There's a dead body in there."

"You don't say."

"You guys can all be standing around like assholes when they get here. You can try to come up with something to say to the police or you can give me the painting and I'll cut her loose. This can all be over in the next two minutes."

"Two minutes? That's a long time." Owen walked off toward the truck. Jonathan didn't know why he needed a closer look, much less a closer smell. He certainly wasn't going to be able to put it out.

Some of the flames leaped off, cutting free from the body of fire before winking out above it. It was oddly beautiful.

Owen went around to the back of the truck. Jonathan could feel the heat from here. It must have been a broiler where Owen was standing.

"What the hell are you doing?" Jonathan called. "Let's get this finished." Then to Carly: "Just bring it to me. Bring it to me and I'll let her go. I'm sorry."

Carly watched Owen, who ignored them both. She plucked at the hem of her T-shirt with her free hand.

But she didn't go to Jonathan.

At the open hatch, Owen laid his arm across his waist, holding back his jacket, almost a courtly prelude to a bow, which he then did, arm extended into the back of the truck.

He came out with a rectangle, cardboard maybe, crossed in duct tape and aflame at one end. He walked around with his torch, away from Jonathan, putting the car between them.

Jonathan was buoyant with adrenaline, as if he were lifting off, hovering slightly beyond what he was actually doing. He couldn't make it mean anything. Was Owen going to start another fire in the grass? "What the fuck are you doing?"

Owen watched the flame at a casual arm's length. Admiring it. Drawing all their attention to its glow.

"Stop! Not another goddamned step. What are you doing?"

Owen cocked his head as if Jonathan hadn't spoken English. And he certainly didn't stop. Across the roof of Jonathan's own car, Owen smiled at him, big teeth flashing. He opened the driver's side and pitched the burning box in with Marcelline and closed the door again.

It was Monopoly. Jonathan was transfixed by the sight of it on his seat. Cheery white and red where it wasn't on fire. GO! on one end, big bold question mark on the other. Indeed. All of life summed up and burning. The leather of the seat melted instantly under it. The steering wheel smoked. The carpet oozed black smoke.

Carly's piercing shriek rent the air and broke the spell.

"Shit!" Jonathan recoiled a stagger step back in horror as Marcelline went wild-eyed, flailing to the short limit of her ties, rough, gagging screams of terror rising muffled through the fabric in her mouth.

The open window beside her sucked at the flame, pulling it toward her.

Owen came around. He'd never broken stride. He slid into the shallow space that Jonathan had left in his small retreat. He stepped between the car and Jonathan with not a flicker of distress spared for the woman about to burn to death in front of them.

Carly was already halfway there. "No!"

She dropped the painting as she ran and it hit the ground, corner first, with a bright, splintering crack. The four-hundred-year-old Flinck disappeared in two distinct pieces into the tall grass.

Jonathan backed off another step, holding the knife out at Owen.

Owen gracefully sidestepped Carly rushing up, tearing at the door, screaming for Marcelline but calling her Emma.

Every nerve in Jonathan's body hummed to an almost-subsonic ring, an internal tornado siren of music. He was vibrating so steadily, the back and forth almost canceled out to a standstill. His knife hand was trembling so hummingbird fast, it was almost steady.

Carly fought against the cummerbund around Marcelline's neck, her wiry little muscles bunching in the strain, her whole body twisting to thrash the cloth loose, coughing out smoke and calling for help.

But Owen ignored her and matched Jonathan's retreat, step for step, herding him away.

Carly pulled Marcelline free, collapsing to the ground with her, pulling at the viciously tight bindings. She unwound the purse strap from Marcelline's ankles and freed the gag. She wrapped up the grown woman in her spindly little-girl arms, their heads together, crying. Marcelline was sobbing into Carly's shoulder, trying to talk between the hitches, reaching for her bag. Carly helped her.

On her knees Carly turned to Owen. "Are you crazy?"

Jonathan walked backward, slowly away, knife out. He shivered as Owen still held his gaze, smiling at Jonathan in the clamor, calling over his shoulder to the rabidly angry Carly, "What? He only gave me two minutes."

Carly jumped up as Marcelline shoved a black something into her hands.

Carly pointed the gun mostly downward, teeth bared at Owen, barrel toward his knees, deciding what to do with her power. She jerked one titch to the right and the gun was lined up on Jonathan.

It had been a horrible feeling looking at the black circle of that barrel in Marcelline's hand the other night. With Carly behind it, it was almost otherworldly. She couldn't shoot anyone. She was just a kid. She couldn't knock anyone out either. Or track him down. Or steal a priceless painting. Twice. Except that she had.

Jonathan took another step back. Everything in him wanted to run, but it would be pointless. Owen would catch him. He raked his mind for one more plan. Just one more. Carly drew the low aim back and forth between the two men.

"Perfect!" Owen was grinning. "Can I have that, please?"

Carly's nostrils flared and she brought the gun up as Owen came toward her. "She could have died!"

"She didn't." Owen put his hand around Carly's, guided it down.

Carly's groan rolled through the wounded low notes and rose to almost a scream. "What is *wrong* with you? All of you?"

"I don't know. But nothing was ever going to happen to her. Not with you around. I knew that."

Their hands moved apart, a magician's trick, and the gun was small and completely steady in Owen's massive fist. And pointed at Jonathan's middle.

Jonathan dropped the knife. Hands out. "Okay. Let me just leave. What difference does it make now? You have everything. There's nothing I can do to any of you."

"True. But how are you going to do that?" Owen asked.

"Do what?"

"Leave. Are you suggesting I give you a lift to the bus station? Your car is on fire."

"You can't shoot me in front of Carly. Or at all. She'll know. That's not right."

"I can't? You burned a dead body in front of her. And, Jesus, look at Marcelline. You beat the shit out of her friend. Held a knife to her throat. You actually told Carly to bring you that painting so you wouldn't kill her friend. But I can't shoot you? Hmmmm."

Jonathan hoped Carly held sway over Owen. She worked quickly on men like them. She'd taken him from wishing his girlfriend were childless to being a content stepfather. An amused one. One who sought her approval. He and Owen weren't so different.

"Carly, listen. Carly, please. Remember what I said about us making ourselves? You have to understand I was going to—"

Owen lowered the gun and covered the distance between them in a few shockingly fast strides. Jonathan's body jerked in opposing impulses, to relax out of the gun's sights and to retreat from Owen's sudden lurch toward him.

Jonathan didn't work out the conflict in time to get clear of Owen's open hand. It crashed against his cheek in a slap that stole his vision briefly. Owen backed up immediately and reextended the pistol.

"Don't you talk to her, you sack of shit."

Owen stepped back and poked at the grass with his foot. He stooped and picked up the larger piece of the painting, then reached again for the splintered triangle of its left side. It had broken off just past the waterwheel at the foot of the bridge.

That corner. The first thing Jonathan had seen poking up from the box in his father's garage. The wedge that had shown in the video as he pulled it up on his computer with the cops behind him. The tattling glimpse that no one should have seen.

Jonathan breathed in a lungful of complicated air. Smoke. The green of trampled grass. Fresh decay. Wisps of clean breeze. Metal and meat.

He watched the maw of the gun never waver off target. Fresh sweat bloomed into his armpits and groin.

"Carly." Owen called to her and she walked over, stricken, mouth like a tragedy mask. Owen gave her the pieces. "I want you to take this to the car. Put it inside and then keep walking down the road. I'll pick you up in a few minutes."

She looked past Owen into Jonathan's eyes.

Alarm blazed through him and thrummed into his fingertips. His calves ached. His blood sizzled under her gaze. He tried to be John, the one she'd laughed with, the one she'd accepted in good faith. He brought the components of her stepfather into his frozen face as fast as he could recall them through the rising yammer of every instinct in his body. "Please."

But Owen called her attention back before Jonathan could work it all to the surface. She looked away. There'd been no spark of recognition. Carly didn't know him. How did it ever come down to Carly?

Her chin was trembling when she looked back at Owen. He held the gun on Jonathan casually, almost invisibly, like an extension of his arm. He might as well have been pointing his finger at him.

"Take it to the car and keep going. I'll be right there." Amazingly, Owen winked. "Go on, Your Highness. One day you'll rule more than you already do. But you need to listen to me just now."

"But Marcelline. What will—"

"Go ahead. It'll be okay."

She did. Jonathan watched her thin back retreat, the big piece of the broken Flinck under her arm, the rest of it, the wooden stake of a Dutch master, in her hand.

Terror, like pain, has a threshold. Beyond it is just white noise. The line slipped under Jonathan's toes and tipped him away from all that he could handle.

Owen took up Jonathan's sight line. His height and breadth eclipsed the light. The air fell just slightly cooler in his shadow.

"Your problem is that you think this means something. That it has to, even for me. That this is dramatic." Owen took one giant mother-may-I-step closer. "It's not."

Jonathan wanted it to be that Owen punched him in the chest. The pain felt like the blow of a hard, heavy fist. But a crash of gunfire split the air simultaneously with the hit. And Owen was still where he'd been. Not punching. Just aiming.

It wasn't possible for it to be what Jonathan wanted, and the center of him was now hot and wet. The middle of him had a new gravity all its own. The world whooshed into him, Jonathan staggered sideways and his knees went loose. He went down to his hip and one arm. He heard a pop in his elbow but didn't feel it. His chest felt solid, flattened, as if he couldn't break open the bellows of his lungs. He rolled onto his back.

Then Owen was all the sky above him. Owen shook his head, mild in his disgust. He put the gun between them. "Idiot."

Jonathan's head snapped sideways with the crash of the second shot.

CHAPTER THIRTY-ONE

Marcelline and Owen hadn't seen each other in more than four years. The last time she saw him, she wasn't convinced she'd survive the next time she did. And that had nearly been true, but in no way resembling what she'd lived in fear of all this time.

The sun lit up the sheen of his dark blue suit. She was bleeding, shaking, stunned motionless in the after-ring of gunshots. Two vehicles were on fire. And he looked as if he'd walked out of a magazine.

He surveyed the truck, measured the column of smoke rising skyward from it, then craned back to check the bend of the road in the distance where it turned toward them.

"We really do have to get out of here," he said, picking it up like the next line of a casual conversation they'd never had.

It was the first thing he'd said to her since he'd told her to get some rest in his guest room. She hurt all over, but it was remote. She wanted to talk to him, wanted to know what he thought about what had just happened, and to know if he understood her part in this.

But the weight of the moment seemed lost on him. Maybe. She felt him not allowing their eyes to meet. He kept a step too far from moving the air around her. He walked past, stripping off his jacket. In Jonathan's car, the flames were halfhearted, smoldering and belching smoke, not even scary compared to their big brothers bellowing in Roy's truck. Owen beat the blaze down with his jacket, then grabbed up the garment bag from the back and pressed it against the seat to finish it off.

The fire snuffed out. The upholstery had holes through to the springs in places, and the dashboard was dusted in soot, but the damage was cosmetic. Owen started the car and smiled at her through the open passenger window.

He popped the trunk and was out again, charred box top in hand. He strode in a full graceful, giant bustle that didn't get any less unreal as he went. How was he unrattled? What was he thinking? He skirted the red and beige glistening clutter in the grass by Jonathan's head and dropped the cardboard next to it.

Marcelline looked for Carly at the edge of the clearing, but she hadn't come back. They couldn't let her see this. Owen walked over and plucked the shredded cheery wrapping paper out of the grass, crossed back, and tossed it into the waiting trunk.

Then he finally looked at her. Everything. He knew it all.

The trees tilted in Marcelline's vision, the fire was above and beside and the sky was in the wrong place. A gray mist pulled the green and orange from the image, speeding in to swallow her.

Owen stepped under her arm to steady her. "Whoa. Whoa. Are you going to lose it?"

Marcelline was okay enough to shake her head. She sucked in a deep shuddering breath.

Owen was looking into her eyes, holding her. For a glinting instant, she wanted there to be more. More to ask. More to know.

More time. But her want deflected off something in him, a wall. A cancellation. And her want was gone.

He steadied her. "Okay, good. We really have to get out of here. And we have to get that out of here." He ticked his head at Jonathan. "Help me." Owen walked over to the body and looked back, surprised not to find her at his shoulder. "Come on. You can hold his legs, if the rest of it bothers you."

When Jonathan was packed away with the burned garment bag and Owen's jacket, they covered the burned seat with the ruined tuxedo.

Owen bent the game box into a scoop and headed back to the red grass. Marcelline closed her eyes against knowing any more about what he raked from the trampled ground. He dashed back to Roy's pyre, with a Monopoly box top full of gore. He tossed it in. Jonathan's brain burning in the fire he'd started. Her legs made the case again for folding. She resisted.

Owen came back from a quick scan of the area. He seemed satisfied. "I can call someone in to take care of this, but I need you to drive the car to the airport. Just park it, leave the keys in the ignition, and get away fast. Text me the space number as soon as you can. Someone will be on standby to get in right after you. I'll pick you up. And then you're done. This is done."

She could only look at Owen in wonder.

"Okay?" he said.

"What about Carly?"

"I'll take her. She's waiting for me. She needs to go home."

"But I can't just leave it like that. I have to talk to her. I have to help her with this."

Owen ticked his head to the side. "I know that. What did you think I was going to do? Let you drive my car? Again?"

Owen being funny. Jonathan dead. The Flinck in her hands and then gone. The gray threatened at the edge of her vision again.

"Can you do this?"

"I've got it." Marcelline rifled through her battered purse for her hotel key. "Go get Carly. Meet me at the Marriott across from the Y. Room 311."

"She'll be fine. I'll talk to her. See you soon. Don't get pulled over."

Samantha would approve of Owen's advice. She closed her eyes and felt the balance in her mind. Marcelline found her handhold on the last part of the story. "Let's go."

CHAPTER THIRTY-TWO

Carly walked away from them, the pieces of the painting nearly weightless in her grasp, as if some essential thing had poured out when it cracked in two. Like it was hollow now.

All this trouble for something so breakable.

But what little weight there was, even in two pieces, had served as an anchor. As soon as she put it in the car, nothing held her to her place. The responsibility of carrying something so precious had been a distraction that kept all the other thoughts away. She had allowed it to do that. She'd bent all of her concentration on it.

But when she closed the door of Owen's pretty car, there was nothing. Or more precisely, there was everything. Carly ran.

Her right knee had been at the top of its pistoning stroke when the first gunshot split the air. A second later when she was skimming the ground, her feet switching places midleap between the footfalls, another sharp crash broke over the noise of the rush and thud of her sprint.

She skidded to a stop, arms wheeling big circles to keep her from pitching over.

She listened. Nothing. If the shots missed, no one was yelling about it. If the shots landed, no one was in pain to cry over it.

She ran faster.

She'd covered most of a mile by the time she heard tires rolling, faint in her wake, the engine hum growing louder as it came closer. Carly wanted nothing more than to be invisible. Other Carly took the reins and made that happen.

She veered off the edge of the dirt track into the trees. She watched the road from behind the trunk of a stout pine. Ridiculous. Cartoony. *Life imitating art imitating life.* She could almost hear Marcelline saying it.

Carly was supposed to wait for Owen. He was coming to get her. That's what she'd agreed to. The yes had made sense at the time. The yes allowed her to leave a situation that she desperately wanted to be away from. Yes to a man with a gun in his hand, before the reality of that gun had blasted a hole into the quiet.

Now the thought of seeing Owen made her want to scream.

But it was John's red car that crawled into view. Carly couldn't breathe. If it was John, then who didn't scream at the gunshots? The two gunshots? There were only two other people. How?

The car picked up speed and Carly tried to shift with the motion of it to stay completely hidden behind the bole of the tree. As the car drew even with her, she risked a peek. It wasn't John at the wheel.

Marcelline was sobbing, not even trying not to, and driving away. Leaving her.

Carly dashed from around the tree, waving her arms to flag her attention, but Marcelline didn't turn her head. She didn't stop. She didn't even slow down.

Carly watched from the middle of the dirt track as John's car receded out of the field and toward the main road. Which left no time to hide again as Owen's car rocketed into view.

She stepped back, ending up at the driver's-side window as he slowed to a stop next to her.

"We've got to go." That's all. After everything, that's what he chose to say.

"I—"

"Get in."

Carly looked back down the road she'd run, then off toward the comet trail of dust that shrouded the back of Marcelline in John's car, growing smaller in the distance.

"Now!" said Owen.

She came around and climbed in beside him. She'd spent a long time in this seat already today, but it was only something she knew, not something she remembered in her mind or body. A story of what had happened. Unreal. There would be no video to show her how she ever sat next to him and did not scream.

"Buckle up."

Carly burst into tears. "She didn't even look at me. She was crying."

"You'll see her again. I'm taking you to her hotel. She'll be back in a little while."

Carly fought the shuddery breaths. "Why was she crying like that?"

Owen just glanced at her.

"Is he dead?"

Owen looked away from the road again, scowling at her, incredulous.

An unpadded avalanche of consequence hit, blow by blow until Carly doubled over onto her knees. John was dead. All of this. Her life. Oh, God, her mom. Carly was so tired.

She didn't feel the bump and rise of the transition to asphalt, but when the sobs had run out, she realized the road was smooth under their wheels.

Owen was rolling up his shirtsleeves. His forearms were ridged with muscle, but pale.

"What happened to your jacket?" Carly risked a likely bad answer on purpose, to test herself for more tears.

"It got burned."

"That's all?"

"Yes."

"Why did you have to kill him?"

Only his right eyebrow acknowledged the question, and they drove on in silence.

When they got as far as the first traffic lights in civilization, he looked over at her again. "You have a very human problem."

"What?"

"You want everything both ways. Or more like you want everything every way. You know what he was. You know what he'd done. You saw what he would have done today. You did see that, right? You watch the shit out of everything. I'm going to have to hope you were paying attention to that."

She was certainly paying attention now.

But he checked to make sure. "Good. It's the only way someone like you gets through this. Did you believe that he would have killed Marcelline if he thought it would've helped him?"

The misery dragged Carly's voice to a place she couldn't get to. She nodded.

"I had what I came for. I had the painting. You needed him stopped."

The peg turned. Owen's voice. The protective curl of his huge shoulders shielding himself. The cramped space between his pained eyebrows.

"You didn't have what you came for. You needed him stopped, too."

Owen's jaw muscles flared. "Fair enough. So I stopped him."

"There wasn't another way," Carly said in something between a question and a declaration.

"He lied. Cheated. Stole. Schemed. And that's only what he did to me. He threatened people, he manipulated them and got some of them killed. He put people in danger who didn't agree to any of this. You. Your mother. He brought it on himself."

It was true. But it wasn't the only thing that was true.

"He was John, too, you know," she said. "Not just Jonathan like you knew him. All of it wasn't fake."

"Perhaps."

She glared at him.

"Fine. He was. I believe you, because somehow I can't help myself. But you have to let him be this, now. Whatever else you want to think of him, you need to make peace with the idea of the Jonathan I knew. Because I'm not wrong either.

"If you want the life you're meant to have, you will hear me. If you blow this up, it will take an entirely different direction. John will have Jonathaned your life, and your mother's life, into something you won't recognize. Ask Marcelline how I know this."

Carly found more tears that ran, slowed, and dried by the time they pulled into the hotel lot. Owen gave her Marcelline's key.

"It's room 311. Go on in. Get cleaned up. Don't call anyone. I'll bring her back, and the two of you will figure out what's next."

"That's it, then?"

"You'll be okay."

She looked at him.

"Truly. You're going to rule the world someday."

"I don't even know where you live." They were in the stupid end-of-phone-calls awkwardness, but times a thousand. "Do you think you will ever talk to me again?"

"God, I hope not."

It caught her off guard. Funny and painful and somehow frightening. "That's mean."

Owen shrugged. It looked weird in his massive chest. "I am not meant for hanging around with. Small talk. I am not meant for Christmas cards and what do you call it? Snapchat. I am not meant for young ladies who will rule the world. This situation needed a good bad guy or a bad good guy. You can decide where you'll put me in this story."

Carly looked at the clock in the dashboard. It wasn't even four o'clock yet. But her mother would be worried soon, if not already. "I have to go home. I have to act normal. Like I don't know. Marcelline will be gone. You'll be gone. It'll be like it never happened."

"No. In some weird way, we'll still be here. Nothing is ever over. It's always happening. Out there in infinity. That's the good news and the bad news and the only useful thing I have for you."

"All this stuff that happened. It'll make me a freak."

"You might very well be. But I suspect not. I said you'll be okay. I didn't say it would be easy. A wise person once told me that sometimes it sucks to be a unicorn."

Owen pulled his phone from the cup holder and tapped away at the screen. "Okay. When you get your phone back, you'll have a text from a restricted caller. I am the original restricted caller." He cut his eyes at her, and it seemed impossible that she felt a smile well up in her face. "It'll tell you how to spoof a number. You can use it to help your mother get through this. I'm sure our friend Samantha will get you started. They'll help you with a story to finish out what happened today. But you're the only one who will know what to make John say in his goodbye messages to help her."

Carly's eyes flooded again.

Owen shook his head. "He's not worth it."

"Are you?"

"I have no idea. But don't let that stop you. I don't think you're going to be able to turn off the waterworks, so you need to find a way to add that into your story, too. Don't try to hide it from Marcelline and Samantha. They'll know what to do with it."

Of all the un-Owen things that Carly could imagine, he swiped his curled fingers over her cheek, taking most of the tears with the stroke. "But be careful with the texts, okay? I don't actually think you'll be an unstoppable menace. It doesn't seem very you. But you're . . . People will be watching you, wanting to connect with you, because of the way you are, because of how you carry it all. If you're not paying attention, you could create an army of unstoppable menaces."

Carly wiped her face the rest of the way dry with her palms and nodded.

"Goodbye, Carly."

"Goodbye, Owen."

CHAPTER THIRTY-THREE

Owen's car slid like melted silver along the curb in the cell phone lot where she'd told him she'd be. Marcelline raked her hair over her bruised face and stepped from the shadow of a tree. She'd tucked in there, going for a look that said casually dedicated to shade and totally absorbed by something on her phone. It kept her away from anyone who might walk by. Her purse was dangling by its stretched and shredded strap. It was all she could do to keep upright. She smelled like smoke and looked like the fighter who didn't win the belt.

He barely had to stop for her and she was already in, slamming the door on anyone who might have been like her, helpless not to stare at the Mercedes as it went by.

"Is Carly okay?"

"She's okay. She knows what happened. . . . What? I didn't go into detail. She's smart. It's not like I was going to get away with lying about it. I think she'll hold. Samantha's going to see to it that her mother gets an email from John's account tomorrow. It'll cover everything. You know Samantha." He slipped a pointed look sideways at her. "It'll be solid. All Donna will know is that he's left them. She'll make it believable."

"This is horrible. Poor Carly."

"She'll be okay," he said. "Our baby. The child we made."

"That's also horrible."

"Okay," he said. "The Flinck is busted."

"I know."

"They'll still pay the four point seven five for it."

Marcelline's mouth went dry. "But you already have it. I was always going to give it to you if I found it. Because of everything that happened. I don't want the money."

He was surprisingly pleased with himself. "If the transaction doesn't go through, they'll wonder. They'll ask. It'll be a thing. And they're getting it for cheap. Trust me, I would pay five million dollars of my own on top of it to never hear another word about the Gardner collection. This is the last piece of it."

"What do you mean?" But her pulse knew what he meant and it ran to tell her at the same time he did.

"That little stunt you and Jonathan pulled back then—"

"Jonathan. Not me. Not. Me."

"Right. Sorry. Habit. But they didn't just get mad. They got obsessed. They wanted all of it. They wanted me to find the whole thing. That's all I've been doing for four years. This is the last one."

She felt ill. Elated. Amazed, but not unbelieving. For everything he was that wasn't good, Owen wasn't a liar.

"They have the Vermeer?"

Owen nodded.

"The Rembrandt?"

"Uh-huh. A couple of the Degas drawings were destroyed over the years as far as I can tell. I tried to see if Jonathan knew any more about it. But this is it. They even have the vase and the flag topper. This piece of shit is the last important one."

"Owen, they can't keep it. Not the whole thing. This is terrible."

Owen flexed his jaw and sped up.

"It has to go back. This stuff is priceless."

"No. Not true. The price is at the end of a transfer code. Four and three-quarter million. Take the money, Marcelline. Help Carly through school or something. Have a life. Get back to your old one if you want. I'm sure Samantha can help you figure out a way to make amnesia sound believable. Or some damned thing."

"What about the story of the murder? That music producer. Some people said there was evidence on it. Blood. I think maybe I saw it. There might have been."

"Would it help you to know that he liked to drug fifteen-year-old girls?"

She stared at him.

He shrugged. "Okay, that's not true. By all reports, he was a lovely guy. His estate still drills wells in Africa with his royalties. But this painting won't bring him back to life, and this has sucked four years out of mine. Leave it alone."

"How do they think somebody won't tip them off to the FBI?"

Owen sighed. "Don't even think about it. You and Samantha are the only ones who know they have the whole collection. An anonymous tip won't be anonymous. And I will not be forgiving. This you owe me. You could take your chances, but I don't recommend it."

"Yeah, but we're not the only ones who know," she said. "You know. You could let them enjoy it for a little while. But they get bored and your specialty is switching out their boredom for a new thing to get bored of. It's the way you get your kicks.

"Wouldn't it be amazing to see how they weave and dodge out of that one? And they would get away with it. You know they would. So would you. They'd love the disaster of it all. And you could give it to them."

The scene passed through his imagination and drew a smile in its wake.

"Leave it alone . . . Emma."

But he was still smiling.

The pain in her bruised face had gone tenfold as the exhaustion sapped the last reserve of her strength. She called up to the room for Carly to meet her at the side of the hotel. She couldn't bear the thought of trying to brave it through the lobby.

Owen pulled his car into the lot, the strange heaviness of the day, these years, this parting, dragging the time down to a crawl. Owen let the car drift to a stop before the last turn at the side of the building.

"Did you ever think we . . . ?" He stared straight ahead.

It wasn't flattering to be the flaw in granite. The only one who could hurt him. It made her chest ache. She didn't look at him, but heard him swallow.

"I would have disappointed you, Owen. You lead with that. Everyone knows it. You scare people. You scare me. Possibilities don't follow something like that."

"If I scared you, you hid it well."

"I know. That's the thing I lead with."

Owen nodded and took the turn around the hotel. Carly opened the side door of the building and peered out.

"Let's not cross paths again," he said.

Marcelline measured his expression for threat. There was none. Just an ending. And even the barest hint of a smile under the surface.

"Yes. Let's not." She pushed the door open, but leaned in, one foot already on the pavement, and kissed his cheek.

She pulled herself out into the late-afternoon sun. The door thunked home behind her.

There was no way to keep the bargain. They crossed paths often, if only in memory, and, for Marcelline, always in the sound of the receding purr of a big engine.

EPILOGUE

At the Isabella Stewart Gardner Museum on a chilly Boston spring day, a young woman moves from the hall surveillance into the frame of the first camera in the Dutch Room, DR Int 1. She crosses the screen from left to right with a long, sure stride that pulls the security chief's practiced eye from his divided attention to his grandchildren's vacation photos on Facebook.

He feels old now, but the job feels new these days with an amiable crush of tourists excited by the saga of the restored collection. It's been all over the news and cable TV specials. An anonymous tip, and then somehow a bunch of rich people made a crime into an act of charity. But at least the artwork was back where it belonged.

Now, hundreds of people a day file across the screens he monitors from the camera room, as he has for years. But this girl is someone you notice. She stands out. Someone you can't not see.

He watches her. She seems familiar, but he can't place it.

She doesn't have an audio-guide handset. She doesn't turn for the Rembrandt or the Vermeer. Everyone goes to the Rembrandt or the Vermeer first. But this one goes straight for the Flinck, back in its gilded frame after all those years, faced out to the far corner of the room as it was before the robbery.

There's a giddiness as she gets close, an electric bounce in her step that makes her seem, for just a few beats, much younger than she clearly is. She's at least college-aged, but for a second she's coltish, not yet grown.

The idea that he's seen her before tickles again at the back of his mind, a déjà vu feeling that hints at security-camera footage rather than the recollection of an actual encounter. She's probably been here before. Maybe that's it.

She pushes aside the plaid flannel shirt tied around her waist to pull a phone from her back pocket to photograph the Flinck. He wonders why. It's not much to look at and it's not one of the famous works. She checks her pictures, her hair a long curtain of blue-sheened chestnut that falls from a strong side part as her head bows over her screen under the camera mounted in the crown molding.

She puts the phone back in her pocket.

She leans in over the cordon, peering closely at the left side of the painting. It had been damaged in its years away from the museum and restored so that the break is all but invisible. She doesn't read the new plaque, but it's as if she knows what to look for.

The young woman steeples her fingers over her lips and stares at it, back bowed in contemplation. When she pulls her hands away, he's almost sure she'll reach out and touch the painting. He can practically feel her yearning to through the lens. She leans in again, plucking at the hem of her T-shirt, shedding nervous energy in the unconscious habit. His hand hovers for the radio to tell the room guard to keep an eye on her. But the look on her face is complicated, reverent. He's reluctant to disturb her.

She straightens and her shoulders rise and fall in a sigh. She snaps her arms straight to drop her sleeves back into place on her wrists. Something catches her eye and she goes to her knee to tie the lace on her combat boot. She pushes up from the floor, and in the swift arc of her turn for the exit, he almost knows where he's seen her before. He feels the shadow of a worry in that faint brush of memory, as if she's in danger. *Run!* he thinks.

But no. She's fine. She's obviously fine.

She crosses the screen, right to left this time. A blur of motion, the math of grace and life. He doesn't know why this young woman makes him smile. She's at the edge of the frame, and then she's gone.

ACKNOWLEDGMENTS

Writing a novel is hard. Once it's done, though, writing the acknowledgments for that novel is pure joy.

I would unquestionably write stories if I lived alone. I would plot to myself with abandon, out loud and pacing. I would compose dialogue with passionate stage presence for an audience of knickknacks and dust mites. I would crow and mutter my inspirations and frustrations to the empty rooms. I would stay up too late. Then sleep too late.

I mean, I'd still act sane in public. But it wouldn't be as good. It wouldn't be as true.

My husband, Art, and my daughters, Julia and Rianne, make life out of what I'd do alone. Their love, brilliance, and enthusiasm make the world better and bigger for everyone, but especially for me. Art has always been my first reader and advisor and he only gets better at it as the years spool out. And I thought it would be weird when my children were old enough to offer insight and input as I write. It's not weird. It's terrific.

My civilian friends who read for me and encourage me in my work, then entertain and move me with their own stories and confidences, they fill out my heart in a way I can only hope I do for them.

Thank you Mary Rollins, Samantha Kappalman, Diane Lopez, Jessica Coffey, Katie Delgado, Kelly Coffey Colvin, Lisa Fitchett, Kristi McCullough, and Jenny and Dave Eccleston. Jeanne Miller-Mason, my mother, is unfailingly wonderful at keeping my writerly spirits up, as are my sisters, Carmen Mason and Natalie Sherwood, too.

On the business side, I am indebted to Karen Kosztolnyik for picking up the book for Gallery, Jen Bergstrom for letting me play in the sandbox again, and my editor, Jackie Cantor, for everything. Sara Quaranta is the Queen of Polishing Touches, and my copyeditor, Steve Boldt, is my conscience at each of our path crossings. So many thanks to every professional who added their expertise to this project. My admiration for what you do to bring stories to the shelves is boundless.

My agent, Amy Moore-Benson, makes business a pleasure. I learn from her, rely on her, collaborate with her, and adore her. My luck in this partnership is a big, shiny talisman against ever feeling too overwhelmed. Always and ever, thank you.

But every time I get to the point in the acknowledgments to where the job meets the soul, to the time for thinking toward my writer-friends, I get a lump in my throat. I am very lucky to know so many wonderful writers.

This book, like any and all of them, had some shepherding from my tribe, and some of that literally, if we capitalize it. I have to especially thank Jay Shepherd for a tireless ear, precision insights on structure and plotting, an inexhaustible well of what-if-this-es, and the not insignificant achievement of finding the perfect title (and epigraph) for this book. Thank you, thank you. My debt is heavy.

Josh Stallings and Nancy Matuszak have earned hazardous duty pay for reading multiple drafts of *The Hidden Things*, and since I pay in affection and admiration, they should prepare to be snowed under with love.

And I am lost without the advice and understanding of these

brilliant writers: Lou Berney, Tana French, Elizabeth Little, Nadine Nettmann, Graeme Cameron, Brad Parks, Coleen Valentino, and Mark Pryor. Thank you, all the way thank you.

Finally, the other group of people who make me glow with gratitude—readers. Thank you for wanting stories. It's not a small thing. It makes us better. I believe that. And I am one of you, too.